LOYAL DE

Loyal Devlin knew which way Lieutenant Hennessy and his men had to have gone—toward Oakland to catch the ferry back to the city. The chase had ended; the hunter was bringing home his slain prey. Only Hennessy had a surprise in store for him.

Loyal pushed the horse hard, spurred by cold-blooded fury. Then he saw them: the four horses and three riders, and the corpse slung like a deer carcass over the saddle. One of the troopers was playing a banjo and singing. Hennessy and the other broke into loud laughter.

Loyal drew his gun. Vengeance would be his and its tool was in his hand. He knew how to hate. Now it was time to learn to kill. . . .

SAN FRANCISCO

The third saga in a blazing new trail of adventure—
FORTUNES WEST

FORTUNES WEST

SAN FRANCISCO

A. R. RIEFE

A SIGNET BOOK

NEW AMERICAN LIBRARY

A DIVISION OF PENGUIN BOOKS USA INC.

PUBLISHER'S NOTE

This book is a work of fiction. Names, characters, places, and incidents either are the product of the author's imagination or are used fictitiously, and any resemblance to actual persons, living or dead, events, or locales is entirely coincidental.

SIGNET, SIGNET CLASSIC, MENTOR, ONYX, PLUME, MERIDIAN and NAL BOOKS are published by New American Library, a division of Penguin Books USA Inc., 1633 Broadway, New York, New York 10019

First Printing, September, 1989

1 2 3 4 5 6 7 8 9

PRINTED IN THE UNITED STATES OF AMERICA

For Jim Allen

In appreciation of his timely and
invaluable assistance in research

A friend in deed is a friend indeed

Stars twinkled against the black sky as a westerly wind whipped over the normally tranquil waters of the Golden Gate. All was quiet except the rattling of a flag rope against its mast at the top of Fort Point. Positioned at the entrance to the San Francisco Bay, the fort was a commanding structure made of brick in Flemish bond and trimmed with granite groins, cornices, and sills. Its seven-foot-thick walls enclosed a paved courtyard, surrounded with galleries of tiered brick arches. Eight-inch Columbiads stared blankly out over the dark water.

The troops in the courtyard were standing at attention as the provost marshal entered on his coal-black stallion. He was followed by the band playing the doleful strains of the "Death March;" then came a guard of twelve armed men, which was deployed diagonally across the open end of the formation to prevent the prisoner's escape. Next four soldiers carried a pine coffin. The eyes of every man at attention were immediately drawn to the box. The condemned man followed, his face deathly white. A guard marched on either side of him, and he was preceded by the chaplain.

Bringing up the rear of this funereal procession came the firing party, made up of six men, one of whom carried a musket containing a blank charge. None of the six knew which was the harmless weapon and each could hope that it was the one he carried. The procession halted and the coffin was set down near the open grave. The prisoner was quietly ordered to sit on it. The torches flickered and all was silent for nearly half a minute.

Commanding Officer Lieutenant Colonel Ewing Bracy stood watching the proceedings, feeling sick at heart. Executing men for desertion was not his idea of military justice, but the orders had come directly from the War Department in Washington and he had no choice but to obey. Since the discovery of gold in the area less than two years earlier, officers as well as enlisted men were deserting at the rate of two or three a month. The War Department justified this severe punishment on the grounds that it would serve as a deterrent to others. Colonel Bracy doubted this assumption, but did not object to the order in writing.

What would have been the use? he thought now, watching the condemned man tremble as he sat on his coffin. What could he write in protest to Washington? However impassioned his arguments against the policy might be, would the War Department change its mind? Bracy doubted it. Just the same, the situation at hand stirred not a little guilt in his heart. He was fifty-six years old and had seen much of war, most recently distinguishing himself at Cerro Cordo in the war against Mexico. War in all its so-called glory was more often than not an onerous job for men in command. But to feel such misgivings in peacetime was disheartening.

As the chaplain came forward to minister to the condemned man, Bracy studied the faces in the flickering torchlight. Some of the men looked appalled, others fearful, as if they were about to witness their own executions. Still others looked puzzled. Some looked resentful, others hugely sympathetic. But to Bracy they all looked as if they'd rather be anywhere else.

Except for the man standing beside him. Second

Lieutenant James Michael Hennessy was less than half the colonel's age and had never seen a battle in his four years of service. Before being assigned to Fort Point, he had served at Fort Sumter, three miles from Charleston in South Carolina.

Hennessy's expression intrigued Bracy. The man appeared to be enjoying this grisly drama. Bracy wondered if he was bloodthirsty by nature, like others he knew, frustrated at missing out on the slaughter in Mexico. Was this a substitute of sorts? Was Hennessy's smirk one of satisfaction? Perhaps he agreed with the War Department's solution to the problem of desertion. Was he one of that sorry breed who secretly revels in the power of life and death he fancies he holds over the men?

Bracy himself could see nothing to smirk about. He didn't even approve of the hour. Men were executed at dawn, not 10:00 P.M. But these days the War Department had ordered that the deserter be tried, sentenced, and executed within two hours of his arrest. Whose idea that was, Bracy could only conjecture. Secretary of the Army Charles Conrad's, possibly; the bantam rooster with the voice like a bay foghorn was well-known as an advocate of iron discipline and harsh punishment.

The chaplain was done ministering to the condemned man. The provost marshal came forward and fixed the prisoner's blindfold. The commander of the guard called for silence. The provost marshal read the official order of execution. It was punctuated by a low grumble from the men looking on.

"Silence," the sergeant in command of the guards shouted.

The condemned waved away a cigarette as the six-man firing party stepped into position.

"Ready . . ."

Hammers clicked in unison.

"Aim . . ."

Everyone held his breath. The blindfolded man was shaking so badly that his knees threatened to give way. The drums rolled on.

"Fire!"

The blast hammered Bracy's ears. He noted that Hennessy's smirk never left his face, nor did it deepen or soften. It was like a mask. The prisoner had fallen. Gasps went up, shouting, protests. He was still alive, bleeding from chest wounds. One shot had also grazed the side of his head. He lay groaning pitifully.

"Put him out of his misery," someone shouted.

Before the last word was uttered Bracy acted, drawing his service revolver and shooting the unfortunate man through the head. The man wrenched, then lay still. A loud babbling broke out.

"Good thinking, sir," burst Hennessy.

Bracy grunted. He had no sensation of "goodness." Revulsion filled his stomach. He didn't respond to Hennessy, didn't even look his way.

"Westerfield," he bawled. "Captain Westerfield!"

A burly, bearded officer—twin silver bars cresting a disreputably rumpled jacket—came bustling up. The surgeon was bending over the body. He examined it and signaled to Bracy that the man was dead. Westerfield snapped off a salute.

"Sir?"

"See that the men are marched single-file past the corpse."

"Yes, sir."

The provost marshal joined them.

Bracy held Westerfield by the sleeve. "No band, no drums, just the usual march. Chalk up another, eh, Roy?" he added bitterly to the provost marshal. "Did you see?"

Provost Marshal Viselli nodded. "Two men in the firing party refused to fire."

"Lock them up. Thirty days, bread and water."

"The condemned man, Private MacGruder, was very well-liked, sir. Very popular."

"I don't give a tinker's dam. See to it!

Viselli saluted; Bracy returned it halfheartedly. He couldn't let MacGruder's buddies off for their dereliction of duty. Not if he hoped to retain the respect of his men.

"I'm going home," he announced to no one in particular.

He headed toward the Sally Port door as Hennessy sidled up to him. Every eye among the assembled men was on the colonel. He felt them all. The majority were critical, some even damning.

"Look at the bastard," murmured one. "Lord God Almighty, power o' life and death."

"Don't blame him, Joe, it was Mac went absent without leave. Colonel sure as hell didn't give him the gold fever."

"Colonel's just follyin' his orders," added another. "Get a load o' Hennessy. Never does miss a chance to lick his boots, does he?"

"Must be he never gets the taste of leather out of his mouth," ventured another man.

"It does set an example to the men," Hennessy said to the colonel, sensing his superior's disapproval as he hurried his step to keep pace with him.

"Does it, James?" was the response. "Maybe it does, maybe I'm all wrong."

"About what, sir?"

Bracy didn't reply. The wind rose as they neared the Sally Port, raising a dancing dust devil. Thunder grumbled over the Golden Gate. It seemed to the colonel to announce to the world that the 182-man complement of Fort Point was now reduced by one. Bracy felt saddened.

In the Jenny Lind Theater the Reverend Samuel Brannan sat forward in his seat and peered down over the brass railing of his box at the audience below. To his right, the crescent of the balcony was filled, displaying a number of the city's notables, meticulously groomed gentlemen, in richly colored brocade silk vests and frock coats, the ladies showing off the latest fashions from Paris. The pit and rear balconies held the common throng, with a sprinkling of ill-clad miners from the diggings in town out on a spending spree.

Looking down, Brannan felt like a king, his subjects at his feet. The impression that the audience was his and expected him to speak flashed through his mind; he inadvertently cleared his throat. Excellent speaker though he was, he was not a particularly attractive man: plain-faced, not handsome, not homely. He affected a close-cropped black beard neatly sculptured around an islet of hair under his lower lip. No mustache. He associated mustaches with miscreants, drunkards, and the like, and his mirror regularly reminded him that the absence of a mustache on his face testified to his spiritual strength.

Along with being one of God's representatives and a forceful and persuasive sermonizer, he was a business entrepreneur without peer in San Francisco: founder and editor of California's first newspaper, the *California Star*, as well as founder and head of both the Law and Order Party and the Vigilance Committee. The latter had been able to keep peace in the streets, where the municipal government and the military at Fort Point had proven so ineffective. He was also a real-estate tycoon, an alderman, and a man who refused to pay taxes and regularly diverted money from his church's property and tithes to his own pockets.

Seated beside him was his wife, Mercy Brannan. How Mercy tolerated her husband was San Francisco's pet mystery. As beloved as he was resented, she was his antithesis in every way. Of course, she was not the first woman in history to share her bed with a man who rated himself considerably higher than did others.

Mercy Brannan loved the theater. She found it a welcome breath of fresh air from the outside world, one to be tasted and enjoyed to the fullest.

On the stage below, the celebrated Drew family, fresh from a triumphant engagement in Kansas City, was preparing to begin the third act of Shakespeare's *Comedy of Errors*. Sam Brannan continued to lean on his elbows and survey his subjects below, a few of whom chanced to look up and recognize him. One man waved greeting. Sam smiled down patronizingly.

"Sit back, dear," Mercy said, "you'll be more comfortable."

"I'm fine and dandy, Mother," he replied.

"You don't look it, you just want folks down there to see you, don't you?"

He straightened and put on an appropriate hurt look. "Fiddlesticks."

"There, you're straight. Now sit back."

She fanned herself with her program in futile defense against the stifling heat of July. The heavy curtain, adorned with a dyspeptic-looking George Washington draped in an American flag against a background of San Francisco Bay and the Golden Gate, rose in jerks, setting the footlight candles fluttering. On stage the actors stood motionless, waiting for silence in order to begin. Before the first line was spoken, the theater owner Tom Maguire, resplendent in his tuxedo, stepped from the wings.

"Ladies and gentlemen, may I have your attention, please? Forgive this untimely interruption. I have an important announcement."

His preamble was greeted with catcalls and objections, rising so quickly in volume that he could not continue. In sudden desperation he tried to shout down the crowd.

"This performance is hereby canceled," he burst.

An even higher tide of objection greeted this.

"Will you all please rise and leave? Your money will be refunded. Simply show your ticket stub at the box office tomorrow morning."

Not a soul stirred.

"Get off the stage, Tom," bawled a voice.

"Show must go on," bawled another.

"Quit holdin' up the works," shouted a third.

By now, his patience fled, he was becoming red-faced.

"Out! Move! Get up and get out of here! There's a fire broken out next door. There's no immediate danger; we have plenty of time to get out before it reaches here. Take your time, move slowly toward the exits, give your neighbor every consideration . . ."

Whatever else Tom was going to say was drowned out by the tumultuous rush for the four exits. Pandemonium reigned, as he stood yelling and gesticulating like a wildman, trying in vain to quell the uproar. Sam and Mercy Brannan looked for the stairs, Sam practically dragging her along to speed her step. Outside the theater in the warehouse next door, the city's fifth conflagration in nineteen months was well under way. In minutes the flames consumed the jerry-built wooden building and began to spread.

The passengers and crew of the *Goldfinder* looked eagerly toward shore. The 700-ton hermaphrodite brig was 139 days out of Boston, survivor of heavy seas off Bermuda and a series of fierce storms coming through the Strait of Magellan. An unscheduled stop at Callao to take on eighty-two Peruvians bound for the California gold fields had swelled the ranks of the argonauts to more than fifteen hundred. As a result, the voyage had taken longer than anticipated and tempers were perilously short. Fights had become commonplace, stealing was rampant, and drunkenness was the order of the day.

An organized fight was under way on the forecastle, the capstan situated squarely in the middle of the "ring", a hatch cover some five feet astern of it, twin iron bollards at the corners and other deck appointments strategically placed, impeding the footwork of the combatants. The fight was over a half bottle of

rye, and who it actually belonged to. Moments before
the bottle had slipped from Loyal Devlin's sweaty
hand and shattered. Wars have been declared for lesser
offenses, and a truism as old as mankind held that if
two men felt inclined to fight, any excuse was excuse
enough.

Devlin had no great itch to fight. He wasn't sober
enough to do his best, and sober as a preacher he was
no great shakes. His opponent, a rangy, bull-chested
carpenter, was even drunker, but appeared to have no
thoughts of delaying things until he got sober. Devlin
wanted only to land, get off this damned tub, and find
his way to Fort Point, to be reunited with his brother,
Tom, whom he hadn't seen in ten years. After the
recent Mexican War, Tom had been assigned to Fort
Point, the recently remodeled military installation on
the site where the old Castillo de San Joaquín had
overlooked the harbor. Originally the Spanish settle-
ment of Yerba Buena, the city had recently been
renamed San Francisco.

But first things first. Devlin and Duckworth, the
carpenter, had stripped to their waists. A rheumy-
eyed and not altogether sober little Scotsman acted as
referee; the fighters stood toe to toe, going at it furiously. Duckworth wanted to take the price of his
bottle out of Devlin's hide; Devlin wanted to get it
over with so he could get on with the business he'd
come thirteen thousand miles to consummate.

Devlin had fought with his fists in half the bars in
Boston and was no stranger to the art. He could see
after the first flurry that Duckworth, although taller
and bigger through the chest than he was, moved
clumsily, and was slow to react. He also seemed overly
protective of his jaw. Was it glass? Devlin wondered,
and resolved to find out.

But Duckworth's reach was about four inches longer
than his, so getting close enough to test his jaw wasn't
easy. When he tried to move in the carpenter would

pound him one-two in the chest, driving him back a step. Devlin could take it in the chest, the upper arms, even the face; his stomach was his weakness. It was somewhat flabby for a man in his prime (he was not yet twenty-six), abused with too much alcohol and too little decent food over the past eight years. Duckworth concentrated on his stomach, belting him again and again, forcing Devlin to fight sideways, turning one way then the other to avoid a direct blow. But even glancing blows sent pain flaring through the area.

The crowd cheered as he sidestepped a lethal blow and countered with a roundhouse left, catching his lumbering opponent in the temple and nearly toppling him. Duckworth staggered and shook out the cobwebs. The crowd cheered louder when he retaliated, a wild swing catching Devlin high on the right cheek. It felt smashed in seven places and immediately began to swell. It hurt like fury. The crowd loved it.

They went into a clinch, both panting like blown stallions. The little referee pushed between them.

"Break it oop . . ."

Glaring at each other, the carpenter lowered his right shoulder and came boring in. Devlin ducked, bringing up his right, pile-driving him full in the heart. Duckworth roared, cursed, and came back at Devlin's face. Devlin staggered back, tripped over an anchor ring, and fell on his back, his head crashing down on an anchor in its cathead. He went out cold.

The crowd roared delightedly. Duckworth raised his fists in triumph, money changed hands as a bucket of water was dashed on Devlin. He came to, sputtering. The referee was leaning over him, his breath fouling Devlin's nostrils.

"You okay, lod?"

The back of his head felt as if he'd been hit with a twelve pound sledge. Devlin sat up rubbing his head gingerly.

"Fire!" someone shouted.

By this time, the *Goldfinder* had drawn within two hundred yards of shore, and the harbor was crowded with ships.

Visible through the maze of masts, flames rose from the heart of the city, sending great black clouds upward into the watching stars.

"Mr. Mitchum, heave to," bellowed the captain from the top of the steps leading up to the afterdeck.

The first mate manning the wheel saluted and obeyed.

"Prepare the hooks," shouted the captain, and crewmen ran to the anchors.

The passengers on deck protested and surged en masse toward the rear of the vessel to confront the captain.

He waved both hands, demanding they quiet down. "I'm not taking her in to berth," he explained. "Looky at them vessels already anchored. They're so close together most are touching." He indicated the fire. "Sparks carried down to the docks on the breeze, they'll go up like tinder, and us too if we get close to 'em. We'll sit out here. Wait it out. Them that can't or won't, can swim for it. My advice is to relax and be patient, your gold's not going anyplace underground."

The passengers roared protest. A half-dozen men started up the steps as if to pull the captain down. He jerked out a pistol, cocking and aiming it at the face of the man in the front.

"Avast and belay, gold bug, 'fore I blow you back to Boston!"

Fort Point was an irregular quadrangle, modeled somewhat after the plan used in the construction of Fort Sumter, South Carolina. It was 150 feet wide, its longest side measuring 250 feet, and the height of its three stories was forty-five feet. Two bastions extended outward, one to the northeast and the other to the northwest; these guns provided flanking fire. Located one above the other facing the Golden Gate were three tiers of gun ports. Located at a level below the topmost tier were walls of dirt, angling away from the fort. The guns had yet to be installed on these barbette tiers.

On the land side, the rear of the fort, a hillock had been raised to a height of forty-five feet. At the southeast corner was the well-protected entrance, the Sally Port. The Sally Port boasted two heavy iron-bound doors, studded with large nails, secured against forcible entry by means of a long iron bar that pivoted on one of the doors. A passageway led to a second set of strong doors. To the right of the inner doors were three prison cells. In one cell languished the men who had failed to properly perform their duty on the firing squad.

The wall on the land side contained shops and living quarters for the garrison. Shops for various utilities, such as wheelwrights, forges, and tools, occupied the first floor; on the second floor were the officers' quarters. Each set boasted two bedrooms and a parlor. The enlisted men's quarters were on the third floor.

Two shot furnaces, each fifteen feet in length, were located in the courtyard. Rainwater caught on the sloping roof was carried through iron pipes to a large storage cistern below the fort.

The sound of gunfire coming from the courtyard so startled Doreen Bracy, the brandy bottle slipped from her hand, spilling at her feet. She quickly retrieved it and knelt, staring at the stain in the carpet. She restored the bottle to the cabinet and went into the kitchen to dampen a rag in soapy water. It was then she heard the single shot following the volley of the firing squad. This puzzled her, but only for a moment. She wet the rag and turned to poking among her herb and spice bottles. She found the cloves and put a few in her mouth to chew. Then she returned to the parlor to attack the stain.

She was working at it without much success when she heard steps outside. Rising, she crammed the rag into her apron pocket, touched her hair, and plumped into a chair. Her husband, Ewing, came in. He looked exhausted. He bent and kissed her affectionately, then made a face, crinkling his nose. But he said nothing beyond greeting her.

She got up. "Sit, dear, you look worn out."

"I need a drink."

"I'll get it." She turned to the cabinet, hesitated, then got out the rye. She failed to see his questioning look.

"A little of the brandy if it's okay," he said quietly.

His eyes found the stain in the carpet as she brought out the brandy. He lifted his eyes from it to the bottle.

"Dorey . . . oh, Dorey . . ."

She'd drunk more than half. "I'm not drunk, I'm not, I'm not," she protested.

"Of course you're not." He got up wearily, took her in his arms, and kissed her.

"I'm not," she went on.

He could see she was close to inebriation. It wasn't the first time he'd caught her in such a state. In fact, it was at least the fifth time in a little more than a week. Brought up in strict Baptist tradition, she had never touched alcohol until recently. Now she seemed to be making up for lost time.

It began when she had gotten word that her older sister had died of diphtheria. She hadn't even known she was ill. She had idolized her sister, Catherine, and for a time the shock of her passing had been almost too much to bear. Ewing was upset over the timing of the tragedy. Their only daughter, Catherine, named for her aunt, was in Kansas City visiting other relatives.

Doreen had wanted to pack a bag and go to St. Louis for the funeral. But Bracy feared the pain of the tragedy and the difficult journey would have been too much for his delicate wife. She was not a strong woman, and she took medication for her heart. He had advised her that under the circumstances, paying her respects in her prayers would certainly be acceptable to God. In the end, she agreed.

But it wasn't her sister's death or their daughter's absence that had turned Doreen to drink. They were merely the final straws. He could see the cause in his mirror. The war had separated them for months at a time. The life of an army wife was marked by separations, hardships, harsh living conditions on the posts, and the absence of feminine niceties that women craved. Doreen had always been able to make do; he had never known her to complain. But it was a life that no woman would envy and none enjoyed.

He helped her up the stairs and got her into bed. She was embarrassed. He sat on the side of the bed brushing her hair for her, looking from her face to a pen-and-ink likeness of her rendered twenty years earlier that sat in an oval frame on the nightstand. She was fifty-four years old now, and the years had not been kind to her. Her lovely smile she would never lose, but age lines assaulted her mouth and streaked away from the corners of her eyes. There was a sadness in her eyes, a broken look. She was drained of her old resolve, which he had always so admired. Drained of hope and of all joy.

"Ready to go to sleep?" he asked.

"You must be," she said. "I'm not tired, not physically . . ."

"We're coming to the end, Dorey. Only two more years. Twenty-eight down, two to go. We'll make it." He squeezed her hand affectionately. "Retirement, pension, a little place all our own, wherever you want to live. You'll have your garden. Won't it be wonderful? Somebody else can fight their wars, buck his head against the bureaucratic wall, shoot the deserters. Oh, God, but I hated it tonight!"

"What happened?"

"We executed another one."

She looked at him to continue. He hesitated to tell her it was he who'd applied the coup de grace. He didn't want to talk about any of it, it was done and over. Until the next one. He shook his head dejectedly.

"It must be horrible for you," she said, "but it does set an example, discourages them from deserting, doesn't it?"

"Everybody seems to think so."

"Except you."

"If it is a deterrent, when will it start to deter? There's too much gold out there, too tempting, too easy to find. I'm surprised we don't have six times as many desertions."

She tried to reassure him, and despite her weariness, her face shone with love. Her most arresting feature were her eyes—as black as ink, her Spanish eyes, she jokingly called them. She closed them now, a contented smile on her lips.

Once more Bracy felt a twinge of guilt. He wished he had more time for her. Perhaps he should take her on a picnic. Doreen loved picnics, and this was the perfect time of the year. He couldn't stop her drinking, but he could make her want to stop of her own volition. He would; then and there he made a pact with his conscience.

He would begin by holding back his own troubles: this desertion business, the other headaches, the ones every post commander has to contend with. The shortage of supplies, of personnel, unqualified officers, troublemakers, the presence of Sam Brannan and others of his stripe in town, who seemed to be put on earth solely to give him fits with their antics, conspired to make a difficult job an almost impossible one. The biggest thorn in his side was Brannan's Committee of Vigilance, a civilized name for an uncivilized gang of roving malcontents out to take an eye for an eye.

But from now on he would hide his discouragement, wrap up his troubles in his old kit bag and smile, smile, smile. He wished Catherine would get home. Between them they'd prop up her mother until she was able to stand on her own again.

A loud knocking threatened to bash in the door downstairs. Doreen woke with a start.

"I'll see who it is," he said. He kissed her. "Sleep."

It was Captain Westerfield with four men. He seemed to have changed jacket and trousers. At least he looked less disheveled. He scratched his beard, his expression apologetic.

"Sorry to bust in on you so late, Colonel, but we just got word there's a fire in town. Big and getting bigger. Started next door to the theater on Montgomery Street and already spread to the Barbary Coast and Chinatown."

"Roust out the second and third platoon. Every man jack. I'll be with you in . . ." He paused, one hand on the door stile, and turned to look back at the bedroom. "On second thought, you take charge. Go straight to Mayor Brenham's house and present yourself. If you can't find him, go to Chief Sanger. Give him my compliments and offer to help the police guard against looting."

"The Sydney Ducks," said Westerfield, nodding.

"They'll be flocking down from Sydney Town to loot and plunder as usual. Likely already started."

"They started the damn fire, always do."

"We don't know that. See that you don't go shooting anybody on suspicion. Get on it fast as you can. Report to me at reveille. Again, no wild shooting. Nobody fires unless they catch somebody in the act. God forbid somebody shoot some fine upstanding pillar of the community by mistake."

"That include Reverend Brannan?" Westerfield asked straight-faced, then breaking into a smirk.

"Stay out of his way if you can, Robert. Do your level best to."

"Yes, sir."

Westerfield saluted, Bracy shut and bolted the door. He poured himself the stiff brandy he hadn't gotten to earlier and stood before the mirror surveying his image. He looked much older than his fifty-six years, his gray sideburns showing signs of whitening, few black hairs surviving among the gray ones. In his younger days, he'd been handsome, dashing even. But they were long gone and now his good looks sagged. He rubbed at the line angling down from the right side of his mouth. He sipped. His glance drifted to the calendar alongside the mirror and Tuesday, July 24, 1851. Catherine was due back in two days. Two days he resolved to stick close to his wife. She needed them both so badly.

He finished his drink and went back up to the bedroom. She was asleep. He sat on the bed beside her and stroked her hair. Outside he could hear Westerfield and his men passing by on the double on their way into town.

———————— ◀2▶● ————————

Sam and Mercy Brannan had gotten out of the theater just in time. Fanned by an onshore breeze, the flames had quickly spread in all directions. Whole blocks were consumed in minutes. Even brick houses crumbled like sand castles. Occupants of iron-framed buildings believed they were safe and remained inside until too late, for as soon as the walls got red-hot, the furnishings would begin to smoke; locks and hinges would warp or partially melt in the heat, doors could not be opened, and those inside found themselves entombed.

The Brannans got quickly away from the conflagration; Sam stopped them short as they turned a corner, preparing to cross Market Street and head down it toward the Baldwin Hotel and their house a few blocks beyond.

"You can make it yourself from here," Sam said.

"Aren't you coming?"

"I've work to do, I have to round up the Vigilantes. We'll be busy tonight. I'll need to borrow a gun."

"Oh Sam, no."

"My dear, the city has to be protected from those filthy mongrels. You know perfectly well, every fire is an excuse for them to prey on the populace. The police are too busy protecting themselves, and the army's useless as always. The Vigilantes are San Francisco's only hope . . . Where are you going?"

"To the hospital, I'm sure they can use two more hands."

"I forbid you! You're to go straight home, do you hear?"

She ignored him and started back the way they'd come.

"Mercy . . . Mercy!"

Loyal Devlin had watched the captain announce his refusal to bring the ship any closer to port. His reasoning made sense, only not to his listeners. They proceeded to jump ship, tossing their belongings into lifeboats and lowering them splashing, ignoring his loud threats and pistol shots in the air. Devlin tossed his bag safely into a boat, then dived into the water and swam to shore.

"Where you off to in sooch a roosh?" asked the little Scotsman who had refereed the fight. He stood on the dock dripping and grinning. Sight of him set the growing bump at the back of Devlin's head throbbing anew.

"To find my brother Tom," he said.

"Mind your bock, Redhead, the town's wide open, ready and waiting to snop closed like a bloody bear trop on oonsoospecting greenhorns like yourself." Devlin laughed and clapped him on the back. Then quickly retrieved his bag, and ran up a side street, passing house after house being swallowed up by the flames. The heat was unbearable; he felt as if his lungs were on fire. People ran about shouting and screaming. He stopped to catch his breath, and a storefront toppled, narrowly missing him as he resumed running.

He watched a family—mother, father, and four young children—escape from a burning house. The parents hurried the youngsters ahead of them to the safety of a vacant lot opposite. Then, to Devlin's astonishment, the father turned back to run into the burning house. Devlin dropped his things and ran up, catching the man by the arm. He tried to jerk free, but Devlin's grip was too strong.

"Don't be a fool, man, the roof's coming down any second."

"My son's in there, dammit, let go!"

"Where?"

"In the back."

"You see to your family, I'll get him."

Devlin ran into the house. It was an inferno; he could hardly draw breath. He cast about blindly, searching for the boy. Finally, he saw him standing in a doorway, his eyes rounded with fear. Devlin grabbed him by the arm and headed back toward the front door. In his haste, he tripped and fell, breaking the fall with an outstretched hand.

Pain exploded in his wrist. It felt broken. Ignoring the pain, he got to his feet and with his good hand dragged the boy outside to safety.

"God bless you," cried the boy's mother, running up to them. "You saved him."

The roof falling ended any further conversation. His back to it, Devlin could see the flames reflected in the woman's horror-stricken face.

"That's that," growled her husband. "Mister, how can we ever repay you? You risked your life."

"You got someplace you can go?" Devlin asked.

"Bertha's sister's house over to Tyler Street. The fire won't get that far, it never does."

"Are you okay?" the woman asked.

"I'm fine," Devlin lied. He picked his things up with his left hand and started away.

"God bless you," she called after him.

His wrist was killing him. And every exposed part of his body felt as if a branding bar were being rolled over it. His lungs burned furiously in his chest; he coughed and coughed to rid his throat of the smoke.

He moved away from the fire, feeling cool air against his burning cheeks. Ahead the lights of a saloon beckoned. He made it up to the door and staggered in, dumping his things on the floor. The place had been converted into an emergency hospital. The stink of carbolic acid filled the stuffy air. Volunteers were bandaging burns, preparing splints for broken limbs, and otherwise attending to the injured that filled the room.

A motherly-looking woman, her dark hair gathered in a tight bun at the back of her head, her eyes pale and as solicitous as her expression, ran up to him.

"I need a drink," he said.

"You look like you need more than that, young man. That wrist needs binding. Look at how it's swollen. Come over here and sit. Amelia! Amelia Davenport, bandage here. The double thickness. Quickly!"

Devlin dropped wearily into a chair.

"What's your name?" the woman asked.

"Loyal Devlin."

"I'm Mercy Brannan. Pleasure to meet you. How'd you hurt your wrist?"

"I fell. I think it's broken."

"You're able to move your hand. Sorry to disappoint you, but it can't be broken. Just badly sprained. Fell, you say? Where are you from, Royal?"

"Loyal."

"Why don't I settle for Red? Good grief but that's red hair. Like it's on fire of its own. From where?"

"Boston."

"Oh, just up the road," she said with a smile.

"My ship just got in."

"You sure picked a fine time to arrive."

The other woman brought up a roll of gauze.

"Hold still, dear," Mercy said. "Be a brave soldier."

He grinned. She was priceless. She wound the gauze around his wrist, binding it securely.

"You look a little peaked," Mercy said solicitously,

cocking her head and eyeing her patient. "Want to lie down?"

"I'm fine."

"You sure don't look it. Your face looks like you've been in three fights. Is that what you came to San Francisco to do, pick fights?"

He told her about his brother.

"My throat feels like somebody's been swabbing it with a torch," he said. "Can I have a drink?"

"You'll have to pay for it."

"I've got money. Scotch whiskey, tumblerful, if you don't mind." He dug out money.

"I don't mind a lick, it's your innards."

She went to get him the drink. She was bringing it back when a young girl filled the doorway. Dressed expensively in a gingham frock with leg-o'-mutton sleeves and a bonnet with a bright-red ribbon, she looked decidedly out of place in this saloon turned shelter. She was blond, with an upturned nose and blue eyes. The sort who's never had to get down on her knees and scrub a floor, decided Devlin on the spot.

"Mother! There you are," she shrilled. Picking up her skirt front, she set sail for Mercy as the woman was handing Devlin his drink. "You had me in a tizzy. I waited and waited for you . . ."

"Betsy, this is Mr. Devlin, come to our burnt-up-Eden all the way from Boston," Mercy said calmly. "Mr. Devlin, my daughter Betsy."

Betsy did not even look at Devlin. She stood frowning at her mother, her little fists clenched white against her hips. "Hello," she rasped.

"Ma'am . . ." Devlin got to his feet.

"Miss," she corrected, still not deigning to look at him.

"Where's your father?" Mercy asked.

"He at least came home. But went right out again

with Mr. Ward and Mr. Scapelli or Patelli, whatever his name is."

"His two henchmen," Mercy explained to Devlin smiling, then sobering and going on to tell him about the Committee of Vigilance.

"Are you or are you not coming home with me?" interrupted Betsy.

"In a little bit. You go ahead, dear. Is the fire starting to burn itself out yet?"

"Not that I could see."

"Then I'd best stay."

As if on cue, two more injured were brought in on litters. Betsy sputtered disapprovingly, then left, leaving Devlin and Mercy without so much as a good-bye.

"Very pretty," he murmured, his eyes on the open doors.

"A bit headstrong, and more than a bit ornery at times." Mercy laughed. "Takes after her daddy. I'll have to leave you now to lend a hand. You really should sip that stuff, not bolt it down like iced tea."

"Yes, mother . . ."

She laughed and left him.

Sam Brannan, Eustace Ward, and Sergio Scapelli marched straight from Brannan's house to his office at the northeast corner of Bush and Sansome streets, only a block from where the great fire continued to rage. There the three were met by more than eighty men armed with rifles and pistols, brickbats, cudgels, and knives. Brought along also a liberal supply of half-inch rope. Brannan mounted a stool in front of his office door and addressed his fellow members of the Committee of Vigilance of San Francisco.

"My friends, I'll not waste time with needless speeches. Our duty is clear. We'll split up into groups of five men each and scatter. Arrest any looters you find and bring them back here to be locked in the storage room. We'll all reassemble back here in two hours, at which time we'll hang the lot. We can handle four at a time using the crossbeam in the shed out back. Good hunting, boys."

A loud cheer went up.

"Show the filthy swine no mercy! They started this fire, by Josiah's curse, they'll pay for it. They will wish to heaven they'd never set foot on a ship to America. Are you with me, brothers?"

Again a tumultuous cheer.

"Go then! And the Squad of Retribution that brings in the most miscreants will earn itself a case of Bushmill's Irish whiskey, compliments of yours truly!"

Another cheer. The men started away.

Brannan stopped them. "Hold it, boys. Before we go, let us invoke the Lord's blessing upon our efforts." He descended from his stool and knelt on the sidewalk. His listeners bared and lowered their heads.

For more than a year the city had been plagued by bands of roving hoodlums. The worst of the lot were the Sydney Ducks. The Ducks were mostly Australians, or English convicts sent to that country as an alternative to prison. News of California's gold had been irresistible to this litter of society. Although some men were not convicts, the great majority came on "tickets of leave."

A disease-ridden, wretched San Francisco slum immediately south of Telegraph Hill was the favorite haunt. Sydney Town was the most dangerous section of the city. From it, the Ducks set forth to prey on anyone who might have money or jewels—or to set fires in retaliation for arrests and set the stage for citywide looting.

By the time Brannan finished rallying his Vigilantes, the whole of Washington Street, Kearny Street, Montgomery, California, and others had gone up in smoke. Presently, with a few exceptions, the entire central city was either blazing or already burned out.

Although volunteers from the various companies fought the fire, valiantly, the situation was hopeless. It had spread too quickly. Some streets ceased burning only when there wasn't a stick of wood left for the flames to consume, and these burned-out blocks served as firebreaks, allowing the volunteers to direct their efforts and rapidly dwindling supply of water at the outer reaches of the conflagration.

When Captain Westerfield and his men arrived in town, the captain immediately sought out Chief Sanger at Police Headquarters. They found him sputtering orders to the last few men who'd showed up, instructing them to round up all the looters they could find in hopes of identifying those who'd started the fire. Sanger was a small man with a distinct military bearing. He was temperamental, high-strung, and not given to mincing words on certain subjects. He stood in the doorway in his shirtsleeves, his face beet-red as he shouted away the last of his men.

"What do you want, Captain?" he barked at Westerfield.

"Colonel Bracy assigned us to help you out, sir," Westerfield replied calmly, at the same time waving away the growling of resentment coming from his men behind him—resentment at Sanger's expression and his inhospitable tone.

"You want to help—"

"Catch looters, sir," Westerfield cut in.

"My boys'll take care of them. You want to be helpful, find Brannan and his cronies. They'll be more trouble than the Sydney Ducks before this night is over. They'll be out for blood. Keep 'em out of trouble if you have to march around town two steps behind 'em."

Sanger was right, but his words did not sit well with Westerfield. The captain was well aware of the fragile relationship between the army and the citizenry. Bracy had already had a couple of run-ins with Sam Brannan and had come away slightly bruised both times. The preacher was making a career out of criticizing what he termed "the bumbling inefficiency of the military," incompetence surpassed only by Police Chief Sanger's "idiots with badges." Clearly Brannan's intent was to discredit both the army and the police in order to elevate his Committee of Vigilance in the public eye. So far he had succeeded handsomely. People looked to the Vigilantes to keep law and order.

Most citizens seemed to have forgotten that it was Brannan who'd led a successful campaign to cut the police force in half in the first place. Under the circumstances, with the Sydney Ducks waiting to pounce, this was tantamount to removing the door to the henhouse. But in a meeting of the Board of Aldermen the year before, his motion was carried, the force was reduced, and San Franciscans became even more dependent on the Committee of Vigilance for their protection.

Westerfield knew that Sanger was in no mood to discuss the situation further. It was either do as he ordered or do nothing, and the latter Colonel Bracy would not accept in the captain's report come reveille tomorrow morning. The chief went back inside, closing the door in the army's face. Westerfield sighed and assembled his junior officers.

"We have no choice but to do as he says. We'll concentrate on the area from St. Marys to the south to Israel Street to the north, Front Street east, Powell west."

"Concentrate on what?" asked Lieutenant Hennessy.

"Look for groups of Vigilantes with captives. Don't confront them. If possible keep out of their sight. Follow them to where they're taking their prisoners. Probably some abandoned shed or house that hasn't been touched by the fire, which means on or close to the outskirts. Surround the place. Do what you can to prevent any lynchings."

Hennessy eyed him jaundicedly. "You mean we're here to defend the bastards that started the thing?"

Westerfield eyed him in like manner. "You're here to do as you're ordered. Get going."

"Yes, sir." Hennessy's expression registered the disapproval his words could not. He turned to the noncom beside him.

"Sergeant Devlin, take your squad over to Montgomery and on out to Front Street. Work up and down Front; send men up the cross streets, over and back."

"And mind your weapons," interposed Westerfield. "This is no rabbit hunt. I want to make that very clear."

"Yes, sir, Captain," Sergeant Tom Devlin replied.

By the time Loyal Devlin had got his wrist tended to and his thirst slaked, it was too late to go up to the fort to meet with his brother. Following a second whiskey, he prepared to leave the Blue Duck. He approached Mercy Brannan, busy bandaging a man's head.

"I'm going now," Devlin said. "I wanted to thank you. It was a pleasure meeting you, ma'am. You should be a nurse."

"Haven't got the feet for it; I'm no spring chicken. Where are you heading?"

"To find a bed."

She finished the injured man's bandage and turned to him. "Don't bet your last dollar you'll find one, what with half the town in ashes and the other half on the way. Why don't you sit down, have another drink, and wait for me?" She glanced about them. "We've plenty of volunteers, I've been at it for hours, and business seems to be getting slack. I doubt I'll be missed. You can walk me home and sleep in the guest room."

"I wouldn't want to impose, ma'am."

"Are you going to be rude and turn down my invitation? After I saved your life? Seriously, you look like you need some clean clothes, and a decent night's sleep. Tomorrow, I'll give you a breakfast that'll stick to your ribs. How does that sound?"

"Sounds great, Mercy."

She laughed and gave him a pat on the back.

Her husband, meanwhile, was in no such charitable mood. His men had shot fourteen suspected looters and rounded up three others. Although he had warned against shooting any suspects, he took the news disinterestedly. From the newspaper office the group marched the three prisoners around back to a building used for storage by Brannan and untouched by the fire. The three were gagged and made to stand facing their judge and jury (Brannan), their wrists tied behind their backs, ankles hobbled to prevent their making a break for it. The Vigilantes stood behind them in a body while Garrett Ryckman, a successful brewer and pillar of the Methodist Church, assumed the role of prosecuting attorney.

The call for a Committee of Vigilance in the face of the ever-inceasing criminal activities of the Ducks and other lawless elements was widespread and insistent. It did not originate in the imagination of hot-headed extremists; it had been strenuously advocated by the newspapers and even the authorities.

The police force had proven all but useless and in many instances corrupt, and when it became known that the Ducks were deliberately starting the fires in order to create opportunity to loot, the public outcry could no longer be ignored.

Few San Franciscans questioned the need for a Committee of Vigilance, but many questioned the group's penchant for summary justice, so strongly advocated by its leader. Balancing off Brannan's avarice, his sanctimonious airs, his loud mouth, his revenue dodging, his abrasive manner, his thirst for blood were his energy, enthusiasm and in some cases spectacular achievements. And at the moment he was in his glory. The torches flickered; he cleared his throat and raised both hands.

"Quiet down, boys, let's get this over with. You men were caught red-handed looting. I won't ask you what you have to say for yourselves, because whatever it might be, it can't obscure your crimes or mitigate them in the least. You are guilty as charged. You are hereby sentenced to hang."

The prisoners struggled with their bonds, mumbling incoherently behind their gags. Quickly hoods were brought up and placed over their heads. Ropes were tied over the crossbeam twenty feet above the floor. Three stools were brought up and the men forced at gunpoint to stand on them. Then the nooses were placed around their necks. Brannan got out his bible and begun turning pages looking for suitable advice to the condemned.

Suddenly the doors burst open, and Captain Westerfield came striding in. His men fanned out on both sides of him, every man his weapon at the ready. Brannan gasped and glared.

"What's the meaning of this? How dare you come barging in here—"

Westerfield's upraised hand stopped him. "No lynchings, Reverend, Chief Sanger's orders. I can appreciate how you feel about these vermin. But it's for a court of law to try them and convict them, not your committee. Now everybody just relax and cooperate. We're going to take them off your hands, march them over to headquarters, and see them locked up."

"You'll do nothing of the kind, Captain," said Brannan icily. "You have no business here. We are a legally constituted authority. In short,"—he leaned forward, aiming the full force of his resentment at the officer—"mind your own business."

Shouts of approval went up from the vigilantes.

Westerfield ignored Brannan and the cheers. "Sergeant Devlin," the captain said softly. "Do your duty."

Tom Devlin pulled his service revolver, walked up to Brannan, and aimed the weapon at the small of his back. The onlookers gasped, but nobody moved, nobody uttered a word.

"Lieutenant Hennessy, remove the prisoners' hobbles and gags and escort them out. Lieutenant Brookens, remain here with the first squad; the rest of you, outside."

They left Brannan furious, but helpless to stop them. Sergeant Devlin was the last to leave. Ignoring the cursing and catcalls directed at him, he marched Brannan to the door, turned him around with his pistol, and slipped outside, closing the door on him.

Westerfield and the rest had already started for the police station. The captain was worried. No doubt he'd done the right thing, but he knew the strained relations between Fort Point and the townspeople were bound to worsen as a result of his actions. He walked beside Lieutenant Hennessy.

"You know something, James, what we need about now is a full-scale attack from the sea," Westerfield said. "A chance to blow the dust out of the guns and heroically defend the city. Save it from pirates or whatever; upgrade our image in everyone's eyes. Right now we're the lowest of the low."

"If you don't mind my saying so, Captain, I think we should have let them have their way with this scum."

"I don't mind you saying so, but you're wrong."

Hennessy shook his head. "Brannan won't stand for this. When things get back to normal, he'll raise hell."

The captain did not reply.

Meanwhile back at the building, Brannan raged. "I have friends in Washington, brothers," he said to the men grouped around him. "Secretary of the Army Charles Conrad, for one. And this high-handed intrusion into our affairs shall not go unpunished. Bracy is behind this; he's always been against us. Well, he's poked his nose in our business for the last time. Tomorrow, I intend to compose a letter to Charles citing Bracy's many derelictions of duty. Make no mistake, I've been keeping a record. I promise you, he'll be out of here bag and baggage before the Fourth of July.

"We'll meet here at nine A.M. tomorrow. Bring your weapons and your friends. We're declaring war on Sydney Town, gentlemen. We'll march on it and capture every Duck able to stand and lynch them en masse."

The reverend's eyes blazed as he raised a fist.

"As God is my witness and my strength, it shall be done!"

As the soldiers headed for the police station, Sergeant Tom Devlin mulled over his own plans. He had completed his last official act tonight. His gear was packed, his savings of $104 were securely buttoned in the breast pocket of his tunic, and he carried a change of civilian clothing. As soon as the detachment got back to the fort and the men retired for the night, he'd be leaving.

He had yet to decide where he would head. He could head east to Grass Valley or Hangtown, or even farther over the mountains to newly settled Nevada. Perhaps north to Oregon or south down across the Colorado river to Chloride. Gold was everywhere, just waiting to be found. Young and old were getting rich as Croesus while here he squatted with the rest of the star-spangled heroes of President Polk's War. Earning the magnificent sum of nineteen dollars a month. He laughed hollowly. Nineteen dollars, exactly half of what he'd have earned had he joined ordnance instead of the artillery.

Now the heroes rested. There was no action—other than picking up the pieces for the police—nor chance for promotion. He had no future beyond watching his beard grow grayer in his mirror with each passing day until they turned him out to pasture with a few dollars, his honorable discharge suitable for framing, and his head filled with dusty memories. Again he laughed bitterly. And wondered if he could wangle a corner room in the Old Soldiers' Home.

They were within sight of police headquarters. No one was about, the meager force was probably still scattered about the city trying to catch looters in the act. Inside, Sanger would be dozing at his desk. Devlin sighed. He had enlisted in the service for that most honorable and respected of reasons: love of country. Tom Devlin, patriot! Served he had, but the war was over. There was nothing to do now but nursemaid the locals and sit and stare at the other soldiers who marched around the courtyard at the fort on dress parade. Boredom weighed like a horse anchor in his heart. And all the while, ten miles away, men were digging up buckets of gold, washtubs full of it.

One thing gave him pause: the word "deserter." They'd write him off; he would effect a complete about-face from the glowing patriot who had enlisted. Would that prick his conscience in the weeks to come? However much gold he found—and he'd surely find his share—would that wipe away his misgivings over deserting?

"Deserter." What a filthy word! And what if they caught him and brought him back? The next digging he'd be doing would be his grave. Devlin thought about the executions he'd seen lately. Was he having second thoughts? If so, the War Department was right and the threat of the firing squad was a deterrent to would-be deserters.

No, by God, he would get out. Tonight. Cut and run. Far enough away so no search party could pick up his tracks. And once he made his pile, he'd leave the country. Perhaps he'd go to Ireland, County Mayo, where his father had hailed from.

They had halted in front of the police station.

Two men were escorting the three prisoners inside. The captain followed. The soldiers waited. Presently Westerfield reappeared in the doorway.

"Listen up, men. We'll be working it a little differently from here on in. We'll spread out, ring the fire, and move slowly forward. Anybody you catch, bring them straight here. Threaten them if you must, but don't shoot. I'm afraid it's going to be a long night."

The men groaned. Devlin looked around at his fellow veterans of the Mexican War. What would they think of him? How would he look, a deserter?

A disgusting word, right down there with "coward" and "traitor."

●◄3►●

The fire began to die shortly after midnight. But
not before eighteen blocks had been destroyed,
mostly in the Barbary Coast and Chinatown. Two
thousand buildings—many not yet a year old and touted
as fireproof—were consumed. Gun barrels were found
twisted and knotted like snakes from the heat; tons of
nails were welded together in the shape of the kegs
that contained them; dozens of "fireproof" safes burst.
Silverware and crockery were found melted and fused
in heaps; preserved meats, unable to stand a second
cooking, exploded.

One hundred and eight people died, thousands suffered
injuries. Loss of property was to be estimated at more
than three million dollars. At the Jenny Lind theater,
The Comedy of Errors turned into the *Tragedy of Tom
Maguire*. The onetime New York City hack driver
turned theatrical impressario saw his pride and joy
burn to the ground.

Nineteen looters were arrested, jailed, and before
the week was out would be tried, found guilty, and
hanged. San Franciscans took their fires—and those
who set them and profited from them—very seriously.

Loyal Devlin awoke shortly after seven-thirty in the
morning feeling refreshed. He found his shirt, socks,
and trousers washed and ironed and hanging over the

foot of his bed. He washed, shaved, dressed, and came out to find Sam Brannan seated at his desk composing a letter.

"Good morning," the reverend said amiably. "Sleep well?"

"Like a top."

Brannan smiled. "I confess I never have understood that term. Tops being inanimate objects, how can they be capable of sleeping or waking?"

Mercy came in to rescue Devlin. He greeted her and thanked her for washing and ironing his things. She led him into the dining room by the arm where her daughter Betsy was already having breakfast.

"Betsy dear, it's polite to wait for our guest to sit down before starting," said her mother.

"I'm absolutely famished, Maw, or I would have. I'm sure Mr. Devlin doesn't mind."

"Not at all," said Devlin.

"See? If you don't like bacon, I'll take yours, Mr. Devlin," said Betsy, readying her fork.

Mercy laughed, a trifle embarrassed, thought Devlin. "Now you just behave yourself, missy. Whatever will Mr. Devlin think of your upbringing!" At which Betsy withdrew her fork with unconcealable reluctance.

The room was beautifully and expensively furnished, Devlin noticed as he sat down. Only the best for the wealthy; and in a month or two, he and his brother Tom would be joining their elite ranks. The tablecloth and napkins were Belgian lace, the sideboard was in the New York Empire style with large panels of flame-grained mahogany columns. The Duncan Phyfe table was older and even more impressive. And overhead hung a Bohemian-style glass chandelier, colored a soft blue in deep-cut patterns. Devlin would not have been surprised to see the governor walk into such a beautifully appointed room and sit down beside him.

Reverend Brannan joined them. Betsy continued attacking her breakfast as if she hadn't eaten in days.

For one so slim, she seemed to have an enormous appetite. Her father studied her indulgently. The maid glided in to fill Devlin's coffeecup.

"I take it the fire's burned out," he said.

"About five hours ago," said Brannan.

"What a pain in the neck," snapped Betsy. "We won't be able to shop for weeks. It was the worst one yet," she added, mumbling, having packed her mouth with toast. "More orange juice!"

The maid came hurrying in to refill her glass.

"Betsy dear, your table manners leave much to be desired," said her mother.

"Pish tush. Do you think my table manners are bad, Mr. Devlin?" she asked coyly. "I think table manners are stuffy. Sit, eat, and get it done with is my motto. And I don't think I'm any less of a lady because of it!"

Brannan chuckled tolerantly; Mercy rolled her eyes.

"We mustn't put Mr. Devlin on the spot, Muffin precious," said the reverend. "Mrs. Brannan tells me you've come all the way from Boston to join your brother. To look for gold, right? Of course, why else? You probably wonder why I'm not out digging with the rest. We've been here since 1846, long before the gold rush, and I'm proud to say these hands have never held pick or shovel."

"No need," commented Mercy dryly. "My husband opened a mining-equipment store ten days after we got here, bought property with the profits, gobbled up more and more—"

" 'Gobble'? Really, my love, you make me sound as greedy as Midas. I'm a businessman as well as a man of the cloth, Mr. Devlin. And blessed with enormous energy. I was born in Saco, Maine, in 1819, and became a printer. Later I embraced the Mormon Church. I'm proud to say I preached the first English sermon in the streets of our fair city and performed the first non-Catholic marriage ceremony. May I inquire, sir, as to your religion?"

Mercy gasped and looked appalled. "You mustn't ask a body that—"

"Daddy," murmured Betsy, equally embarrassed.

"It's okay," Devlin said. "No harm. I'm a Roman Catholic."

"Ah . . ." Brannan had a barely recognizable expression of disapproval on his face, which swiftly became one of pained tolerance. Devlin nearly laughed aloud. "As the good book says," his host went on, "we're all God's children."

"Amen," said Mercy.

Betsy smiled. Her father frowned at her briefly, then went on to enlighten their guest regarding his other accomplishments since settling in San Francisco.

"Two weeks ago I ran for governor of California."

Betsy giggled. "He got one vote."

"I keep telling you that's not the point," her father rasped sternly. "The point is, Mr. Devlin, as I'm sure you see, Samuel Brannan is ever ready, willing, and able to serve the populace." He wiped his mouth and put down his napkin. "Now, if you'll all excuse me, I'll take my coffee into my study and finish my letter."

"Daddy's writing to the secretary of the army to get rid of the colonel at Fort Point," said Betsy. "He sticks in his craw."

"Crudely put, muffin precious, but not altogether wrong. Though I'm sure you're not in the least interested in our problems with the army, Mr. Devlin."

"*Your* problems, Sam," said his wife, "not ours."

"They are the problems of every conscientious and loyal citizen of San Francisco," burst Brannan irritably. "If you'll excuse me, sir."

"Most of us are grateful for the protection of Fort Point," added Mercy when her husband was out of hearing. "What little peace we enjoy the soldiers help keep. More eggs, Loyal?"

Mercy Brannan's gratitude for the presence of the

army would have done Colonel Bracy's heart good, had he known of it. But he had arisen three hours earlier and had no such consolation. Westerfield had brought him the news of the events of the night before. Now the two stood at the corner of the courtyard watching the men, many only partially dressed, others literally asleep on their feet.

"Well you did the right thing," Bracy stated. "You certainly couldn't leave them there to be hanged. Knowing Brannan and his friends, they wouldn't bother with proof of guilt before hanging a man. You remember the last fire, last Christmas? One of the Vigilantes shot and killed a sailor because he caught him with a torch in his hand."

"Sir?" asked Westerfield, utterly mystified.

"In the act of lighting a cigar," Bracy went on. "Sufficiently incriminating to warrant killing him in cold blood, evidently."

The breeze was coming from the south, wafting the acrid odor of charred rubble. The flag on the top level flapped listlessly. The first sergeant called for attention and began calling the five A.M. roll. Bracy only half-listened, letting his thoughts drift back to Doreen, still asleep when he'd left, and Catherine, who'd be coming home sometime tomorrow. Not a moment too soon, he thought wistfully.

"Danforth, C. W."

"Ho . . ."

"Deming, R. T."

"Here."

"Devlin, T. W."

No response.

"Devlin. Sergeant Thomas Devlin."

Nothing.

The first sergeant was suddenly looking exasperated. "Anybody see Devlin? Speak up, dammit!"

Bracy and Westerfield walked over to the sergeant.

"You heard the man," Bracy said. "Any of you boys who are buddies of his know where he is?"

"He came back with the rest of us around thirteen hundred hours," said Westerfield. "Matter of fact, I saw him go into his quarters." He pointed at the third level of arches above them. "He rooms with Sergeant Aronian. Sergeant, where is he?"

"Don't know, Captain," said a dark-skinned, slender man in the second row. "When I got up this morning, he wasn't there. I figured he'd already turned out."

"Was his bed slept in?" Bracy asked.

"Come to think of it, sir, I don't think so."

"Oh, Christ," Westerfield muttered.

"Lieutenant Hennessy," snapped Bracy.

Hennessy came rushing up, nearly tripping over his own feet in his haste. He snapped off a salute. Bracy returned it halfheartedly.

"James, take two men, check Devlin's quarters, bed, footlocker. Report back after breakfast call. I'll be in my office. Sergeant Aronian, you go on upstairs with them."

"Here we go again," Westerfield murmured gloomily.

"We'll see," said Bracy, striving for optimism in his tone.

"We sure will," responded the captain.

In his heart the colonel agreed. By 6:00 A.M. Sergeant Thomas William Devlin, a veteran of five years service with the U.S. Army, two years in action in Mexico, recipient of four battlefield commendations for conduct above and beyond the call of duty, thrice wounded in action, was officially listed as a deserter.

At five past ten Loyal Devlin, clean-shaven, hair neatly combed, clothes pressed, boots blackened with the Reverend Brannan's Ball Polish, accompanied by Betsy Brannan hanging onto his arm, appeared at the Sally Port door and asked to be taken to the man in charge. The two men on guard smiled.

"If you mean Colonel Bracy, he's in his office," said the taller one.

"I do believe that's who he means," said the other.

"He's in charge, all right, ain't he in charge, Heck?"

"That he is."

"Will you two clowns stop shilly-shallying and let us in?" Betsy snapped irritably. "They're pulling your leg, Loyal," she added, as if it were a revelation.

Given directions, they made their way to Bracy's office. A guard blocked their way, but obligingly stood aside when Devlin explained their presence. He opened the door for them. Inside they were met by the colonel's striker.

"We want to see the colonel," Betsy announced.

"I have to ask what for."

"It's personal, 'sir'," she gushed.

"I'm not an officer, you don't have to call me sir."

"Howard, what's going on out there?" called the colonel from his inner office. He appeared. Devlin apologized for barging in without an appointment and introduced Betsy. Bracy stiffened visibly at the name "Brannan."

"And I'm Loyal Devlin," continued Devlin.

Bracy's jaw dropped, but he speedily recovered.

"Come in, come in. Shut the door, please."

The office was typical of a post commander's: the desk cluttered with reports, orders, and other papers. Framed, autographed photographs of Generals Winfield Scott, Stephen W. Kearny, and Zachary Taylor plus a narrow, extremely long panoramic photograph of a field artillery regiment, complete with equipment dominated the walls. On one corner of the desk stood a miniature brass howitzer, on the other portraits of Bracy's wife and daughter.

The colonel looked exhausted to Devlin, not just the fatigue that comes from lack of sleep, but that which results from excessive tension and pressure. He arranged a chair for Betsy; Devlin took the other one. He explained why they'd come.

"You're Sergeant Devlin's brother . . ."

The colonel looked surprised by the fact.

Devlin nodded. "We haven't seen each other since before the war, sir," he explained. "I wrote him I was coming, but knowing the mails, my letter's probably still trying to catch up with me. I'd like to see him."

The colonel didn't respond.

"If he's busy on duty, I can wait, of course."

"He's . . . not busy," said Bracy. "I'm afraid he's away at the moment."

"Away?"

"Ah, up north . . . Portland. Detached duty. He'll be back in a couple of days. It seems you're right, your letter hasn't gotten here yet. If he'd known you were coming, he'd have said so and we'd have sent someone else."

Bracy hated to lie, but he wanted to be sure about Tom Devlin before he spread the word. "As soon as he gets back, I'll tell him you're here, of course."

"I've waited this long," said Devlin, "a couple more days won't be so bad."

Bracy got up and offered his hand. Devlin shook it. "Mr. Devlin, Miss Brannan, it's been a pleasure."

"I'll check back tomorrow," said Devlin, "if that's okay."

"Make it the day after."

They passed Captain Westerfield as they left. The captain nodded and went into Bracy's office. The colonel closed the door.

"You know who that was?" Bracy asked rhetorically. "Sergeant Devlin's brother, come from the East for a family reunion."

"Good God, what marvelous timing. Did you tell him?"

Bracy sighed and gazed silently out the window at the empty courtyard.

"Did you?" Westerfield repeated.

"No. I . . . Look, maybe the sergeant hasn't deserted. Maybe something happened to him last night."

"In his quarters? Sir . . ."

"The sergeant's brother will be back here day after tomorrow looking for him. If, in fact, Devlin has deserted, I'll tell him then. No harm waiting to be sure before breaking the bad news."

"I suppose you know what you're doing, Colonel."

Again Bracy sighed. "Look, the man walks in here out of the blue to see his brother. He hasn't seen him in six years. What am I supposed to say, how do you do? Welcome to California, and your brother's just deserted? We're looking for him, if we find him he'll be shot by a firing squad?"

"I see what you mean. It's a pickle, all right, but see here, you're acting like *you're* to blame. Blame the sergeant, he's the one mucking things up."

A knock sounded. It was Sergeant Nowakowski, Bracy's striker.

"Sir, Reverend Doctor Anderson and four other gentlemen want a word with you. They say it's extremely urgent."

A harried-looking little man, with a clerical collar at the bottom of his round pink face and a gleaming pate at the top, pushed past the striker.

"Colonel you must do something. At once! Call out your men. Stop them, stop them!"

"Take it easy," murmured the colonel. "What are you talking about?"

"The Committee of Vigilance. They've declared open war on Sidney Town. They're out to shoot or hang every man they find and to destroy the whole area."

A man nearly two feet taller than Anderson stepped forward.

"Jake, Artemus, and I are members of the Committee of Vigilance. And we're as sick and tired of the lawlessness and fires as the next man. But we don't abide wholesale slaughter! When we heard about it, we went straight to the reverend here."

"Fighting lawlessness with lawlessness is no solution, Colonel," shrilled Anderson. "The police don't dare lift a hand against Brannan's gang. You're our only hope. In the name of God, do something."

"Sergeant," bawled Bracy.

Nowakowski pushed through the knot of men blocking the doorway.

"Howard, get hold of the bugler, tell him to sound assembly. Every man's to drop what he's doing and fall in. On the double. Armed and prepared to move out."

"Yes, sir."

E ven before the sun rose workmen began to rebuild the city. Within weeks, the rubble would be
cleared and any number of new buildings put up.
Again. Five devastating fires; after each one the pref-
erence for masonry and stone in rebuilding greatly
increased. Thick-walled, iron-shuttered, tile-roofed brick
fortresses, similar to Reverend Brannan's house sprouted
up. Many merchants relocated closer to the outskirts
of town, to the windward.

The platting of the city hindered fire prevention.
San Francisco had originally been laid out as a hamlet-
port, with narrow streets and alleys. From 1845 on it
had grown enormously and too rapidly. Now it boasted
nearly fifty thousand residents. On any normal work
day the narrow streets were clogged from dawn to
midnight. When fire struck it was nearly impossible to
move people with their effects out of the central city
to the safety of the outskirts.

Loyal Devlin and Betsy Brannan left Fort Point
arguing. Having claimed possession of the handsome
young visitor, Betsy loudly insisted that he stay on as
the Brannan's house guest. Devlin refused to take
advantage of Mercy's hospitality. If it took him all
day, he'd find a hotel that had escaped destruction and
get a room.

As they drove back together to the house, so Devlin

could pick up his things, he abruptly changed the subject.

"What do you think of Colonel Bracy?"

"What do you mean?" Betsy crinkled her brow.

"Anything strike you as strange about him? Am I imagining it or did he seem a little shaken by our visit. He seemed evasive, even ashamed."

"Why on earth should he be ashamed?"

"Didn't you think he behaved oddly?" asked Devlin.

"No. He told you your brother's away, but he'll be back. What's odd about that? They're always sending soldiers off on some kind of mission or something. Oh pish tush, will you look at that!" She pointed to a rubble-strewn area. All that was left of the building were the charred remains of the back brick wall. "MacIvitty's is burned down! Wouldn't you know. The only decent dress shop in the whole foolish town. Burned down. If that isn't the limit. Just my luck!"

"Just poor MacIvitty's luck."

"He's dead, the new owners just kept his name."

"They'll rebuild. Everybody always does, your father says."

"But I won't be able to buy a stitch for weeks and weeks!"

Devlin chuckled. "That *is* bad luck. A crime."

"I'm serious!"

"Don't be. Think of the poor owners. You're inconvenienced, but they're out of business."

Betsy didn't seem to resent his chiding her. From the reaction on her face, she liked it. She held his arm possessively. In fact, she had hardly let go of it from the moment they'd left the house. Devlin got the feeling she wanted to appropriate him for her own. He'd bet that she was fed up with spineless men who overindulged her. Too bad he wasn't interested. She *was* pretty, but he'd come here with things to do other than take up with the first pretty girl he met. He'd connect with his brother Tom, talk him into resigning from the army, and they'd go off and dig for gold. Soon they'd be so rich they'd be able to buy and sell the Reverend Brannan.

"Aren't you the quiet one all of a sudden?" Betsy commented, breaking into his thoughts. "What are you thinking about?"

"Tom."

"I guess it must be hard being separated from your brother for so long. I wouldn't know, I'm an only child."

"Are you really?"

The sarcasm went over her head. "It's not easy; Daddy spoils me something awful. If it wasn't for Maw I'd be the most hateful little beast."

"Your mother's one great lady, Betsy."

"Daddy's the most successful man in the whole county, and one of the richest. Everybody knows him. He's head of the Committee of Vigilance, you know. If it wasn't for the Committee of Vigilance San Francisco would be an absolute jungle and we'd all be dead. He's very rich."

Devlin only smiled.

Many members of the Committee of Vigilance shared the Reverend Doctor Anderson's associates' views and refused to march against Sydney Town. But more than four times as many nonmembers assembled in front of Brannan's office. Irate citizens came in droves and within half an hour nearly six hundred men, armed, angry, and emboldened by their numbers and their purpose, were ready to "clean up" Sydney Town.

Most of the Vigilantes were not criminals but men fed up with San Francisco's legal system. And tired of seeing lawyers defend well-heeled criminals with legal quibbles and delays. The courts were inefficient and in many cases corrupt; juries were packed and witnesses bought off. And the police were for the most part either helpless or indifferent to the problem.

The people themselves complicated the problem.

The imperfections of the jury system were particularly flagrant. "Jurying" was, for some, a way of making a living and in many cases not an honest one. It wasn't easy to get respectable, responsible men, especially hard-working merchants, to neglect their businesses in order to serve. People excused this reluctance with the argument that it took only one rascal to pack a jury. This was indisputable, but turning their backs on the system only encouraged tampering.

So it was natural that people came to look on the Committee of Vigilance as a last-resort protection against lawlessness. Brannan interpreted public approval as a mandate to deal with matters as he saw fit. If anyone disapproved of his methods, the devil take them.

The Ducks in Sydney Town got wind of the impending attack, and most of them went to ground. About twenty assembled at Madame Reiter's Bagnio and prepared to defend their loot and their lives.

On the colonel's orders, Captain Westerfield led a four-man detachment into the city ahead of the rest to intercept the Committee of Vigilance before it left Brannan's office. They arrived too late. The Vigilantes were already on the march that would take them up Sansome Street and west across Vallejo into the heart of Sydney Town. Ordered to quick-march, the soldiers caught up with their quarry just two blocks below Vallejo, where the Vigilantes had stopped to allow Brannan to welcome additions to their ranks. The crowd by now was so large it blocked the entire intersection. Brannan had just finished loudly welcoming the new volunteers when he espied Westerfield and his men coming at a run.

"Look there, my friends," he bawled from his perch on a Pears Soap box, brought along solely for that purpose. "Just as I expected, our 'friends' from Fort Point have come to join the fray. Welcome, Captain. What kept you?"

"Reverend, I'm not going to mince words with you." Westerfield struggled to catch his breath. "This assembly is illegal, this is a mob. I know what you're up to, and I'm giving you five minutes to disperse. Go about your business, go home if you got a home to go to—"

"Ahhhh, how apt," boomed Brannan. "How singularly appropriate. Did you hear the man, my friends? 'If you've got a home to go to.' How many of you do? Raise your hands."

Few hands went up. A roar of disapproval filled the air, drowning out Brannan's words as he tried to continue. He gesticulated and shouted and finally got his listeners' attention.

" 'Illegal,' Captain, is that the word? You call this lawful assembly illegal? You're wrong. The Committee of Vigilance is duly constituted, recognized and respected by the authorities—such as *they* are." He paused for the loud laughter. "And this morning we have a job to do. You're welcome to join us, but if you don't, see that you don't interfere."

"Rabble-rousin' sonovabitch," burst the corporal standing beside Westerfield.

The captain spun on him angrily. "Shut up, idiot! One more word and I'll put you on report."

As he spoke, men on the fringe of the crowd detached themselves from it and began forming a circle around Westerfield and his men. Somebody fired a pistol in the air.

"You heard the reverend, soldier boy. Turn 'round and get the hell out'n here if you don' wanna see blood."

"Yours!" bellowed somebody behind him.

Everybody laughed. Nobody smiled. Westerfield appeared unfazed. His orders were to delay them in order to give the colonel and the main force time to surround Sydney Town. He stalled for time.

"Sir," he said to Brannan, "we don't want trouble

any more than you. You're all decent men who are fed up with this terrible situation—"

"That's enough soft soap, Captain." Brannan was glaring. "This is our business, kindly keep your distance. Attention, everybody, let's proceed. Walter, Herbert, keep them surrounded for ten minutes. Until you hear the shooting. You know where to find us."

"Yes, sir, Reverend."

"You're a fool, Brannan," snapped Westerfield.

Brannan ignored him. The march resumed, the men breaking into a raucous rendition of "Yankee Doodle." But as the crowd turned the corner, a hush settled over it. About twenty yards stood four artillerymen. Before them sat a howitzer, primed and ready, capable of hurling two twelve-pound balls a minute.

Suddenly there was a loud explosion, and a burst of blue smoke whooshed over the heads of the astonished Vigilantes. They panicked and scattered; Brannan was hard-put to restore order and reassemble them. But after a good deal of shouting and threats, he managed to do so.

In the meantime Colonel Bracy, clad in his dress blues, appeared. He stood in front of the still-smoking howitzer, his buttons glinting in the sun, his sword at his hip. His eyes bored into the minister's.

"Colonel Bracy," said Brannan.

"Reverend. Lovely day."

"Isn't it, though?"

"Perfect in all respects, but for the burned smell, wouldn't you say?"

"I would indeed, Colonel."

"Have you by chance seen Captain Westerfield and his men?"

"We met them on the way and had a brief chat. No harm has come to them. None will come to you and your men, Colonel."

"I'm sure of that."

The two men faced off, with half a block separating them. As they talked, soldiers drifted into view behind Bracy, until more than fifty had assembled. If Brannan was impressed, he gave no indication.

"Colonel, you're obstructing our way and delaying our mission."

"Not delaying it, Samuel, more like nipping it in the bud. Gentlemen, your attention please. I'm going to ask you to lay down your weapons. Guns, knives, whatever you're carrying. You have thirty seconds. Lay them down, turn around, and get out of here."

Not one man behind Brannan moved. He laughed.

"Ewing, either my men have been stricken deaf or they have no intention of obeying your orders."

"Perhaps I can persuade you, Samuel. Would you men behind the good reverend open it up so he can look back through the street behind you?"

Once more Brannan laughed derisively. "Do as the colonel says, brothers."

He turned and looked toward the rear, as did everyone else. A double rank of soldiers, fifty-six men with upraised rifles cocked and ready, greeted his eyes. The crowd gasped.

"Say the word, Reverend Brannan, and as soon as you've put down your weapons my men will lower theirs and you can leave. Then we can all leave peacefully."

"You wouldn't dare, Bracy."

"Major Downing!"

From behind the double rank came a deep voice, its tone awesome and intimidating.

"Ready. Aim. Fire!"

Fifty-six men fired at once, at the last second elevating their rifles slightly. The sound was deafening; confusion erupted. The crowd scattered. Within seconds Brannan stood alone, the breeze flapping his coat, a solitary, forlorn figure.

"You devil," he rasped. "This is the last straw. I've

put up with your interference for the last time. You're finished. I've already written a letter to the secretary of the army, an old and dear friend. Other letters will follow from every important personage in this city. All demanding that you be relieved of your command. You're as good as out of here, Bracy, to be replaced by a true professional, someone capable and sympathetic to our plight. A man over whom the lawless will have no power."

On he raved. It was one of his more eloquent tirades, heavily laced with venom, loaded with threats, abundant in insult and sarcasm. But gradually his listeners left, leaving the street empty until well into his speech a barefoot little girl in a ragged dress came into view at the corner of Pacific and Montgomery. She carried a hoop and stick. She stood spellbound, hanging on to his every word.

◄ 5 ►

Colonel Bracy left a platoon encompassing Sydney Town and returned to the fort. Loyal Devlin roamed about canvassing the few hotels still standing, including the Parker House in Portsmouth Square. At every front desk he was told that the usual price of a room to miners with their pockets full of pay dirt—thirty-seven fifty a week—was now doubled. For Devlin it was a lesson in how conscientious, enterprising business people can take immediate advantage of a catastrophe. He settled for a flop in a fifty-man dormitory on Chestnut Street, about ten minutes walk from the fort. Price: six dollars a week.

Sam Brannan took his fury and frustration back to his office. He soon decided that getting rid of Bracy wasn't enough, he'd launch a campaign to close Fort Point permanently. He would rid the city of every blue uniform. He wrote a second letter even more fiery than the first, already in the mails.

He had nearly finished his second letter when his secretary came into his private office to announce that Mercy had stopped by.

"Bring her in, bring her in . . ."

He held a chair for his wife. As she sat, she surveyed the cramped little office, clucking softly but resisting comment on the disarray. Her husband was a pack rat; he never threw anything away.

"Ahem, listen to this, my dear. I sometimes think I'm an even better writer than I am an orator."

He read his letter. Her expression did not alter in the slightest throughout. She let him vent his anger before responding.

"It sounds awfully strong."

"It's got to be strong. How else can I get results?"

" 'Cure the cancer afflicting us all?' Really, Sam . . . The idea to get rid of the troops, our only real protection, is absurd. You're going off the deep end, dear."

He let this pass. He told her about the most recent confrontation, justifying his actions with all the arguments he could think of.

"Sam Brannan, we've been married twenty-three years. In twenty-three years I've seen you do some silly things, but this takes the cake. When word gets around town that you've sent a letter like this one you'll be a laughingstock. You're criticizing the federal government."

"Is the federal government above criticism? Shouldn't it have to answer to the people? Don't decent, hard-working taxpayers have a right to complain?"

"That's not what I'm saying. I just don't think you should scramble out on a limb, then saw it off. I guess fighting fire with fire works with a fire, but not with the Sydney Ducks. Leaving us unprotected, you're playing right into their hands. And lots of folks will say the same."

"Anyone so inclined is a coward and a traitor to the cause."

"If the cause is bloodletting and lynching, then I'm both. Come, take me to lunch. And tear that up and toss it in the waste."

"I will not. And I can't take you to lunch. I have to go over to Rincon Point. There's a choice piece of property up for grabs, and I mean to grab."

"After lunch. Let's go."

"Oh all right, all right, all right! The sacrifices I make for this family, it's a wonder I get anything done . . ."

Colonel Bracy was nobody's fool, least of all Brannan's. The reverend told him outright he'd already complained to the secretary of the army. Bracy had been in the military long enough to know that protecting one's rear off as well as on the battlefield was an unwritten rule of survival. He decided to describe the confrontation in detail in his weekly report—including the firing of the howitzer. His friend, General Isaac Kinsolving at the War Department, would read it and pass it on to the secretary of the army.

He was at his desk composing the report when his striker interrupted him. It was getting on to noon hour.

"Excuse me, sir, there's a policeman outside asking to see you."

"Show him in, Howard."

Bracy recognized his visitor, Sergeant Hooper. He knew him as an honest man and Chief Sanger's right hand—a good policeman, but almost comically careless about his appearance.

Hooper came slouching in looking uncharacteristically serious. "Colonel, the chief is meeting with the mayor at headquarters in about half an hour, and he wants you to sit down with them. It's about this to-do this morning with Brannan and the Viggies. There's talk around town there's gonna be more trouble."

"There's not going to be, Hoop. I've got men watching Sydney Town who can handle anything that crops us."

"For now, maybe, but Sanger and his honor want to work out some kinda strategy for dealin' with the Viggies in the future. And they want your two cents' worth."

"Figure out a way to get a halter around Brannan, huh?"

"That's it all right."

Bracy sighed. "It's like belling the cat."

"Can you come?"

"Let's go." Bracy set off with the sergeant.

Devlin moved his things into a locker in the dormitory and went out for a drink. He set out in a southeasterly direction, walking through the fire-ravaged central city. When he came to the Blue Duck, he went inside. The only sign that it had been pressed into service as a temporary hospital the night before was the bloodstains on the floor.

Despite the earliness of the hour, the bar was lined with patrons and most of the tables were taken. He found an empty place beside an off-duty corporal drinking his lunch with his sidekick, a private.

The bartender recognized Devlin from the night before and greeted him affably.

"How's your wrist doing, Boston?"

"Not bad. Whiskey." He placed a paper dollar on the bar.

"Find your brother?"

"Not yet. The colonel up at the fort told me he's up in Oregon. Supposed to be back tomorrow or the day after."

The two soldiers were listening.

"Oregon?" the corporal asked Devlin. "Oregon?" he repeated to his buddy.

"Portland," Devlin said. "Say, do you boys know my brother? Sergeant Thomas Devlin?"

They exchanged looks. The private shook his head.

"We know Tom Devlin," said the corporal, "and he ain't up to no Portland. Old Tom's gone lookin' for gold."

"Deserted," said his friend. "Last night."

Devlin gawked.

"The colonel told me—"

The corporal shook his head. "Hell, three of the boys are out lookin' for the sarge this minute, and I pray they don't find him. Because if they do, he's a dead man. They shoot deserters these days."

"Amen," said the private. "You wouldn't catch me desertin'. With my luck they'd find me before I got as far as North Beach, Chrissakes."

The Corporal forced a laugh. "You and me both."

Devlin was stunned by the news, and anger began filling his head like a liquid. He was suddenly livid. The bartender had set his drink down for him. He waved it away, snatched up his dollar, and ran out.

The two guards outside the Sally Port were the ones who'd been on duty when Devlin and Betsy had come earlier. Both recognized Devlin but shook their heads. One barred his way.

"Provost marshal's orders, sir," said the other apologetically. "We're not supposed to let anybody from town in, not unless we've been told you're coming or you're the police."

"I have to see Bracy," Devlin snapped.

"He ain't here," said the other. "Gone into town." Devlin's eyes took on a suspicious look. "Swear to God, police sergeant come and got him."

"When's he coming back?"

"Dunno," said the other. "Might be back already." He pointed down the road. "That's his house facing the other way, the one with the red tile roof and the flowers. He coulda come back without us seeing, stopped off home. He does that."

Devlin thanked them and started back the way he'd come.

He was surprised when his knock was answered by a young woman. Her hair was a profusion of jet-black waves that contrasted with her eyes, the color blue of a sun-bleached sky. Her cheekbones were too high, too prominent, sending long shadows down her cheeks; her jaw was boxy, almost defiant. Her coloring was pale bronze, as if she'd been out in the sun and tanned and let it fade. Her lips were a trifle too full. She was thin and nearly as tall as Devlin's six-foot-even. Her shoulders seemed somewhat wide for a woman, her hands were slender. She was stunningly beautiful.

"I . . . beg your pardon," stammered Devlin.

She looked distracted. "Yes?"

"I'm looking for Colonel Bracy."

"My father's not here. He and Mother are both out."

"I'm Loyal Devlin."

Her attention focused on him. She held forth her hand and smiled.

"Catherine Bracy," she said as he shook it. "Come in and wait if you want. Is he expecting you?"

"No. But it's rather important. He wasn't at the fort."

"Then he's in town. He'll probably stop in on the way back."

Devlin tried not to stare, but he was mesmerized by this woman. The corners of her mouth came up in a smile. She was beautiful, just beautiful, and her voice was low and seductive. And her eyes! He'd never seen such long lashes.

The parlor looked as if a whirlwind had struck, whipped about the contents of two large suitcases, and left.

"Don't look," she said. "I just got home from a trip." She started to move an opened suitcase from a chair to the floor so he could sit. He helped her set it down. "Is there anything *I* can do for you?"

"No, thanks, it's—"

"Personal, of course. Man talk. Would you like some coffee? I could use a cup. I came all the way from Kansas City." She set her hand to the small of her back and leaned against it. "I never want to see the inside of a stage coach again. It was almost nineteen hundred miles."

She talked over her shoulder on her way to the kitchen and gestured for him to follow. He could not take his eyes off her. He busied himself helping her make the coffee.

"Traveling by stage rearranges all the bones. Even your fingers. Honestly. I don't know how older people stand it. Have you ever had the pleasure?"

"Not yet. I came by ship from Boston."

She had lit the stove. He filled the pot with water. She poked through the bread box.

"I'm afraid we don't have anything to go with it."

"Just coffee's fine."

"You've come from Boston, you said? That must have been fun."

He grinned. "If I ever decide to go back, I guarantee it won't be the same way."

She smiled, and he felt his cheeks tingle slightly. She asked about his trip, and he soon found himself telling her everything: the voyage by sea, his dreams of finding gold with his brother Tom, his home in Boston. He wanted her to know everything about him. But then they got to talking about the fire.

"It looks even worse than the last one," Catherine said. "Each one is worse than the one before. Which doesn't seem to discourage people from rebuilding. Fuel for the next fire. What did you do to your wrist?"

"Fell on it."

"It looks painful."

"It's just a sprain."

"Who doctored it?"

"Nursed. Mrs. Brannan."

"What did you think of her?"

"She's wonderful."

"Everybody adores Mercy Brannan. And did you meet her husband?"

Devlin nodded. "She put me up at the house last night. We all had breakfast together."

"So you've met Betsy, too. Pretty, isn't she?" She smiled. "So what did you think of her father?"

"Unusual man."

Catherine laughed. "Now, there's an understatement if I've ever heard one." She had added cream and sugar to her coffee and stared blankly into the cup.

"Sam Brannan and my father despise each other. Perhaps that's a little strong, but they do see things differently. *Every*thing." She shrugged her shoulders. "Now tell me about your brother Tom."

He did so, omitting what he'd learned at the Blue Duck earlier. He saw no need to involve her in his brief with her father. It did threaten to make things awkward, though. And he'd certainly hate to see anything come between him and this beautiful creature. Maybe it'd be wiser to hold off talking to the colonel. Do business in a businesslike setting, not the man's home. Besides, the walk back to the fort and this delay had cooled him off considerably. He finished his coffee, complimented her on it, and got up.

"Where are you going?" Catherine looked surprised.

"I can see your father at the fort."

"Are you sure there's nothing I can do? Anything you want me to tell him?"

"That's very kind of you, but it's strictly between—"

"My, my, it really does sound serious. Does it have to do with your brother?"

Something clicked in Devlin's heart. Since he'd arrived, the only person he'd met he felt comfortable with had been Mercy Brannan. But Catherine Bracy was making him feel even more comfortable, and he was exceptionally attracted to her. He could see that she liked him, too, and it couldn't hurt to have her as an ally.

"Your father and I spoke earlier," he began. "He told me Tom had been sent up to Oregon, that he'd be back in a day or so. I found out about an hour ago that he lied to me. Tom lit out, and your father knew it."

"He's deserted?" Catherine looked startled by the news.

"That's what I heard. Why would the colonel lie to me?"

"My father's not a liar," she said defensively.

"If you don't believe me, ask him yourself."

"If Tom deserted and my father knew, I'm sure he had his reasons for not telling you."

"What the devil reason could there be!" Devlin snapped.

"When you see him, ask him," she snapped back. "Until you do, don't go around accusing him."

"He's a damn liar! And I'll tell him to his face. Stay out of it, it's none of your business."

"You've made it my business; you told me, remember? You call my father a liar and blame him for what your brother's done. Tom's deserted! You don't like the word, but that's what he's done. Gone out looking for gold like the rest."

"If he catches him and stands him up in front of a firing squad, it'll be the last man he'll ever murder. I'll raise a stink all the way back to Washington, so help me God! I'll start right here in town with his friend Brannan. He's editor of the paper, right? I can see the headline in his paper: 'Bracy Executes Mexican War Hero.' "

"Get out of here!"

"I was going, you stopped me."

"I didn't 'stop' you; what are you doing, blaming me as well as my father? Blame your brother. Anybody with brains enough to tie his shoe knows what he's letting himself in for when he runs away."

Devlin waved this away. "Don't defend your old man to me. And what are you, judge and jury? Petticoat God Almighty? Do you go to all the executions? Is the firing squad a highlight of the social life around here?"

He flung open the front door to discover the colonel and Mrs. Bracy coming up the walk arm in arm.

"I want to talk to you." Devlin snarled. "Right now."

Catherine had followed him to the door.

"Pay no attention, Daddy."

"Colonel!"

"I'll see you at the fort later, Mr. Devlin," said Bracy.

"Catherine! Sweetheart!" he burst out.

The two of them rushed past Devlin to embrace and kiss her. He turned to watch briefly; they ignored him, save for a withering glare from Catherine over her father's shoulder. Devlin stormed off, heading toward the fort, resolving to wait for the colonel in his office, by the Sally Port.

Maybe if he waited long enough he'd cool down, get control of his temper, and when Bracy did show, he'd talk to him in civilized fashion. Instead of knocking him cold.

6

The Reverend Samuel Brannan sat opposite his wife at lunch and watched her attack her salad with startling fury. They were having lunch at "their" table by the front window in Ransom's Restaurant on Post, across the street from Union Square. He knew it was only a matter of minutes before she turned her fury against him. She must have heard about the attack on Sidney Town.

"How could you do it?" Mercy finally asked.

"What's that, my dear?" he replied, feigning innocence.

"Don't play games with me, Samuel Brannan. You know exactly what I'm talking about: rabble-rousing and marching on Sidney Town. You could have gotten yourself killed—not to mention your followers. You have a family. Don't you ever stop to think of either of us?"

"Ssssh, people are looking this way, dear."

"You call yourself a man of God . . ."

" 'Call'? I like that. It happens that the Vigilantes are the last line of defense in this city. The police, the army—"

The look on his wife's face stopped him cold. "I don't want to talk about the Vigilantes or the police, I want to talk about you. Only you. Whenever trouble crops up, whenever the Vigilantes get involved, you lose control. You go wild."

"I like that!"

"Let me finish. You do. I know you better than you know yourself. I've seen responsive crowds go to your head, election triumphs, business successes. But nothing like when you play general in your private war against Sidney Town. You become more bloodthirsty than the most barbaric despot. I'm sick of it. So is Betsy."

"You don't understand, neither of you."

"I understand the situation better than you think. What has all the commotion gotten you? What have you changed? Nothing. Things are as bad now as they were before the Vigilantes got together. In some ways worse. Listen to me. Instead of voting to cut the police force, you should vote to double it, for pity's sakes! You should be working side by side with Colonel Bracy and his soldiers instead of against them. But no, that's not enough for you because you'd have to share the limelight."

"That's a terrible thing to say to your husband."

"I'm telling you the truth because I'm your wife."

He sighed martyrlike. "Why don't we just drop it and enjoy our lunch? We don't agree, we obviously never will."

"Sam, please, I beg you. Stop this vengeance before you or someone else gets hurt. It's reached a point where I expect to open the door and see them carry your body in on a board."

"You're overreacting, dear."

"I'm not. You're always at the front of the pack, exposed, in danger. Hasn't it occurred to you that you've become their number-one target? Good Lord, they've probably put a price on your head. A hundred dollars to the one who blows your brains out."

"I'm not afraid. Never. 'Be strong and have a good courage, fear not, nor be afraid of them: for the Lord thy God, he it is that doth go with thee; he will not fail thee, nor forsake thee.' Deuteronomy . . ."

"Thirty-one, verse six, I know. In other words, there's nothing I can say to change your mind."

"Our ship is on its true course, my dear; we need only time, patience, and the guidance of the Lord to bring us safely to port."

"Eat your soup, it's getting cold."

Tom Devlin got out of the city as fast as he could. Heading south, he was halfway to Redwood City by sunrise.

He had stolen a horse, reasoning that the army owed him that much for his years behind brass buttons. He knew that Hennessy would be after him shortly after roll call. Hennessy, the bloodhound. He'd brought back two or three deserters. No doubt he was beginning to get good at it. Knowing him, he enjoyed the hunt.

Well, this was one fox he'd never catch. The only way Hennessy could pick up his trail would be if he struck it rich. Really rich, a bonanza. Word would get around like wildfire. He'd worry about that when the time came.

Up to now they were catching roughly one out of nine or ten deserters. And Tom Devlin had no plans to be one of the unlucky ones, like Joe MacGruder. Poor Joe, the funniest man on the post; he always had everybody in stitches, even the brass. Didn't tell jokes or stories, just saw the funny side in everything and made a crack in that raw, gravel voice of his. Everybody in stitches, even the colonel. Now Joe was gone and all the laughter with him.

He dug his heels into the little mare's flanks. It was another five miles or so to Redwood City. Ten or fifteen beyond before he could turn the corner at the south end of the bay. It might be wise to head north, all the way up to Martinez, before cutting east. It was a long jaunt—more than forty miles—but it might be smart. Most runaways headed east as soon as they got around the bay. Hennessy knew that, and he'd probably never think anyone would bother going all the way back up to the top.

The more he thought about it, the more sense it made. He had to be a fox to outwit the bloodhound, and this fox was new at the game. His every move had to be carefully planned. No rushing things, no mistakes, none.

He slowed his horse to save her. He probably wouldn't get to Martinez until sundown. He could buy what he'd need there, starting with the most important piece of equipment: a pie tin. It was said you could wash a shirt, feed a mule, or fry bacon with it, as well as pan your fortune. Panning was the simplest method, but some said far from the easiest. It meant hours of squatting in freezing water, rotating the pan until your arms got numb and your knees and the backs of your thighs ached like fury. He would start with panning at first and see what happened.

It was going to be a scorcher of a day. Tom could already feel the sun cooking his face. His hand slipped down to feel his canteen. It felt cool. He could do with a swig, but his throat would have to wait. First, he had to stretch the miles between him and Hennessy. He planned on riding until the horse showed signs of tiring. And that wouldn't be for a while.

He passed through Redwood City, feeling a little easier as the town began shrinking behind him. He thought about his brother Loyal. When he made his strike and could relax a little, he'd write to him and talk him into coming out. They could work side by side. Loyal would love it. They'd collect a fortune and leave the country for a year or two, then return to Boston and live like kings.

He smiled at the thought. He only hoped that Loyal would understand his "leaving" the army. —he couldn't bring himself to call it desertion. Loy had always looked up to him, respected, admired him, especially since the folks had passed on. All the family they had was each other. They'd always been close, until he'd joined the army.

That was the key to explaining his leaving: he'd joined, he'd fought, he'd unjoined. The army wouldn't buy it, but Loy would; he'd understand.

He thought about Martinez. When he bought his supplies there maybe he should invest in a mule. Almost every prospector had one; handiest animal going. How could a man carry 300 pounds of gold on his back?

He thought about Colonel Bracy and envisioned the look on his face when this Devlin didn't answer at roll call. He'd be furious, and hurt. They'd been together more than four years. They respected each other. He had to be the last man Bracy would think would light out.

"Sorry, Colonel, nothing personal."

Loyal Devlin could have kicked himself for sounding off at Catherine Bracy. Not that she hadn't provoked it with that temper of hers.

Now he'd probably never see her again. He was surprised by how disappointed he felt.

He waited for the colonel over an hour, managing to regain little control over his anger. When Bracy finally showed up, Devlin had to hold himself back from having it out then and there.

"Come inside," the colonel said quietly, coming up. "We can talk in my office."

Devlin followed him in; neither spoke. The colonel preceded him into headquarters. His striker jumped up saluting.

"At ease, Howard. Any messages?"

"No, sir, but Captain Westerfield was asking after you, sir."

"Give us ten minutes, then get him."

Inside, the colonel gestured Devlin to a chair. He ignored it.

"I'm not staying, I just want to get one thing straight."

"I lied to you," said Bracy, turning his attention to correspondence on his desk, responding without looking Devlin's way. "Your feelings are hurt."

"Don't talk down to me, Bracy. I'm not one of your tin soldiers."

"Shut up and sit down."

"I'll stand."

"You can do back flips for all I care. Now let me explain. When you came in here this morning asking after your brother, I told you he'd been sent up to Oregon. I'd already had him listed as a deserter." Bracy took a deep breath. "Your brother and I go back a long ways, to the summer of forty-six. If circumstances were diffcrent, we might have been the best of friends. As it was, we were close, believe that or not. Believe this: when he didn't answer to his name this morning, I felt like I'd been punched in the heart."

"Like it was your son," said Devlin sarcastically.

"Exactly." His tone softened. "Then you showed up, and I lied to you." He looked past Devlin to make sure the door was closed. And lowered his voice. "If I'd told you he'd deserted, you'd have immediately gone out looking for him. That'd be just dandy for us—not very good for Tom. Our search party would have followed you. Easier than following his cold trail, don't you think?" Bracy shook a finger. "I stuck my neck out. For him, not you. And if you ever tell a single soul what I just said, so help me God . . ."

Devlin scoffed softly. Bracy frowned, annoyed.

"You don't believe me."

"I don't even know you."

"You think I like bringing men back and shooting them down like dogs? I despise it. Every execution makes me sicker than the one before. But orders are orders. And responsibility's responsibility, and Tom threw his overboard. You've a problem with me? Blame him."

Devlin thought it over.

Was Bracy leveling with him? Whether he was or not suddenly didn't seem important. Only Tom. He had to find his brother. To hell with digging gold, better they get out, or . . .

"What?" asked Bracy.

Devlin looked Bracy straight in the eyes. "What if I find him and talk him into coming back. Would you still shoot him?"

"Of course not! Good God, man, what do you think we are, savages?"

"When I go out, your men will follow me."

"Lieutenant Hennessy's already out. Way ahead of you. I won't be sending anybody else."

"Will this Hennessy catch him?"

"He's caught others, but Tom's a lot brighter than most. That's what surprised me, his deserting. That and because he's been in so long, with such an exemplary record. It proves one thing: nobody's immune from gold fever. I'm surprised every man here hasn't flown the coop."

Bracy stood up. He offered his hand. Devlin shook it. Bracy grinned.

"Good hunting."

"Thanks."

"Beat it."

Devlin started for the door. He stopped with his hand on the knob and turned, suddenly sheepish. "Can I ask a favor? Would you mind apologizing to Catherine for me?"

"Glad to."

"I got pretty steamed."

"I can't guarantee she'll accept it. My little girl has a mind of her own."

"I noticed."

Bracy laughed. Devlin exited, and Westerfield, who had who been waiting in the outer office, came in.

"Close it."

"What's he doing back here?"

"Nothing." Bracy got right down to business. "I guess you heard, I just came back from a meeting with the mayor and Chief Sanger. They want us to post men in town on a regular basis."

"We don't have the manpower."

"That's what I told them. Until we do, we'll have to put it on hold. There's more. Sanger's planning a secret sweep of Sidney Town. He's a fool if he thinks it won't get back to the Ducks. Half his force is taking money from them. I tell you, Robert, this mess is getting worse by the hour."

"Did either of them say anything about the Vigilantes?"

"The chief topic of discussion."

"Do they have any hope of disbanding them? Or at least getting rid of Brannan?"

"We all agree on that, but we don't know how. Brannan's got his tight little coterie of loyal followers. Still . . ." Bracy paused, narrowing his eyes. "I've an idea. I should have thought of it at the meeting. How many Vigilantes on the committee all told, would you say?"

Westerfield shrugged. "Eight hundred? A thousand?"

"Not that many; maybe seven hundred. With four hundred loyal to Brannan. And three hundred who can't stand him and only stay on out of community spirit or the hope that someday they can squeeze him out. Now how can we get those three hundred to come over to our side? Work with us?"

"Good question, Colonel."

"What if we *could* gradually draw Brannan's support away from him, eventually leave him hanging out to dry?"

"Great! How?"

"I'm not exactly sure, but I think we're on the right track. Only how do we take away his support without making him look like a martyr? His favorite role. And, remember, he's beloved by the people. He may be a hypocrite, and a tax dodger, but he's given more to San Francisco than anybody. When a new mother around here names her little boy Samuel, it's not after Sam Houston."

"Maybe we'll get lucky, maybe in the next broil he'll get himself killed. He's always up in the front."

"And always protected by his friends. Like the king going into battle. He's got a new bee in his hat, he wants to get rid of me."

"What's new about that?"

Bracy told Westerfield about Brannan's threatened letter campaign and his own strategy for defense against it.

The captain reacted in dismay and disgust. "We have to explain to the War Department that we're only doing our jobs? Goddammit to hell!"

"What time is it?" Bracy asked.

"Going on four."

"The police are going to start sweeping Sydney Town at six sharp. I promised Sanger thirty men in addition to the boys on lookout down there now."

"You think the Vigilantes'll butt in?"

"Don't you?" Bracy got up stretching and yawning. "I'm going down to the house. Catherine came home a day early."

Westerfield brightened, as might be expected of any interested admirer.

"Stop by and pick me up at twenty to six," the colonel went on. "Issue every man twenty rounds. And pick and choose, Robert. No hotheads, no blood lovers looking to make another stripe; this could get messy without our making it so. If Brannan shows up, I can almost guarantee it."

7

Sergeant Joseph Aronian was an unwilling member of Lieutenant Hennessy's chase team. He'd never gone out deserter-hunting before—and Tom Devlin was a friend of his. He hated the idea of chasing somebody with whom he'd gotten drunk, whored around, and fought side by side against Santa Anna. If they caught up with him, what would Tom say when he saw his old bunkie?

A corporal and private, both regular members of the bloodhound's search team, brought up the rear. Aronian rode in front, beside Hennessy. All the way down from the fort, he'd been sneaking glances at the lieutenant, noting the unmistakable air of determination about him. . . . If necessary Hennessy would ride to hell to catch his prey, Aronian was sure. Not that the lieutenant had any special dislike for Devlin; it was more a matter of pride. The more feathers in his helmet, the sooner a silver bar would replace his gold one.

Redwood City was awakening when they rode in. A woman emptied a tubful of wash water out her front door, an old man in long johns and ragged, holey pants, wearing bright red suspenders, stretched and yawned as he gently nudged a small dog out the door with his foot. Upstairs windows opened, curtains fluttered, bedding flopped over sills to air, somebody shouted, somebody else laughed, a well-dressed man sporting a slouch hat so large it dwarfed him bent to unlock the door to the drugstore. The lieutenant hailed him, pulling up sharply and getting down.

"Good morning, sir."

The man came over to them, and Hennessy described Devlin in detail. Each detail set the man shaking his head anew.

"I've been up two hours," he said finally. He pointed to an upstairs window in the building directly opposite. "That's my room there. The window's been open all night. I would have heard anybody riding through. Nobody did. Not in the past two hours."

"Maybe he circled the town," said the corporal.

"Thank you, sir," Hennessy said to the man. He drank from his canteen, all four watching him, recapped it, and mounted his bay. "Let's go."

As they headed out of town a thought occurred to Aronian. Perhaps he had been ordered on this mission precisely because he was a friend of Devlin's. Maybe the colonel hoped his presence might prevent a shootout. He could talk to Devlin; Hennessy certainly wouldn't bother. Aronian felt a little better about his duty, thinking of it that way.

Four miles beyond Redwood City Hennessy pulled up. "We'll circle the end of the bay and head up the other side," he said. "But only as far as Niles. Then cut east. Search the Hangtown–Grass Valley area first. I've got a sneaky feeling about this pigeon, boys. He's hungry; I bet he stops at the first panning site he comes to to try his luck. We're going to get him."

"If he spots us coming, he'll come up from the creek shooting," warned the private. "He ain't like the others, who gave up without a fight." He leered. "What if he forces us to shoot him, sir?"

"He won't, he's not stupid."

"If we get him cornered, he'll be desp'rate. He'll shoot. We sure can't shoot back to miss, can we?"

Hennessy smiled and lectured with a finger. "You make sure you shoot first. I couldn't care less whether we bring him home sitting his horse or slung over it. Nor does the army."

"We're supposed to bring him in alive," Aronian said.

"Who says?" piped the private. "What's the difference between us shooting him and the firing squad?"

"That's not the point," said Aronian caustically.

Hennessy nodded. "The sergeant's right, soldier."

Aronian heard him say it, saw him nod, but with more like sarcasm than conviction in either. They *wouldn't* kill him, he wouldn't let them. Only how could he stop it, especially if Devlin started it? If Hennessy even suspected he was trying to save Devlin's butt, he'd put him on report as soon as they got back. Get him court marshaled for sure.

Jesus Christ, he thought wearily, forty-eight possible roomies and I get Tom Devlin.

Loyal Devlin returned to the dormitory. The man in charge, a small, balding, mousy individual with one eye that appeared too tired to straighten itself in its socket, looked up from the sign-in book.

"I'm checking out," said Devlin.

"You just checked in."

"Change in plans."

The man shrugged and scanned the page in front of him. "I can't give you your money back. It's against the rules. You signed in for a week."

"I know. Do you know someplace I can buy a halfway decent horse cheap?"

The man scratched his head. "Your best bet would be down near Sydney Town: Miller's Stables. It's the biggest in the city. Jake Miller's supposed to be a fair man, honest. You go down Columbus till you come to the Church of St. Francis of Assisi, turn left there, Vallejo Street. Jake is on the corner of Kearny and Vallejo. There's a big sign, you can't miss it. If the place is still standing. Just be careful."

"Why?"

"I told you, that's Sydney Town. It's rougher than the Barbary Coast and, son, you *look* like you just stepped off the boat."

"I can take care of myself," Devlin said, hoping he could with his still aching wrist.

"Sure you can," the man said generously.

It was close to six when Devlin arrived at Miller's Stable.

Jake Miller was nowhere about, and his elderly evil-smelling assistant informed Devlin that the boss would be back in ten minutes. Across the street, the Down Under Bar beckoned. Devlin went in. It looked nothing like the Blue Duck; it was seedier. The ceiling was so low he could almost reach up and touch it, and the smell of stale liquor combined with the stink of vomit almost made him sick. But by the time he got up to the bar, he'd become used to it.

The bartender was a woman. She was an imposing figure, tough, with bleached hair, leathery skin, and a beauty mark the size of a nickel. She looked at him as if she hated the sight of him.

"Scotch," he said.

She took his dollar and poured, emptying the bottle. She said nothing. There were seven other customers in the place. They had all looked him over when he walked in; now they behaved as if he wasn't even there. All seven drank alone; there wasn't a whisper of conversation. Devlin figured five minutes had gone by; recalling the clerk's warning about Sydney Town, he resolved to drink up and head back to the stables to wait for Jake Miller.

He swallowed half his glass, then emptied it. The

instant he set it down a dozen hammers flew from the center of his brain in all directions and began pounding his skull. The bartender was staring at him, her face blank; then she broke into a smile. He saw it start, before his eyes rolled back in his head, burst crimson, and the world blew up.

8

C olonel Bracy and Chief Sanger walked side by side. The police and more than a hundred soldiers had assembled at the corner of Sansome Street and Vallejo and started the sweep through Sydney Town. They searched the area in small mixed groups to impress the Ducks with their solidarity. They searched everywhere. But most of the suspects had been forewarned of the sweep and had gotten out of the area.

The man in charge of each team carried a copy of Chief Sanger's list of suspects, complete with known aliases. The chief and the colonel were realists; they didn't expect to apprehend even half the names on the wanted list. But only a few would do to impress the Ducks that the authorities were going on the offensive.

The object of the effort was to put on a show of unified strength. The sweep would also show the public that the police and the army weren't sitting on their hands waiting for the Vigilantes to take the initiative. Sanger was optimistic about the results; Bracy, less so. But by six-thirty P.M. eight suspects had been captured, and squealers had given the sweepers leads on more than a dozen others.

A team led by Provost Marshal Viselli invaded a Kearny Street bordello. The odor of cheap incense greeted them. The soiled doves and their customers protested loudly. Fights broke out. One soldier was badly scratched, and two policemen were bitten. A burly giant battled three policemen and finally had to be clubbed into submission. But not before he gave the Provost Marshal a black eye and a knee in the crotch.

Order was eventually restored, the house was searched. A rear room was broken into. Spirit lamps burned feebly, scorched shallow saucers and long-stemmed pipes were in evidence, a sickly sweet smell struck the intruders' nostrils. A boy no older than fourteen had picked up a dipper, placing the sharp end of it into his saucer, picking up a drop of gumlike opium. He held it over the flame, turning it slowly. The drop was beginning to whiten, soften and swell when a soldier knocked the dipper from his hand. They ransacked the room, smashing the lamps and saucers and other paraphernalia; buckets of water were brought in and dashed on the addicts. They were turned out; the boy was taken into custody, then released to his mother, the whore who had scratched the soldier.

Loot from the fire was found in house after house. Even food had been pilfered.

Some of the Ducks tried to make a stand. Their ranks were swollen by others, many of them new arrivals from Australia. All were well armed; the old hands knew every nook, every cranny, every house, a distinct advantage over their pursuers. Shots rang from one end of Sydney Town to the other. Residents of Chinatown, two blocks below Sydney Town, gathered along Broadway Street to watch the conflict, oohing and ahhing at the smoke from revolvers and rifles in the manner of spectators at a fireworks display.

When one team of police and soldiers broke into a warehouse, it was greeted by four men armed with shotguns. They fired point-blank, killing one policeman and wounding two others before the intruders could find cover, fight back, and finally overpower them. One Duck, seeing that he was about to be captured, set his pistol to his temple and blew his brains out.

The colonel and the chief, meanwhile, reached the corner of Vallejo and Grant Streets to be greeted by sight of some five hundred Vigilantes led by Brannan. They were coming from Little Chile. They were armed, spoiling for blood, and pushing an odd-looking contraption.

A portable scaffold, the noose swinging ominously. On either side of it men pushed large coal carts. In one a piece of canvas covered what looked to be two bodies.

"Pay no attention to them, brothers," bawled Brannan. "Just keep moving. Keep—"

It was as far as he got. A loud clamor interrupted him. The din of trash-can lids being beaten rose above it and a swarm of club-swinging Ducks came pouring out of upper Grant Street. The two sides came together, bashing heads, shooting, slashing with knives, pounding with clubs. Chief Sanger blew and blew his whistle, collecting police and soldiers around him. The battle soon spread in all four directions away from the intersection. Two men with rifles appeared at the third-floor windows of a partially burned building. Both fired at Brannan. Amazingly both missed; and four of Brannan's followers leapt to form a human wall to protect him. Others fired back at his would-be assassins. One was hit and fell out the window, landing headfirst in the street. His head smashed like a melon. The other withdrew.

Sanger could barely make himself heard above the noise of battle. He yelled orders. Bracy repeated them. More soldiers and police came running up at the sound of the whistle.

They tried running into the thick of the fray in a flying wedge in an effort to separate the two sides. But by now the Vigilantes and the Ducks were so interspersed, it was impossible to part them. Bracy signaled his men to pull back; Sanger did also.

"We'll surround them," yelled the colonel.

It took about five minutes to get their men into position. In that time combatants on both sides were killed and seriously injured. Although the Vigilantes vastly outnumbered the Ducks, few knew how to protect themselves. Many were in their sixties or older, their zeal unmatched by their strength or stamina. They quickly became exhausted and were forced to withdraw.

The battleground was finally surrounded, and both sides forced to quit. But not before Brannan had been stabbed in the shoulder and smashed in the hip by a club or ax handle. He lay bleeding in the street.

The waves beat against the cliff in slow succession, each one pounding, sending brilliant orange flashes skyward. A mile out to sea a man was swimming, lifting his leaden arms, struggling to pull himself shoreward. He had swallowed too much water, he was half drowned, his body felt like a boulder. The water pulled him down, only his arms and his ebbing will kept his head above the surface. He eyed the cliff ahead. A mile that may as well have been a hundred, a thousand. In his pounding heart he knew he'd never make it. Water rushed into his mouth, down his throat; he tried to spit it out, but could only get part of it up. His temples throbbed so he feared his head would split. He grew weaker, weaker . . .

A wave carried him upward and down into the trough. Beneath him invisible hands rose and gripped his ankles. He thrashed and thrashed trying to break free, but they pulled him down, pulled him under, his mouth again filling with water. It poured down his throat; he choked and choked and fought for breath. The sea closed over his head. Down, down, down.

*   *   *

At the same time the battle was being brought to a halt, four policemen and six soldiers entered the Down Under Bar and Restaurant. The woman stood behind the bar wiping it with a filthy rag, ignoring the intrusion. Then a man fitting the description of a suspected bank robber came through a door in the rear. He took one look and tried to run back, but they grabbed him and pulled him struggling and protesting toward the front door. He was hustled off to the holding pen set up and heavily guarded behind St. Francis Church. The sweepers ran up the stairs and began going through the rooms on the second and third floors. In a large room on the third floor they found twelve cots. Eight were occupied. On each was a man bound and gagged. Some were unconscious, others blearily awake, struggling feebly with their bonds.

Captain Westerfield gaped.

"What the hell?"

Sergeant Hooper came up to him. "We got here just in time, these boys are getting ready to go to sea."

"A press gang?" Westerfield looked mystified. "They don't shanghai men in this country."

Hooper snickered. "They didn't for the past thirty years; now it's started up again. Blame the gold rush. Ships land here, the goldbugs get off and half the crews with them. Shipmasters can't keep full working crews on board worth a damn. They offer them six times their pay, the men turn them down. What do they need with thirty bucks a month when they can get rich in thirty days a few miles inland?"

Westerfield recognized Loyal Devlin's red hair. He lay motionless. The captain took off his gag and untied him.

"Hey, Devlin . . . Hey . . ."

Hooper shook his head. "He's out of it, Captain. Drugged. Look at him, he looks dead."

"He's breathing."

"Barely . . ."

"His left leg looks dislocated," Westerfield said.

He glanced about them. The other captives had all been freed. Two were able to sit up. The sergeant shook his head.

"They knock them out downstairs with laced hooch, bring them up here, bind and gag them, and off they go on the midnight tide. By day after tomorrow they're halfway to Valparaiso. This boy looks bad off. We'd better get him to a doctor."

9

Tom Devlin came within sight of Martinez at 8:30 P.M. intent on stopping to equip himself with the bare necessities. He wouldn't splurge on a mule. Rumor said that even the oldest and most decrepit beast fetched seventy-five dollars. His most expensive purchase would be a ten-dollar eight-quart pie tin—popularly known hereabouts as a gold-washing pan. That first full pan was the aim and dream of every goldbug. Eight quarts of gold was worth $2,500.

He had not yet decided where he would stop to try his luck, but far from Martinez, east at least fifty miles, then either north or south. If he found no gold there, he'd make sure to move even farther from San Francisco. He needed to keep out of Hennessy's way for at least one full week. By that time somebody else would have deserted. This didn't mean that he'd be completely safe from capture—the searchers would continue to scour the gold-bearing areas, regardless of whom they were after—but fresher quarry would succeed fresh quarry.

"Makes this deserter that much staler."

"Deserter." He must stop using the word, stop even thinking it. He wasn't one. He was a civilian-by-choice. Not bad. From now on that's what he'd call himself.

He had prepared well for his new work, reading everything about prospecting he could get his hands on. Off-duty in town at a bar he listened in on the miners' conversations. He recalled one in particular. One miner had discovered gold up near Truckee. In an ingenious fashion. He had been panning in a stream, gradually moving down it. He came to where it had changed course, the old branch drying up completely. There he'd found an old, dry sandbar. He shoveled the sand into a blanket and tossed it in the air to be winnowed by the wind, and down fell the heavier gold. In two days he'd collected $10,000 worth. The amount may have been exaggerated, Devlin had thought at the time, but the method was foolproof. Plus his winnowing-mining removed the lucky fellow from the competition crowding the streams.

Devlin had also overheard a vital bit of information. It was generally agreed that a man working from dawn till dusk was lucky to find a half-ounce to an ounce ($8 to $16) a day. This was the rule-of-thumb minimum needed to sustain a man in the field, what with the inflated prices for food, equipment, and other essentials. If a man couldn't average half an ounce a day for a month, he'd find himself in trouble.

One thing he had to guard against: so-called lump fever. Of all the diseases afflicting prospectors, none was more widespread than the rumor that a big strike had been made someplace nearby. It was claimed that the haste with which miners abandoned one claim to go in search of a better-paying one elsewhere was the main reason why so few struck it rich.

The sky was darkening rapidly, boiling black, when Tom Devlin dismounted in front of Martinez's general store. He quickly hitched his horse and walked inside. The man behind the counter looked more like a gambler than storekeeper. A small diamond horseshoe stickpin gleamed at his chest; his fingers were slender and supple like those of a professional dealer, and on his right pinkie a diamond the size of a pea sparkled. He had to be at least seventy years old.

" 'Evening," murmured Tom, glancing about the place.

Every shelf from floor to ceiling was crammed with merchandise, all the way around to the door at his back. The ceiling was festooned with tools and containers of every size and description. He set a list on the counter. The storekeeper got out a pair of gold-filled spectacles and sent his skinny finger down it item by item, mouthing each one silently.

"What do you need with a washboard?"

Tom grinned.

"Oh, hell," the man went on, "I know what it's for, it's just that you can get by without it. I'm here to equip you, not skin you. You can get by with half the stuff you got down here." He looked up, his eyes dark, sharp, ferretlike. "You in the market for a burro? A mule?"

"Not right away."

"Then give your horse a break. All you need is a pick, a shovel, gold pan, decent rifle, ammunition, couple of drawstring bags for the ten thousand in gold you're going to find." He leered, showing a missing tooth. "Grub for three weeks, coffeepot, the usual." He held out his hand. "I'm Ira Jack Fayles."

"George Houlihan." Tom lied.

"Where you from, George?"

"Massachusetts."

Ira Jack Fayles came around the counter. He was suddenly eyeing him questioningly. "You do have cash money."

"Enough."

Fayles began collecting items, setting them on the counter, pointing out things for Tom to pick up and add to the pile.

Tom watched as Fayles glanced out the door at his horse. Tom wondered if he recognized it as government issue. He'd probably seen any number of them before; half the goldbugs coming through Martinez must be deserters, if not from Fort Point then Fort Mason or posts to the north and south. Did doing business with a deserter bother him? Whether it did or not, Tom thought, he shouldn't let the possibility bother *him*.

While Fayles was adding things up Tom's eyes wandered to the framed certificate hanging between two sets of shelves behind and above the storekeeper's head. An honorable discharge from the U.S. Army.

Fayles noticed him noticing. "Twenty years in the cavalry," he said proudly. "That was a thousand years ago. I got out in fifteen. I served with Andy Jackson. New Orleans."

"Must have been pretty rough going."

"It sure was at the Rodriguez Canal. Were you in Mexico?"

He had stopped his adding. His full concentration was on the conversation. Tom suddenly felt like a butterfly at the moment the pin is inserted, but could see no way of flapping free.

"I was. From start to finish."

"You're deserting."

It was a statement, not a question. Devlin didn't reply.

"They'll come after you."

"I know." He indicated the list. "Can we settle up? I—"

"You have to make tracks, I know."

They stared at each other. "You'll tell them, won't you?" Tom said resignedly.

There was contempt on the old man's face as he opened a drawer and fumbled about inside. He brought out a small silver medal, an eagle on sheaves of wheat, below it Old Glory suspended vertically down to crossed sabers double looped to an oval displaying stars.

"I earned this at the Rodriguez Canal. I carried four of my wounded comrades to safety."

Tom held up a finger. Going outside, he searched

through a saddlebag. He came back and laid the identical medal on the counter. Fayles did not react. He restored his medal to the drawer and went back to totaling the purchases. He said nothing further, beyond announcing the figure the items came to.

Tom paid and rode off. Bringing out his medal had to be an old routine for the storekeeper, calculated to make deserters feel ashamed. Only this time he'd been matched. Did it surprise him? Did it kindle a small flame of sympathy?

He pushed the incident from mind and concentrated on Hennessy. If he and his men did venture this far north, they'd be sure to question Fayles.

If eventually they did catch up to him, he must remember to ask if Fayles was any help to them.

When Loyal Devlin came out of his drug-induced stupor, his mouth felt as if it were stuffed with cotton batten. His head was buzzing aloud, and his first impulse upon awakening was to throw up. He inhaled deeply, sucking fresh air down to the bottoms of his lungs, and presently the nausea began lessening. He tried to move his legs, but only the left one responded. When he finally managed to move the right, he cried out in pain. He threw aside the sheet to see his right knee heavily wrapped. It looked badly swollen.

Through the fuzziness in his brain, his nausea, and the suddenly erupting pain in his knee, it all came back to him. He recalled finishing his drink at the Down Under Bar. That woman must have put something in it to knock him out. From that point on, things were blurred. He dimly remembered struggling with two very big men. They were trying to pull him upstairs. Just before they got him to the top, he jerked free, but in turning and trying to run down, he fell and tumbled all the way to the bottom, landing with his right leg under him.

"Good God, what have I ever done to get such a run of luck?"

There was a bright side, however. He'd met Catherine Bracy; whether they'd ever see each other again seemed doubtful, and if they did, would she speak to him? He told himself that her father was now on his side; would that help the cause?

"What cause is that, Devlin?" The voice belonged to Mercy Brannan, his angel of mercy. Devlin vaguely recalled being brought to the Brannans' home. When was that? He had no idea. Through the closed door beyond the foot of the bed he could hear the muffled ringing of a small bell. Followed by a familiar voice.

"Mercy! Mercy! More tea, please. Mercy!" Reverend Brannan. Also bedridden, from the sound of it. "Mercy!"

"Coming, coming—I'll be right back, Devlin."

Devlin could hear her running to the door across from his own, opening it. He strained to hear but heard nothing further. He went back to breathing deeply, hoping it would chase his headache. After a few minutes the door opened again. It was Mercy.

"Good morning, how do you feel?"

"Don't ask. How did I get here?"

"Doctor Slocum. He took care of both you and my husband. He didn't know who you were or where to send you. The only hospital in town burned down." She smiled. "And the Blue Duck hospital was closed to everybody but drinkers. He asked around, I gather; somebody must have told him you'd stayed here. I know it wasn't Sam."

"Mercy!"

"Oh, do shut up, Sam Brannan, for pity's sakes!" She opened his door; bed and patient were out of the line of Devlin's sight. She called up the hallway. "Emma, would you drop what you're doing and come see what he wants now?"

Devlin heard him protest; Mercy ignored him and closed his door again.

"What happened to him?" Devlin asked.

"Somebody stabbed him in the big to-do in Sydney Town last night, and somebody else gave him a great good lick across the hip with a two-by-four, it looks like. Luckily it's only badly bruised. The wound in the shoulder's a lot more serious. Doctor Slocum says it's clean and it'll heal okay, but it'll be stiff as a plank the rest of his days. Lyle Slocum didn't say so, but I think he's lucky he's got a 'rest of his days.' "

Devlin threw off the sheet down to his waist.

"What are you doing?" she asked, her expression announcing that she knew very well.

"I have to get up."

"Your knee is badly strained."

"Got any crutches?"

"Even if I did, I wouldn't give them to you. Do you understand English? You're not going anywhere, you're not leaving that bed."

He explained about Tom. Mercy listened but remained unmoved.

"I have to find him before the soldiers."

"Even if you could find your brother, how do you expect to help him in your condition?"

"I can ride a horse, shoot."

"You'd be more hindrance than help. He travels fastest who travels alone. Haven't you ever heard that? Relax. Are you hungry?"

"Thirsty," Devlin said.

She got him a pitcher of water. Out of courtesy he asked about the reverend.

"Oh, I suppose he's in pain. But his second 'defeat' in the same day must hurt a good deal more. I only hope we can keep him in bed the rest of the week. Out of mischief. I wish I could drum it through his skull that he's playing a dangerous game."

"That could be what he likes about it."

"I'm sure." She stood at the window looking out at the rubble-strewn city. "I wish we could leave here. It's getting so I despise California, which is really a shame. It used to be so peaceful around here before the Ducks came, before gold was discovered in the area."

He finished his second glass of water.

"I really should leave," he said. "I hate to impose a second time. You've got your hands full with him."

"You're staying, and that's that. Now how about some bacon and eggs? How do you like your eggs?"

"Mercy! Mercy!"

10

C hief Sanger was invited to the Bracy house for dinner two days after the Battle of Sydney Town. Between the police and the army the field was finally cleared, the casualties dragged off, and order restored, if only temporarily. The next day the Ducks discreetly kept to themselves, the Vigilantes left them alone, busying themselves tending to their wounds and praising each other for their heroism. Hero of heroes, thanks to his shoulder wound, was their leader.

The chief arrived promptly at six and cocktails were served in the parlor. The colonel invited Catherine and Doreen to join their guest in a drink. To his relief, his wife declined and busied herself in the kitchen, monitoring the progress of a roast, and barring Catherine, politely rejecting her offer of help.

The chief and the colonel agreed that no miraculous solution was possible for the problem of the Sydney Ducks. To Bracy's mild surprise, Sanger then turned to Catherine to ask if she had any suggestions.

"I've thought about it, of course," she said. "Who hasn't living here? I think the federal government should stop the Ducks emigrating from Australia. Close the doors and lock them."

"It's been tried," Sanger said.

"Only to prove it doesn't work," added the colonel. "Any more than you can keep Mexicans from illegally entering down below. Unfortunately, the authorities in Australia are only too glad to get rid of the Ducks —they've said so in print. They don't care where they go as long as they do."

"That most of them wind up here in San Francisco doesn't matter beans to the governor of New South Wales," added Sanger.

"But they're Australian citizens," persisted Catherine. "Why can't they be rounded up, put on a ship, and sent back? They can't be prevented from landing in their own country."

Sanger shook his head. "If they were thrown out of California, Australia is the last place they'd go to. Most are ticket-of-leave men."

He got out a cigar and after asking Catharine's permission to smoke lit up. "We could load them on ships, I suppose, but once they got back, what's to prevent their turning around and coming right back again? No, I think if there's an answer to the problem it's here. I'm sorry to say a big part of it is our system of justice; it's riddled with corruption. My boys catch a Sydney Duck or any other criminal in the act, he goes to court and winds up walking free. If we had a ninety-percent conviction rate instead of ten percent, we'd lick the thing inside of six months. And might even discourage others from coming here."

"That's true," said the colonel.

Catherine frowned. "What you're saying is that we're as much to blame as they are. That's disgusting!"

The conversation was interrupted by a crash from the kitchen. The colonel and Catherine rushed in and found Doreen lying unconscious by the sink. The colonel bent over her. Sanger filled the doorway.

"Help me, John," said the colonel. "We'll get her into bed. She's hit her head . . ."

"She's barely breathing," rasped Catherine, feeling her pulse. "Look at her!"

"Get her medicine," snapped her father. "Hurry!"

Doreen began coming around just after they got her into bed. She looked to be in pain.

"You hit your head when you fell," explained the colonel.

"Hard," she whispered. "I was standing at the sink peeling the carrots for the roast. I don't know what happened; the kitchen started spinning, I suddenly felt weak as water, my knees gave way."

"Sssssh."

Catherine gave her her medicine. The bitter taste etched sharp lines in her face, but she got it down.

"Just let me rest a few minutes," she said. "The roast is about done."

"You stay here," Catherine said sternly. "I'll take care of the dinner. Try to sleep. After, I'll bring you some beef broth. If you feel up to it."

"Maybe a little. I'm so tired. I feel so foolish. I apologize, Chief."

Catherine tucked her in. At the door her father spoke in low tones. "I'm going to the fort to get Doctor Wilcox." After a quick apology to Sanger, he left.

The chief, sensing his host's concern, begged off dinner, promising to return when Mrs. Bracy was herself. Catherine was relieved when he left.

Her father arrived minutes later, Dr. Wilcox in tow. Wilcox was in his forties, a career man and Bracy's field surgeon during the war. He was unostentatiously patriotic, and Bracy was very fond of him.

"I assume she's taking her medicine regularly," he asked after examining the patient, who was now resting.

The colonel nodded.

"Will she be alright?" asked Catherine.

Wilcox looked from her to her father, then shrugged. "Her heart is no worse than the last time I examined her. But no better either. She could live another forty years; I've seen such cases. But she must take good care of herself, not overdo things, not worry too much."

"She complained of feeling weak just before she fainted," said Catherine. "I wanted to give her some broth."

"Fine," said Wilcox. "Just don't wake her up. It's better she sleep."

"What about her medicine?" the colonel asked.

"Wake her up to take that."

He asked when she'd taken the last dose. When Catherine told him, Wilcox suggested waking her at two in the morning for another teaspoonful.

Catherine persisted in worrying. "Doesn't she look awfully pale to you?"

Wilcox nodded. "Patchy. Like she's been drinking." Wilcox did not meet the colonel's eye. "I wouldn't worry, though, her color'll come back with her strength. Make her stay in bed."

Wilcox left.

The colonel closed the door and leaned against it.

"Something I forgot to tell you, sweetheart. Young Devlin asked me to apologize to you for what he said." He managed a grin. "Calling me a liar. He had every right to, I did lie to him." He explained why. "Anyhow, he's sorry he lost his temper."

"If you run into him again, tell him I apologize for losing mine. We were pretty hard on each other. I'd call it a draw."

"He's determined to go out after his brother, of course. I didn't even try to talk him out of it. None of my business. Nice boy, he's got grit. I wished him luck. That's not as hypocritical as you might think. This is one I really and truly hope James Hennessy doesn't catch up to. Tom Devlin was a good soldier," he added wistfully.

He took her in his arms and kissed her forehead. He held her, searching her eyes. "There's something you should know."

He told her about catching Doreen drinking.

"It's not the first time, I'm afraid, only the first time I caught her."

"How do you know that?"

"I've smelled cloves on her breath four or five times." He sighed. "I could empty out the liquor cabinet, I suppose, but that'd be the same as saying I don't trust her. Then, too, if she wants it bad enough, she can get it anyplace."

"When did you first notice the cloves? Before or after I went away?"

"After. It's all been during the month you were gone. I blame myself. You know she's never been content as an army wife. What woman is? It's my fault she's gotten herself in a hole, and it's up to us to help her up out of it."

"But carefully."

"Very."

They discussed it well into the night. At two, they went in together to give her her medicine. She was awake, and her color had returned. She seemed rested and her smile was natural. Catherine warmed up the broth and made toast with her mother's favorite marmalade. She ate well for a "lazy bones" as she described herself.

The colonel did not fall asleep until almost three in the morning. Over his own and Doreen's protests, Catherine dozed in the chair in her mother's room.

Earlier that same evening, Betsy Brannan had returned home from a full day's shopping. Dropping her purchases on a chair in the foyer, she sailed straight to the guest room to see how her handsome house guest was progressing.

By the time she walked in, Devlin was itching to get up and out after his brother. He had already decided to take her into his confidence, hoping that honesty would win him an ally to his cause. He asked her to get him three things: crutches, a horse, and a pistol.

"Your mother wants to keep me here a week," Devlin explained. "By then Tom could be back here in front of a firing squad. He's alone out there, he'll need help. I've come halfway around the world . . ."

Betsy hardly heard what he said.

She was studying him as she listened, slipping away as she drifted into fantasy. He was so handsome, his arms so deliciously muscular, his chest broad and full. The sight of his bared upper body set her tingling. Betsy felt a sudden urge to lay her hands against his chest and send them wandering up to his shoulders, down to his lean, flat stomach. There was no place she would not send them. Loyal would respond, closer and closer their lips would come until they touched in a passionate kiss.

Her heart drummed in her breast. Thundered! That he didn't seem to hear it astonished her. She imagined him undoing the buttons of her blouse. She could feel his body heat blending with the building fire of her own. Take me, I'm yours, I'm yours, she wanted to cry out.

"If you won't help me, Betsy, I'll just have to do it all myself. You can make it a lot easier."

"What? I'm sorry . . ."

She hadn't been listening. She seemed mesmerized by him, Devlin noticed. When she came in, her cheeks had been pale; now they were flushed and her forehead gleamed with tiny beads of nervous perspiration. Although the heat of the day had passed and it was cool in the room, she continued to sweat. Devlin sighed deeply. He'd been around enough to know that Betsy Brannan had one and one thing only on her mind.

Damn, he thought, would he have to make love to her to get her to help? In his condition? And to the daughter of his savior, Mercy Brannan? Again he began describing the situation. Stressing the urgency, he pleaded for her help.

"If I could leave tonight, I know I could catch up

with him before they do. It's tonight or never, Betsy."
He spoke deliberately, hoping to get her attention.

Betsy suddenly caught herself, as if realizing she was
becoming a spectacle was enough to snap her out of
her fantasy. "You don't even know where he's heading. You're a stranger. Besides, Maw would have an
absolute fit. She's become terrifically fond of you,
you know. You should hear the way she carries on."
She smiled engagingly. "Goodness knows what the big
attraction is."

"She'd never know you helped me, I certainly
wouldn't tell her. A crutch, a horse, and a gun, that's
all I'll need. I have the money."

Betsy considered for a moment. "Gregory Miller
could get a horse for me. He's an absolute simp, but
he's crazy about me. He'd jump off a cliff if I asked
him. His daddy's stable is the biggest in town. It's up
by St. Francis' church."

"I know, I've been there."

"I suppose he could get me a gun, too. And you'll
need ammunition, won't you?"

"All you can get."

"I suppose I can find crutches. Would a cane do?"

"Yes, yes."

"Daddy has one from when he turned his ankle and
tore the ligaments last Christmas." She giggled.

"That'll do fine. Just so I can take my weight off my
knee."

"Does it hurt terribly?"

She had come forward, as if interpreting his desperate need for help as an invitation. She stood over him
and brushed his hair back from his forehead. Her
hand lingered a bit too long.

"I know your wrist hurts, too, but is the rest of you
all right?"

"Yes. Can you get everything tonight? I could leave
as soon as it gets dark."

"Oh, not tonight, please. I'm totally worn out from

shopping. I couldn't walk another ten feet, honestly. I must have walked a hundred blocks. First thing in the morning. It's better. You need rest yourself. I'll sneak the gun in in my big bag and the horse'll be waiting down the street by the sign post at Turk and Market. It's only a block." She pointed at the west wall of the room.

A knock sounded.

"Betsy, are you in there?"

"Maw," she rasped, wide-eyeing him.

She scurried to the door, unlocking it, swinging it wide to be greeted by a suspicious look on her mother's face. Mercy was balancing a dinner tray.

"Why did you lock the door?" her mother asked.

"Mr. Devlin and I were talking personal and private, and you know what a nosy Hogan Daddy is."

"That's no way to talk about your father. What are you two up to? Are you planning to help him light out?" she asked Betsy pointedly. "Don't. Doctor Slocum's orders are bed rest for at least six more days."

"Pish tush," snapped Betsy. "What does he know? He's so old, half-blind, his hands shake so—"

"Don't you dare, Devlin," said Mercy, leveling a threatening forefinger at him. "If I catch you setting one foot out of that bed, so help me I'll tie you down with the clothesline."

He laughed and made light of her suspicions. The three of them talked for a while, Mercy switching the subject to the melee in Sydney Town. Devlin mostly listened, concentrating on wolfing down his meal, so famished was he.

He blew out the lamp around ten o'clock. Betsy had stayed a few minutes after her mother left with the supper tray. She promised that a horse would be at the corner of Turk and Market, saddled and ready to ride, and she'd have the gun and cane for him at 7:45

the next morning. He gave her sixty dollars. She refused it.

"Daddy's rich, he can pay, even if he doesn't know about it."

"No Betsy, I pay my way."

She stuffed the money in her bodice and left. Leaving him with emotions decidedly mixed. He'd much rather get out tonight, but he was in no position to make demands on her cooperation. Still, it was discouraging. By the time he got started, he'd be three full days behind Tom and searching an area as vast as New England that he'd never before set foot into.

Of course there was the off chance that in looking for Tom he might run into Bracy's men. He'd have no trouble identifying them. How many groups of soldiers would be out combing the territory? If he spotted them first, he could follow them. Or should he?

He lay awake thinking about his brother and the dangerous situation he'd put himself in. When he did catch up to him, he planned to persuade him to come back voluntarily and give himself up.

When he caught up was the height of presumption. Everything appeared to be against him—including the fact that he'd never ridden a horse in his life. He hadn't the nerve to tell Betsy that.

Sleep knocked softly at the door of his mind, but he pushed it away and thought about his big brother. Tom, his protector against the bullies, his confidant, mentor, idol, friend. No other boy had a brother to compare with him. Nine years separated them, perhaps that was why Tom treated him more like his son than his younger brother. Maybe, too, because their father wasn't interested in either of them, so that out of necessity they had drawn close to each other. They had stayed that way over the years—until Tom had decided to enlist.

Tom had announced his decision to join the army at the dinner table. Mother didn't like it; it frightened her. Their father had been indifferent to the idea. True, by then he was entering the last stages of lung cancer and had given up on life. He had no interest in his work or family. And Mother was so concerned with him, she seemed detached from everything else— even her sons. And she was to die herself accidentally two months before Father died.

Loyal remembered sitting with his full dinner plate before him, listening to Tom's announcement and thinking how bad his timing was. Their father's days were numbered, the doctor had told them flatly that he wouldn't last till the end of the year. Later he had asked Tom why he couldn't wait till it was over. He remembered his answer word for word. "He's my father, I love him. But he's going to die, and none of us can prevent it. The war's begun, they need me and now; that can't be put off."

This had annoyed him, he recalled. He asked him if he was afraid that if he delayed leaving he'd miss out on his share of the glory. At this Tom had stared at him in such a way it made him feel like he was shrinking down into his shoes. "I'm not enlisting for the glory," he'd said. "I'm enlisting because my country needs me."

Loyal had believed him.

So what had happened? The last he'd heard Tom had been as loyal and patriotic as ever. It seemed as if his triumphs in Mexico had elevated his self-esteem and reinforced his convictions. And although he himself had come to California to talk Tom into leaving, he'd never dreamed his brother would chuck it all like this. Loyal had hoped the government would bend the rules for one who'd volunteered and served his country so heroically. Tom *was*, after all, a war hero.

So they'd let him out, his discharge tucked in his pocket, and off they'd go to dig for gold. It seemed so easy.

Only Tom had deserted, casting a whole different

light on the thing. What had happened to change Tom's outlook? He knew his brother wasn't rash or impulsive. Something must have happened to embitter him against the army. Or was it just the gold? Sitting around fantasizing, picturing piles of nuggets lying about just waiting to be gathered up must have been a tremendous temptation. Who could blame anyone for going after it? Isn't that why Loyal himself had come?

Loyal drifted off to sleep finally, thoughts of his brother floating through his mind.

Devlin did not hear the soft padding of slippered feet approaching his door, the knob being turned, the door easing open. Moonlight poured through both windows. Betsy stepped into a pool of it and undid her peignoir. The two halves fell apart as she slipped it down her shoulders. She came forward and stood at the end of the bed. She reached down, found his foot under the covers, and pinched his great toe. He stirred.

"Shhh, silly, you'll wake Maw. She's right next door."

Devlin blinked rapidly, drew in his breath, and gazed down the length of his body to the foot of the bed. There she stood completely naked. Her small breasts were bathed in moonlight, lending them a metallic sheen, her nipples pink and erect. She was grinning saucily. Without a word, she came around the bed, whipped back the covers, and climbed in beside him.

"Betsy . . . ," he began feebly.

"Sssssh." She set a finger against his lips. "I promise I won't hurt you. I'll be very careful."

"We can't do this."

"Maw wouldn't approve." She giggled. "Daddy would have kittens. But what they don't know won't hurt us, right? You just relax, I'll do everything. You, you gorgeous animal, are going to heaven!"

She reached down his stomach, located his organ, and began stroking.

"Oooooo," she cooed, and whipped her tongue lasciviously.

"Betsy, no . . ."

"Ssssh, don't say you don't absolutely love it. You mustn't fib."

He was erect, hard as a bolt; she threw the covers back, got up on her knees, and kissed and licked him. Then she threw one leg over and mounted him carefully, easing slowly down. She moaned as she lowered and lowered. Until they touched and locked. She began gyrating, writhing, beginning to moan and suffer deliciously, passionately.

She was wild; he was afraid she'd start screaming, so violently did she react. He grabbed her shoulders to get control of her, but could not. There was no controlling her now—nor him. Up and down she pumped, pounding. In seconds it became not male and female in the act, but war, one side overwhelming the other.

He flung his load, thrashing into her, slamming against her own. His hand flew to her mouth to cover her scream, killing it in her throat.

On and on she pounded, tiring not at all, but gradually exhausting him. She seemed unaware that he was even present. She cared only about what he could give her. She had reduced him to a state of total subservience.

He thought he would pass out, and still she bounced and gyrated tirelessly.

"Betsy, please!"

Up she jumped, and threw herself off him, leaving him freed and panting. Sweat glistened on her like a second skin.

"Did I hurt you?" she whispered, her lips close to his ear.

He didn't answer. All he wanted was out of the room, away from this attacking lioness. But it was not to be. Already she was preparing to renew the assault, fondling him, working him back to erection

"Let's rest a bit," he murmured.

"Later, you can sleep the whole night. Remember,

quarter to eight at Turk and Market. The cane and the pistol will be there, too."

It was a threat. Devlin knew if he failed to jump through her hoop, he'd find nothing but the signpost tomorrow.

She went back at him.

He had no idea of the time when she finally got enough and left. His mind felt like mud. She had dismounted after her fourth or fifth time; by then he'd lost count. He hadn't the energy to respond when her tongue attacked his in a final passionate kiss.

She left with a kittenish wave and triumphant leer. The spider and the fly, he thought murkily and rolled over on his bad knee. He yelped in pain and rolled back to try to go to sleep.

Colonel Bracy sat at his desk a troubled man. Preoccupied with his wife's problems and the state of city, he could not even bring himself to pick up the sergeant major's morning report in front of him.

Howard stood in the doorway saluting. His homely face seemed to say he felt for his superior, and sympathized with him for whatever was troubling him.

"Sergeant Aronian to see you, sir."

"Send him in."

Aronian came in disheveled, discouraged looking. He wiped the sweat from his forehead.

"Lieutenant Hennessy sent me in to report, sir. I left them up at Antioch. It's just east of Martinez."

"I know where it is, Sergeant. No sign of Sergeant Devlin, I gather."

"Something, sir."

"You spotted him?"

"Not exactly.'

"Spit it out, son."

"Lieutenant Hennessy got a hunch that he might head north up the other side of the bay, him, Tom being smarter than the average guy. We stopped in Martinez early this morning. The old man who runs the general store was opening up. Hennessy questioned him."

"Had he seen Devlin?"

"Yes. He'd stopped there to buy stuff late the night before. Just before closing time. He described him to a tee. But it was funny."

"Funny?"

"Hennessy had to ask the old man a few times before he'd answer. By the way he hesitated, it was almost like Hennessy was torturing him to make him tell what he knew. I never saw a man hate telling something so bad. Then Hennessy asked him what time Devlin came through, and he hesitated again before he said. Then Hennessy says, 'Are you sure?' like he thought maybe he was lying, and the old guy got really hot. Started cursing like a mule skinner, blasting the army. Like he was carrying a grudge. Only why did he tell us he saw Dev? He could have lied. Anyway, Hennessy finally calms him down and tries to butter him up some. He thanks him and says he's doing a service for his country, and that starts the old man off again. He reaches in his pocket, pulls out the silver medal of valor, throws it on the ground, smashes it with his heel, and stomps back into the store."

Aronian could see that Bracy was only half-listening; he had turned in his chair to consult the map. He fingered Martinez and Antioch to the right.

"That's it, sir," said Aronian, "but they're not there now."

"I should hope not."

"They're combing the area to the east. Hennessy says if they don't find somebody who's seen him, they'll start working south." He paused and shook his head. "I'm sorry, I still can't figure out that old man throwing down the medal like he did. Walking off, leaving it in the dust. Hennessy figures Dev gave it to him in exchange for goods. How else would he get one?"

"He might have been in the army."

"He didn't look like it. He was old."

"So's the army, Sergeant. Is that it?"

"Yes, sir."

"Thank you. Go get yourself cleaned up and get some sleep. Dismissed."

Aronian left.

Catherine came in. She looked as weary as her father felt. He gestured for her to close the door.

"She woke up about an hour ago and took a little of the broth. She's in good spirits."

"For your benefit, dear."

"She's terribly weak. I left her dozing; I can't stay, I just came up to let you know."

"Byron Wilcox usually finishes with sick call around noon. He promised he'd check on her. Catherine, I've been thinking about the drinking. I think instead of us watching her like hawks, it'd be better if we removed the temptation."

"I already did. Emptied every bottle down the sink. Only it says the same thing."

"That we don't trust her."

"I just hope it doesn't get to the stage where she's hiding bottles all over the house. That would be horrible. I'd better get back."

"I'll come home with Byron."

She leaned over the desk and kissed him, cradling his cheek in her slender hand. Going out, she paused with one hand on the doorknob. "Did they catch up with Sergeant Devlin?"

"Not yet. His brother might be the first to. He's bright and tenacious. I'm sure he's very resourceful. What was your impression of him?"

She shrugged. "He was nice enough, I guess. When he wasn't snapping. Talk about Irish temper . . ."

The colonel smirked. "His or yours?"

Loyal Devlin climbed out the window moments after Betsy came back to say good-bye.

"I'll see you again," she said as he lifted his bad leg over the sill. It was not a request, more like a command.

"I'll probably be back," he responded off-handedly.

"I love you, Loyal. You're my new beau. I know you have to go, but you must come back. Promise me."

"I promise."

"Faithfully."

"Faithfully."

She had had the presence of mind to bring the cane to make it easier for him to get to Turk and Market and the waiting horse. She also gave him a practically brand-new Whitneyville Walker. A six-shot, single-action percussion revolver, .44 caliber with a square-backed trigger guard and nine-inch octagonal barrel. It was the largest and heaviest of the Colt handguns, weighting more than four pounds.

"It's a cannon," he marveled.

"Will it do?"

"It's beautiful, a godsend. You were up early this morning."

"Six o'clock. Duty calls. Now yours calls; and when you've finished, you'll come back to me. Remember, you promised." She kissed him good-bye.

He left, hobbling along, pulling himself forward with the cane. Gregory Miller must have been the putty in Betsy's hands she'd as good as declared him to be, for when Devlin got to the corner of Turk and Market there stood his horse. It was a superb gelding, wearing a gourd-horned Mexican saddle that looked highly serviceable and extremely uncomfortable.

He had to hand it to Betsy, she had come through brilliantly. He owed her one—not a wedding ring, for certain—but he was definitely in her debt. And knowing her, she'd make good use of it.

Since it was his right knee that was injured, he managed to mount the horse well enough. The first horse he had ever mounted, he didn't have to remind himself. But the saddle felt like cast iron and bulged in all the wrong places. His injured leg hung down, putting strain on his knee, until he succeeded in fumbling his foot into the stirrup. He squirmed in the saddle, hoping he could adjust his rear end to it, but it was useless.

There were saddlebags; in one was a box of ammunition, two corned-beef sandwiches, and some beef jerky. In the other he found a full canteen and a map of northern California with the gold fields shaded in pencil.

"God bless you, Gregory Miller. Betsy, marry the poor man."

Betsy. Soreness erupted in his crotch at thought of her again. For a spoiled and self-indulgent twenty-one-year-old, she had acquitted herself astonishingly well between the sheets. Thinking about it, he marveled that he'd survived. He wondered if she slept with Gregory. Probably not; her sort usually teased a good deal more than they delivered.

"With certain exceptions, of course."

He was riding out of her life. Although he knew she expected him back. He was her property. When he didn't return—and he could see no reason to—she'd be furious. She might even come looking for him. Sneak out on her parents. She wasn't the brightest girl he'd ever come across, but she had enough sense to keep her intentions secret from her mother. And what would Mercy think of him if and when she did run away?

He'd miss Mercy; furious didn't describe what she'd be when she walked in and found the bed empty. She'd be hurt, would she be resentful? She was too big to be either, but she *would* worry. He disliked the idea of burdening her, she had enough to contend with with the reverend. As soon as he caught up with Tom he must find some way to get word back to Mercy that he was fine and grateful to her for all she'd done for him. When she ran out of temper, she'd understand.

He headed down Fifth Street. By the time he got to Howard, two blocks below Market, it was clear that he was kidding himself; his knee was killing him; with every jounce, even at a trot, pain knifed through it. It was all he could do to keep from screaming. He wouldn't make it to the outskirts of town.

He turned the horse around and got carefully down, getting out the cane as he did so, and easing his weight from his right leg to his left. He was sweating furiously. He walked the horse back to Market and up the way to the house. Maligning the fates, damning his luck, feeling the fool. Mercy stood in the doorway.

"Your breakfast is getting cold."

Tom Devlin had ridden almost sixty miles after turning south at Antioch. The horse appeared even tireder than he was. He lay over, concealing himself and the horse behind a mass of boulders which afforded him excellent cover and a good view of the road about thirty yards away. It was getting dark. Since leaving Martinez the night before, he had come to a decision. The great gold hunt could wait; first and foremost he had to shake Hennessy. Permanently, if possible.

Hennessy would lead him on a chase for at least a week. By then, he was sure to turn his attention to the next deserter.

To Tom's knowledge Hennessy had never chased a man longer than a week. Realistically, Tom had no guarantee he wouldn't this time, but the odds that the lieutenant would give it up did look to be in his favor.

So there it was, he reflected as he set about feeding the horse. If he continued to be scrupulously careful, attentive to details, and above all, patient, he'd eventually beat the hunter. Hennessy would have to give up. Then Tom could turn his efforts to prospecting.

One small cloud marred the horizon of his hopes. He was beginning to experience regret over his decision. Not the shame that he'd felt earlier. This was different; this was ruefulness that came from forsaking all that he had valued for so long. Never to feel the flush of pride at sight of the flag being raised. Never to receive the admiration and respect of civilians as he marched in dress parade. Never to see his honorable discharge framed and displayed, where friends and strangers alike could see and admire it. All of these things were in ashes now, and he'd struck the match. It filled him with great sadness.

What if he called a halt to it right now. Gave himself up. What would Bracy do? Thirty days bread and water, demotion to private? Worse? Would they kick him out with a dishonorable discharge? The colonel could take the position that even if a deserter had a change of heart, having slipped once he'd be likely to do it a second time. Whatever the punishment, it would be tough enough to give the next man second thoughts before he walked away. Would going back to be kicked out be worth it?

It would not. He'd keep on. He'd committed himself and he'd stick by his guns. If you deliberately jump into the water, you swim.

Finally he slept.

Four days passed, and Tom continued moving south, at the same time drifting eastward toward the Nevada border. He was not inclined to cross it to begin his digging there; his principal concern continued to be to throw off his pursuers. For the time being, he only wanted to eat up time until the next man at Fort Point took it into his head to desert.

Late in the morning of his fourth day back, Slocum removed the wrapping in order to test Loyal Devlin's wounded knee.

"How long before I can walk on it?" Devlin asked anxiously.

"Before you went off skylarking, I would have said five or six days; now you can figure twice that, if not longer. Maybe this'll teach you to do as your doctor tells you. That hurt?"

"Owwww!"

Mercy came in; she had overheard the brief exchange.

"He doesn't listen to what anybody tells him," she said. "He knows it all. Mr. Pighead Personified!"

Betsy appeared behind her mother, who had heard her step and looked around at her.

"Of course," Mercy went on, "if he didn't have somebody in cahoots with him, he wouldn't have made it out of the yard. Still, I can't say I was surprised." She turned for a second look at her daughter. "Just disappointed."

"Oh, how was I supposed to know he didn't even know how to ride a horse?"

Devlin held his tongue during this interchange between mother and daughter. What did it matter? All that was important to him was Slocum's prediction as to the duration of his confinement. His situation was certainly ironic. In the past five years, the worst injury he could remember was a black eye suffered in a bar fight in Brockton. Since coming to San Francisco, in less than a week he'd been knocked out by an anchor, sprained his wrist, gotten himself drugged and his knee so messed up he couldn't walk. It was almost as if the city was lying in ambush for him.

It was going on a week since his brother had taken off. Tom could be halfway to Denver by now. Or Canada. Mexico. Loyal feared they'd never see each other again. Perhaps his wisest course would be to board the first ship home. At least then—if Tom did manage to get out from under his troubles and wrote— he'd be there to receive the letter.

Another idea came to mind: investing in a buggy to go with the horse. A buggy would be fine, no strain on his knee. But he quickly rejected the idea. A buggy was excellent where the roads were okay, but useless when they turned into trails and paths, dried-up streambeds, and the like.

He thought about Betsy. She had been visiting him nightly since his return; he had no way of preventing her. Maybe she had fallen in love with him. Already she was ordering him about as if he were her personal property. She had yet to ask him if he loved her; she apparently took it for granted. He pitied the poor soul she would one day marry.

Loyal was scrupulously careful in his conversations with her. He was on the front burner at the moment so he cooperated, having no choice but to. But for one so petite, she had an unusually large thumb, plenty of room for him under it.

"What's the matter with you?" her mother asked, steel-eyeing him.

"Nothing."

"You look like a whipped dog."

"I feel like one."

"Cheer up."

"Gregory Miller promised to take care of your horse until you're up and about," blurted Betsy. "And only a dollar a day for food, water, and a stall. The regular price is three dollars, but he's doing me a favor." She wrapped the tip of her finger around another, as if it were he.

"Gregory's a nice boy," observed her mother.

"He's an absolute simp. His clothes don't fit, he spits when he talks, and he has a huge Adam's apple. A girl would have to be absolutely, totally desperate to take somebody like that seriously."

"You took him seriously enough to use him," snapped her mother.

Betsy rolled her eyes, dismissing Gregory Miller from her life and the face of the earth at the same time.

Catherine sat by the parlor window curled up on the divan reading Dickens' *Martin Chuzzlewit*. But only scattered phrases registered in her brain. She was worried about her mother, who sat across from her in the rocker, sewing. Catherine's eyes rose again to look at her. Her mother had come a long way and seemed almost herself again; her energy and optimism had returned. All of which should have been encouraging to Catherine, but glancing at her now, Catherine saw none of the favorable signs—only her mother's heart pumping, overworking, tiring.

Catherine had read the same paragraph for the third time when her mind wandered on to thoughts about Loyal Devlin. Not for the first time had she thought about him. Every time he came to mind, she consciously tried to drive him out, but in that she had yet to succeed. His Irish stubbornness seemed equal to his Irish temper. Again and again she asked herself what was so intriguing about him? She'd known better-looking men, taller, more sensitive, more attractive. The only thing that made him different was his striking red hair. It looked like a torch emerging from his scalp. True, his eyes were unusual; when he looked at her, they took hold. She had found it hard to tear her eyes away.

And that temper. She chuckled to herself. His or hers? as her father said. Loyal Devlin. Why she thought about him at all, let alone so often, mystified her. The chances of their even seeing each other again had to be nil.

"Would you do me a favor, dear?" her mother asked, shattering her musing. "Next time you go into town, would you stop by Clennan's and get me four yards of Hamburg edging and a large spool of gray thread. I'm running out."

"I can go now."

Before Doreen could reply, there was a knock. It was Captain Westerfield. From the twin silver-embroidered bars on his shoulders to his neatly pressed dress blues, to his gleaming Jefferson boots, he was a model soldier. In his hand was a bouquet of downy violets and ferns.

"Robert," Catherine said in surprise.

"Catherine . . ." He glanced about the room self-consciously. "Am I interrupting anything?"

"Of course not," said Doreen. "How lovely. How sweet of you."

She took the flowers and went into the kitchen to fill a vase for them.

Westerfield spoke in low tones. "I was sorry to hear about . . ." He nodded toward the kitchen. "I wanted to give you a little time to catch your breath. How is everything?"

"Getting back to normal."

"Can you leave her by herself?"

Catherine glanced toward the kitchen. Her mother was returning, holding the vase of flowers at arm's length.

"Just lovely. How nice to see you again, Robert. You two haven't seen each other in what . . . ?"

"Thirty-seven days," he said promptly.

She tittered; Catherine smiled.

"My, my," said her mother. "And how many hours?

Dear, why don't you two take each other into town
and get those things at Clennan's for me? I'll be need-
ing them sooner than I figured."

"Will you be okay?"

"Of course."

"We won't be long," Westerfield promised.

He helped Catherine into the buggy.

"I don't like leaving her alone," she said, "but I
should. It'll be good for her morale to be free of her
watchdog. I don't think there's any danger. She's not
due her medicine until four o'clock, and we should be
back long before that."

"I missed you dreadfully," he blurted.

"I . . . missed you, Robert."

"Not dreadfully, I'm sure."

He was feeling sorry for himself—not especially ad-
mirable in a man, but she understood. She sympathized with him. He loved her, even worshiped her.
He had not asked her to marry him yet, but he was
leading up to it. It wasn't anything he said or did, but
a woman knew; Catherine could sense it intuitively.
She dreaded the day she would have to turn him
down. There was no way she could accept. She liked
him immensely, but she just didn't love him. And
never would. Love wasn't an acquired emotion, despite what some people thought. It was either there at
the start of a relationship or it wasn't. Their kisses
were all one-sided. She was sorry now she'd let him
kiss her the first time, but she'd done so and hadn't
the heart to stop him now.

Out of sight of the house, he stopped the buggy and
took her in his arms, kissing her as passionately as he
was capable. She felt sorry for him.

They headed for Larkin Street. For some time both
were silent, as if each of them were waiting for the other
to begin.

"It's true," he said at last.

"What is?"

"What they say about absence making the heart grow fonder. Was it true for you?"

"I'm very fond of you, Robert, you know that."

"Oh, God . . ."

"What?"

"Why not come right out and say it? You don't love me, you never will. And why can't I accept it? Why go on and on kidding myself? How can it ever be any different? Why don't I face it and accept it, right?"

Catherine slipped her arm through his, squeezing it affectionately. "Don't be such a grump. I did miss you; not a day went by that I didn't think about you. I missed our moonlight walks on the beach, the Sunday-afternoon rides in the country, the picnics. I missed your smile, your warmth, your caring."

"My love . . ."

"Please."

"I'm not giving up, Cathy. Don't expect me to. You're all I want in this life. We'd be good for each other. There's no prince charming to come riding up on a snow-white charger to whisk you off to paradise. Not that you don't deserve one, but those things just don't happen, not in real life. People have to settle. Life isn't a romantic novel. Beside, you're practical, just like your father. That's just one of the hundred things I love about you. You're not a dreamy-eyed schoolgirl. Give yourself time and you'll learn to love me. Love is something that can grow. It doesn't always spring up like a mushroom. It hardly ever—"

"You're probably right."

He brightened; her heart sank. What on earth had made her say that? Why give him hope where there was none?

"I won't rush you," he went on. "I haven't up to now, have I? I'm the most patient man alive. I can wait; I made up my mind to that a long time ago."

Again, silence. Larkin Street beckoned. They started down it toward Jefferson, crossing it. Suddenly, Loyal

Devlin popped back into her mind. She tried to dismiss his image, but could not.

"Did they catch Sergeant Devlin yet?" she asked.

"No."

Good, she thought, maybe Loyal will find him first.

"Do you know him?" Westerfield asked.

"No, but I met his brother. He came to the house looking for Daddy. He's gone after the sergeant."

"No he hasn't."

"He did. He left the day of the uproar in Sydney Town."

The captain shook his head and told Catherine about finding him upstairs over the saloon. He described the condition he was in.

"You're wrong," she interrupted, "that couldn't have been him."

"Oh, it was him, all right, no mistaking that red hair."

"My God. What happened to him? Where did you take him?"

"The police did."

"To the hospital?"

He shook his head. "It burned to the ground in the fire."

"Can you find out where they took him?"

"I suppose. Sergeant Hooper would know. Only, why?"

"No reason, only that I feel sorry for him. He's had nothing but bad luck since he came ashore. Where could he have gotten to? And is somebody taking care of him?"

"Boy, you are interested, aren't you?"

"No. Just concerned."

They had crossed Beach Street.

"Clennan's is on the right," she said quietly, "just before you get to Hyde Street."

Like Lazarus rising from his grave, Sam Brannan rose from his bed of pain. He dressed himself and walked somewhat unsteadily out of the house over his wife's shrill protests and even louder threats. The time was two minutes past nine at night. Earlier, Dr. Slocum had examined his knife wound and declared that it was healing "splendidly," and wrapped his shoulder in an ascending spica bandage. After Slocum left, Brannan added a sling, a visible badge of his heroism in the recent fray for all of San Francisco to see.

"Important business," he called back over his bad shoulder to his wife. "The war goes on, the walking wounded must respond when duty calls."

"You're a fool, Sam Brannan, utter and complete!"

He acknowledged this assessment with a backhand wave, got into his buggy, and drove off. During his confinement he held four separate meetings with Eustace Ward, Sergio Scapelli, and other ranking members of the Committee of Vigilance. He had directed them to set up permanent headquarters on Sacramento Street in a converted liquor warehouse. This they had done, encircling the building with sandbags and naming it Fort Gunnybags. An alarm bell and a single cannon were mounted on the roof.

It was to Fort Gunnybags that a group of Vigilantes brought a tall, muscular Australian by the name of

Claud Allworth. Allworth had been caught stealing an iron cashbox from the Long Wharf office of a shipping agent, who also happened to be a Vigilante. The agent spotted the thief trying to escape in a rowboat. He was caught by a boatman and turned over to the Vigilantes.

By the time Brannan got to Fort Gunnybags, double taps had already been sounded on the fire bell and more than two hundred members rushed to the fort where Allworth had been taken. Hearing of the incident, Chief Sanger hurriedly collected twenty men and rushed to the fort. They pounded on the door demanding the prisoner. The Vigilantes ignored them and proceeded to question the shipping agent and the boatman who'd caught Allworth. The accused was speedily and unanimously judged guilty. Sam Brannan pronounced sentence in as few words as he was capable of, just short of six minutes, applying a sacred seal of approval to the committee's action.

Sanger and his men were still pounding the door when Brannan emerged showing off his sling, basking in the adulation of the crowd that had gathered for the spectacle. He informed one and all of the committee's decision. Everyone except Sanger and his men shouted approvingly.

At midnight, the Vigilantes marched—with Allworth in the center of the throng—to Portsmouth Square. A crowd of Sydney Ducks had meanwhile come down from Sydney Town, bent on rescuing their friend. They rushed the marching column, but were easily repulsed.

At two minutes past midnight a noose was placed around Allworth's neck and he was dragged up to an old adobe house, a relic of Mexican days. The rope was tossed over a projecting beam. Brannan silenced the crowd.

"Any last words, fellow?"

"You bet, you bible-beatin' son of a bitch! Go to hell and take your rotten soul with ya."

This brought a pious smile to Brannan's face. "Get it over with, brothers."

Twenty Vigilantes hauled the kicking, gurgling Allworth into the air. There was no death cap to hide his face. The raucous crowd became suddenly silent, so quiet one could almost hear the heartbeat of the man standing beside him. Looking on helplessly, Chief Sanger lowered and shook his head, unable to tolerate sight of the doomed man's swollen and purple features. He was left to hang until daybreak, when a man showed up to cut the body down.

In a little more than one hour a criminal had been caught, tried, and executed. Most San Franciscans cheered, but others—a small but vocal minority of private citizens—objected to the execution. The penalty for the crime was excessive. The enthusiastic supporters of lynch law answered this with the argument that Allworth was a hardened criminal and deserved hanging on many other counts.

The next morning, however, a hastily convened coroner's jury sided with the minority, and named several of the committee members as having their hands on the rope—and Sam Brannan as the individual responsible for orchestrating the lynching. Chief Sanger went in person to Brannan's house to arrest him.

Colonel Bracy got wind of the arrest from Captain Westerfield, who had heard about it in town earlier that morning and had seen Brannan being marched into police headquarters in handcuffs. The colonel's reaction to the news came as no surprise to the captain.

"Dammit!"

"What do you think the chief will do to him?" Westerfield asked.

"I doubt if he knows himself."

"He deserves what he has coming."

"You're missing the point, Robert. John Sanger is playing right into Brannan's hands, making a martyr of him. The son of a . . . Brannan'll milk it for every drop. This could turn out the most glorious day of his life. John'll be lucky if they don't take his job away from him. And if they do, you can bet Brannan and his mob will handpick his successor." He whistled softly. "Wouldn't that be all we'd need?" He stood up and buttoned his tunic.

"Where are you going?" Westerfield asked.

"To talk to John. Holding Brannan is the absolute worst thing he could do. Take over for me. Remember, today's the day we test-fire all cannon, every piece. You'll be in charge. Howard . . . Howard! Get my horse!"

By the time the colonel got to police headquarters, a public statement bearing 219 signatures had arrived on Chief Sanger's desk. All the signers held themselves "equally responsible for the act of justice meted out the night before." Sanger held it up for the colonel's perusal. Bracy read the opening sentence and waved away the statement.

"We have to talk, John," he said.

"I know what you're going to say," said Sanger, fending him off with both hands. "I shouldn't have arrested him. Well, I did, and I wasn't wrong to. It was long overdue. Ewing, I'm supposed to be the law in this town. We're trained professionals. We're supposed to be in charge, and we haven't been since the committee was organized. Brannan and his henchmen do as they damned well please. They run this town. They're the law. We stand by with red faces looking like idiots. Little boys in the street poke fun at us. 'Brass buttons, blue coat, couldn't catch a nanny goat.' I'm sick of it, goddammit!" He pounded the desk, his face reddening, jowls quivering.

"I know," said Bracy, "I understand—"

"Like hell you do!"

Bracy gestured toward the statement. "Whether I do or not, that paper cinches it. You can't make the charge stick. Any judge you take him to will have to let him go. Calm down, man, you're taking it much too personally."

"How am I supposed to take it? How do you? He's making you look just as foolish."

"At least I can accept it. We can't win, not this time."

"Not ever!"

"John . . ."

"I'd like to run that sanctimonious, hypocritical bastard out of town on a rail, that's what. I'd give six pounds of raw flesh to." He had risen from his chair; he sat slowly, setting his elbows on the desk, lowering his head between his hands. "I've been a cop my whole life. Proud to be. There's supposed to be a majesty to the law. We're designated as the upholders of it. Isn't this a democracy? Am I wrong? Tell me!

"Goddammit, I've got a mind to chuck it. Get the hell out of here. Take my wife and mother-in-law and head back East. Let Brannan find somebody else to wipe his shoes with, ridicule, make a laughingstock."

"Let him go, John."

"All right, all right!"

He got wearily to his feet. He snatched up the statement and ripped it to pieces.

"Wallace!"

A policeman who looked to Bracy to be about sixteen came running in, chewing furiously.

"Spit out that damn gum, you look like a damn camel. Let the prisoner go."

"The reverend?"

"The reverend!"

"But . . ."

"Do it, dammit!"

They sat in silence listening to the faint jingling of the keys, the door being unlocked and squeaking open. There was a trenchant pause, a laugh barely audible, and the door was closed. Brannan came in all smiles, pretending surprise at sight of the colonel.

"Ewing, what an unexpected pleasure. Are you two enjoying your usual morning tête-à-tête? Or should I call it a council of war? Do I have you to thank for my release? Or did you have a change of heart, John?"

"Just get out of here." Sanger was crouching like a toad over his desk glaring, seething. "Beat it."

"Come, come, John, we mustn't be a sore loser. Although if you think about it objectively, as I know you eventually will, there's no possible way you can win. Who was it that said public opinion is more powerful than the biggest sword in the strongest grip? I might add it's also inexorable. As the public sees it, you've made a terrible mistake. Will they forgive you? I wonder. Ewing, what do you think?"

"I think you ought to do as he says and leave."

"Hear that, John? Loyal indeed is the ally who never disagrees." He started off swaggering. At the door he paused and turned back to them, reveling in his triumph. "One last bit of advice, John," he said quietly, his tone as pained as his expression. "Next time, why not take a moment to assess your priorities before you take action? Before you duplicate this sorry blunder. Try to remember, the Sydney Ducks are the enemy, not my Vigilantes."

Sanger started up from his desk.

"Ahhh," Brannan gushed, "anger. Ever the last refuge of the humbled and abased."

Sanger swore, snatched up his inkwell, and threw it. Brannan ducked; it struck the wall inches from his head, spilling ink down it. He laughed and went out. The moment the door closed a loud cheer went up outside.

"Don't let him get to you," said the colonel. "He's not worth it, and he's not forever. A lot of people in this town are getting fed up; they're beginning to see that the bloody approach to the problem is dead wrong."

It was salve to cool and soothe a wounded ego, but Sanger wasn't buying it.

Bracy got up, patted him on the back, and left. A hundred men were milling about outside, collecting around their hero, cheering and congratulating him. Four policemen on their way inside to go on duty were roundly hissed and insulted. At the sight of the colonel, Brannan's supporters scowled and shook their fists. The insults "tin soldier" and "traitor" rang in Bracy's ears as he made his way through the gathering. He walked as if he were alone in the street.

14

The fifty-pound ball rolled down the barrel of the eight-inch Seacoast howitzer, one of twenty-eight eight inch Columbiads arming the top tier. Traffic was being warned off the Golden Gate by means of twelve floats with flying pennons. The loaders stood clear. Captain Westerfield took four steps back and joined the crew, jamming his index fingers into his ears.

The gun was fired. The ball whooshed forward over the placid water and arched, landing two thousand yards distant in a small white splash. The two loaders, both new recruits serving for the first time on gun duty, cheered and moved toward the smoking muzzle.

"Hot stuff," Westerfield warned.

They hesitated, waiting until the howitzer alongside theirs in the line was fired. Then they set about swabbing the barrel. The gun was rolled back; the captain leaned over and squinted down the barrel.

"Ball runned out straight as a string, sir," commented the sergeant commanding the crew.

"Clean," Westerfield murmured approvingly, and moved on to inspect the next gun as the one beside it was fired.

"Can I ask somethin', sir?" called the sergeant after him, a lean-jawed man affecting an expression of unrelieved puzzlement. "Why waste the ammunition? Every gun in every tier works fine. Got to, we keeps the barrels shinier than a catfish's ass."

"Colonel's orders, Walter, and he gets his from the brass back East. You can't tell if a whistle'll blow if you don't blow it, right?"

The sergeant didn't understand.

"We've got to be prepared," Westerfield continued. "We've got a city to defend."

" 'Gainst what?" piped a private.

Westerfield grinned. "That, soldier, is the question. But who knows what might come slipping through the Golden Gate in the dead of night, primed and ready to blow us all to the stars?"

"Canadian gunboats, right?"

The others laughed.

Doreen Bracy could hear the sounds of the cannons as she got down on her knees and thrust a hand under her mattress. She searched and found a full bottle of Lefleur French brandy, cached there against the possibility of her daughter disposing of all the liquor in the house.

Her ailing heart beat faster and her hand trembled as she uncorked the bottle and half-filled the tumbler she had brought upstairs from the kitchen. Moving to the window, she sat in the wicker chair. From the window she could see the road coming up and out of town, passing the front gate and continuing on to the Sally Port door.

She stared at the amber liquid in the glass on the sill and put her hand into the pocket of her apron to make sure the cloves were still there. Slowly she reached for the glass and closed her hand around it, her eyes still transfixed by the contents. Into the tumult of her thoughts came visions of Ewing and Catherine.

Then the glass reclaimed her attention; it held her spell-bound. She had started drinking on impulse, a spontaneous and daring exploration into the unknown, and discovered its magical properties. Alcohol had

shortened the long, boring periods when Ewing was at
work and Catherine away. Liquor dispelled her loneli-
ness; it had became her companion and friend, de-
pendable, reliable. As she grew more susceptible to its
blandishments, her dependency on it increased until it
became her master. It mastered her now, urging her to
pick up the glass.

Tears welled in her eyes, dimming sight of the road
below. One, then another, slid down her cheeks. Her
hand trembled as she picked up the glass, spilling a
few drops on the sill. This slightest of slight accidents
was enough to break the spell. The contents of the
glass no longer held her gaze as the drops became the
focus of her attention. She went to get a cleaning rag
and wiped the sill. Wiped and wiped and wiped it.
She cried until she caught herself, stopping, stiffening,
the rag slipping from her grasp to the floor.

Again the brandy took her attention. Again she
picked it up, holding it to the sun, viewing the sun through
it. Her tears came more profusely now; her cheeks
glistened. She continued to cry.

For Loyal Devlin the days up to this morning had
slugged by. But this glorious morning found him waking to discover that no pain, not even numb discomfort, filled his bad knee. He immediately got out of
bed, tested the joint, and found it strong enough to
support him. He cheered, bringing Mercy running. He
threw his arms around her and hugged her till she
squealed. Then he announced that he was fit to travel
at last.

"I'm off!"

"It's not even nine days," she said reprovingly.

"Who cares how many? Knees can't read calendars.
See for yourself, I'm as good as new."

"Admit it, that knee's killing you."

"I can't feel a thing, not a twinge."

He had sat down in the rocking chair. Capping the

cane with both hands and resting his chin on them, he looked up at her with a twinkle in his eye. Part relief, she decided, mostly mischief. And yet she was pleased for him.

"Don't mind me," she said. "I admit I overworry about you. Only because you're a babe in the woods."

"I like that."

"I mean it. Go if you have to. But I'll never forgive myself for letting you if word comes back that you got your head shot off out in Cut Throat Bar, Chicken Thief Flat, Poker Flat or some other hellhole of a mining camp because you couldn't run fast enough with your bad knee. The Lord'll never forgive me, I'll never forgive myself. I feel like a general sending a raw recruit into his first battle."

"I'm going to find Tom, not pick a fight. Is Betsy up? I want to thank her for everything and say good-bye."

"She's up and out. Gone into town."

"Will you say good-bye for me, and to the reverend?"

"She should be back in a couple of hours."

"I can't wait. You understand."

She was gazing fixedly at him. She tried a smile that didn't quite make it; she shook her head. "Will we see you again?"

"If we come back to San Francisco, this'll be my first stop. To visit my friends and tell them all about my adventures. Show you all the gold we've dug up."

"Never mind the gold, just find your brother and get out of California before the army catches him."

Loyal got to his feet, the cane clattering to the floor. He held her hands and kissed both her cheeks.

"You take care of yourself, Red. I'll say a prayer for you. I'll even go to St. Francis and light you a candle, isn't that what you Catholics do? I like it, it sounds . . . effective."

"One for me, one for Tom. Mercy, I want to pay you for my keep."

She waved this off, refusing to take a penny. She saw him off with a smile, a wave, and a heart over-flowing with misgivings. The boy didn't know how to ride a horse, shoot a gun, or even the territory he was venturing into. He was still not 100 percent recovered, and he'd be looking for a needle in a whole field full of haystacks. Beyond all that, she thought, would he even make it out of town?

Or would he meet with yet another accident?

Second Lieutenant James Hennessy, Sergeant Aronian, who had returned from Fort Point and the two en-listed men were continuing the search for Tom Devlin into the second week. Hennessy could see no reason to give up the search: nobody else had deserted and Colonel Bracy didn't need them back at the fort. Fur-thermore, Devlin offered a singular challenge to the bloodhound Hennessy. He had been the first to go out of his way, all the way up to Martinez, in an attempt to throw them off his track. He was smarter, tougher, and more resourceful than the rest. As Hennessy saw it, his scalp would be the finest to hang from his belt.

He had them searching in the vicinity of Mt. Diablo, south of tiny Antioch, east of the Bay. They had been moving from camp to camp, questioning prospectors. Hennessy's experience helped him to fine-tune his in-terrogating. After all, he was asking perfect strangers to inform on their fellow goldbug; many were loners, not a few on the run themselves, and understandably suspicious of blue uniforms. Second only to the gold they sought, what they wanted most was to be left alone. Getting information out of such men took ingenu-ity, tact, and above all, a distinct talent for lying.

The lieutenant questioned one seedy old-timer work-ing a shaft by himself, accompanied by only his burro. Hennessy described Devlin. His listener leaned on his pick, scratched his hindside and his beard, chased away a horsefly, and narrowed his eyes in thought.

"Whatcha want him fer?"

"Rape," Hennessy said.

The man whistled softly.

Sergeant Aronian looked at the ground at his feet. The two enlisted men fought back smiles.

"Do tell. Injun?"

"A white girl. Only fourteen. We have to find him. Last we heard he was heading for the gold fields. We've been looking for him for nearly a month. I hate to give it up, I have two daughters of my own."

"What kinda bastard would rape a little girl?"

"My feelings precisely, sir. You can understand why we want to bring him in; he's given every man at Fort Point a black eye."

"Lotsa boys pass through. Was he in uniform?"

"We don't know; probably not. As I say, think of a shanty Irish face: round and red, blue eyes, brown hair longer than most, almost down to his shoulders. His shoulders are unusually broad. And, sir, I might add that it's not the first time he's raped."

"You mean he's been gettin' 'way with it right along?"

"He's new to the post. The colonel had no idea of his . . . until this. Then it all came out; men who'd known him down in Mexico . . ."

"Lemme think. I believe I did see such a man. Broad, broad shoulders. That I recollect, and that he didn't have no mule. Nine outta ten come through got some kinda beast o' burden. Yes, sir. He walked his horse through; I remember noticin' his army saddle. He didn't speak when I hailed him, just waved. He was passin' just as I come outta the adit. Early in the mornin'."

"When?"

"This mornin'. No more'n four hours ago." He pointed. "Last I seen he was headin' toward Bethany."

"Any particular diggins, do you think?"

"They's everywhere over thar. Five hunnert places. Farther on over the border into Nevada they's gold and silver. I wisht I had a true line on him fer ya, I sure hope you catch the sonovabitch."

"We will," said Hennessy. "And thank you, sir; when we do, and when I tell her mother and daddy how you helped us, they'll be really appreciative. God bless you."

Tom Devlin had been heading toward Bethany, but long before he got within sight of it, he turned the horse northward in the direction of Grass Valley. For no special reason other than to respect the rule he had promised himself he would observe four days earlier: whenever he saw somebody, whenever they saw him, he'd ride out in one direction and, as soon as he was out of their sight, head in another.

Loyal Devlin, meanwhile, had hitched a ride on an ice wagon from the Brannan house to Miller's stable. His gear slung over his shoulder, cane in hand, he got down from the wagon, thanked the driver, and turned to enter Miller's. A familiar figure was passing. It was Catherine Bracy.

"Mr. Devlin. Are you all right? I heard you hurt yourself. Again."

"More like continuously," he joked. "I'm okay now, thanks, just picking up my horse, heading out."

"After your brother."

He nodded.

Catherine twirled her pink-and-white lace parasol over her shoulder. She wore a beribboned straw bonnet and blue silk pelisse over a blouse and full skirt. He caught himself ogling. And wondering. She and Betsy had to be close to the same age, but in terms of maturity there was a decade between them.

"Excuse me?" He hadn't been listening.

"Where are you heading?" Catherine repeated.

"I have a map."

She drew closer to him, looking up the street and

down as she did so. Two small children were playing with a ball in front of a church, but no one was within earshot. She nevertheless lowered her voice.

"I shouldn't be telling you this, but . . . Well, my father happened to mention at the dinner table that one of the men who'd gone out with Lieutenant Hennessy had come back to report. He said your brother had stopped off in Martinez to buy supplies. Let me see your map."

They found Martinez. Devlin seemed skeptical.

"Don't you believe me?" she asked.

"Of course, it just seems so far out of the way."

"Which could be intentional on his part. It's a start; where he headed from there God only knows."

"Can I ask something personal? Does your father usually talk about army business at the table?"

"Almost never, which is why it stuck in my mind. I think he did it on purpose. I think he wanted me to tell you. Daddy's a career man, but a very decent human being. Not that he excuses what your brother did, but he certainly wouldn't be happy to see him punished. I don't like James Hennessy. He's got a vicious streak and a taste for his superiors' boots. I hope he doesn't find him."

"We have something in common, after all." Devlin smiled warmly and held out his hand to shake hers. "Thank you, Catherine."

"You're welcome, Loy—"

A shrill voice interrupted them.

"There you are, you rascal!"

Betsy Brannan almost tripped in her haste to join them, quickly taking possession of Devlin's free arm.

"Naughty man, running out without even saying good-bye!"

The look on Catherine's face spoke volumes to Devlin, not one paragraph favorable. He felt ridiculous.

"Betsy," she said quietly, "you're looking well. Good luck, Mr. Devlin, I should be going . . ."

"Wait!"

She walked off. He took a step after her, but Betsy tightened her hold on his arm.

"Loyal, what are you doing? I chased you all the way up here to help you with Gregory. You don't even know him; you've never set eyes on him. My dear—"

"Will you stop that!" he burst angrily.

Catherine had reached the corner and turned to cross the street. Not yet far enough distant to be unable to overhear them. She turned and looked back at him with the same expression Betsy's unexpected arrival had stamped on her face. A mixture of disappointment and shock.

"Look at me when I'm talking to you. Loyal."

"What is it?"

"What were you talking about with her?"

"Nothing."

"Secrets, secrets, right?"

"She happened to overhear her father mention the name of a town Tom passed through."

"Do you think she's prettier than I?"

He ignored the question and started for the stable office. She clung to his arm. A tall, muscular-looking man with a wild mane of coarse black hair appeared in the doorway. He greeted her, she let go of Devlin's arm.

"Gregory Miller, this is Loyal Devlin, our house guest. He's all better, he wants his horse and saddle and gun and things."

"Mr. Devlin."

They shook hands. Gregory Miller had a grip capable of bending horseshoes.

"Isn't he handsome, Gregory?"

Not knowing quite what to say in response to this, Gregory stood aside, held the door for them, and in they went.

* * *

Catherine approached a large brick building, apparently untouched by the recent fire. Above the entrance a gilt-on-black sign proclaimed Hurdle's Drug Store. In the display windows, pillboxes and bottles vied for attention with trusses, knee and ankle supports, and other devices. In one window was a sign announcing the availability of Bohner's Raspberry Lemonade Essence. Inside, a Sunshine stove centered the hardwood floor. Shelves filled with nostrums climbed to the tin square ceiling on three sides. Overwhelmed by the quantity, Catherine studied the labels in obvious confusion.

A bald clerk greeted her amiably, asking if he could help her. It was not the easiest question to answer.

"I'm looking for something that'll cure . . . drinking."

"A boozer."

His bluntness mildly annoyed her; still, calling a card by its suit was no crime. He indicated a group of boxes on the third shelf down from the ceiling directly behind him.

"Ormsby's Remedy for Intemperance, Hooker's Cure." He took one down, showing her the label. "Matthews' Liquor Specific, endorsed by the Chicago Temperance Society. White Star Secret Liquor Cure, German Liquor Cure . . ."

"Do any of them work?"

"Any one's as good as any other. They all use pretty much the same ingredients."

"But do they cure people of drinking?"

"Sometimes. It depends upon the patient. Mind really does work over matter, you know, that's a known fact."

"You mean essentially they're all useless."

"I didn't say that. If the drinker wants to quit"—he held up the German Liquor Cure again—"this will help him. If he doesn't, nothing will."

"I understand."

"How bad is he? Your husband?"

Catherine stared through him.

"It's none of my beeswax, right? Try this one. I understand it tastes awful, but that's what the manufacturer intends. Everybody thinks the worse medicine tastes, the better it works. This is supposed to increase one's appetite for food instead of booze."

She paid one dollar for a box containing forty-eight doses, wondering as she gave him the money if she'd succeed in getting her mother to take even one. It was all so discouraging. Wasn't everything today? Seeing Loyal Devlin with Betsy Brannan, the way she had her hooks into him, was a shock, as well as a disappointment. Still, why should it be? What did he mean to her? She had learned he had been taken to the Brannans' house, and that Mercy had taken care of him while his knee mended. Apparently he had gotten friendly with Betsy as well. Which, knowing her, was scarcely a surprise. Only where did that leave poor Gregory Miller, who always seemed to be standing on the sidelines? Mr. Unrequited Love.

"Thank you, I hope it works for him," said the clerk, shattering her musing.

Colonel Bracy got a much-needed lift to his spirits in the form of a letter from his good friend and fellow Mexican War veteran, General Isaac Kinsolving, in Washington. It was not yet ten days since Bracy had dispatched the report on the "cannon confrontation" with the Committee of Vigilance when Brannan had threatened to send letters of complaint to Secretary of the Army Conrad; so neither report nor letters could possibly have reached Washington yet.

Kinsolving's letter was just a friendly note, a reminder that Bracy was still in his thoughts. One part in particular caught his attention:

. . . I do envy you your distance from this flaming cauldron. We're suffering through an horrendous heat wave. People are dropping like flies. You can carry a freshly laid egg in your hand from Constitution Avenue up 6th Street, and by the time you get to K Street it will be baked, I swear. More than half of our staff has either suffered heat prostration and been put to bed, or fled to the nearest waters for relief, leaving operations to stagnate until the monster leaves town.

How I envy you your cool winds off the Golden Gate, the mild winter temperatures, the comfortable summers, the eternal balminess. Especially when I think of some of the posts out there in New Mexico and Arizona, the accursed heat, eternal dust, scorpions, rattlesnakes. And in Dakota Territory it's the terrible winters, the hardships, and everywhere the red man. Everywhere except Fort Point. What a post, what a jewel! No headaches, no confrontations with savages, no bothersome emigrants, desperate renegades, unscrupulous Indian agents, foreign interlopers. No disease, no frostbite, no heat prostration. Only the splendid view, the tranquil Pacific, and one gloriously sunny day following on another. I could go on and on, you lucky rascal, but all I'm doing is making myself more jealous. I trust that every night when you say your prayers you remember to thank your stars for your great good fortune.

Ever sincerely yours,
Isaac

P.S. Miriam joins me in sending love to Doreen and Catherine.

The door opened. It was Howard.

"Sir, it's Captain Westerfield, says it's urgent, sir."

Bracy half-rose and, leaning over his desk, called past him. "Robert . . ."

Westerfield strode in, face flushed, eyes anxious.

"Sir, something's going on out in the Gate. We just finished bringing in the marker floats after the gun test and two very strange-looking ships have shown up. They came around Point Bonita. Can you come up and have a look?"

Three officers were standing studying the ships through binoculars when they got to the top level.

"Major Downing," said the colonel, addressing the tallest of the three, "you're our resident naval expert, what do you make of them?"

Downing lowered his glasses. "It's hard to say, sir. Neither one is flying a flag. Their gun ports are closed."

"Let me have a look."

Bracy adjusted the major's binoculars and scanned the topmasts of the first vessel, then her decks from bowsprit to stern. He then shifted to the smaller ship following it. They had entered the Golden Gate and started across it, heading eastward. They stopped, one behind the other, both presenting their starboard sides to the fort.

"What do you think they are?" asked the colonel.

Downing shrugged. "Could be anything from Greek to Siamese. Could be pirates, maybe even a Chinese warlord."

"Pretty far from home, wouldn't you say?"

"It's still possible. They're both fair size. I'd say the bigger one is about two thousand tons burden. Both are standing pretty tall, which means light draft. No heavy cargoes."

"They're opening their gun ports, Colonel," said another man, continuing to peer through his binoculars.

Bracy took another look through Downing's glasses. The starboard port covers on both ships had been raised, but the guns not yet moved forward.

"I count eighteen on the one in the lead," Said Downing.

"Lieutenant," said Bracy to the third officer, "get downstairs and shake up the furnaces. I want them hot in fifteen minutes; throw whiskey on the coal beds if you have to. And make sure the lifts are working. I want red-hot balls up here on the double."

Bracy resumed studying the ships.

"They seem to be waiting for the fog to come in before they attack."

"Why?" asked Westerfield, looking puzzled. "They won't be able to see us any better than we can them."

"They know where we are, Robert, and we're a lot bigger target than either of them. Oh, oh . . ."

Suddenly, a third vessel appeared, coming around Point Bonita. It was much larger than the first two and carried four masts. Downing focused his glasses on it, Bracy having handed them back to him.

"Fore-and-aft rigged," said Downing. "A brigantine and heading this way. Looks like it's getting ready to take the stage."

"Captain Westerfield," snapped Bracy, "alert the bugler. Man the guns. Double quick!"

The fog rolled in pocketing the three ships. The fort prepared itself. The twenty-eight forty-two-pounders and two twenty-four-pounders in the lower tier, the twenty-eight eight-inch Columbiads and two twenty-four pounders in the second tier, the twenty-eight eight-inch Columbiads, two twenty-four-pounders, and nine ten-inch Columbiads in the third tier were speedily manned and loaded.

In the nick of time. From out of the gray shroud came the roar of cannon. The salvo wooshed over the fort, exploding fifty yards beyond the man-made hill butting up against the rear wall to the south.

The second salvo emerged from the fog with devastating accuracy, slaming into the top tier, killing two entire crews and destroying two forty-two-pounders. The cursing and screams of the injured and dying rose in chorus. The colonel, standing between the two battered guns, stared back unflinchingly at the surviving crew members who had turned from their guns to question him with their eyes.

"Hold your fire," he snapped.

By now the hot-ball buckets had come up with their first loads. Men, standing on either side of the muzzles, lifted the buckets by means of four-foot handles, fitting the protruding tongue to the muzzle, tilting the bucket, sending the red-hot fifty-pound ball rolling down the barrel. The fog broke again to reveal the brigantine standing 150 yards out starboard on a direct line with the fort. Her gunners let go a third salvo. Once more the top tier was hit, but with less damage than the previous salvo.

"Prepare to fire," bawled the colonel. "Hot balls only. Try for her main deck. Aim . . . ready . . . Fire!"

The last word was not out of his mouth when the fog closed, obscuring the ship. The hot-ball cannons roared. The cold-ball guns chased a volley immediately after them. The breeze blew the smoke back over the fort, bringing with it the acrid stench of powder. Litter bearers had come up and were carrying away the dead and wounded. The wind had come to life and was now blowing the fog before it and creating a noticeable swell. The ship reappeared. Black gaps yawned in her side, four separate fires blazed on her main deck, her poop was completely demolished, and one of her four masts was gone by the board. The gun crews cheered loudly as a second mast toppled.

The concentrated destruction seemed to momentarily freeze the aggressors at their guns. Again the colonel barked an order. The second and third tiers fired. Most of the balls sailed harmlessly through the open space created by the fallen masts, but one ball found her mizzen-topgallant mast. Down it came, bringing the rigging with it.

"Concentrate on her gun ports," boomed the colonel.

The order was repeated to the tiers below. The ship was suffering badly in her hull and lower masts, and along with two of her four masts, her gaff and head braces were also shot away. But she appeared in no immediate danger of sinking, although the loss of canvas had slowed her and affected her maneuverability.

All three tiers fired. When the smoke cleared, it revealed every brace and most of her rigging destroyed, rendering it impossible for her to move out of range.

On deck, fire still raged. Two hot balls had found their marks, igniting two new fires, the flames shooting up followed by billowing black smoke. Men began jumping overboard, many over the starboard rail in full view of the fort's gunners. Others battled the davits holding the lifeboats, one then another dropping into the water. In the water some men splashed about helplessly; others swam for shore.

"Major Viselli," barked the colonel. "Detail twenty men to round them up. Lock them in the cells. Any officers you find, bring them to headquarters under guard. They're to be held there till I'm done here."

Meanwhile the other two ships had raised anchor and looked to be making a run for it. Both had been standing a thousand yards off watching the battle. And out of it for all intents and purposes, only not out of range.

"Fire a pattern surrounding them," Bracy ordered. "Try to encourage them to stay where they are. One salvo, then, if they keep going, blow them out of the water."

The order was given, the second tier firing. Thirty guns. Twenty-nine sent their charges sailing out to encircle the two vessels. One gun blew up in its carriage, sending chunks of metal in all directions. The concussion felled two men, killing them instantly. A third caught a trunnion squarely in the neck, severing his head. He stood headless, blood spurting, until his legs buckled. Miraculously, no one else was hurt other than the three.

15

In his newspaper office Samuel Brannan heard the guns and ran out into the street. At police headquarters Chief Sanger and a number of his men did the same. People all over town stopped what they were doing to listen to the booming. Loyal Devlin on his way south heard it as did Catherine Bracy arriving home.

Each of them heard the cannons but neither's curiosity was sufficiently strong to dismiss their thoughts of one another. Devlin had said his good-byes to Betsy; actually, it was she who had carried the burden of the parting, and in such melodramatic fashion it was all he could do to stay and hear her out. Riding away, his thoughts immediately went back to Catherine. Betsy had interrupted their good-byes; not that it would have gone beyond a friendly handshake and her wishing him well, but until Betsy showed up it had been a chance to talk freely although how far he would have carried it was moot. All that he knew for certain, thinking back on it, was that seeing her again had the full effect he'd imagined it would. At first sight of her his heart had come alive. At sight of Betsy, he felt nothing.

He wished he didn't have to go, not until he and Catherine could spend more time together. He knew what he felt for her now could grow, become a fire. But he had to think of his brother.

Entering the house, it struck Catherine that Loyal Devlin was practically all she'd thought about all the way back from the drugstore. Now her mother demanded her attention. She looked at her purchase, wondering if it would prove at all beneficial. At this point anything was worth trying. She put the box back among her other purchases.

"Mother. Mother?"

No answer. She went about the house calling, then into their bedroom. The room reeked of liquor. The tumbler lay on its side on the windowsill. On the floor underneath it lay the empty bottle. Doreen was face down on top of the bed. Catherine had to look around the door to see her.

"Mother!"

Her heart snapped; she looked dead! She ran to her and set her ear against her back. She was breathing. Slowly, gently, she turned her over.

"Mother . . ."

Doreen opened her eyes. Catherine threw her arms around her, holding her tightly, rocking her.

"Oh, Mother."

She gazed into her eyes. They were red and puffy from crying, her face red, her cheeks tearstained. The stench of liquor in the closed room was so strong it stung Catherine's eyes.

"How could you?"

"I didn't," Doreen murmured thickly.

Catherine sighed. "You promised."

"I didn't drink it. You must believe me."

They heard pounding in the distance.

"What's going on?" Doreen asked.

"I don't know. Target practice, I guess." Catherine got up from the side of the bed. "Try to sleep. I'm going up to the fort and get Doctor Wilcox."

"What for? I haven't been drinking, I swear. I . . . I poured a glass. I was going to, but I stopped. I did, honestly. I accidentally knocked over the bottle."

"And the glass?"

"I guess. I don't remember. I have a headache."

"I don't wonder."

"I didn't drink any of it!"

"All right, all right, if you say so."

"I didn't!"

"Ssssh, calm down."

Catherine noticed the cloves that had fallen out of her mother's apron pocket, scattering on the coverlet. Doreen saw.

"I got them. I was going to drink, but I didn't. Smell my breath. Oh, I started to sip, I admit it, but I stopped. Only a sip. I didn't swallow. Not one drop. I swear, Catherine! As God is my witness . . ."

"If you can't fall back to sleep, at least stay here and rest. I won't be long."

"I don't need the doctor, dear, please!"

"Do you have any more bottles? Tell me honestly, I must know."

"No. Just the brandy. Dear, you won't tell your father, please? I didn't drink it, not really. I'm telling the truth; you do believe me. Say you believe me."

Catherine was looking down at her pityingly. She said nothing. She kissed her mother's forehead, covered her with the twilled blanket folded at the foot of the bed, and went out, leaving the bottle and tumbler where they lay.

Outside, people from town were streaming up the road toward the fort, turning off about a hundred yards beyond the Bracy's front gate and heading down to the beach. Catherine espied Gregory Miller with Betsy and her father. They didn't see her, and by the time she got to the road she lost sight of them.

"Where's everybody going?" she asked a middle-aged man in his shirtsleeves, shading his eyes with an outrageous-looking floppy-brimmed hat. "What's happening?"

A younger man walking beside him answered. "Battle's going on, can'tcha hear?"

Catherine shook her head. "It's target practice."

He laughed scoffingly. "My Aunt Hannah! It's a real battle. Three ships attacked the fort. They sank one, blew her clean outta the water, so they say. Hurry up, Marcus," he said to his older companion, who was lagging behind. "We'll miss all the fun!"

She stood watching them hurry off. A battle? Unbelievable. The whole town was turning out to watch. Catherine clutched the front of her skirt and ran past the point where the crowd was leaving the road, heading to the right and the beach below. By the time she got up to the Sally Port door she was gasping for breath.

"Let me in!"

"Sorry, Miss Bracy," said both guards at once. They looked at each other; one went on. "Major Downing's orders. Nobody's to enter. You better go, it's dang'rous 'round here."

"I have to see my father!"

"Colonel's up on top giving the orders. We can't talk to him now, nobody can."

"I need Doctor Wilcox. Get him for me."

"No can do, miss," said the other guard. "He's busier'n a one-armed apple-picker. We got us some bad wounded."

"Daddy!"

"He's okay."

"We're real sorry, miss, but orders are orders."

She got control; she nodded slowly. "Of course."

She started back toward the house. The pounding persisted. The people bound for the beach to watch had broken into a run.

On the top level the order was given to rake the

smallest of the three ships. It and its companion were now making a run for it in earnest, the larger of the two in the lead. It was a two-masted brig with a spanker aft. The peak had been hit about a third of the way up its mast; the sail drooped uselessly down to its balance reef. The ship's fore skysail and fore royal had been shot away and flames leapt from her quarterdeck. Men were beating at the fire with blankets. Lifeboats from the sunken ship floated about, picking up the last of her survivors.

The top tier Columbiads were loaded and aimed, targeting the trailing ship. Two balls struck her bow, taking away the bowsprit and with it the flying jib and outer and inner jibs. The fore skysail collapsed. Both ships had long since stopped returning fire and were concentrating on getting out of range.

One last ball boomed out over the water, coming from a gun near the center of the first tier line. So late it brought a derisive cheer from the crews when it landed harmlessly well beyond the trailing ship.

"Hold fire," bellowed Bracy, and the order was repeated down the line and to the crews below. "My God," he gasped. And he pointed off to the right.

Nearly a quarter mile of the narrow beach was mobbed with people, women carrying umbrellas and parasols, some with camp stools, many with binoculars and telescopes. Butchers selling food moved among them shouting their wares. Westerfield had come up alongside the colonel.

"It's like they were watching a fireworks display," rasped the captain.

"People are insane," the colonel said irritably. "I swear. Touched in the head. Still, why should it surprise me? They gathered like that at Waterloo to watch Napoleon against Wellington. Lined both sides of the battlefield and watched like it was a horserace.

"Listen, men, this idiotic whatever you want to call it is over! From all appearances, we're the winners."

A cheer rose.

"Captain Wilcox," called the colonel.

Major Downing came forward, saluting. "He's down in the infirmary, sir, we've got about twenty wounded."

"How many dead?"

"Around eleven."

"Around . . ."

"They've already started checking crew by crew. We'll know exactly in a few minutes, sir."

The colonel nodded. "At least half a dozen up here alone. Where's Viselli? Has anybody seen the provost marshal?"

"You assigned him to round up the prisoners, sir," said Westerfield.

"Right. You take over here, Robert. Set the men to cleaning and mopping up. Brookens, Drabecki . . ." The colonel beckoned to two second lieutenants, one of whom looked as if he was suffering powder burns on both cheeks, so blackened were they. "Come down to the office with me."

The bigger of the two men was a giant. He stood about six-foot-eight and weighed well over three hundred pounds. He wore a blue coat with mammoth side pockets and brass buttons and white duck trousers. He was completely bald. Both he and his much shorter and slighter companion were dripping wet. A private stood behind them, his hand on his pistol. Howard saluted as the captain and the two junior officers came in. Bracy flung himself into his chair and purposely delayed addressing the two prisoners or even looking at them, instead addressing himself to Brookens and Drabecki, discussing the battle. The provost marshal came in. He saluted.

The colonel nodded. "At ease, Roy. How many prisoners?"

"About thirty, sir, and we're still rounding them up.

These two are the only officers. Neither one speaks English."

At sound of the word both leered.

"What do you speak?" the colonel asked. "Any civilized language?"

"French, sir," Viselli said.

"Is that so?"

Bracy got up, came around his desk, and leaned back against it, folding his arms and studying the big man, then his companion, getting as much disdain as he could muster into his expression.

"You speak French, Roy? Does anybody?"

Howard cleared his throat noisily. "Corporal Bissonette does, sir. Like a regular frog."

"Find him. On the double."

Corporal Bissonette came in two minutes later, during which time Bracy and the two lieutenants continued their discussion of the battle, completely ignoring the two prisoners.

"Corporal, I understand you speak French?"

"Mais, oui, mon colonel."

"Not to me, to these two. I want you to question them. I want to know where they're from, what they think they're doing here, why they attacked—everything. Ask the big one. Are you the captain?"

The man leered. *"Amiral!"*

"My mistake, Admiral."

The man sneered and muttered in French. Bracy was only able to make out two words: *"Bouton"* and *"cochon."*

"What's he saying?" he asked Bissonette.

He lowered his eyes.

"What?"

"He called you a pig with brass buttons."

Bracy glared. "Tell him I said he stinks worse than rotten fish, and that if he doesn't get off his high horse and cooperate, I'll have the skin flogged off his back before I hang him."

The colonel studied the big man's eyes as the corporal turned his words into French. He saw not a glimmer of fear. Bissonette questioned him. As he answered, the prisoner never took his eyes off Bracy, never took the sneer from his mouth.

"He says they're from French Indochina, sir. It's his private, personal fleet."

"Pirates," interposed Bracy.

Bissonette went on. "They sailed from someplace called Phan something to Perth, Australia. They lay over there. It was there they heard about the gold rush here. People told them San Francisco was where most of the gold ended up, that the streets were paved with it. They crossed the Pacific."

"And attacked us," interrupted the colonel. "Brilliant. Ask them why."

The admiral responded in rapid French, like peas shooting out of his mouth. Bracy nodded.

"He figured if they could knock out the fort, the city would be easy pickings."

"He says they cleaned out Youanmi in Western Australia, got themselves a fortune in gold nuggets. Wiped out the town."

The Frenchmen leered and spoke again. His companion grinned and nodded.

"What's he say?" the colonel asked.

"He says they're prisoners of war."

"What war?"

"He says they have to be fed and treated as prisoners of war. And if you torture them, if you so much as lift a finger against them, you'll have to answer to the French government. He wants you to contact the French ambassador in Washington. He says you'll take your orders from him. He says . . ."

"He says, he says. Roy . . ."

"Sir?"

"Put these clowns in irons and lock them in the

storage room across from the magazine. You, what's your name? Ask him, Corporal."

"Amiral Antoine Henri Etienne Gustave Marcel Delamasse," snapped the Frenchman.

"So you do understand English. Okay, Antoine . . . My God but you stink! *Parlez-vous* soap? Corporal, tell him he's to be locked up until we execute him." Bracy looked toward Viselli. "Give him a little something to think about, the murdering son of a bitch. Corporal, tell him we don't consider them prisoners of war; they're pirates, and they'll be treated as such."

"Pirate is the same word in French, sir," said Bissonette.

"Nobody's contacting the ambassador. In case he's forgotten, his ship is at the bottom of the Strait and the other two are heading back the way they came."

Again Bracy watched Delamasse's eyes as the corporal translated. They smoldered with anger. He looked on the verge of exploding.

"One more thing. Roy, if either of these two so much as sniff at you on the way over to the storeroom, you have my permission to shoot 'em through the head. Tell 'em, Corporal."

Translated, this brought a torrent of abusive-sounding French from Delamasse's fat lips. He stood glowering at Bracy; his fists were the size of twelve-pound howitzer balls; he took one step forward, bringing them up. The guard behind him whipped out his weapon and set it so hard against the small of his back it jerked him straight. He froze, his enormous shoulders sagging.

Both of them were taken out. Bracy then dismissed Lieutenants Brookens and Drabecki, after he'd directed them to make the rounds, assess the physical damage to the fort, and get up a written report "for the War Department." Captain Wilcox came in as they left. He looked haggard. His hands were smeared with dried blood.

"I lost two of the wounded. Both had stomach wounds—not a chance in hell of saving either of them. All told, I count sixteen dead."

"Good God," groaned Bracy.

"Ewing, what in the name of Joshua's bones was it all about? Who were they? Where did they come from?"

Bracy told him.

"They're maniacs," burst Wilcox. "*Locos rematados*."

"Whatever they are, they came halfway around the world to kill sixteen men."

"And twenty wounded, three badly. I don't know if they'll make it, Ewing."

"Roughly fifteen percent of our roll-call strength." He erupted. "Goddammit to hell!"

Howard appeared in the doorway looking a little shaken by the outburst.

"Sergeant Aronian, sir, reporting in from the field. Just this minute got in."

"Not now, Howard. Tell him . . . Oh, what the hell, show him in. Byron, go back to the infirmary and do your damnedest for those that are the worst off. I'll be over in a little bit. What a day! Sergeant Aronian."

"What happened, sir? Pirates?"

"Never mind. Where's Hennessy gotten to? What's happening?"

"I left them at the Malakoff Diggings. Down near Ingomar. It's the farthest south we've looked."

"Any sign of Devlin?"

"People have seen him, at least claim to have, but we haven't got close. Hennessy figures he's still running. At least there's nothing to indicate he's stopped to dig or pan."

"How long has it been so far?"

"We're into the second week, sir."

"Okay." Bracy began drumming the desktop with his index finger. "You get yourself cleaned up, get something to eat, get some sleep. Tomorrow morning go back and rejoin them. Tell the lieutenant to call it off. We lost sixteen men in this attack, even more than that wounded. We can't afford the luxury of men running around looking for deserters. Two weeks, two years, you may never find him. We win some, we lose some."

"Sir, Hennessy is dead set on running Dev to ground. Real determined."

"I don't care what he is, Sergeant. My orders are give it up, all four of you come on in."

"Yes, sir."

Catherine had returned home. When she walked into the room to check on her mother, she found that the angle of the sun had changed while she'd been away. Now its burnished copper rays struck the bureau mirror opposite the front window, rebounding and flooding the room.

Identifying what she had failed to notice before: a large light-brown stain on the hardwood floor under the windowsill at the mouth of the empty bottle, and a smaller one honey-coloring the normally white surface of the sill itself beside the overturned glass. One glance confirmed that both bottle and tumbler had been full, or nearly so, when they were upset.

Doreen had been telling the truth.

"And I accused her," Catherine gasped. "As good as called her a liar to her face."

Her mother was asleep. She bent over and smelled her breath. She detected liquor, but very faintly, nothing like the smell that still lingered in the room. She looked down at the cloves scattered near her apron pocket, some at the opening, some still down inside. Taken together they'd make a small handful. She could smell no scent of cloves on her breath, which meant, as her mother had insisted, she had not taken a drink, only a sip. Thus there'd been no need to chew the cloves.

Also, Doreen had not behaved like someone who'd been drinking. Her speech was clear, and although her eyes were red and puffy from crying, they lacked that glazed, empty look that comes with drunkenness.

She sat caressing her mother's hair and pushing it back from her forehead, which glistened with sweat. Her breathing struck Catherine as slightly labored, her bosom heaving, holding, subsiding. She felt her hands; they were cold.

"Mother . . . Mother, wake up."

She awoke, her eyes roving the room as she threw off the cobwebs and got her bearings.

"Catherine . . ."

She sat up. Catherine fluffed and propped up her pillow for her. Doreen's hand found her forehead. She seemed confused.

"Mother, I'm sorry I accused you of drinking. It was stupid of me, I was wrong, I apologize."

"I told you and told you."

"You did. I wouldn't listen."

"You thought I was lying."

"That's not it . . ."

What else was it? she thought drearily. Doreen was staring, appraising her with uncharacteristic coldness. She obviously felt hurt and seemed to be striving to generate indignation.

"What's that in your bag?" She pointed to the reticule at the foot of the bed, where Catherine had set it when she'd come in the first time. "That box."

"It's . . ."

"Let me see it."

"It's nothing, Mother. It's . . . I thought it might help."

"German Liquor Cure," Doreen read, "stops the craving for liquor instantly and stimulates the entire system to healthy action. Craving, dear? This is for drunkards, people gone off the deep end. I'm no drunkard. Do you think I am? I don't. I'm sure your father doesn't. Oh, once or twice I've drunk a bit more than I should have, but to accuse me of being a drunkard . . ."

"Of course you're not."

"You seem to think so. Why else buy this stuff? This . . ." In a burst of petulance she threw the box against the wall.

Catherine retrieved it, setting it on the bed out of her reach.

"Throw it away," said her mother irritably. "Take it back where you got it and get your money back."

"I will."

"Whatever possessed you to buy it in the first place? What were you thinking? How very heartless of you not to trust me. You don't, you don't listen to me, you plot behind my back to trick me into taking some foul medicine. Not even medicine, some filthy concoction; Lord knows what's in it. But worst of all, you think me helpless."

"I don't."

"You do. You think I'm not in charge of myself, not competent, not strong enough. Who says *you* are? Who elected you my keeper?"

It was getting out of hand. Doreen was taking refuge in her resentment, ascribing blame to Catherine. She carried on for a few more seconds, her voice becoming shriller, then stopped abruptly, as if realizing that her accusations of unfairness were themselves unfair. She lowered her face into her hands and cried.

Catherine patted her shoulder, then took her in her arms.

"Listen to me shouting at you like a fishwife," Doreen murmured haltingly. "When all you're doing is trying to help. I'm so sorry."

She brought her hands slowly down.

"Why don't you lie back?" suggested Catherine.

"No, I'm not tired. I want to talk. About something you and I have never discussed." She paused. "The guns have stopped, do you hear? For good, it sounds like."

Catherine told her what the guards had said at the Sally Port door.

"Father's all right," she added quickly.

"Are you sure?"

"Yes." She smiled. "It's not Cerro Gordo or Vera Cruz, just a tempest in a teapot. If they haven't sunk the ships, they've driven them off. What was it you wanted to talk about?"

"What I think has happened to me and why. Your father could have resigned his commission three years ago, you know. He'd finished twenty-five years. We talked about it, but you weren't home at the time. He wanted to stay in five more years for thirty."

"For a bigger pension."

"Not because of that, because . . . You know how he feels about the army. That it's a privilege to serve, not an obligation. It used to be. Remember the little house in Laurel Heights back in Arlington, Virginia? How I adored that house. Remember the day after Christmas five years ago, the day he left for the war? Captain Ewing Bracy. If he wasn't the smartest-looking, the handsomest officer in the whole army. I remember the other women's faces. Your father was very handsome, dear."

"He still is."

"Oh, no, not like he was. Anyway, off he went, and us two worried our selves sick waiting for his letters. You remember how they used to come in batches? That infuriated me. But it was only for a few months, then the war was over and he came home all in one piece and we were posted to Fort Bragg. Then in May of forty-nine we came out here. He could have gotten out the year before, but didn't, and can't for two more years now." She paused and looked about the room. "We three had such high hopes for this place, didn't we? San Franciso was supposed to be a sleepy little port, the beautiful Pacific, marvelous weather all year round. Only it didn't turn out so marvelous. It turned out to be hell. The gold rush started everything downhill."

Catherine could see that she was working herself back into resentment, getting angry again.

"Mother . . ."

"Let me talk. The gold rush brought all sorts of riffraff to the area, those criminals from Australia. The way they settled in the very heart of town. And the fires began, and the Vigilantes, and this terrible fighting among ourselves. That rascal Brannan is also to blame. Every time there's trouble he's either leading the way or stirring it up behind the scenes. And that scandalmongering rag of a newspaper of his; the way he criticizes the army, ridicules your father. People read it and believe it."

"Calm down."

"I won't! I never thought I could hate a fellow human being, but I despise that man. Mercy Brannan has to be a saint to put up with him. I hate him for what he does to your father, he and the rabble that follows him around and does his bidding. I believe poor beleaguered John Sanger is the only decent man in the whole city. Mayor Brenham's about as helpful as a stick. I blame the gold: people carrying on like the beasts of the jungle, Brannan catering to everyone's basest instincts. I hate it here. Hate it!

"When General Kinsolving wangled Fort Point for your father, we were both ecstatic. He was in seventh heaven. It was supposed to be *the* prize command; and it was, until the gold. Poor Isaac. To this day I don't think he realizes what he got his old friend into. They write back and forth, but I'm sure your father doesn't complain.

"Those months he was away in Mexico we worried ourselves gray, didn't we? But it was bearable. Other families had husbands and sons and brothers go off to fight. We were all a sort of fraternity, banded together with the same aim and purpose: to wait and hope and pray and be proud, oh, so proud. Caesar's wife couldn't have been prouder than I was of your father. Now I see him every day; his side of the bed's not empty night after night; we eat together, we talk. He's here. And it's ten times harder because I can see what it's doing to him. It's eating him up. He's fifty-six and he looks seventy."

"He doesn't."

"He does! I'm sorry, but he does. You don't see him as I do, you don't look deep into his eyes and see the anguish, the suffering, the frustration. Oh, the frustration! And you don't remember Virginia. He used to walk straight as a ramrod; now he walks like an old man. And he's miserable. The deserters are the last straw. He doesn't talk about them, but I know. That horrid firing squad. The War Department's making him shoot his own men. It's as if he pulls the trigger himself. Some of them he's known since Mexico. Catherine, it's killing him. It's making him into an ogre, a monster in everybody's eyes. He can't sleep nights. Oh, I hate this post, this town, Brannan, the Australians, the gold, gold, gold. If Isaac Kinsolving had the faintest idea . . . What time is it?"

"About seven."

"Oh, Lord, here I sit prattling and any second your father'll be walking in wanting his supper."

"I can make it."

"No, you go and meet him. Walk back with him. Cheer him up. He's always terribly down at day's end. It's because he gets so tired. And he loves your father-and-daughter walks and talks." She drew an affectionate hand down Catherine's cheek. "You're so good for him, dear, so much better than I am."

"Nonsense."

"I'll warm up what's left of the roast chicken."

Catherine started up from the bed.

"Dear . . ."

"Yes, Mother?"

"Don't say anything to him about this, okay? Nothing happened, isn't that so? Nothing did, cross my heart. I'll pick up in here."

"Are you sure you don't want to see Doctor Wilcox?"

"What for?" Doreen snapped irritably. "What do I need with him?"

"All right, whatever you say."

Her mother walked her downstairs and to the door. Seeing her out, she asked Catherine a question; it was entirely unexpected and not a little jarring. "Have you decided what you're going to do about Robert Westerfield?"

"Do?"

"Don't be coy." Her mother shook an admonishing finger. "He's crazy about you, dying to marry you. Catherine, you *do* love him."

"No."

Doreen looked startled.

"He knows I don't." Catherine went on. "We have an understanding; I guess you could call it an emotional arrangement. We're good friends, but that's as far as it goes."

"That sounds so cold."

"Perhaps, but it's for the best. The way it has to be."

"Your decision, I gather. Is there somebody else? Someone I don't know?"

"Yes. No."

"Which."

"Nobody else. But that doesn't mean I have to love Robert, does it?"

Catherine smiled and kissed her good-bye. Doreen suddenly looked anxious, as if, reflected Catherine, her daughter's last chance for happiness had tumbled into the abyss. She'd be an old maid the rest of her life.

"I don't mean to pry, dear, but I am your mother."

"And I'm glad you care, I am. It's just that like a few million other girls I'm still waiting for the right man. Don't worry, I think he'll come back."

"Back?"

"I mean along."

Catherine went out through the gate and up the now-deserted road toward the fort. Her father emerged from the Sally Port door, returned the guards' salutes, saw her, and waved.

Would Devlin come back, she mused? And if he did, to whom would he be returning—Betsy Brannan or her?

━━━━━━━━━━━━●◀ 16 ▶●━━━━━━━━━━━━

C olonel Bracy toured all three gun levels the next
morning inspecting the damage. Majors Downing
and Viselli accompanied him. Four guns had been
destroyed in the attack, including two forty-two-
pounders. A Seacoast howitzer weighing nearly three
tons had been struck in the muzzle and blown clear of
its carriage against the rear wall on the top level. Two
mobile powder magazines fashioned of sheet metal
were blown apart. The flagpole fell victim to a ball.
The granite seawall withstood the attack stoutly, but
the upper structure of the fort, built of brick, suffered
some heavy damage. Two ton of brick would have to
be brought in to repair it; the damaged guns would
have to be replaced.

The damage to the crew was much worse than the
damage to the facility. Bracy visited the infirmary and
spoke to the men, praising their bravery, assuring
them that they would have the best of care during
their recovery. For most it was their first action. For
the others, it was the first action they'd seen in four
years. The colonel was deeply affected by the suffering
of the wounded, and furious with the self-styled "admiral" and his henchman, Captain Armagne. The attack was incredibly stupid, doomed to failure from the
outset. Lives had been needlessly sacrificed on both
sides. Coming out of the aftershock of the bloody

affair, Bracy regretted that the two prisoners in the storage room had not drowned when the biggest ship went down. However, the colonel's vexation did not extend to Delamasse's men in the cells.

"I thought about them at breakfast this morning," he said to Downing and Viselli as the three of them left the infirmary and headed toward the storeroom where Delamassse and Armagne were being held. "I think we should ferry them over to Sausalito, give each of them three days' rations, and let them loose. They can find passage home, go out and dig for gold, or march to Alaska for all I care."

"What about the big man and his pal?" Viselli asked. "You won't let them go."

Bracy scowled. "Not before I boil them in oil. The thing of it is, whatever we decide, we'll have to get brass permission. I'd like to toss them in John Sanger's lap, but it wouldn't be fair."

"Sir," said Downing, "the pirates that attacked New Orleans and along the coast of North Carolina were tried by civil courts. Even today they're tried by civil courts in European countries, even England."

"Be practical, Major, do you honestly think anybody in San Francisco would be willing to take them off our hands?"

"They attacked the fort to get to the city," Viselli said. "Delamasse admitted that, didn't he?"

"Frankly, I don't want to get rid of them, Roy. Would you want me to? You think the men would? No. I'll deal with them."

"How?" Downing asked.

Bracy didn't answer; he had no answer. The guard at the storage-room door came alive, presenting his rifle in salute. He let them in. They stiffened and gasped at the sight that met their eyes. Delamasse sat slouched in a corner, his coat off and draped over him, asleep. In the center of the floor lay Armagne—dead. His head and face were drenched with blood. His friend had pounded him to death and, from the welts on his throat and neck, strangled him also. His head lay awkwardly, his neck obviously broken. Bracy knelt and lay a hand against his bloodstained forehead.

"Still warm. Wake up Admiral Stink. Let's hear what he has to say."

He proceeded to wake Delamasse himself, striding over to him and kicking him hard and repeatedly in the thigh. He jumped up glaring and rubbing his upper leg. Spouting French. Bracy did not speak. He pointed to the dead man. Delamasse's eyes rounded in astonishment.

"Que"—

"Speak English, you phony bastard! What happened? Why'd you kill him?"

"I? *Absurde*. Crazy!"

"Let's get out of here. Guard . . ."

"Sir?" The guard came in.

"He's dead, he killed him. Obviously. Did you hear anything?"

"No, sir. Jesus . . ."

"Get back outside. I'll send a litter around for the body. Keep a sharp eye on this one when they take the other one out. Give him half a chance and he'll do the same to you."

"Absurde!" roared Delamasse.

"Shut up! Come on, boys, it stinks to high heaven in here."

They walked back to headquarters, Downing on one side of the colonel, the provost marshal on the other. Both marveled at the change that had come over Bracy. His step was lighter, he walked with his shoulders squared, his chest out, a smile that came dangerously close to a leer wreathing his face. There was a new brightness in his eyes.

"Thank heaven for timely favors," he murmured. "I do believe Mr. Stink has just solved our problem for us."

"Why the hell do you think he killed him?" Downing asked.

"Who cares? Roy . . ."

"Sir?"

"Draw up a formal charge of murder."

"Just one?"

"It's all we'll need. We'll assemble the men in the courtyard and go through the legal mumbo jumbo after lunch. Then shoot him."

Downing and Viselli exchanged glances behind the colonel. Downing shrugged; Viselli crinkled his brow and tilted his head one way, then the other.

By the time Loyal Devlin reached Martinez, he was ready to shoot his new horse with his new pistol. He dismounted in front of the general store, his legs numb beneath him. He stood suffering in the bright, white afternoon sunlight, the object of everyone's attention. Some tittered, some shook their heads in pity, some looked anxious for him, one man roared with laughter and slapped his thigh.

Devlin ignored them all, took a deep breath, slowly straightened, and manfully pulled himself with the cane into the store. Ira Jack Fayles eyed him from behind the counter with mild sympathy.

"Smarts, eh?" Fayles said quietly.

"Ooooo," Devlin murmured through his clenched teeth.

"I'd offer you a chair, but I'd rather you didn't knock my block off for a wiseacre."

"I'll be all right. Until I have to get back on. It's my first time on a horse."

"I'd never have guessed."

"Does it ever go away? I mean, do you get used to the saddle so you can ride without it killing you?"

Fayles laughed good-naturedly. "I recommend you stay out of it at least one full day. Heal, brother, heal. When you do get back on, it'll hurt, but nothing like now. First time's the worst."

He was studying Devlin's face.

"Do I know you?" Fayles asked. "Your face is sure familiar. Oh, my yes, family resemblance."

"You've seen my brother." Devlin brightened through his discomfort.

"He came through a week ago. And the soldiers chasing him right after."

"Did you tell them you saw him?"

Fayles nodded sheepishly. "Hey, I didn't desert."

"Did you have to tell them? Did they threaten you?"

"No. I felt it was the right thing. I *had* to tell them. But, truth is, I've regretted it ever since."

"That won't help my brother."

"There's no way they could have caught up with him."

"There's always a way. If they do, he's got you to thank."

"Hey, all I did was tell them he passed through. I didn't know where he was heading, I don't think he did. At the time, I had my reasons for telling them. Maybe not good enough for you, but they were for me. If you can't accept that, too bad. So, you want to buy something or what? I'm a busy man."

"You look it. There's more dust in here than outside." Devlin turned and retrieved his cane, but before he took a step, he leaned back against the counter, gripping it backward.

"Easy, fella," cautioned Fayles. "You won't even make it to the door. If I were you, I wouldn't try. Come back here, I've got a cot in the storeroom; you can lie down."

"No, thanks," rasped Devlin.

"Be smart, man. You can hardly stand. Lie down, rest your rump, get some sleep, take a break until tomorrow morning. When you ride again, it'll be sore, but not as bad as now. And you'll make up the lost time in short order. Riding until you split isn't going to help him any."

"I have to find Tom."

"Try tomorrow. Come around here. And stop looking at me like you want to beat me to death. I didn't do a damn thing you wouldn't have if you'da been me."

"I wouldn't have told them. There was no need."

Fayles flared back. "How in hell do you know that?" He pointed at his heart, then his head. "How do you know what's inside here? In here? Never mind, you wouldn't understand. Only he did. Yes he did! Are you coming or aren'tcha?"

When Sergeant Aronian told Lieutenant Hennessy what Colonel Bracy had told him to tell him, the bloodhound took it less than gracefully.

"The dirty dog! How dare he pull us off? We've been eating dust for going on two weeks."

"That's why, Lieutenant," Aronian said mildly.

Hennessy's reaction to his words was not unexpected. The sergeant had caught up with him and the others about ten miles southeast of Martinez, in gold and silver country. Goldbugs were everywhere. They cluttered the landscape in the hectic quest for their fortunes. Never before had Hennessy seen so many prospectors. And most seemed to be meeting with some success.

The previous night, it struck Hennessy—and not for the first time—that he was working the wrong end of the rope. By now, he knew the gold fields as well as any argonaut. If *he* had deserted the first time Bracy had sent him out hunting fourteen months ago, he'd now be wealthy as Dives. Living in a mansion anywhere he pleased. Wealthy beyond his wildest dreams. Well, he didn't take off, and because he hadn't, he felt more strongly about catching Devlin. It had become a matter of pride, of honor. Not only because he hated to fail, but also because the more deserters he caught the fewer would try to desert. He—and he alone—had the power to cure this cancer of desertion.

Damn Bracy! Talk about kicking the props out from under a man. This was the thanks he got. How many other officers would ride out after deserters? How many men would volunteer to undertake such a thankless assignment and give it their all?

"Not a goddamn one!"

Both enlisted men jerked their heads up sharply.

Aronian looked confused. "Sir?"

"Nothing."

"I'm sorry to be the one to bring the bad news," said Aronian.

"I'm sure you are, Sergeant."

Aronian's eyes slitted. "I'm only the goddamn messenger, don't go shooting me, 'sir'."

"I'm just burned up," said Hennessy. "I know Bracy lost men in the attack. Still, that's no reason to bring us back. How can four men replace thirty-six? He should apply to his friend Kinsolving for replacements."

"That's none of my business, sir," said Aronian. "All I know is what he told me to tell you."

Hennessy got out a cigarette stub, pinched both ends, and lit up. "What he told you to tell me," he repeated. "Should I be wondering what you told him?"

"About what?"

"Don't be dense, Sergeant. Did you, for example, hint that we weren't getting anywhere? That we're not having any luck at all? In short, did you plant the idea in his head to pull us in?"

"Like hell I did!"

"A simple yes or no, Sergeant."

"When we get back, ask him."

"I'm asking you. I know, like hell you did." Hennessy sneered and turned his back on all three. He puffed and drew deeply, blowing smoke at the sun. "Incompetent fool. How Bracy ever got command of a post has to be the mystery of the age." He turned to face his men. "All right, mount up, back we go."

Not a mile north of Hennessy, Tom Devlin was tending to his horse. She had been limping. He found a pebble embedded under her shoe.

The sergeant had come to a decision. He'd been on the run for almost two weeks, and the creek he'd just passed about a quarter mile back looked promising, no doubt because he counted no fewer than seven men panning it. He glanced about and espied a grove of trees about two hundred yards ahead. He would camp there for the night.

First thing in the morning he would go back to the creek and launch his quest for his fortune. His horse whinnied. He laughed.

"You agree? You approve? Good girl."

Pirate Leader Executed by U.S. Army

Admiral Antoine Delamasse, leader of the pirate fleet that attacked Fort Point yesterday, was today executed by a firing squad. He was convicted of attacking the fort as well as murdering his fellow pirate while both were held in the same prison cell. Little is known of the details leading up to the execution, other than that the two men were captured and imprisoned by Colonel Bracy. It is presumed that a court-martial took place, the guilty verdict handed down, and the firing squad carried out the punishment forthwith.

This newspaper does not question the wisdom of the colonel's action. The pirates killed and wounded more than thirty soldiers in the attack.

But certain issues do come to mind. Why a secret trial? And was it properly conducted? Were Colonel Bracy's superiors in Washington informed of the attack, the capture, and the colonel's decision to execute his prisoner so quickly?

No one questions the colonel's patriotism or

expertise. But what of his judgment? In this instance, did he act in haste?

There now remain many unanswered questions. Was Delamasse acting on his own or on behalf of some foreign government? Could he have been employed by some sovereign power that covets our gold and other resources? Could Delamasse have had links with the Sydney Ducks in Australia? It is well known that a small group of powerful individuals controls the Ducks in Sydney and elsewhere in New South Wales. Has the colonel questioned any of the denizens of Sydney Town in this regard?

Unfortunately, with both men now dead, these and other questions must go unanswered. So, may we humbly offer the good colonel some advice? In future matters involving the welfare and safety of our city, why not take us into your confidence? Enlighten the police and the Committee of Vigilance as to your intentions.

Let us like the Israelites of old work together in harmony and mutual trust toward our common goals.

Catherine Bracy set the *California Star* on her lap, shook her head and tsked disapprovingly.

"That man elevates hypocrisy to a science," she said. "Ingratitude, thy name is Brannan."

Her father smiled. "Are you quite sure he wrote it?"

"Who else would? He writes exactly like he talks: windy, pretentious, demogogic . . ."

"I don't need his gratitude, dear," said the colonel. He chuckled. "It'd be the kiss of death."

"*We* don't need him," said Doreen.

Mercy Brannan read the article aloud at Sam's behest at the dinner table. He listened, beaming proudly.

Betsy ate. Mercy finished, crushing the paper as she lowered it. "Sam Brannan!"

He flinched at her tone. "You don't think it's superb? My best piece ever?"

"I think it's sanctimonious drivel. Uncalled for, unfair, ungracious. Must you stab the poor man? Hasn't he enough to contend with?"

" 'Stab'? Really . . ."

"Really! What would you call it?"

"You don't get the point, my dear. It's not accusatory, not at all. What it is is a plea for future cooperation. Give it here."

She crushed the paper completely and flung it to the floor.

"Shame on you! I hate to say it, but at times you can be downright insidious. You should write an article of appreciation, for pity's sakes, an open letter thanking him for defending the city. They paid a heavy price; they deserve praise, not abuse."

" 'Abuse'?"

"Do you suddenly have a hearing problem?"

"Isn't that a bit strong? I merely—"

"I know what you merely." Mercy tossed down her napkin and got up.

"What are you doing?" Betsy asked, stopping her soup spoon just below her lips.

"I've lost my appetite. Excuse me, I'm going upstairs."

"My dear," began Brannan.

She left bristling and without so much as a glance back at him. Betsy called after her.

"Can I have your mushrooms?"

Other San Franciscans read their copies of the *California Star*. Brannan's loyalists on the Vigilance Committee saw nothing abusive in the article. To a man, they agreed with their leader's every point. Reverend Doctor Anderson and his parishioners, John Sanger and his men, Mayor C.J. Brenham reacted with varying degrees of disapproval and resentment toward

Brannan's observations. His detractors agreed on two points: there was little they could do to shut his mouth. There was less they could do to quiet his newspaper. The weekly *Star* printed letters to the editor, but none that took issue with the editor's opinions. This was left to the *Alta*, a triweekly publication, the *Pacific News*, and the daily *Herald*. The *Alta* leveled its biggest guns at Brannan personally, but hesitated to criticize the Committee of Vigilance. The other two papers also hesitated, opting to adhere to a precept as old as the printing press: bucking public opinion was the shortest route to red ink. But Brannan's excesses, and in this instance his arrant hypocrisy in "demanding" Colonel Bracy's cooperation, did not pass unnoticed.

Lieutenant James Michael Hennessy, the bloodhound, and his men returned to Fort Point as ordered. Hennessy took his time coming back, dallying in Redwood City for a whole day to assemble the arguments he planned to put to the colonel against being called in. When Bracy walked into his office a few days after the *Star* story appeared, he found Hennessy waiting for him.

"Good morning, sir!" Hennessy sprang to his feet and snapped off his sharpest salute. "Reporting back as ordered."

"Welcome home, James. At ease, sit. You must be exhausted."

"Not really, sir, we've gotten used to the rigors of the trail."

"No luck this time, I hear."

"Not yet, sir. A shame, too. A particular shame."

"How's that?"

"Bringing Devlin back would have discouraged a lot of them from attempting to desert."

"Perhaps, but I need the four of you back here more than I need him. Sergeant Aronian told you what happened to us. We're short sixteen dead; seventeen, Private Sánchez died of his wounds this morning,

and twenty laid up, unfit for duty. I gave you what
. . . twelve days?"

"Eleven."

"More than the usual week."

"And don't think I don't appreciate that, sir. It was
very gracious of you."

Bracy eyed him quizzically. "Gracious? Devlin
deserted."

"Quite right, sir. Wrong word, sorry."

"I wish I could have let you stay on a few more
days, but you're to be in charge of the damage
repairs on the top level. The bricks and mortar came
in late yesterday; there'll be a crew of eight civilians
and an equal number of our men. The workers have
their own foreman, but I'm putting you in overall
charge. Get it done, quick as you can. I don't like
civilians on the premises— not that I expect any trouble from them—but they're always a lot looser about
things than we are."

"And they're a bad influence on the men."

"They can be. Anyway, see to it, would you? And
glad to have you back."

"Glad to be back, sir." Hennessy was on his feet
and saluting again, so sharply that Bracy feared for his
shoulder joint. The colonel returned it. Hennessy went
out, taking with him all the reasons he'd prepared
against being brought in from the field. He'd failed to
voice even a single one.

"Damage repairs," he muttered. "Watchdogging a
bunch of common laborers. Wonderful. While Devlin
goes free as a jay. I'll get you for this, Bracy. So help
me, I'll fix you if I end up bleeding for it. Some post
commander you turned out; you couldn't command a
church choir. What a crime."

" 'Morning, James, welcome home."

Passing him, Captain Westerfield greeted Lieutenant Hennessy amiably, jerking him out of the black
hostility engulfing his tangled thoughts.

"Good morning, sir," he responded brightly. "Thank you, glad to be back. If I may say so, you're certainly looking fit, sir. Everything's going well, I trust."

Neither Devlin brother knew anything about the pirate attack or the execution and editorial that followed. While Loyal recovered in the rear storage room of Ira Jack Fayles' general store and mentally prepared to remount his horse, Tom set about panning Vitreol Creek.

According to what he'd learned, it was the best way to start. He had accumulated an impressive store of "overheard know-how"; now he would put it to work. He knew that the first place prospectors looked was in the streambed placers. In these poor man's mines, gold could be uncovered without expensive or cumbersome equipment. But you had to be able to recognize gold when you saw it, and not confuse it with fool's gold or mica.

It was easy to identify; you need only bite down on a bit of it. It was soft and bent easily without breaking. It was the only yellow metal that could stand pounding with a hammer without shattering. Under pressure, bits of gold tended to meld into one piece. Under virtually all conditions pure 24-carat gold maintained its own identity. It would not rust or tarnish, even after lying for centuries in water filled with minerals. Gold would quickly amalgamate with quicksilver on contact, a single property that was a great help to prospectors. Tiny particles of placer gold that could not be picked up with the fingers could easily be picked up with a blob of mercury. The two metals could be separated just as easily by squeezing them in a chamois bag; the mercury oozed through the pores of the leather, but the gold would not.

Aeons ago, gold-bearing rock had risen in molten form from the depths of the earth, driven upward by the powerful, violent forces that built mountains. Miners called the rock gangue. Secreted in it was gold. Wherever the gangue was exposed to the weather, erosion gradually broke down the rock, releasing the indestructible gold within. Rain and mountain streams carried the gold downhill. Nuggets and large flakes of gold traveled only short distances, but the tiny light particles called flour carried much farther, sometimes even as far as the ocean.

Experienced prospectors kept an eye out for places where rivers suddenly widened, slowing their currents; for gravel bars protruding into the bend of a stream; for transverse ridges and potholes in streambed rock. All of these were natural traps for gold.

Two men were already at work when Tom arrived, both younger than he—partners from Illinois, they told him. They had been panning for five weeks.

"Any luck?" Tom asked.

"Some," said the older one, a chubby, fresh-faced individual about Loyal's age without a tooth in his mouth. "We found us a right good pothole last week, but it petered out real quick."

"Peters out is what a mine does, George," his partner corrected him. He was a gaunt wraith who walked as if he'd just been told that the world would shortly be coming to an end.

"Anything can peter out, Leland. Luck, happiness, pothole gold." He glanced at Tom. "That pothole sure did in a hurry."

"Do you mind if I—?" Tom began.

"Nope. Free country."

For a few minutes he stood on the bank watching them work. Each held a three-inch-deep basin like his, measuring about ten inches across its flat bottom and about fifteen inches across the top. They shoveled sand into the pan, submerged the pan in the stream, and revolved it slowly with a flipping motion that washed the light sand and silt over the rim. It took upward of ten minutes to wash the pan clean of everything but a spoonful of heavy residue called the drag. Then, with a skillful flick, first George, then Leland, fanned out the drag on the bottom of the pan, revealing a tiny comet of gold specks. These they picked out with their knives and stashed in a bean can, the gleanings to be transferred to leather pouches when the day's work was over.

Tom started panning. Within minutes his hands were as red as theirs. And freezing cold, so cold his teeth began chattering.

"Cold, eh?" called Leland good-naturedly.

"Not bad," Tom said.

"Freezing," George said. "You'll get used to it. Take you about fifty panfuls."

Tom knew that in a day spent squatting in a cold mountain stream, a miner could go through about fifty panfuls of sand, and he would make his pay if he averaged ten cents' worth of gold per pan.

Each comet of colors he brought to light in the bottom of his pan he carried to the empty prune-juice bottle he carried in his pocket. By the time the sun reached its zenith, he'd accumulated less than one-sixteenth of an inch of tiny gold specks. From noon until sundown he barely doubled his stash. When the three of them quit for the day, Leland and George invited him to share a bottle of Booker's rye by their campfire. One swig was enough to tell Tom that Mr. Booker's pride burned a trifle too hot in his throat. He bid them good night and rode back to his own campfire.

It had turned out something less than an encouraging first day, but he resolved to be realistic. Rome wasn't built in a day, neither would Thomas William Devlin's fortune.

But the following days proved no more productive. By noon of the fourth day, the contents of his prune-juice bottle had ascended to just under one-fourth of an inch. He announced that he was moving on.

"Man, you're in a big hurry to strike it rich," observed George.

"Got to be patient," Leland said.

Tom nodded. "I mean to be. Only not here. I figure I'm better off looking around."

"Suit yourself," Leland said, and spat into the stream of his dreams.

"Well, let me ask you something," Tom said. "The three of us have been working this stream for three and a half days together. Counting just those three and a half days, how much gold have you found?"

They looked at each other and back at him, sharing an expression that told him with no uncertainty that his point was well made. Both got out their bean can and, sure enough, the contents equaled only twice what was in the bottle.

"We're still sticking here," said Leland. "The time you take riding around looking for another spot is time wasted."

George agreed. "We figure you're better off panning *some* gold, even if it's no bonanza. Some's better than nothing."

Tom disagreed, but said nothing. He wished them luck and said good-bye.

The next day found him twenty miles to the north, almost the same distance from Martinez as he had been at Vitreol Creek, only in the opposite direction.

Catherine Bracy lay in bed in darkness, thinking what had lately become her most dominant thought. In spite of all her efforts to evict him from mind, Loyal Devlin was her main preoccupation. *He* was "out there" looking for his brother. He'd probably never find him. He seemed to have no idea what a sprawling vast country it was out here. And he was certainly in no condition to be traveling by horse. When she'd bumped into him on Vallejo Street, he was carrying a cane. Had his knee really recovered, or had he told her he was fine just to avoid talking about it? He didn't look well, even paler than the last time she had seen him when he came to the house. Of course he had been confined to bed for some time. Confined to Mercy's care—and Betsy's. How well had they gotten to know each other? Was he interested in her? She obviously was in him, the way she was clinging to him. He hadn't looked interested, but then what man would with another woman looking on?

She recalled their first meeting. She was moved by his eyes, their frankness and the wistful look in them. Before she even realized it, she'd been taken with him. She hoped he'd find his brother right off. Once reunited, they could do their prospecting, find their gold or not, and he could get it out of his system. He didn't impress her as the prospecting kind. She had always thought of prospecting as a lazy man's get-rich-quick undertaking, even though her father insisted that most prospectors worked like Trojans trying to make a go of it.

Her father had also mentioned that James Hennessy and his men had come back, leaving Sergeant Devlin breathing room, at least for the time being. There was nothing to prevent Hennessy's going back out after him when the men wounded in the attack recovered and things got back to normal.

Still, her father had never sent the bloodhound out twice after the same deserter. Although in this case the prey was a noncom, the highest-ranking deserter yet. When would the first officer be added to the list? Wouldn't it be ironic if James Hennessy took it into his own head to desert?

Loyal Devlin.

"Damnation!"

All told, she'd been with him less than one hour, and she'd never known any man to have such an effect on her. Every day she seemed to think about him more than the one previous. It was like he'd left something in her head that came alive at the least provocation and took over her.

"It's only because I feel sorry for him."

As she would for a poor lame puppy, or a baby bird fallen from its nest. And yet how could she feel sorry for someone so exasperating.

"Get him out of your mind," she warned herself.

"Catherine?"

She stiffened. It was her father at the door.

"Are you okay?"

"I'm fine."

"Can I come in?"

He sat on the edge of the bed. He smelled of tobacco. Unable to sleep again, he'd been sitting up with his pipe. The moonlight lent him a ghostly gray look, perfectly suited to his expression. Her mother was right: lately he seemed to look permanently weary.

"Bad dreams?" he asked.

"No, I haven't been asleep yet. How is she?"

"She's asleep. I envy her. Is something the matter?"

"Not really." She avoided his eyes.

"Something is, then. Don't worry about her, dear, or me."

"When the damage to the fort is repaired and the wounded have recovered, will James Hennessy go back out looking for Sergeant Devlin?"

"You're worried about his brother."

"Not at all," she said too quickly. "Just curious. After all, he's an innocent bystander. He's not really part of the war between the army and the sergeant."

"I'm afraid he is now, now that he's chosen to go after his brother. But I think the 'war,' as you put it, is over. Chalk up another one that got away."

Catherine noticed her father didn't seem too upset at the idea.

"I wonder if it turns out to be worth it to them," she mused. "I mean the ones that don't strike it rich. I wouldn't want to live the rest of my life looking over my shoulder. Is there a time limit for desertion? Say after seven years, does the army drop all charges?"

"There can't be," her father said. "It wouldn't make sense. When a man deserts and isn't caught, his only punishment comes from his conscience. And it can be pretty hard on him, depending on the individual, of course. If he knew he'd be off the hook after a certain amount of time has elapsed, he'd look forward to it, knowing that if he can hold out till then he'll be safe. It's like the difference between being imprisoned and knowing when your term will be up, and not knowing."

"Do you think most of them still worry after the first few weeks? Especially out there?"

"I would. But I have a feeling it's not Sergeant Devlin you're worrying about, but his younger brother."

"Loyal. Not exactly."

"But he is on your mind. You like him, don't you? I know he likes you. I knew that when he asked me to apologize to you for him."

"That doesn't mean beans. He doesn't even know me; we don't know each other." She blocked a yawn with her fist. "It's late."

He grinned. "You'd prefer not to talk about him, I understand." He got up, bent over, and kissed her lightly on the forehead. "Sleep tight. He'll be fine; he's a big boy, he can take care of himself."

"I wonder."

Dear Editor,

I have been stationed at Fort Point since before gold was discovered in the area. It is no secret that at that time the number of desertions began to rise dramatically. Colonel Bracy dispatches search parties under Lieutenant James Hennessy to look for deserters. But finding them is a difficult, all-but-impossible task. A few have been captured, all thanks to the lieutenant's dogged determination. Now, unfortunately, the colonel has seen fit to curtail the effort. From now on, deserters will need only get out of sight of the fort to be free to make their way to the gold fields, without worrying that they may be caught and brought back to face the firing squad.

This change in policy can only pave the way for a dramatic increase in desertions. The armed strength of the fort will diminish, and the safety of the city will be put at risk. Can one, for instance, imagine what would have happened in the recent battle with the pirate ships had only half the guns been manned?

I urge you to print this letter in the hope that it will alert your readers to the dangers posed by the colonel's new "let-them-go" policy. As a loyal, patriotic American, serving in the greatest army in the world, I believe our first priority is the protection of the people. With all our resources, with our full strength. Official capitulation to the greed of malcontents is simply unacceptable.

This is not intended to criticize Colonel Bracy as an officer. I take issue only with his leniency in dealing with those who would desert.

Yours respectfully,
A deeply concerned soldier

Sam Brannan couldn't sleep either. The letter in his hand had been slipped under the office door just before he left the newspaper for the day. He held it as he would have held Victoria's crown. It was a gift from the Almighty, dropped from heaven into his lap. Another arrow in his quiver, ready to shoot at Bracy's reputation.

He was still waiting for Secretary of the Army Conrad's replies to his two letters of complaint, as well as to those sent by his friends. The front-page article had been generally well-received, despite his wife's disapproval. The colonel was on the skids. Brannan hoped he'd be able to send Bracy sliding out of Fort Point, out of California, perhaps, God willing, even out of the army.

"He's old enough to retire."

He read the anonymous letter again, savoring every syllable. It was well-constructed and clear. It made its point and without anger, insult, or sarcasm, leaving little chance that anyone reading it might feel sympathy toward the colonel. He wondered who'd written it. Whoever he was, it was clear he hated Bracy as much as Brannan did. What luck! Furthermore, he made an excellent point: the fewer the men available to the colonel, the greater the risk to the community in the event they were called upon to defend it. Of course, replacements for the deserters could arrive, but they'd still be tempted by the gold.

Brannan was not choosy as to how to get rid of Bracy; any means would serve. And this letter could only help.

"One more arrow in his heart. 'Whoso diggeth a pit shall fall therein.' "

He would print the letter in Thursday's edition—after reworking it, of course. Brannan smiled in satisfaction.

"By all means, next Thursday's paper. A pity we have to wait five whole days."

Loyal Devlin was finally getting accustomed to his saddle. It was proving a painful period of transition without a doubt, but each day he suffered less. His knee and wrist had recovered, and he'd thrown away the cane. Now, early in the afternoon under a ferocious sun, he headed out of Antioch toward Mt. Diablo.

Ira Jack Fayles had given him sage advice in addition to the cot—and a map that was far superior to the one Gregory Miller had given him. It showed not only the gold areas, but every creek and stream where he'd be most likely to find Tom. At the moment he was following Mortality Creek, which, the map indicated, would run out about four miles ahead. A mile or two beyond the dry-up point lay Sunshine Creek. He had already stopped to question at least twenty prospectors. None had seen Tom, but nearly all offered advice on where he should look. The consensus was that he should head south along the inner rim of the gold fields down to Governors Flat. Then circle the end of the fields and come back up the outer edge. On both maps the fields assumed the rough shape of a hatchet, with the handle ending at Governors Flat. The hatchet stood well over two hundred miles tall and from the edge of the blade to the back of the handle was about a hundred miles.

It was a daunting undertaking.

It could take him a year to track Tom down, perhaps two. How he'd support himself over such a length of time he had no idea. He regretted not buying a pan from Fayles. Whenever he stopped to rest the horse, he could take time out to pan the stream he happened to be riding along.

It was funny that he was even considering it. He had no great itch to prospect for gold—certainly nothing like what Tom must have felt when he lit out. Maybe it was something one developed. Still, the gold was a distant second to finding Tom. He would simply keep looking, holding body and soul together with spit and string, as his mother used to say whenever his father lost his job. Live off the land. If he did find his brother, they'd prospect together. Either way, he could see no chance of getting back to San Francisco to Catherine.

Beautiful. The sight of her when she opened the door and fixed her eyes on him had galvanized his heart. He'd never known a woman that affected him as she had. So speedily, so powerfully. The night before he had dreamt of her. They had made love in, of all things, a rowboat drifting down a quiet stream canopied with branches heavy with apple blossoms.

She had been incredibly passionate. He supposed Betsy Brannan could be described as passionate, but so different from Catherine in his arms in his dream. Betsy exploded, Catherine smoldered, and the effect on him was as different as they were from each other. Betsy was a romp; she didn't give anything, she only took. Catherine, he knew, would give and share, equal contribution to mutual fulfillment.

"You're becoming a bloody poet, Devlin."

He would make love to her again tonight. He would smell her sweet flesh, feel her mouth against his, feel her heart thunder against his own. He imagined her shudder ever so slightly as he drew her close, feel the tingling warmth of her thighs as his exploring fingers aroused her. His own thighs would ignite. A long, passionate kiss would signal the next phase. He'd enter her—the glorious act. She would be his to love forever.

Somehow he had to find Tom, and fast. Then he'd make plans to meet him wherever he was heading and ride back to San Francisco. Back to Catherine to tell her that he loved her, ask her to marry him. Would she say yes? He'd be able to tell from her eyes before she said a word. Was her heart his?

Reality, callous and heartless, struck like the anchor hitting the back of his head.

"Get wise. She doesn't even know you're alive."

It was true; by now she had probably forgotten him. When she saw him with Betsy, she must have assumed they were involved with each other. She certainly hadn't lost any time getting away. And he hadn't seen her since. Again he speculated on what the next few minutes would have brought had Betsy not shown up. At least he'd have been able to say good-bye properly, thank her in more detail for what she'd done for him. Thanks to Betsy, he had been denied.

What a way to end what really hadn't even started.

"Brilliant observation, Devlin! You do have a way with words."

He wished he had a picture of her. To take out every so often and study, admire, nourish his dreams. He got out the map Fayles had given him. From his present location he calculated it to be well over a hundred miles back to the city. He didn't care if it was five hundred; he was going back. Find Tom first and explain. Then head back to her, his brother's horse laugh ringing in his ears.

Did she have a steady boyfriend? he wondered. The thought sent an icicle through his heart, prompting a soft groan.

Tom Devlin tried his luck in a dozen creeks, but it failed to improve. It was too early to get discouraged, he reasoned, but he had hoped that he might make his strike early, thereby enabling him to get out of California before Hennessy got on his track.

He rode out one morning toward distant Sacramento, intending to follow the Sacramento River and cross it before he came within sight of the city. It hadn't rained in weeks and the road boiled with dust. Behind him it rose in a dun cloud, obscuring the sun. Ahead the land rose in a jumble of hills. He followed it at a leisurely jaunt. He rounded a mesalike hill studded with boulders and came upon a mine. To the left of the entrance stood a mangy gray stallion swishing away flies with its tail. It was hobbled and nibbling on the dried grass. On the other side was a pile of timbers. Lying against it were two picks and a D-handle, round-point shovel. Over the entrance a board was nailed and burned into it was a name, "The Dorothy."

Devlin's horse whinnied greeting to the gray as he pulled up, which immediately brought a man out of the darkness. Carrying a shotgun. From fifteen yards distant it looked huge. Up it came blowing, whistling a shot past Devlin's ear so close that for an instant he thought he had been hit. Too late he ducked.

The man came running toward him. "Hands up!"

"All right, all right." Devlin raised his hands. "Careful with that thing!"

"Who are you, what do you want?"

"Not a damn thing. Just passing through. Will you please put that thing down? You make me nervous as hell."

The gun did not lower. The man continued to eye him suspiciously, confirming one assumption in Devlin's mind: This man had gold to protect—or at least thought he did.

"Can I lower my hands?"

"No. Higher!"

"For Chrissakes, they don't go any higher. Goddamn but you're jumpy. Can I at least get down?"

The man didn't answer. He was old; Devlin figured at least seventy. And he looked as if he hadn't slept indoors in thirty years. His skin was the color of a saddle; there was no way the sun could burn it any darker. He was small-framed and short, but with wide shoulders and an impressive chest for one so old. His legs bowed like no legs Devlin had ever seen. He wore a battered derby. He came up to Devlin, menacing him with the shotgun.

"Get down."

Devlin did so, and was immediately relieved of his pistol and rifle. The miner flung away one, then the other.

"Now can I lower my hands?"

"Okay, but don't try any nonsense. You do and I'll blow your brisket through your vertical timber."

"Are you this touchy with everybody who happens by?"

"Not touchy, just careful. You're trespassing, son, this is my claim. Officially recorded in Martinez." He gestured toward a sign nailed to a stake standing behind the stallion. Partially hidden by the creature's rump, Devlin hadn't noticed it. It said: "Claim Notice. N. L. Van Sickle of Penn. takes this ground; jumpers will be shot."

"I'm no jumper. Like I told you, I just happened by."

"That's what they all say."

"I swear."

"That, too."

Van Sickle was peering into his eyes, looking for the glint that betrayed a lie. He evidently failed to see it. He nodded and lowered his weapon.

Devlin let out a long, audible breath. "My name is Tom Devlin." He held out his hand.

Van Sickle looked at it, sank his upper false teeth into his lower lip, and shook hands. "Northgraves Llwellyn Van Sickle, Junior." He grinned, showing his full set of false teeth. Lending his face the momentary look of a skull. "Enough names for three men, right? My friends call me Punk."

"Pleased to meet you, Punk."

Punk was now looking past him at his horse. "Which fort did you come from, soldier?"

"Point."

He asked Devlin if he was in the war, where specifically, what battles, questions designed to test his honesty and reinforce Punk's apparent growing impression that he was not a jumper, being able to look him squarely in the eye when he denied the accusation. The conversation turned to the inevitable topic. Devlin was asked if he'd had any luck in his first week in the business. He got out his bottle, holding it up.

"That's a week?" Punk's eyes looked almost fearful. "That's not even a teaspoonful."

"Sorry to disappoint you."

"Don't be touchy. I'm sympathizing with you, not poking fun. Can't you tell the difference? Where'd you find it?"

Devlin told him. Punk nodded every few words. Devlin began feeling foolish, as if he should have known better than to pan the creeks he'd panned.

"There isn't enough gold left in the waters to fill a cup. Not around here. It's in the ground. It's in this hill. Come here, let me show you something. You know anything about geology? No, you just know what you overheard the panners tell one another in the bars in the city, right? Most of which is hot air. And panning isn't gold-mining; any woman, any child five years old can stand in a stream and wash out sand and gravel to get a few specks. Mining, working a mine, is man's work. But most men are too lazy and don't know what to look for because they don't know the first thing about geology."

He had walked Devlin over to his campfire. Out of a canvas sack he brought a piece of quartz the size of his fist.

"Do you know what this is? And please don't say a rock. Geologists call it a gossan. Miners call it an iron hat."

It was decomposed, honeycombed, porous, and rust-colored.

"You know what that red means? It indicates oxydized pyrites. Oxydized pyrites are generally a sign of a vein. You'd be amazed what the surface can tell you about what's underground. You see these hills and ridges? They're influenced by the angle of the rock beds." He demonstrated, angling his hands. "By the relative hardness of different ones, by the folds and the fissures and other signs of weakness. See that ridge? That's where this piece came from. Down under it there's a vein."

"Pure?"

"Oh, lovely. I can see you know less than nothing."

Devlin bristled. "I don't claim to know anything."

"You'd better not. The answer's no. It'll be a mix with gold in it. How much, how extensive, I won't know till I find it. I will, I'm getting close. I can almost smell it."

"Where did you learn geology?"

"Back in Homestead, Pennsylvania, in the public library. Never got past the fifth grade in school, but I'm not stupid. I taught myself geology. It's the most sensible, clearest, most truthful science there is." He toed the ground. "This land, any land, can tell you all about itself if you've got eyes and know the difference between a hole and a hill, between quartz and sandstone."

"How long before you locate the vein, do you think?"

"Anytime now." Punk had laid the shotgun down on the sack. He stood with his arms slack. He lifted his hands, working his fingers slowly and wincing. "If my mitts don't give out on me."

"Arthritis?"

"To beat the band. The old-age affliction. I'm seventy-six. There are times my fingers are stiff as stove bolts. Can't move them if my life depends on it. And you wouldn't believe the pain. When it's really bad, I soak them in Epsom salts water. It helps a little. Chewing poke root helps too. Prickly ash bark. Even wintergreen leaves. But there's no cure, I sure haven't found any. I'm at the stage now where I can't hold a pick or shovel more than half an hour at a time. I'm still strong enough; strong as a plowhorse; no aches or pains, except these." He held up his fingers. "How are your hands?"

"Okay. Fine."

"Your back?"

"I'm in decent condition."

"How old are you?"

"I'll be thirty-four this coming Wednesday."

"Alone in the world?"

"I've got a younger brother back in Boston."

Punk said nothing further for fully twenty seconds, contenting himself with staring at Devlin. "I'd like to

offer you a business proposition. How about throwing
in with me?"

"Partners? Equal?"

"Equal. Fifty-fifty. All the way, from the vein to the
bacon. You contribute your hands and your back, I
contribute my know-how and my mine, the Dorothy.
Named for my mother, rest her poor soul. Dorothy
Munster Van Sickle. A saint, a true believer, mother
of fourteen, burier of three husbands, maker of the
tastiest loaf of wheat bread in Allegheny County." He
thrust out his hand. "Is it a deal, partner?"

Devlin hesitated, then shook hands. More gently
than the first time.

"It's a deal."

◄18►

San Francisco had almost completely resurrected itself, providing—as her most vocal pessimists observed—fresh fuel for the next conflagration. Fort Gunnybags stood idle, the bell on the roof waiting to summon the Vigilantes to their next combat. Fort Point was repaired; normal life resumed. A corporal and a private, the Callahan brothers, failed to answer morning roll call and were duly classified as deserters.

Lieutenant Hennessy was summoned to the colonel's office before leaving to search for the two. Already present when the bloodhound walked in were Major Downing and Captain Westerfield. Hennessy pulled up sharply at the colonel's desk and executed a salute that could have shattered a two-by-four.

"At ease, James," said Bracy. "Have a chair."

It wasn't until Hennessy sat down between the other two officers that he noticed the newspaper on the colonel's desk. It was open to the letters-to-the-editor page. His eyes fixed on the letter with the black margin, then lifted to appraise the colonel's expression. He saw no irritation in it, but he was uncomfortably aware of an iciness emanating from the captain to his left and the major to his right. No such coldness came from the colonel, however. Hennessy relaxed. Suspicion fell safely short of proof.

"Whoever he is, he didn't even have the guts to sign his name," said Westerfield.

Bracy shrugged. "How could he? Why should he? He doesn't need credit for it to make his point. And he does make his point. James, have you seen this?"

He handed the paper to the lieutenant. Hennessy feigned reading it and gasped.

"Disgraceful! Disgusting! Sir, if I may say so, the scoundrel who wrote this deserves to be horsewhipped. Nothing less! And kicked out of the army. Yes indeed, dishonorable discharge."

"Take it easy, James," said the colonel mildly. "You've made your point. Any idea who might have done it?"

"I can think of a round dozen men off the top of my head, sir. Unfortunately, I wouldn't be able to prove it. Not without a thorough investigation. Any accusation would have to be backed up."

"With proof, right."

Hennessy softened his outrage. "I could question my men. They'd have a hard time keeping something like this secret from me. It only took one to write it. But you know yourself, it's almost impossible to keep a thing like this to yourself. You have to tell somebody, or burst."

"Do you really think so? If you wrote it, would you tell anybody?"

"I . . ." Hennessy half-laughed. "Of course I didn't write it."

"Of course not." The colonel addressed himself to the others. "That's all, boys, you can go now."

Westerfield and Downing saluted and withdrew, but not before the captain got in one last shot.

"Colonel, if you want, we'll assemble the men in the courtyard and read the thing out loud to them."

"Read their expressions," Downing said.

Bracy shook his head. "I don't think so. Tomorrow it'll be yesterday's news. A week from today most people won't even remember it. I take it with the well-known grain of salt. Whoever he is, he's not the first man to find fault with his superior." He smiled. "Just the first to do it in print. There's another angle. Maybe one of us didn't write it. Maybe Brannan did. He's twisted enough to cook up something like this."

They left. Bracy gestured Hennessy back into his chair, then folded the newspaper and filed it in the wastebasket.

"The Callahan brothers—Corporal Timothy, Private Dennis—left hearth and home for more profitable climes. Take your men and go after them."

"Sergeant Aronian, sir?"

"No. The only reason he went along last time was because he was such a close friend of Sergeant Devlin's. Speaking of Aronian, how did you two get along out there?"

"Excellent, sir, the sergeant's a fine soldier. Credit to the unit." Hennessy got up. "Will that be all, sir?"

"That's it. Now that ten of the wounded are fit for duty again, we're no longer strapped. And did I tell you we're getting six new seasoned gunners in from department headquarters?"

"Wonderful! Colonel, about our being called in, I want to say I understand completely. I did at the time. When Aronian came back and told us, the first thing I said to him was, That's the way it goes, blame it on the pirates. I try very hard to be philosophical, sir. That's my nature. As to the Callahans, sir, they should be easier to track down. They'll definitely stick to-gether and they look almost identical. Anybody who sees them will remember them. Well, sir, I'm off." He started for the door.

Bracy called, stopping him. "One last thing. Tell whoever you leave in charge of your platoon about the letter. Some of the men may not have seen it." He reached into the basket, retrieved the newspaper, tore out the letter, and handed it to him. "Tell him to post it in the barracks. Tell him if he hears anything to let Captain Westerfield know. Would you do that for me?"

"Of course, sir, happy to. And good luck to you. I hope you find out who did it."

"Oh, I think I know who did it, James."

Hennessy looked nonplussed. "You do?"

"Yes."

"You mean you have a good idea. Strong suspicion."

"Neither one, James. I know."

"May I ask who, sir?"

"You know him as well as you know me . . . better."

Hennessy swallowed. "I do?"

"Yes. Godspeed, James. Good hunting."

"I take it you prefer not to say."

"Prefer not. For good reason, I have no proof. As you said before, you can't accuse a man without proof. Oh, you can, but it makes no sense to." He grinned. "I know who wrote it, James, I just can't prove it."

"Well, I sincerely hope you get the proof, I do indeed. Good-bye, sir."

"There's another possibility, of course."

"What's that, sir?"

"That I get whoever it is to confess."

"That *is* a possibility, sir."

"You think so? If you were guilty and I couldn't prove it, would you confess?"

"Well . . ."

"I know, you're not the one. Thank goodness for that, eh? Good-bye, James."

Hennessy went out.

Bracy laughed lightly, then louder and louder yet, uproariously. The door opened two inches revealing his striker's wide eye. He opened the door further. Both eyes were wide.

"Anything wrong, sir?"

"Nothing, Howard. Private joke."

"Yes, sir."

Howard closed the door.

Bracy got a rein on his hilarity. " 'I sincerely hope you get the proof, I do indeed, sir.' I'll just bet you do, my boy. And if I didn't have a load of better things to do, I just might. Lieutenant Boot Licker!"

The door flew open. It was Howard again.

"You wanted something, sir?"

"No, Howard. Yes, Howard." He came around the desk and joined him at the door. He indicated a spot near the edge of it inside. "Get a hold of a door bolt. Install it right about there. I want to be able to lock the door from inside. If anybody wants to come in, they'll have to knock, understand?"

"Yes, sir."

Catherine came rushing in. "Daddy, come quickly, it's Mother. She's . . ."

She glanced at Howard, who stood looking dumbly.

The colonel nodded and followed her, suddenly drained of all the humor Hennessy's performance under the gun had inspired. "We'll pick up Doctor Wilcox at the infirmary," he murmured.

19

"**T**ell me exactly what happened," said Byron Wilcox quietly, his tone deeply sympathetic.

Doreen lay on the bed, fully clothed, in a drunken stupor. Catherine, her father, and the doctor stood outside the open door, the colonel holding the empty bottle Catherine had found on the floor beside the bed.

"I was downstairs," she said, "dusting in the parlor. She had gone up about half an hour before. She was going to change the beds, collect the linens to wash, and straighten up. I could hear her walking about, then it was quiet. I didn't think anything of it. My mind was on other things, I'm afraid. Then I heard a loud thump, like a heavy shoe dropping. But right after I could hear her walking again, so I didn't think anything of it."

Wilcox took the bottle from the colonel and sniffed it. "Rye whiskey."

"When I finished with the parlor," Catherine went on, "I went to the foot of the stairs and called up, asking if I could help her up there. When she didn't answer, I went up. She was fast asleep. I tried to wake her, but couldn't. I panicked, ran out and up to the fort."

"You didn't panic. You did what anybody would have," said Wilcox reassuringly.

The colonel shook his head. "So we're back to square one." He looked to the doctor for agreement, but Wilcox said nothing, didn't even nod. "Let's go downstairs."

"I'll be down later," said Catherine. "I want to undress her."

"There's no need," said Wilcox. "Just cover her with that blanket."

Father and daughter shared the high scallop-back tête-à-tête. The doctor sat facing them in the colonel's tabouret chair.

"What can we do?" Catherine asked.

"Nothing," said Wilcox flatly, to their surprise. "I had hoped she'd respond to your love and attention, but she hasn't. Before I go on, please believe me when I say neither of you should take this as your failure. There's only so much loved ones can do. All you can really do is hope and pray.

"I've done quite a bit of reading on the causes of ebriety. My dad was a drunkard. There's a lot of myth associated with the disease, a lot of poppycock. Right now she's in an alcoholic coma . . ."

Catherine started, her fingers going to her lips.

"Oh," Wilcox went on hastily, "she'll come out of it, all right, but in an awful state: feverish, exhausted, sick and giddy, ears ringing, with a violent headache. And her heart is pumping much too hard, which is the big worry. Drinking is her escape hatch. From what, who can say? She could even be punishing herself for something. Of all the drugs men use, alcohol is the most insidious, I think, because it has social approval. And because the discomforts resulting from overindulgence are readily removed for the time being by getting drunk again."

"Vicious cycle," said Catherine.

"Exactly. And each repetition more enfeebles both the will and the judgment. The only hope of relief is rigidly enforced abstinence. Face it, she's become a chronic drunkard, and anyone in that condition has to be regarded as temporarily insane."

"Isn't that a trifle strong?" the colonel said.

"No. My advice is to place her in an asylum until such time as she regains sufficient self-control to enable her to overcome her need for drink."

"No," burst out Catherine. "I won't have her stuck away in some dismal hole with a bunch of raving lunatics."

"Dear," whispered the colonel, "hear what he has to say."

"I won't. She's lying up there like she is because I was downstairs paying no attention. I was lax. It's *my* fault, not hers."

"It's nothing of the kind," said Wilcox. "That's nonsense. You can't stand over her twenty-four hours a day, seven days a week. It's better for her if neither one of you is around." Catherine started to say something. He stopped her with his hand. "I know, you're going to say she needs her loved ones for support and all of that. You're wrong; you're her crutches. She needs to stand on her own two feet. She needs to be cured. Do either of you know Doctor Lyle Slocum? His office is on Sansome. He has a younger brother in Sacramento who's also a doctor. He runs a private asylum for confirmed drunkards. I supposed you could call it a hospital."

"Sacramento's a hundred miles from here," said Catherine.

"He's got an excellent reputation, a high rate of success. She belongs under his care, and the sooner the better. I can make the necessary arrangements."

"No," said Catherine, "she's not leaving here. Certainly not all the way to Sacramento."

Wilcox put up his hands. "It's up to you two. With Donald Slocum she stands a chance of licking it permanently, a very good chance I'd say. If she stays here . . ."

"We've got to think of her, dear," said the colonel quietly, setting his hand on Catherine's.

"I am," she snapped. "You make it sound like I want to keep her here against her will. This is where she belongs . . ."

"Catherine," said Wilcox, "your mother is seriously ill. She needs help badly and time is vital. If she goes on like this, in a few weeks she'll be beyond help. You can spend six hours a day looking for concealed bottles, you can follow her around town, you can sleep in the same room with her, but when the urge is on, she's going to drink—and there's no way in hell you or anybody else will be able to stop her. You'll be playing a game and she'll be a lot better at it. A lot more clever."

"I can move into her bedroom."

Wilcox got to his feet. "It's your decision. I can't do anything for her. Your German Liquor Cure is obviously useless. You don't throw cups of water on a forest fire. Sir, if she were my wife, I wouldn't hesitate. I'd get her up there as fast as I could."

"We have to, Catherine," said the colonel, "we have to."

The quartermaster got hold of a canopy-top surrey touted as one of the most comfortable vehicles of its kind. It had wide upholstered seats and handled well with a light touch. It was ruggedly constructed, the springs made of the finest steel available, its clips, bolts, and forgings of the best Norway iron.

Colonel Bracy would have liked to have sent Dr. Wilcox along as the women's escort, but felt that he could not spare him. Instead, he selected Captain Westerfield. The journey would take three days over, three back. A ferry made four trips daily from San Francisco to Oakland. From Oakland to Sacramento the roads would be fairly good since the weather had been dry all summer long. The overall distance from San Francisco to the capital was ninety-one miles.

When Doreen Bracy recovered her sobriety and had been told of her fate, she agreed to cooperate. As usual, she was deeply embarrassed over what she'd done. Furthermore, she had the good sense to admit to herself that her illness was now beyond her control. She had only two worries over entering the hospital.

"How long must I stay?"

"We don't know, Mother. Doctor Wilcox says there's no way of knowing."

"What he really means is it's all up to me."

"However long it is, it's the only way."

Her second concern was not as easy to allay.

"You'll be staying with me, dear," Doreen declared flatly.

"I want to, I really do, but he says it's better for you if I don't."

"Why?"

Catherine couldn't think of a convincing reason, beyond Wilcox's belief that separating Doreen from her "crutches" would hasten her recovery. In any event it was one of Dr. Donald Slocum's rules, and Doreen would be obliged to obey.

The colonel came down to the ferry dock to say good-bye. He stayed to watch the ferry depart on the trip across the bay to Oakland. The weather could not have been more cooperative. A gentle breeze came off the water, cooling the area. He stayed until the ferry shrank into a shapeless blot, then returned to business at the fort.

Later that afternoon Bracy released his prisoners. The pirates were let out, escorted to boats, given rations, and ordered to cross the Golden Gate to Sausalito. They were also advised not to return—under threat of being shot on sight."

Bracy stood on the top level with the provost marshal and Major Downing watching the pirates ordered by their escort into their boats. Old Glory flapped noisily overhead; the breeze was stronger now and raised dust devils that danced and died. The sun's reflection off the brass barrels was painful to the eyes. One after another the lifeboats shoved off, heading across the Golden Gate.

"I wonder if we'll see another letter in the *Star*, about this," mused Major Viselli aloud, grinning as he said it.

Bracy shook his head. "I don't think so, Roy. I think our mystery letter-writer is otherwise occupied at the moment."

"How do you know that, sir?"

"Intuition."

Downing chuckled.

Viselli looked from one to the other. "Do you know who wrote that letter, Colonel?" he asked pointedly.

"Look at them," said Bracy, raising his binoculars. "They've stopped, they're gathering around."

As they continued watching, four men dived into the water. Three more followed.

"What the devil are they doing?" Viselli asked.

"That's where their ship went down," said the colonel. "With the gold from that town in Australia Delamasse told us they plundered."

"Youanmi," said Downing. "They're nuts."

Bracy smiled. "Are they?"

"Should we fire one down there and get them moving?" Downing asked.

Bracy shook his head. "No need. They'll get discouraged and give up. How deep is it out there?"

"I don't know exactly," said Viselli, "but at least fifty to seventy-five feet."

They watched the pirates dive unsuccessfully for about ten minutes before giving up and resuming the trip across the bay. The colonel was on his way downstairs to his office when a dispatch rider came dusting up to the Sally Port door. Minutes later Bracy opened a letter from General Isaac Kinsolving. The second paragraph riveted his attention and lifted his heart in his chest.

. . . I gave the secretary of the army your report on the situation out there. He told me he had already received not one but two highly critical letters from a Reverend Samuel Brannan, also other letters from Vigilantes playing the same sour note. I've taken it upon myself to act as your *amicus curiae*. I pointed out what you're up against, the gold rush, the Australians, and the like. Secretary Conrad knows Brannan (with scant affection and less admiration, I gathered). We discussed things for almost two hours. He feels, as do I, that you should be left free to captain the ship as you see fit.

So rest easy, my friend, no one here will pull the plug on you or pay any attention to anyone out there who'd like us to.

The colonel heaved a long sigh of relief.

Meanwhile, Sam Brannan was reading a letter of his own.

. . . Secretary Conrad thanks you for your good letters. He has read them both and has given considerable thought to your advice for improving the situation in the city. All of your suggestions have merit but one. He disagrees that San Francisco would be better served if Fort Point were closed, or at the very least Colonel Bracy be replaced as post commander. The Secretary feels that both suggestions are not in the best interests of the community. Colonel Bracy has an exemplary war record, and his record as a post commander, both here in the East and in San Francisco, is without blemish. He enjoys the full support of the War Department and this office.

> Yours respectfully for the
> Honorable Charles W. Conrad,
> Secretary of the Army,
>
> A. Forbush
> Secretary to the Secretary

P.S. Please be advised that the letters from your associates with the Committee of Vigilance have all been answered. Again, thank you for your interest.

Brannan crushed the letter, let forth a string of words wholly unexpected from a man of the cloth, and headed for Sacramento Street and Fort Gunnybags.

20

Tom Devlin stood at Ira Jack Fayles' counter and reviewed his list a second time. His new partner had sent him into Martinez to shop for groceries, two new picks, and other necessities. At first Devlin had balked at going, but then figured that by now the bloodhound had to have given up. He had nothing to fear in Martinez or anywhere else, he reassured himself. Also, he wanted to satisfy his curiosity. Fayles had all but promised him he'd tell Hennessy he'd been by when the search party showed up; Devlin wanted to find out if he'd actually done so. Not that it mattered at this stage, but Tom was curious.

He had been in the store almost ten minutes, and Fayles had yet to bring up the subject, in spite of having recognized him the minute he walked in. Devlin took the reins.

"Did Lieutenant Hennessy show up after I left?" he asked.

"He did, and yes, I told him you'd passed through. I said I was going to, didn't I? Didn't you believe me?"

"I figured you might have had second thoughts."

"You figured wrong."

"Proud of yourself, aren't you?"

"Actually, no. I regretted it."

"I'll bet."

"Hey, it's water over the dam. He didn't catch you, did he?"

"No thanks to you."

"Did your brother catch up with you?"

Devlin's mouth dropped open. "My brother? What are you talking about?"

"He came through a few days ago."

"That's baloney, he's in Boston."

"The hell he is. And it *was* him, I could see you in his face right off." Fayles went on. Devlin listened, visibly stricken with disbelief. "Where was he heading?" Tom asked.

"How the hell would he know? He was looking for you."

"Jesus, he could be all the way down to Arizona by now."

"Or up in Oregon."

"Did he say he might stop in on his way back?"

"No."

Devlin borrowed a pencil and paper and drew a crude map showing Martinez, Antioch, and other towns in the area and located the Dorothy in among them as accurately as he could.

"Give him this if he returns," Devlin instructed the old man. "If he can find these hills, he'll find us. If he shows up."

"I'll see that he gets it. Nice boy. I put him up out back overnight. He's got grit."

"Did he happen to mention when he got to San Francisco?"

Fayles told him the night of the fire and of the accidents that had delayed Loyal's leaving town. Two other customers came in separately. The storekeeper broke off at sight of them. "You got everything on your list?" he asked Devlin.

They settled up. The horse would be well loaded going back, but it was only about ten miles. He col-

lected most of the groceries and started for the door.
A man was coming in. He looked familiar, shockingly
so. Devlin's eyes started from their sockets.

Captain Westerfield!

Westerfield couldn't help but recognize him, but
gave no sign that he did. None. Looking through him,
he passed by close enough to brush against him and
approached the counter. Outside the store Devlin caught
his breath. His mind was racing as he filled his saddlebags. A surrey was parked a short ways from his horse
at the hitch rail. The faces of the two women sitting in
it were hidden in shadow, then the younger one turned
her head, bringing her face into the light. He recognized her. Catherine Bracy.

Devlin hurried back into the store to get the rest of
his packages. Westerfield was still at the counter, his
back to him. Devlin excused himself, the captain moved
aside, and Devlin picked up what was left and went
back out. Two minutes later he rode off.

The captain had bought two cold bottles of root
beer for the ladies and a handful of Pearl stogies for
himself. He reappeared with the opened bottles and
got back up alongside Catherine.

"Did you notice that man that just rode off?" he
asked quietly, so that only she could hear.

"I didn't pay much attention," she said.

"That was Sergeant Thomas Devlin."

"Are you sure?"

"He recognized me; you should have seen his face.
It was him, all right. Cathy, where are you going?"

Catherine had jumped out of the surrey and rushed
into the store.

"I'll only be a minute," she called over her shoulder.

Inside, Fayles was talking to a customer at the
counter. She ran up to him. "Excuse me . . ." The
customer looked slightly upset at the intrusion, but
moved aside for her. "That man that just left, did he
happen to mention if he's seen his brother?"

"No, he hasn't. He didn't even know he'd left Boston till I told him. His brother came through a few days ago," he explained.

"Did he say where he was going from here?"

Westerfield had come up behind her. Her attention on the storekeeper, she failed to hear him.

"No," answered Fayles. "But if he does . . ."

"Please tell him Catherine Bracy was by. We're on our way to Sacramento, but we'll be coming back through here—won't we, Robert?"

"I suppose."

They exited. Catherine could feel the captain's eyes boring into her, questioning.

"You seem very interested in his brother," Westerfield said.

"I am."

This mildly startled him. She sensed that he wanted to unleash a flurry of questions, but was holding back. He helped her up onto the seat.

"What was that all about?" Doreen asked.

"Nothing important, Mother," said Catherine. "Robert, what did you say to the sergeant?"

"Not a thing. It was one of those times when you have to make up your mind in a split second. I thought to myself, I've got him dead-pigeon. I just have to disarm him. Only, then, what? We have to get to Sacramento, we can't let him hold us up. So I made believe I didn't recognize him. Cathy . . ."

"I know what you're going to say." She laid a reassuring hand on his. "Don't worry, I won't tell Daddy. Mother won't either, will you, Mother?"

"My dear, I really don't know what you're talking about. If you're not going to drink your root beer, hand it back."

Catherine laughed and did so. "Let's go, Robert. If we're lucky, we'll make West Pittsburg before dark. We can take the ferry across to Collinsville first thing in the morning."

*   *   *

Devlin rode slowly on his way back to the mine, tempted to pinch himself. Had it really happened, or was it the sun? No, it was Captain Westerfield. Who else wore artillery red, two bars, and beard enough for two men? What had passed through his mind to keep him from grabbing him? Did he pity him? Did he figure Hennessy had tried and failed, which, by the rules of the game, should entitle the fox to his freedom?

"No. If the colonel ever found out, he'd shove his bars down his throat. He'd bust him to private."

Maybe Westerfield disliked Hennessy as much as everyone else, and given the chance to bail him out, he chose to pass it up. Or maybe it had nothing to do with Hennessy; maybe he just couldn't see taking excess baggage along with the two women, complicating whatever they were doing. Still, there was nothing to prevent him from having the local law lock him up to pick up on his way back from wherever they were heading.

He had always liked Captain Westerfield. He was a fair man and a good officer. He more than liked him now. At the moment his feelings for him approached something akin to reverence.

Forty miles south, heading southeast, further stretching the distance between himself and his brother, Loyal Devlin stopped by a creek to water his horse and his own throat. The sun was descending; to his left, sinking below the ridge of the Diablo Range, it sent wide golden swaths over the dusty land into the shadowed valley to the east. A solitary prospector stood knee-deep in the water examining the sand and gravel in his pan disconsolately. As Loyal watched him he exploded, cursing, flinging the pan, contents and all, to his right. He came striding out of the water, muttering angrily.

"No luck?" Loyal asked.

The man glowered. "What do you think? Hell, I ain't found 'nough to fit under my thumbnail in a goddamn week anna half. Ain't none left. Not in California. I been up to Benton Creek and down to Hubbard and evvy water between. Nothin'! No more'n six specks average. I could starve to death and wither away to dust at this goddamn rate."

"It's just a streak of bad luck."

"Bad luck your asshole, sonny boy. It's the goddamn story o' my life. I ain't seen good luck since I come into the goddamn world. I been livin' hand-to-mouth so long it's a goddamn wonder I got any fingers left. If I had a gun I'd blow my head open. Only I had to sell my gun for bread and beans; now they're gone. Goddamn sonovabitch!"

"Hey, wait! Are you just going to leave your pan there? Let me get it for you." Loyal splashed across the creek, retrieved the pan, and was about to return when he spotted something bright yellow in the sand and gravel that had spilled out when the pan landed. He scooped it into the pan and brought it back. "There's gold in there."

"I'll be goddamned, so there is. Look at that, must be close to a quarter of a ounce." Overcome by a burst of exhilaration, he splashed back into the water, washed out the gold, deposited it in the little leather sack suspended from his belt, and scooped up another panful in the identical spot. "Goddamn, talk about the turnin' worm. Look at that, more! This damn hole's chock fulla it."

Loyal congratulated him, then asked if he'd seen Tom. The man hadn't seen anyone fitting the description and didn't even look up when he told him so. "I got me a goddamn freshwater bonanza here. I'm gonna' be rich."

Horses were approaching, coming from the southeast. Loyal shielded his eyes and recognized blue uniforms with red piping. He sucked in a breath sharply. Bracy's men out looking for Tom! It had to be them. They were slowing. The lieutenant in the lead raised his hand, halting the other two. He brought his horse ambling up.

" 'Afternoon, mister."

"Lieutenant."

All three were looking at him strangely. He didn't need any of them to say why. Tom's face was rounder and had seen more years, but their features were all but identical: from the color of their eyes to their aquiline noses, firm-lipped mouths, and pugnacious, challenging chins. The lieutenant removed his gauntlet and offered his hand; Loyal shook it. Hennessy introduced himself for no special reason, reflected Loyal, but to encourage him to identify himself. To confirm his suspicions?

"You're . . . ?" Hennessy asked.

"Nobody important," said Loyal.

That was stupid, he thought; it was as good as telling Hennessy he knew he recognized him as being related to Sergeant Thomas Devlin. What other reason would he have for hesitating to tell him his name? And at this point, a phony name would never make the grade.

"Name wouldn't be Devlin, would it?" Hennessy smirked. "I heard that the sergeant's brother had come to town. Still looking for him, are you?"

"Whatever I'm doing is no business of yours."

"It is if it turns out you're hiding him," said Hennessy evenly. "Shielding a wanted man's a criminal offense. We can't do anything to you, but the police in San Francisco sure can. Chief Sanger and the colonel are very close; they cooperate with each other in everything. Including deserters."

Loyal ignored him and mounted his horse. The prospector, meanwhile, had not so much as turned his head to watch the conversation. He was far too busy. Loyal turned his horse about, heading it southeast, in the direction Hennessy and his men had come from. The lieutenant, the corporal, and private turned their horses around.

"Mind if we tag along?" Hennessy asked.

"I do. Let's get something straight: I'm not wanted by anybody. You hassle me, you'll answer to Colonel Bracy. Stay out of my way. If you follow me, somebody could get hurt, is that clear? Back off, Lieutenant." Loyal sent his hand to his gun.

Hennessy sniffed and turned from him to the man in the creek. He described Devlin. The man shook his head until the bloodhound was done. "I just finished tellin' him I ain't seen such a man."

Hennessy described the Callahan brothers.

"Nor them neither."

"Thank you."

Hennessy and his men rode off to the northwest.

Colonel Bracy hated being alone in the house the first night. To keep from talking to the four walls he invited Captain Wilcox to supper. The captain left early to make last rounds of his patients, and the colonel went to bed. As he expected, he couldn't sleep. The certainty that he alone was at fault for Doreen's condition nagged him unmercifully. Why hadn't he seen it coming?

Catherine didn't blame him. But the fact that she didn't only reinforced his belief that he was at fault and she had taken pity on him. He had spread himself so thin he had no time left for his wife and daughter. All the while he rationalized his behavior by telling himself and them that it was for them that he worked so hard. Well, it wasn't for them, it was for the War Department, that nebulous entity in distant Washington, most of whose members didn't even know he existed. More than post commander he was father confessor, monitor, director, disciplinarian, mediator, and wore a dozen other hats. He was no better than the Reverend Brannan himself, God forbid, so little time did he devote to his family.

And Doreen suffered, and this is what it had finally come to.

The next day was Sunday. Inspection day. After breakfast the enlisted men busied themselves with fatigue duty, cleaning up the courtyard and the gun tiers. They swept out their quarters, arranged their bunks and accoutrements, and put a shine on all metal and leather equipment. Buttons, buckles, boots, and shoes were polished with spit. Mess equipment was scoured with dirt—knives and forks by simply plunging them a few times into the ground.

Following two hours of preparation, the men marched to the courtyard and formed up to await the colonel's arrival. With Major Downing and First Sergeant Dietrich, Bracy walked up and down the lines, inspecting the arms, equipment, and uniform of each soldier. When he was done, with the major and the sergeant he stepped to the front of the assembled company.

"Tench-hut," barked Major Downing. "Stack arms, unsling and open knapsacks, lay them on the ground for inspection."

The colonel checked the contents of each knapsack by poking among them with the tip of his sword. But his mind was miles from the inspection. It sped to Sacramento and the hospital and waited there for Doreen and Catherine to arrive. The tip of his sword uncovered a dirty sock. He failed to notice it.

"Ahem, sir," Downing said, derailing his train of thought.

The sock had been concealed under a freshly laundered layer of clothing. Bracy raised his sword, the sock hanging from the tip. The men closest to the offender tittered as he blanched.

"Silence," snapped the colonel. "Is this yours, Private?"

"Yes, sir."

"It's filthy. Aren't you afraid it'll dirty your other things?"

"Yes, sir. No, sir."

"Which?"

"Yes, sir."

"Sergeant . . ."

Dietrich stepped forward. "Sir?"

"When inspection is over, see that this man gets a bucket of water, a bar of Globe Brag Soap and a good stiff brush. You'll spend the rest of the day scrubbing the enlisted men's quarters, understand?"

"Every . . . ? Yes, sir."

Inspection ended, the men reslung their knapsacks, recovered their arms, and were marched back to quarters. The colonel, the major, and the sergeant made the rounds: the cells, the kitchen, other facilities, coming at length to the infirmary, where Dr. Wilcox was carrying on his own inspection. In the dim yellow light from the two end windows the two lines of beds with their heads to the walls showed more than half-empty. Only four men of the wounded in the battle were still under Wilcox's care, and two of these were due to be discharged that afternoon.

"Corporal Hogan's pelvis is knitting very well," said the doctor in a low voice. "And Private Danaher's skull fracture is coming along. I want both to stay at least one more week."

The colonel spoke kindly and comfortingly to each of the men in turn. They appreciated his solicitude. He turned back to the doctor.

"We'll be on our way, Byron. Major, let's do quarters next."

They proceeded to the enlisted men's quarters, where, with the men standing in their assigned places, the colonel examined floors, bunks, and furnishings. It was tedious work and his mind was not on it, any more than it had been in the courtyard inspection. He finished inspecting the officers' quarters around noon. Sunday afternoon was normally free time. Men did as they pleased, some going into town to church. The colonel stayed in his office, preferring that to going home to an empty house before nightfall.

He sat at his desk thinking of his wife. If sending her to Sacramento didn't work out, he'd resign his commission. He could see no other choice. Isaac Kinsolving would understand and help him sever the red tape that always accompanied such decisions. He'd get out, get Doreen and Catherine out of here—back to Virginia, possibly. That was where Doreen had been the happiest, back before the war.

He'd let her decide where they'd settle.

Damn but the hours went by slowly, as if each one was carrying a week on its back. Three days to Sacramento, and how long would she be there? How long to cure her? God only knew. Byron Wilcox had no idea. Perhaps a month. Perhaps six? God forbid!

At three o'clock, he gave up battling his worries and called Howard in. "What are you doing?"

"Nothing special, sir."

"I'm going into town. I'm going to church."

"You, sir? Excuse me, I just meant—"

"You've never known me to go to church, right?" The colonel smiled tolerantly. "I only go when I need it. Pretty poor excuse for a Christian, wouldn't you say?"

"Oh, no, sir."

"If anybody needs me, I'll be home around six. You don't have to hang around. If you've got something better to do, go and do it."

"Yes, sir. Thank you, sir. I've got a girlfriend."

"Good for you. Is it serious?"

"Oh, yes, sir."

"Get out of here."

He skedaddled. The colonel laughed. His first laugh since his family had left for Sacramento. He sobered. He had a girl once, too, the prettiest little thing, so alive, so vivacious, and they were so in love. No two persons in history, in all recorded time, had ever been so in love.

"Will you marry me, Dorey MacLaughlin?"

"I will, Ewing Bracy, I will, I will, I will!"

21

Devlin arrived back at the Dorothy to be greeted by a whooping Punk Van Sickle. He was clutching a rock twice the size of his fist, dancing about like a dervish and yelling at the top of his leather lungs.

"What the hell . . ."

"I found the vein! Look at this, look! Quartz riddled with gold, crammed with it, a fortune. Come inside, come in, come in. Move."

Inside the adit the lantern glowed feebly. Punk turned up the flame and led Devlin down the narrow way to the back wall. He handed him the lamp and picked up a pick. "Stand back . . ." He swung, struck the wall and loosened a quantity of rock. Down came half a dozen chunks, sending up a cloud of dust. He grabbed the lamp from Devlin and illuminated the vein.

"It's almost a foot wide. Look, it crosses the ceiling, comes down this wall, tails off right about there. We'll work on the wall. Thomas, it could go on for a hundred yards. We may not get up to the ceiling till Christmas. Isn't this beautiful? Isn't it sacred?"

"It's great."

"Partner, with your hands and back and my know-how, we're going to be in the deepest clover in North America."

"Where do you bring the ore?"

"To the nearest stamping mill. You've got to take

this in to the assay office in Martinez right away and
get a reading on it. Bake Myers'll do all his tests on
it to determine how much gold it'll yield. And unless
my eyes deceive me, there's silver in there too. See
those little flecks? Not as much as the gold, but some.
Bake'll charge you ten bucks; you got ten bucks?
Okay, it'll take him a couple hours, at least. When
he's done testing, he'll be able to tell you how much
gold per ton. And the coin value. For gold and silver.
You pay him, he'll give you a certificate. Make sure
it's numbered and that he signs it at the bottom."

"What if it doesn't turn out enough to make it
worth mining?"

"That could happen, but I don't think so. These
chunks are loaded. I can smell it. Take the biggest one
there."

"Let me unload the saddlebags."

"Just throw them on the ground. I'll unload them.
You get back there fast as you can."

Loyal, meanwhile, had given up his elaborate and
time-consuming plan for circling and working his way
through the camps. Instead, he turned about and headed
in a northwesterly direction toward Martinez. When
the road straightened, which it did about half a mile
from the creek, it ran for nearly two visible miles. He
could see no dust, no sign of Hennessy and his men.
He wondered if they'd given up completely on Tom to
concentrate on the Callahan brothers. Probably not.
Any deserter would do for Hennessy.

He continued in the direction of Martinez. He seized
on a hunch. Tom had passed through Martinez, and
had gotten to know Ira Jack Fayles. It was just possible that after leaving town, his brother hadn't wandered too far from the area. If that were so, it was
very possible that he'd return to the town for supplies
when he needed them. He had waited until Martinez
to supply himself the first time. If he stayed within

twenty miles or so, it seemed only natural that that would be where he'd return to when he needed more supplies.

All Loyal hoped and prayed was that he would catch up with him before the soldiers. He recognized a snake when he saw one, and Hennessy had all the qualifications. He was obviously the shoot-first-and-ask-questions-later type of hunter; the colonel had made a wise choice. Going after deserters wasn't a job most men would relish, but Hennessy clearly loved it. And the two men with him seemed to be just as short of the milk of human kindness as he was.

"Tom, wherever you are, mind your back," he whispered.

Tom Devlin reached Martinez and Bake Myers' assay office. He got the results, paid for the certificate, and left town without even looking in on Ira Jack Fayles. Punk's enthusiasm was infectious and Devlin wanted to get back as fast as the horse could carry him with the good news. The gold assayed at 8.08 ounces per ton, plus less than one ounce per ton silver, with a $160 coin value for the gold.

It was nearing midnight by the time Loyal rode into Martinez. He stabled his horse and splurged on himself, taking a one-dollar hotel room that he could ill afford. He might have taken advantage of his friendship with Fayles and asked for the back storage-room cot for the night, but the store was in darkness and the door locked when he tried it.

He had an early breakfast, his first decent meal since leaving the Brannan house. He stopped in to say hello to Fayles and was greeted like a long-lost brother. Fayles was beside himself with excitement. He quickly got out the crude map Tom had drawn and spread it on the counter.

"The name of the mine is the Dorothy. It's the x, right here. Think you can find it?"

"You bet!"

"Look for these hills he marked in here. He says if you can find the hills, you can't miss the mine. Let me do something here that may help you." He got out a pencil and inscribed a compass. "That's almost exactly north, so the other three have to be close to perfect. You got a compass? Let me get you one."

He got out an open-face compass set in a brass case with a ring and a silvered metal dial, measuring less than two inches in diameter.

"How much?" Loyal asked.

"Thirty cents."

He paid him, hefted the compass, then shoved it in his pocket. "Oh, boy, I'm catching up with him at last. At long last!"

"He'll be out there waiting for you. Go across the street to Hurley's Saloon and get yourself a bottle. You two will have yourselves a high old time celebrating."

"I'm going to do just that. Yes, sir. Thanks again for everything, Ira, you're a true friend."

The old man waved off the compliment. "Pshaw, I just can't resist taking pity on a helpless greenhorn. Good luck, Loyal, and if you two happen back this way, stop in and visit, hear. I'll be mad as hell. Oh, I almost forgot, a young lady was asking for you."

"I don't know any women out here."

"Well, she sure knows you. Tall, slender, hair as black as a grackle's wing, beautiful."

Loyal gasped. "Catherine."

"That's the name she gave me. She and an older woman and an artillery captain came through yesterday—on their way to Sacramento, she said. She said if I see you to tell you she'll be coming back through."

By now Loyal had all but seized him by the front of his shirt, he was so excited.

"When?"

"Maybe we can figure that out. Where'd she come from?"

"San Francisco."

"It's over ninety miles from Frisco to Sacramento; figure with stops and delays thirty miles tops a day in a surrey. If she doesn't stay there more than a few hours, turns around, and comes back, she should be coming back through here in four days. Possibly five."

"She asked for me? Really?" Loyal couldn't believe his luck.

Fayles leered. "What did I just tell you? So where will you be heading now? For the mine or Sacramento?"

"The mine, but . . . Let me make a copy of this map. You hang on to it, give it to her. Tell her . . . Wait, I've a better idea; four days from today I'll come back here to meet her."

"I get the feeling you two really want to get together." Fayles grinned. "I can see the big attraction on your part, but what about her?"

"Thanks."

At the Dorothy, the contents of a bottle of Old Tartan Scotch saved especially for such an occasion had been emptied in celebration of the discovery. The assay certificate hung by a nail over the entrance to the adit, official testimony to the wealth locked in the rock within. The celebrants' exuberance ran out with the liquor, and suddenly sober consideration of the situation took over. Devlin's first concern was that of every miner who strikes it rich.

"How do we protect it?"

"The claim's legally staked, Thomas, officially recorded with four witnesses; all we have to do is work it." Punk slapped him on the back good-naturedly. "You've got nothing against working it, do you? If a man stakes a claim and doesn't show up for ten days or two weeks, anybody can take it over. Legally. Naturally, claims can be bought and sold, but like I said, any transaction has to have witnesses, at least two. If anybody comes along and tries to jump us, even if

they shoot us both, there's no way they can take over.
When they start taking out the gold, word can't help
but get around. The authorities will hear about it.
Somebody's bound to check the claim ownership in
the records and the law'll have the scoundrels dead to
rights."

"A lot of good that'll do us if we're lying behind one
of these hills with the buzzards picking at our bones."

"Thomas, the system is self-protective. The prospectors know the rules and ninety-nine out of a hundred
abide by them; the one who doesn't risks harsh justice
if he's caught jumping a claim. If other prospectors get
wind of it, they'll avenge it before the law in Martinez
gets its hands on him. Mining's a proud fraternity; bad
apples are an embarrassment and the boys think they're
better gotten rid of than put up with.

"Besides, it's not like we're unarmed. We got
your rifle and three pistols between us. How do you
feel, partner?"

"A little woozy."

"Me, too, must be the Old Tartan. Let's catch us a
couple hours' sleep, work out the fuzz, then get to
work." He lurched slightly getting to his feet. He
turned and addressed the entrance, removing his derby,
holding it to his chest reverentially. "Dorothy, mother
of mine, your wandering boy is home at last. Take me
to your bosom, open up your heart."

They slept, awoke, and worked through the night.
The dew sparkled on the grass, the air was sweet to
the taste and uncommonly still. The sun was just beginning to peer over the Sierra Nevada, rising to flood
the San Joaquin Valley, when they finished breakfast
and resumed working.

They had been at it less than two hours when they
heard the sound of hooves coming from the direction
of Martinez. Devlin snatched up his rifle and cocked
it as the rider came barreling in.

"Loyal! Boyo! God Almighty! Loyal! Loyal!" Tom

threw down his rifle and ran over to his brother. They threw their arms around each other, hugging, dancing, roaring happily.

Punk watched, leaning on his shovel and chewing a sprig of dried grass.

"Punk," said Tom finally, "meet my baby brother, the boyo, Loyal Richard Devlin. Come all the way from Boston, Mass. Boyo, Mr. Northgraves Llwellyn Van Sickle, Junior, Esquire, my friend and my partner."

They shook hands. For the next fifteen minutes Tom assaulted Loyal with questions—about the letters, his trip, San Francisco—leading him step by step up to the present. Then he turned the conversation onto himself.

"You must have heard I deserted."

"Yes."

Punk interrupted. "You boys could use a little privacy. If you'll excuse me, I'll take my morning constitutional."

"It's okay, Punk," Tom said. "It's no deep dark family secret. I don't feel ashamed of it; maybe I should, but I don't, not much."

As he spoke, he looked straight at Loyal, looking for reaction to his words: either sympathetic understanding or disapproval. But all he seemed to be getting was the old expression of hero worship. So Loyal's first words surprised him.

"How come you didn't hold off till I got here? And get out, you know, legally?"

"I already told you, I didn't get your letter. I didn't know you were here until a couple days ago. As to getting out legally, as you put it, I did think about that. There was no way I could have worked it." His tone was taking on an edge of resentment. "My mistake was reenlisting. I shouldn't have. I signed up for four more years, only to change my mind. Well, you know the rest. It's done, Loyal, it's over. If I can live with it, you should be able to."

"That's not it! I don't care about that. The army doesn't mean a tinker's damn to me. You did more than your share, you had every right to get out. Only . . ."

Tom stood hands on hips eyeing him, his ruddy face drawn taut with seriousness. "What is it, then?"

"Hennessy's after you."

"Not anymore. He gave up last week; he never chases more than a week."

Loyal told him about his meeting with the bloodhound and about the Callahans. Tom wanted to know exactly where he'd run into Hennessy and which direction he'd taken when he rode off. Loyal told him. Tom nodded.

"They're probably working the area south of Martinez and Antioch. I wonder where the Callahans headed? Funny, if somebody was to ask me which man in the whole garrison would be the next to chuck it all and take off, I would have said Tim Callahan. And Dennis with him. I don't think they've been separated since birth. Are you hungry, boyo?"

"I ate in town." Loyal's attention had drifted to the mine and the certificate above the entrance. "Any luck yet?"

"All the luck in the world," Tom said.

"You're looking at the gateway to a bonanza," Punk said. "All we have to do is break it up and haul it out. We could use a little help." He winked at Tom.

Tom nodded. "I'm in for one half. I'll split with you. Okay by you, partner?"

"It's your half. Let's drink to it. Oh, oh . . ." He held up the empty bottle of Old Tartan.

Tom laughed.

Loyal signaled patience and got a full bottle of Old Tartan out of his saddlebag.

"I like this boy already," chortled Punk. "I like his taste in hooch."

* * *

Sam Brannan summoned his followers to a meeting at Fort Gunnybags. The Vigilantes' numbers had swollen to more than eight hundred. Brannan arrived in an uncharacteristically foul mood. The response to his letters to Secretary of the Army Conrad, coming not even from the man, but from some faceless underling, was a painful blow to his hopes for tilting the balance of power in the city in favor of his committee.

He ascended his favorite Pears soap box and loudly called for attention. He cleared his throat theatrically and assumed his martyred look. He held up A. Forbush's letter. Around him torches licked the darkness, illuminating a sea of upturned, mortally serious faces.

"Gentlemen, I won't bore you by reading this 'note of rejection' from Secretary of the Army Conrad. It's downright insulting. I can conclude that the army is only interested in protecting its own. It doesn't care about the citizens, our loved ones, that it's commanded by law to protect. Bracy stays. The garrison stays. So where does that leave us?"

Two loud groans were followed by a loud, angry rumbling.

"Your attention, please. It leaves us back where we started: on our own. Battling the incompetence of the police, the persistent interference of the army, the wickedness and abuse of the criminals in our midst. Three against one."

More and louder rumbling.

"Brothers, God helps those who help themselves. Ours is a perilous situation. But if you think about it, one fact emerges with striking clarity. Thanks to our numbers, thanks to public approval, thanks to right that makes might we are the power!"

Cheers greeted this statement, and somebody began pummeling a bass drum at the rear of the gathering. A gesture from Brannan stopped it. The crowd quieted.

"Our enemies and their allies can be dealt with. We can and we will rid our city of the Sydney Ducks.

"Brothers, what I am about to say is for your ears only. We within these walls are of a single mind. One purpose: to cleanse our city once and for all. Sydney Town is our cross, our Sodom, our Gomorrah. Brothers, recall to mind the words of the scripture. 'The sun was risen upon the earth when Lot entered into Zoar. Then the Lord rained upon Sodom and Gomorrah brimstone and fire from the Lord out of heaven. And he overthrew those cities, and all the plain, and all the inhabitants of the cities, and that which grew upon the ground.' Genesis, nineteen, twenty-three through twenty-five.

"Brothers, the Lord will not rain brimstone and fire down on Sydney Town. He leaves it to us to bring it down, to expunge it from our midst and send our enemies fleeing. The harbor is cluttered with abandoned ships. You can see them a distance of a quarter-mile. Seaworthy ships, vessels that can carry hundreds of undesirables back to where they came from. How is this possible? How can we effect their departure? Not by the means we have already employed, not by marching on Sydney Town and routing them.

"I propose a whole new approach. A political approach. We will never rid ourselves of the scum that infests us until we get rid of their protectors. I say we replace Mayor Brenham, replace Chief of Police Sanger, and neutralize the colonel and his tin soldiers. Without Brenham's and Sanger's support, the army will be reduced to the role of interloper. Under a new mayor, with a new, more cooperative chief of police, we will stand united against our common foe. As we now stand against him. Since the army refuses to eliminate the garrison, it is our responsibility to dismiss it from our affairs. Ignore its presence, block its interference, render it neutral."

Uproarious cheering. In the forefront of the gathering a number of hotter heads began chanting, calling for immediate confrontation. The chorus was quickly taken up by others. Brannan tried to stifle the uproar, but he could no longer make himself heard. The crowd surged to the doors; all sorts of weapons appeared. The doors were flung open, and the crowd poured out, gathering in the street. Brannan was swept along with the crowd. Pushing his way through to the curb, the minister turned, raised his hands, and called for quiet and attention.

"Brothers, brothers, you're running amok. Listen to me. It's too soon! We'll deal with Fort Point in due time. First, get rid of Brenham and Sanger. Not by force, not this way. By popular mandate. The will of the people! Listen to me, listen!"

He could not get their attention. His pleas were ignored, his last few words were lost in the rising cry.

"To the fort, the fort!"

The mass of humanity moved west along Sacramento Street, picking up curious onlookers along the way. Brannan managed to push his way to the forefront, seizing a torch and swinging it aloft. His reasoning was simple, his conclusion speedily arrived at: if he could no longer control them, he must lead them.

At the corner of Larkin and Sacramento he swung right, heading up Larkin toward the fort. By now his followers had increased to more than a thousand, with others joining them, coming in from every street they crossed.

Colonel Bracy was home alone sipping brandy and catching up on his personal correspondence when a knock startled him so he dropped his pen. It was his striker.

"Major Viselli sent me to get you, sir. Trouble, big trouble, out in the water."

"Slow down, Howard, start again. Slower. What's out in the water?"

"Boats, barges, rafts, just about everything that can float, sir. The townspeople, mostly the Viggies. Yelling, carrying on, throwing rocks; demanding to see you."

"It sounds like they want my scalp."

"The major says you better come quick."

He jammed on his cap, hastily buttoned his tunic and buckled on his sword. He followed Howard up the road to the Sally Port door, past the two guards and inside and hurried up the stairs to the top tier. The sight that met his eyes astonished him. Howard had not exaggerated. At least sixty craft, from canoes to a massive coal barge, were assembled in the water below. Hundreds of torches blazed; a thousand men glared upward, shouting obscenities and threats and shaking their fists. Stones bounced harmlessly off the seawall below. Others flew overhead, striking the low wall at the rear. Two of the guns were already manned. The gunners looked back at Bracy expectantly. The electricity charging the air was so powerful he almost expected it to begin crackling in his ears. Major Downing came striding up, his face grim. He saluted halfheartedly.

"They're demanding to see you, Colonel. But if I were you, sir, I wouldn't get too close to the wall. We can handle them."

"We will, but not that way. Is Brannan down there?"

"Yes, he is, sir," said the provost marshal. To Downing's manifest dismay, Viselli moved the colonel between two Columbiads to the wall. He pointed. "See that rowboat to the left of the little sailboat, the white one?"

"Okay, Roy, get back. All of you stay back, I'll handle this. Everybody keep your hands off your weapons. There'll be no shooting. If it becomes necessary, we'll fire an eight-inch over their heads, but only as a last resort. Understand? Major Downing, you're in charge, I'm holding you responsible."

"Yes, sir."

"Roy, you stay here with me, the rest of you keep back. I'll talk to them and try to get them to disperse."

"They're in no mood to talk, sir," said Downing.

Bracy turned back around and faced the water. He held his hands up for attention. The crowd ignored him. The insults and accusations became louder, nastier. Then Brannan spoke.

"Brothers, brothers, brothers, give the colonel a chance. Let's hear what he has to say. Quiet!"

"You first, Samuel," Bracy said, gesturing invitation. "It's your show."

"No show, Ewing. This is serious."

"What do you want?"

"We're here to strike a deal with you. Hear me out before you decide."

"Go on."

"We ask only one thing: your promise, first verbally, then in writing, that from now on you and your men will confine your efforts to the defense of the city from attack by sea."

The crowd cheered wildly. Again Brannan quieted it.

"Whatever happens in town, you will stay out of it. Whatever steps the Committee of Vigilance takes against the criminals, you will not interfere. No one will interfere. Mayor Brenham and Chief Sanger are to be replaced shortly; the people—"

It was as far as he got. A single shot rang, coming from well back in the armada. It stiffened Viselli, Downing, and the others in surprise. It struck the colonel in the chest. Shocked disbelief seized his features as his hand flew to his chest. Blood seeped gleaming through his fingers. He coughed, groaned softly, and fell.

22

Major Richard Downing had wisely kept his head
when his superior was hit and went down. The
first reaction of the soldiers, however, was to shoot
back. Downing raised his hands.

"Hold your fire! Don't return fire!" he commanded.
Then he knelt beside the colonel, took off his own
jacket, balled it, and placed it under his head. He
unbuttoned the colonel's jacket and pressed his hand-
kerchief against the wound. Bracy groaned; his cheeks
were chalk-white and his eyes floated uncertainly in
their sockets. He was in obvious agony, fighting for his
breath. He looked to be sinking fast.

"Easy, sir," murmured Downing. Then he reared
up sharply. "Don't just stand there gawking, somebody go get Wilcox. On the double!"

Brannan called up from below. "What's happening
up there? Ewing, Ewing, are you all right?"

No one even looked down at him. Everyone was
frozen, in place. The stretcher arrived; Dr. Wilcox
came puffing and perspiring up the stairs after it. He
gasped at the sight of the colonel. He examined the
wound, Downing and others crowding around. Wilcox
waved them back irritably.

"Give the man air, dammit!"

Again Brannan called up from below. "Ewing?
Ewing?"

"Somebody shut that idiot up," snapped Viselli. He jumped up himself. "He's badly hurt! Are you blind? Didn't you see? Are you satisfied, you bible-beating horse's ass! Get the hell out of here, all of you. You've got ten minutes to clear the water. Ten minutes to target practice."

"It was an accident," Brannan responded. "One of the boys lost his head."

"Which one?" boomed Viselli angrily. "Point him out!"

Not surprisingly, no one seemed able to identify the culprit.

"Ewing, this is Samuel Brannan speaking. It was an accident."

"Ten minutes," Viselli repeated. "Closer to nine now . . ."

"You can't, Roy," Downing said. "You heard what the colonel said."

"Relax, Major," was the terse response. "They'll leave. How's he doing?"

"Not good," Wilcox said. "It looks to be dangerously close to the right ventricle. Upward angle, deep, too deep. I got to get it out of there. Pronto." He supervised the moving of the colonel onto the stretcher. "Pick him up very slowly. Careful, keep it level. Take him down to the infirmary. Gently now. Go slowly, mind the steps. Keep the lower end up high as you can. You there"—he singled out a private—"go ahead of them, make sure the way is clear."

"Yes, sir."

"I'll follow you two down. You'll be all right, Colonel. We'll have it out of there in jig time. Deaden the pain. Don't strain, breathe easy.

"I'm coming," said Viselli.

"You're not," burst Wilcox. "I don't need any of you. I'll be at least an hour. I don't want any interruptions. I don't care if the damn pirates come back. Who's in charge?"

"What's going on up there?" Brannan bawled from below.

"Me," Downing said to the doctor.

"No shooting . . ." murmured Bracy feebly; his voice sounded like it was coming from a great distance. The effort proved too much for him: his eyes shuttered, his head fell to one side.

"Good God," rasped Downing.

"He's only fainted," Wilcox said. "Okay, let's go—and careful, careful."

In the water below the armada was breaking up, all of the craft excepting Brannan's rowboat moving to the right in a body, approaching the beach.

Brannan raised his torch. "I demand to know how he is. How bad is it? Is he dead? Did it kill him?"

Viselli leaned over, glaring down at him, drew his pistol, laid it on top of the wall, and set his hand over it. "You scum get onto your oars and get the hell out of here! You've got sixty seconds. Move, or so help me God, we'll shoot that tub out from under you and let you drown."

Brannan bristled and shook his fist. "How dare you address me in such a manner! What's your name?"

Viselli aimed, cocked, fired. The bullet whizzed by Brannan's hat. He yelped, ducked, and his hat fell off into the water. The two men at the oars began pulling for their lives.

"My hat! My hat!"

He looked ludicrous, down on his knees, reaching for his hat, which was floating off upside down. He caught a face full of water from one of the oars and sputtered loudly. Nearly everyone was at the wall watching. No one laughed, no one even smiled. Viselli turned from the sight. The stretcher had disappeared down the stairs, the doctor following.

"The poor soul," Downing murmured, shaking his head. "His wife in the hospital, his daughter on the way back. To this. The poor girl, I wonder if she'll get here before he—"

"Shut up, Richard," snapped Viselli. "Don't talk like an idiot, don't even think that."

Below in the infirmary, the time of the knife turned out briefer than Wilcox had anticipated. He located the ball in his second try. By then, the patient had lost a great deal of blood. Shock appeared imminent. His skin had taken on an ominous gray hue, that of a corpse. Wilcox noticed it and sighed. It was a look he knew well. He had come to view it as the signal that death's bright angel had arrived. It was out of his hands now.

The battle had begun. Wilcox could only hope and pray that Bracy had the will to fight off that angel of death. The enemy with no heart, no feelings, no compassion, no respect for the colonel's courage, and was unimpressed by his indomitable spirit. He saw only a life hanging precariously, like a ripened apple from its twig, ready to fall. Wait, and into his grasp it would drop.

Having done all he could do, Wilcox stood watching his patient take shallow, halting breaths, again and again expecting his next one to be his last. The bloodied ball lay where he had set it on his instrument table. He examined it, then flung it away angrily. He pulled up a chair and sat watching, the bogey of his helplessness gripping his heart.

A knock sounded.

"Go away. Leave us alone!"

23

News of the turmoil afflicting the city the night before had not reached Martinez, much less the Dorothy, when the critical fourth day, the day of Catherine's return, as predicted by Ira Jack Fayles, arrived. The three partners were finishing breakfast when Loyal announced his intention to go into Martinez.

"I'll probably be gone all day."

"Boyo, what in the name of all that's holy can you find to do in that dinky little hole to consume an entire day?" Tom asked.

He explained. Tom and Punk listened, both fighting back grins.

"Sounds to me like an aggravated case of infatuation," Tom said to Punk.

"Sounds to me like you're sticking your nose into my business," said Loyal tightly.

"Oooooh," Punk said, and rubbed his hands briskly. "Go to it, boys."

Loyal shook his head and got to his feet. "I'll be back when I get back. Anybody need anything? Oh, you two don't mind my taking a day off, do you?"

"Of course not," said Tom. "Doesn't everybody work three days and take a day's vacation?"

Loyal rode off without looking back.

"Look at him, Punk. I don't think he'd ever seen a

horse, let alone a saddle, till he got out here. Now he rides like he was born in it. Let's go to work."

Loyal got to Martinez in less than half an hour. Ira Jack Fayles had not yet opened for the day, so he wandered about town for a while. Finally he spotted the storekeeper approaching his door. He crossed the street.

"Is this day four?" Fayles asked, his eyes twinkling.

"Don't you start ragging me. I should have kept my mouth shut to my brother, only I had to tell him why I wanted the day off. Congratulate me, I'm a full partner."

"In a hole in a hill."

"A working gold mine, Ira Jack. Mr. Van Sickle claims that by the end of the week we should get at least ten thousand out of there."

"Good. Get rich quick, go back to San Francisco, marry the girl, raise a family, open a general store. You coming in?"

"I'd just be in the way. I'll wait across the street in front of the saloon in the shade. It's going to be another scorcher."

He whiled away the morning sitting with his back against the front of the saloon in the shade of the overhang. Waiting with ever-increasing impatience, sneaking glance after glance up the road that led to West Pittsburg, and the ferry crossing to Collinsville. He pictured her and the captain boarding the ferry. How often did they run? Would they arrive in time to catch one? Or would they be too late and have to wait half a day for the next one? Had they crossed the night before? They must have. So they'd started out this morning from West Pittsburg. How far from there to here? Eight miles, ten, twelve? He should have asked Ira Jack.

Afternoon pushed the noon hour behind it. He passed up lunch, too excited to eat. Shortly before one, thunderclouds began assembling, coming across Suisun Bay to the north. If it started raining, they'd be caught in the middle of it; it could pour buckets and they'd have to stop and find shelter. And if it did rain, how long would it last? He cast another anxious look overhead. The clouds were thickening to form a solid blanket; from the look of it, it could rain through the rest of the day and all night.

"Please hold off."

Why such a worrywart all of a sudden? Black as it was overhead, there was a side to the situation so bright it dazzled. An incontrovertible fact: Catherine wanted to see him again as badly as he wanted to see her. The harsh words between them were a thing of the past; they'd been that when they met in front of the stable. He'd seen the concern in her eyes and knew it was for him. She cared; if enough, it could blossom into love. The old saw made sense: absence really did make the heart grow fonder. He knew what it had done to his heart.

He was dying to see her. It wouldn't be for long. An hour? Not that long. He could stay all night, but she had to get back. However long they had would be enough for now; it would hold him. Like a long, cool drink of water on a day like this, it would sustain him.

Again he looked up the road. There was no sign of a surrey. A farm wagon had come trundling into town carrying a heaping load of manure accompanied by legions of flies; a democrat wagon had come in; a man leading four unsaddled mustangs came through from the opposite direction. Four prospectors arrived, heading straight for the office four doors down from the general store. Above its entrance a weather worn sign proclaimed: "B. Myers—Certified Assayer."

At two o'clock he got up and went across the street and into the store. Fayles had five customers, a startlingly fat individual who looked like a circuit judge and two pair of ladies. He beckoned him up to the counter. "No luck?"

"Not yet."

"They could have stayed overnight in Sacramento. Would you like to wait in the back in the storeroom? It's cramped, but it's cooler than outside."

"No, thanks. I'm watching the road, I want to see them coming. I just came in for something to chase the dry out of my mouth."

Fayles grinned. "Is it the heat, or are you nervous?"

"Got any chewing gum?"

He bought a pack of White's Yucatan Gum and went back out chewing. The sky had become black as a coal hole, lightening to gray toward the edges. Not a sliver of blue could be seen. But the stormcloud was moving slowly southward. A few drops fell, pocking the dust in the street, but then it stopped. By the time he started on his third stick of gum, the storm had moved well out of town. Preoccupied with watching the sky, he failed to see the small dust cloud coming from the northeast. When he did notice it, it had drawn to within half a mile. His heart jumped and thundered; it was a surrey.

He watched it come to a stop in front of the store. He could see the captain; Catherine sat beside him in shadow. She got down and went into the store without turning to look. He spit out his gum, took a moment to spruce his clothes and run his fingers through his hair, and started across. As he went around the horse, the captain nodded greeting.

"Hello," Loyal said awkwardly. "How was the trip?"

"Not as rough as it was sad. We left her mother at a hospital there."

"Oh." He suddenly felt stupid.

Westerfield nodded toward the door. "She's waiting."

"Right."

He could feel tingling start in his cheeks. He reached the door and was about to enter when the captain called to him.

"Good luck, fellow." He smiled wryly. "I hope it's better than I've had."

Loyal waved and went in. She was standing at the counter talking to Fayles, her back to Loyal. He threaded his way through the merchandise and was almost up to her when she heard his step and turned. Her smile in greeting turned his heart upside down in his chest.

"Why don't you two go out back to the storeroom?" said Fayles. "Give yourselves a little privacy.'

Neither seemed to hear him, so engrossed were they in each other. But they did as he suggested. Loyal held the door for her.

"I can't stay long," she said. She suddenly seemed nervous. "My father's home alone. Robert and I took my mother up to Sacramento for treatment. She's . . ." She sighed lightly. "She has a problem with drinking. Daddy's worried sick about her, naturally. I have to get back and tell him everything's okay. It's going to be, I hope and pray. I was worried about you."

"I'm okay. I found Tom."

"Good, good, wonderful! That's a load off your mind."

He started to tell her about the mine, but stopped abruptly. It wasn't what he wanted to say, what he'd waited all these hours to tell her.

"I missed you so," he said abruptly. "The way you left that day when Betsy came along. So suddenly. There was so much I wanted to say. I love you." Loyal was shocked at his boldness. But he knew in his heart it was the truth.

"Loyal . . ." Catherine threw herself into his arms.

All his pent-up feelings for her growing in his heart now burst free. "Love you!" he burst. "Darling . . ."

He kissed her passionately. She trembled as she yielded, holding him as tightly as he held her. Finally, they pulled themselves apart.

"Oh, Loyal, I love you too."

"Catherine, Catherine . . ." Loyal touched her silky black hair.

"I've never felt like this about anyone. I can't get you out of my head. I've no control, I can't stop myself," she finished breathlessly.

"Today was a year. I thought you'd never get here, that you'd taken a different route, that you were staying, that I'd never see you again."

"This is crazy, you know. We're crazy. We scarcely know each other."

"It *is* crazy. I come all this way looking for Tom. And find you."

"Kiss me."

They kissed and separated slowly, reluctantly.

He held her hands and gazed into her eyes. "You're so beautiful."

"I must look a wreck. I haven't slept in days. Loyal, I have to go."

"We haven't even had five minutes."

"I know, but I must. When will you be coming back to the city?"

"As soon as I can." He brightened. "I'll leave tomorrow morning. I'll just tell them to count me out. I don't care about the gold, I don't care about anything, only us."

"Come straight to the house, promise? I'll make sure I'm home."

Loyal kissed her good-bye. She left, and he stood in the storeroom doorway watching her go. She turned and waved before she got into the surrey. Fayles finished with a customer and came over.

"I take it she was glad to see you."

"I'm in love, Ira Jack."

"I should hope so, the way you look. The way you're behaving, it's either love or tick fever. Same symptoms."

"Thanks for everything. I'm always thanking you

for something. If this keeps up I'll have to give you a share of my share. I'll see you."

Outside, he watched their dust rise and settle. The sky was blue again, the sun fierce, the air sweltering. To the south the stormcloud was no bigger than his thumbnail. What would Tom say when he told him he was leaving? That he was in love and was going to be married? He'd probably laugh till he choked. Let him. And as far as the mine was concerned, they didn't need him. And he didn't need the gold.

He'd already found his treasure.

"I love you, Catherine Bracy Devlin."

24

Tom Devlin took the assay report down from the nail over the entrance to the mine, folded it, and handed it to his partner.

"Keep it somewhere safe and dry. No point in advertising our good fortune, right? Wouldn't want to put temptation in somebody's way."

"I agree, Thomas." Punk cast a look at the growing pile of ore. "We've got to think about getting our ore to the nearest stamping mill. Closest one is down below in Concord. The biggest in the region. People claim it can produce as much pure in six hours as a whole flock of arrastras working 'round the clock can produce in a month. We need a good sturdy wagon. Like a coal wagon."

"Can we get one around here?"

"You can get almost anything if you pay for it," Punk said, "I've seen them in Martinez."

"How much?"

"The best ones don't come cheap. There's no coal around these parts, so anybody selling them knows what they're going to be used for. And that if you need one, you can afford to pay top dollar. We'll be lucky if they only triple the price on us."

"How much?" Tom repeated.

"Over a hundred." Punk spat, took off his derby, wiped the lining with his bandanna, and restored it to his head at a cocky angle. "Look at it this way: it'll carry a heckuva lot more than two mules can. Besides, you don't have to feed it, and it won't keep you awake nights braying. And a pair of mules'll run you a good twenty dollars more."

"I should go into Martinez right now."

"Okay. There's only one other thing. Talking about mules, we'll need at least two to pull the darn thing."

"So why not buy the mules and forget the wagon?"

"We'd be shortsighted to do that. I know, this is getting expensive."

"Between us we don't have anything close to a hundred bucks."

"We've got a million, Thomas. Our credit is excellent." He grinned. "Good as gold."

The sound of a horse could be heard.

"That'll be Loyal," Tom said happily. "Coming home from his tryst. I wonder if he's still single?"

"Now don't start teasing him, he's liable to get mad and knock your block off."

But it wasn't Loyal who came riding in. Tom's heart sank when he recognized who it was. His hand started for his gun as Hennessy pulled up.

"Don't do it, Sergeant," Hennessy said, holding up both his hands. He pointed toward the hill to their left, then another larger one to the right. "Boys!"

His men rose, leveling their rifles at Devlin.

Punk muttered and spat viciously.

"Come down and join us, men," sang Hennessy.

"You're trespassing, soldier boy," rasped Punk. "Turn around and get out of here, all of you."

Hennessy had fastened his eyes on Devlin and held them there.

"Tell the old coot to stay out of what's none of his business, Sergeant."

"Who you calling old coot?"

"Easy, Punk, I'll handle it," Devlin said, returning Hennessy's stare.

The corporal and private came hurrying, taking up positions on either side of the bloodhound. They held their weapons with the muzzles dipping slightly, fingers curled around the triggers.

"Take out your gun, thumb and forefinger, and drop it on the ground, Sergeant."

"Do like he says," snapped the corporal.

Devlin dropped his gun.

"Kick it away."

He did so.

"Good, excellent. Well, here we are at last; it's been a long two weeks; you've been a very clever fox. But of course, in your heart you knew it had to end up like this. You're not stupid. Not like the Callahans; we just let them run for awhile, we can collar them anytime." He took a step closer, then another, bringing himself to within ten feet of Devlin. "You're the prize."

"You're not taking me in, Hennessy."

With indescribable swiftness, his hand a blur, Hennessy drew and fired point-blank. Two shots in the heart.

"Great God Almighty," burst Punk. "You bastard! Murdering pig! You killed him in cold blood." He started toward Devlin, lying where he'd fallen.

"Stay where you are," ordered Hennessy. He blew the smoke from his gun and restored it to its holster. "Killed him in cold blood? I disagree. I did nothing of the kind. What say you, men?"

"Self-defense," said the corporal. His companion nodded.

"Liars! Bastards! Cold blood! Cold blood!"

The old man lunged at Hennessy. Again the lieutenant drew, two more shots slammed everybody's eardrums. Punk stopped, seized his stomach, and crumpled in a heap.

"Pick the sergeant up and sling him over his horse. Tie his wrists so he won't fall off. Let's get out of here."

"How come you shot the old man?" the private asked.

"What old man? I don't see any old man. I don't see any witnesses. Corporal, bring me Devlin's gun."

He fired it twice into the ground.

"He shot first, I retaliated," he explained.

"Self-defense," agreed the corporal.

"Just in case some nosey parker at the fort gets the bright idea to check his gun," Hennessy said. "Let's hope they do check it. Shove it back in his belt; with any luck we can make Oakland by dark."

They pulled out with their burden, leaving Punk lying in a glistening pool of his own blood.

Loyal did not push his horse on the way back to the Dorothy. He was preoccupied, his heart celebrating the discovery that Catherine felt as strongly about him as he about her. Reflection on the possible consequences of his promise to give up his share of the mine and return to San Francisco was slow to come, but come it did about halfway back. Tom wouldn't laugh this time when he told him; more likely he'd be furious. He and Punk could work the mine without a third hand. But in honesty he could not flatly say they didn't need him.

And what lay ahead? He could go back easily enough, only what, then? What, to begin with, would he do for money? He'd have to take the first job he found. He had less than thirty dollars left of the money he'd brought with him. He had to eat and put some kind of roof over his head; he couldn't sponge off Catherine. What a way to launch a relationship!

There was no shortage of jobs in town. Storekeepers, builders, even the police force were having as hard a time as the ships' captains hanging on to help. But he could make more in a week working with Tom and Punk than in a year in any sort of work back in the city. And Tom wouldn't hesitate to tell him so. He'd do everything he could to keep him from leaving.

"What should I do, horse? What do *you* think?"

There was one sour apple in the barrel Loyal could

see no way of avoiding. Given that he was practically a pauper, he could hardly ask Catherine to marry him. Any man who did such a thing had to be thinking only of himself, and was a fool to boot. What should he do? Shuttle back and forth between the mine and San Francisco? Maybe Tom could figure something out; at least he could be objective. If he wanted to be. Tom wouldn't want him to leave them, but knowing his brother, he'd only press his objections up to a certain point, then try to help. That was his way, and over the years it was one of the things that made Tom so exceptional.

God, but it was great to be back with Tom again! The gold aside, he hated to leave his brother—and after only a few days. Of course, he could come out and see him; Tom wouldn't dare show his face in town.

Well, they'd just have to talk it out. Between them they'd come up with some kind of solution. He wouldn't leave without Tom's blessing.

As he approached the mine, it took Loyal a full minute to register what he saw before him.

The old man lay in a pool of blood.

"My God! Punk! Punk! It's me! What happened?"

He ran to the old miner and knelt beside him. Punk stirred and groaned. "Funny . . . crazy . . . been poor . . . all my life . . . finally found the pot . . . a week . . . not even . . ."

"Where's Tom? Tell me!" Loyal grabbed him gently by the shoulders.

"And they do this . . . to me."

"Did they take him away? Tell me!"

Loyal cradled the man in his arms, blood seeping from his wound warming Loyal's forearm. Blood trickled from the corner of the old man's mouth, trailing down.

"I'm . . . going . . . going . . ."

"Tom! What happened to him?"

"Shot . . . killed in cold blood . . . took away bod . . ." Punk stiffened, then relaxed, slumping like a half-filled grain sack.

Loyal closed Punk's eyes and lay him down, fury building in his soul. That bastard Hennessy and his men must have found his brother and killed him in cold blood—and poor Punk, too. Loyal mounted his horse, checking his gun as he settled into the saddle. He knew which way they had to have gone: southwest toward Oakland to catch the ferry back to the city. The chase had ended; the hunter was bringing home his fox. Only he'd never get there; he'd never see San Francisco!

Loyal pushed the horse hard, vengeance kindling in his gut. He'd never felt such cold-blooded fury before. Hennessy would pay for his brother's life—in blood.

It wasn't long before Loyal caught sight of the four horses and three riders. His brother slung like a deer carcass over the saddle. The three had to have been moving at a good clip to get so far in such a short time, he decided, but now they were loping along. Drawing closer, Loyal saw that one was playing a banjo and singing. Hennessy and the other broke into loud laughter.

He came pounding up behind them. Hennessy heard, turned, and fired—but too hastily, carelessly, missing. Loyal aimed and fired back. The lieutenant shrilled like a girl, gaped, and dropped. His foot caught in his stirrup, and his horse dragged him bouncing along. The other two reacted in panic. The one with the banjo had dropped it; both went for their guns. Again Loyal fired, the bullet zipping between their heads.

"Don't pull, don't dare, I'll kill you two like I did him. Raise your hands. Do it!"

They raised their hands. The corporal had been leading Tom's horse; when the shooting started, he'd dropped the reins just as his buddy had dropped the banjo. The horse ambled to the side of the road, stopped, and began to graze.

"Don't shoot! Don't shoot, Chrissakes," burst the corporal. "We didn't do it. Hennessy shot him, he did, we didn't do nothin'. Swear to God Almighty!"

"We didn't," bellowed the other fearfully. "It was Hennessy. Shot him in cold blood. We just watched, we couldn't do nothin'!"

"Cold blood," asserted the other, nodding vigorously.

Loyal hesitated. Pulling the trigger, killing Hennessy had been so sudden, so unexpected. But immensely gratifying, venting as it did his boiling rage, his hatred and frustration. He was surprised at the powerful surge of twisted satisfaction he felt—the kind that comes with vengeance taken.

But now it struck him like a hammer that he had killed. Had willfully, deliberately taken a human life. A poor excuse for one, no doubt, but a life nevertheless. It shook him. Nausea flared in his stomach.

"Don't kill us," pleaded the private. "Don't!"

He eyed one, then the other. "Drop your guns."

He fired over their heads. They dropped their rifles, then their pistols.

"Now get out of here!"

Again he fired over their heads and they took off. By this time Hennessy's horse had stopped, its rider's ankle still caught in a stirrup. The horse stood rearing its head, tossing its mane and whinnying about thirty yards beyond Tom's horse. Loyal walked over to his brother. He untied his wrists and, easing him out of the saddle, laid him gently on the grass. Kneeling, he placed the flat of his hand against his heart, bringing it away crimson. He drew him up to a sitting position, holding him tightly in embrace.

He hugged him. And cried.

25

Loyal went through Hennessy's pockets before drap-ing his body over his horse. He found nearly forty dollars; he took it. When one man murders another, the least he can do is pay for his victim's funeral. And Tom would have a funeral. He'd be buried properly in hallowed ground with a priest officiating.

He led both horses with their burdens back to the mine. First, he buried Hennessy in a shallow grave. The shock that had struck when he realized he'd taken another's life had now passed, his hatred for Hennessy barring it from reentering his conscience.

He dug a second grave for Punk. Before interring him, he went through his pockets. He found seventeen dollars and change, a rusty pocket knife, an oval min-iature of a pleasant-looking woman, a pillbox contain-ing seven tiny white pills, and the assay report neatly folded in his back pocket. On the third finger of his right hand was a Masonic ring. He placed the minia-ture on a chain around Punk's neck and restored the knife and pills to his pockets, but took the money and the report.

After he buried Punk he started out for Martinez, deciding that Tom's final resting place might as well be there as San Francisco. He figured the farther from Fort Point Tom was buried, the better he'd like it. Ira Jack Fayles introduced Loyal to the local undertaker, a young man with the requisite somber air of his calling, along with a taste for black attire.

Martinez had no Catholic priest; the only clergyman in town turned out to be a Baptist minister. Tom wouldn't mind a non-Catholic clergyman. He wasn't exactly a devoted churchgoer and would doubtless have agreed that whoever received his soul at the other end wouldn't be all that particular as to the denomination of the one who'd formally dispatched it.

Tom Devlin was buried early the next morning in a corner of the shabby little cemetery. So the sergeant's remains became one with the earth, leaving his younger brother the sole survivor of the clan; leaving behind as well a gold mine with a million-dollar potential.

It was only after the funeral that Loyal thought about the mine at all. Someone would probably come along, see the two graves, come to the logical conclusion, and take over. Common sense insisted that Loyal should go and get his name on record as the rightful heir and owner. But he couldn't be bothered. When he told Catherine, she'd probably think he was crazy. Maybe he was. Only his few days' experience as a miner had confirmed one thing: it wasn't for him. He wanted to get back to San Francisco to see Catherine. Besides, before any of this had happened, he had decided to quit. Hadn't he been on his way back to tell Tom just that?

As he headed out of town, he became aware that somebody was following him. It was Ira Jack Fayles.

"You forgot something, Loyal, your mine. It's yours now. Are you just going to ride off and leave it?"

"I can't work it, Ira Jack, and I don't want to. I don't have the heart to, not now."

"It's still yours. It's a bonanza, isn't it?"

"I guess."

"You guess? Look, why don't I buttonhole Joe Schaeffer at the records office, tell him what happened, get your name down as the rightful owner, and go out there myself and clean up."

"Clean up?"

"Don't be dense: take down the signs, seal the entrance. It'd only take a couple of handfuls of black powder to do it. I've got black powder in stock. Think it over, son. What the world at large doesn't know can't deprive you of what's rightfully yours. Someday you may decide to come back and take another crack at it. It'll be there waiting intact. What do you say?"

"I hate to put you to all that trouble."

"It'll be fun. I love to blow things up. And I'm the one who'll have to do it; that's the only way we can keep it our secret, right?"

Loyal pressed money on him in payment for the black powder. Fayles accepted it, but nothing in addition for his labor. Loyal thanked him again and continued on his way.

It was still light out when Catherine and Captain Westerfield drew up in front of the house. Her knock went unanswered. She got out her key, then changed her mind.

"He must be still in his office," she said. "Let's go on up."

The Sally Port door guards admitted them. Inside, they headed for the office, running a gauntlet of curious stares. The colonel's striker answered Westerfield's knock.

"Who is it, Howard?" Major Downing called from inside.

The provost marshal was with him. Both men's faces sagged perceptibly as they recognized her.

"Where's my father?" she asked Downing. "What are you doing at his desk?"

"I'm in temporary command, miss."

"Is he away?"

"No, miss, he's . . . in the infirmary."

"He's sick? What happened?"

"He's not sick," Downing went on haltingly, casting a sidelong glance at Viselli, asking his help.

"He's been shot," said Viselli. "One of the Vigilantes—"

"My God!"

Before he could add explanation, she ran from the room.

Westerfield called after her. Then turned back to Viselli. "What happened?" Both started to tell him. "Never mind, later . . ."

Catherine, meanwhile, had arrived at the infirmary to find the hospital steward sitting playing solitaire at Captain Wilcox's desk. The colonel lay dozing on a cot in the corner, a sheet drawn up to his chin. A damp cloth had been laid across his forehead. He was sweating and looked alarmingly pale and drawn.

Catherine gasped. Only four of the twenty-two beds in the patient room adjoining were occupied. The doctor was nowhere about. The steward jumped up when she came running in; she brushed past him to the cot.

"My God! Where's Doctor Wilcox? Don't just stand there, tell me!"

"He's . . ."

Wilcox came bustling in, Westerfield right behind him.

"Catherine, sit down, please. Calm yourself."

"He's badly hurt, isn't he? Isn't he? He's going to die."

"Please sit down. George, leave us alone."

The steward went out, Wilcox told her what had happened.

She half-listened, getting up, moving back to her father's side. She felt his forehead with the back of her hand. "He's burning up! Can't you do something?"

"I've done everything I can."

"He's dying."

"He's hanging on."

"Hanging . . ."

"Will he make it?" Westerfield asked.

Wilcox shrugged, turning away from the patient. "He's trying his damnedest to. I got the bullet out, but he lost a lot of blood. But, Catherine, he isn't always like you see him now, honestly. There've been three or four times when he's been awake and able to speak. And when he does, he's perfectly coherent. And this morning he was able to take nourishment."

"He should be home in his bed," she said.

The mere suggestion seemed to horrify Wilcox. "No, no we mustn't move him. Not two feet. He's starting to knit. True, his temperature's up and refuses to come down. I've tried everything I know to bring it down, but it doesn't stay." He showed his hands helplessly. "He's very strong, though, much stronger than he looks."

"How do you know that?" she said, then softened her tone. "You can't do a thing for him, isn't that what it comes down to? He could be dead in an hour, in five minutes."

"Cathy, please," interposed Westerfield. "This isn't doing either of you any good."

"Brannan did this," she exclaimed, turning toward Westerfield. "You heard. Maybe he didn't actually fire the shot, but he's the cause, the rabblerousing bastard. Bastard!"

The colonel groaned lightly and stirred.

"Ssssh," cautioned Westerfield. "Let me take you home. You're worn out, you can nap—"

"Nap? Are you serious?"

"I'll fix us something to eat. You can come back at taps."

"I rather stay. Brannan! God how I hate that man!"

"Please come back to the house," persisted Westerfield.

She finally gave in. She kissed her father, thanked

Wilcox for all he'd done for him, and went out. They walked silently into the house. It was so empty it felt like a tomb to her. The first thing Catherine noticed was the writing materials on the desk, and a letter her father had started to her mother.

She picked it up, started to read it. Tears dimmed sight of the words. She put it down. Westerfield laid a tentative comforting hand on her shoulder.

"She's expecting to hear from him," she said. "He promised to write every day. When she doesn't hear, she'll know something's terribly wrong."

"You can write her."

"It's not the same."

"I mean, imitate his handwriting. That way she'd never suspect."

"I guess I'll have to. She can't not hear from him; it would be like he deserted her. In her condition . . . Oh, Robert, I am tired. I feel like I'm going to collapse."

"Go upstairs and lie down."

Loyal arrived back in San Francisco late in the afternoon. He rode through the city without stopping, coming within sight of the Bracy's house. No one answered when he knocked, and the door was locked. He debated whether or not to go back to town, but despaired of finding Catherine. He went on up to the fort and asked to see the colonel.

"Colonel Bracy's in the infirmary," said one of the guards. "He can't see nobody."

"He's dyin'," said the other.

"You don't know that for sure, Amos Redding. Nobody knows, not even the sawbones."

"I know what Major Downing said."

"What does he know? He don't know beans."

Catherine must be with her father, Loyal concluded.

"Can I have a word with What's-his-name, Westerfield

then? Tell him it's Loyal Devlin. We know each other, sort of."

One of the guards went to get the captain. Loyal waited, pacing back and forth, speculating on what had happened to the colonel. He hesitated to ask, preferring to save the question for Westerfield. He finally appeared.

"Catherine's with her father now," he said.

"How's he doing?"

"Frankly, I have no idea, apart from that he's still in danger. Cathy's beside herself."

He seemed to imply that Devlin had shown up at the wrong time. Obviously, he wanted Loyal to leave them in peace for now. But Loyal couldn't wait. She needed him, and now. Perhaps he could lift her spirits. He had no idea how, but he'd try anything.

"Can't this wait?" Westerfield asked pointedly.

"No, she expects me."

"I don't doubt she did, but she didn't expect to come home to this."

"Captain, can't we let her decide?"

Westerfield smiled thinly. "Since you put it that way . . ."

Catherine was sitting beside her father. He was awake. Loyal averted his eyes at sight of him. He looked as if he didn't have two drops of blood left in him. His lips moved, but nothing came out, and he was sweating furiously. Her back to the door, Catherine had no idea he'd come in until the doctor approached him.

"I'm sorry, you can't come in here, fellow."

She turned. "Loyal!"

His arms were around her, hugging her tightly. She was suddenly on the verge of tears.

"He's very very bad, very weak," she whispered. "He just can't seem to bounce back. He has no strength left."

Loyal looked at Wilcox. The doctor looked away.

His awareness of his helplessness couldn't have been more evident if it were printed on a sign on his chest. She eased out of Loyal's embrace and turned back to her father. He had fallen asleep again.

"Young lady," said Wilcox, "I want you to go home now and get some sleep before you pass out. You're heading for a nervous breakdown. That's what you're courting, I promise you. There's absolutely nothing you can do for him."

Her expression said he was getting nowhere.

"When will you try to feed him again?"

"When he wakes up. Catherine, the more he sleeps, the better for him." He looked to Loyal. "Be a good fellow and take her home. Right now."

"Darling?" he whispered.

She sighed and nodded. She went back to her father and kissed him and left with Loyal. They started across the courtyard.

Soldiers milled about in twos and threes. A knot of junior officers were heatedly discussing something close by the shot furnaces, as they passed by.

Suddenly, one of the soldiers shouted, "It's him!"

The corporal and private stood pointing at Devlin, stopping all conversation and bringing Major Downing and Captain Westerfield hurrying over.

"That's the guy that murdered the lieutenant, Major," burst the corporal. "It's him, I swear to God."

"No mistake," snapped the private.

They flanked the two officers and continued to jabber accusations. The corporal scowled viciously.

"Don't you say you didn't, you murderin' scum!"

"What's going on?" Catherine asked. "Who are these men, Robert?"

"Did you shoot the lieutenant?" Westerfield asked Devlin.

"In self-defense. He shot my brother in cold blood and tried to kill me."

"Damn lie," interrupted the private, then caught

himself and looked at Catherine sheepishly. "Sorry, ma'am, but it's the God's truth: the lieutenant never shot the sergeant. Did he, Billy?"

"No, sir, Major."

"Liars," rasped Devlin. He started for them. Westerfield blocked his way. Devlin glared past him at his accusers and went on. "Hennessy shot Tom's partner after he killed Tom. Because Punk had seen him do it. Hennessy and these two tramps were in too much of a hurry to leave. They didn't check on the old man; he was still alive when I got back. He died, but not before he told me what Hennessy did. Shot one, then the other. Unprovoked, without any warning."

"It wasn't like that at all," bawled the corporal. "The sergeant panicked. He shot first, wounded the lieutenant, too. Hennessy had to shoot back in self-defense. He killed the sergeant, sure, only it was self-defense. Then, when we was bringing the corpse in, this one here caught up with us guns blazing, killed the lieutenant quick as you can spit. Woulda killed us too, only we got out of there. Isn't that so, Billy? Isn't that the way it was, honest to God?"

"That's it," said the corporal, glaring defiantly at Loyal.

"You jackasses . . ."

"Take it easy, Mr. Devlin," said Downing. "I'm afraid we're going to have to hold you for the police."

"Wait a minute," said Catherine. "It's his word against theirs."

"I realize that, Miss Bracy. I'm not accusing you, Devlin. I'm not making any judgment."

"We're tellin' the bald truth, sir," exclaimed the private.

Downing bristled. "Shut up, you two." He looked back at Devlin. "The thing of it is you're a civilian, whatever happened happened off the base, that makes this a police matter."

"He just told you what happened," snapped Catherine. "Weren't you listening?"

"He's lyin', he's lyin'," shrilled the corporal.

"Chief Sanger'll sort it out, Cathy," Westerfield said.

"No!"

"It's all right, darling," said Loyal wearily. He set his hand on her arm. "There's nothing to worry about, I can prove everything I say."

"Captain," said Downing, "take the pris—take him into town. Explain the whole thing to Chief Sanger. He'll ask you for a statement, Mr. Devlin. Corporal, Private, I want written separate statements from both of you, no comparing notes. You, Corporal, go into my office. Private, you go back to your quarters. Captain Westerfield . . ."

"Sir?"

"Come straight back. Get a good night's sleep. Immediately after roll call tomorrow you're going out after the Callahans with these two."

"Yippee," burst the corporal.

"Major . . ." began the captain.

Downing gestured appeal for no argument. "Please, somebody's got to take over for James Hennessy. If we don't at least take a stab at it, it'll only encourage others to desert."

"Yes, sir."

"We'll find them Callahans for you, sir," said the private. "For sure, just like we found the sergeant."

"Didn't I just give you two an order?" Downing jammed his fists into his hips and steel-eyed them.

"Yes, sir. Yes, sir."

They saluted and sped away in opposite directions.

Catherine approached Westerfield and Devlin. "I'll come with you into town," she said.

Westerfield looked to Downing for help; he got it from Devlin.

"Stay with your father, Catherine, I'll be okay."

"Can we have a minute, Robert?"

Westerfield started toward the passageway leading to the Sally Port door.

Once they were alone, Catherine threw her arms around Loyal.

"This is insane," she cried. "Why are they accusing you? What can they possibly gain?"

"They're out for vengeance. When I caught up with them, they ran like rabbits. They had me four guns to one. Yet they ran. I intimidated them, embarrassed them . . ."

"You shouldn't have come back."

"Catherine, they know what happened. They're lying to protect themselves." He half-laughed without smiling. "They showed up back here without their weapons. I wonder if anybody asked them why? I wonder if they've trumped up a story to explain that?" He held her and kissed her, feeling Westerfield's eyes jabbing his back. "Oh, I left my horse tied to your gatepost. Would you?"

"Of course." She kissed him.

He waved listlessly, smiled, and went to join Westerfield.

— ●◄ *26* ►● —

The Brannans sat at dinner. Mercy was preoccupied and poking at her salad. Betsy was attacking a small mountain of beef and vegetables; the reverend was on his feet, and slicing the roast with the dexterity of a gifted surgeon.

"We've already gathered over two thousand signatures," he said proudly, pausing to assess the effect of his words on his listeners. "Our goal is ten thousand."

"It doesn't make a lick of sense to me, Sam Brannan," Mercy rasped. "Why on earth replace John Sanger? Or Mayor Brenham, for that matter? Who can you possibly get who'll do a better job than Sanger?"

"Nobody's questioning his capabilities, my dear—only his allegiance. You really do miss the point. You're suggesting there's something vindictive behind our effort. Nothing of the sort. It's merely that Sanger and his honor stubbornly persist in taking an altogether different view of our problem than the people."

"Than you do, you mean. Betsy, dear, stop smacking."

"Than I, the members of the Committee of Vigilance, and the public in general. Our two thousand signatures aren't just Vigilantes, my dear. Most are people in the street. Those who've suffered the most at the hands of the Sydney Ducks. Make no mistake,

261

they're behind us. You'll see when we get five, ten thousand signatures on the recall petition."

"I wouldn't crow too soon."

"I'm not crowing. For the first time in years I'm feeling an overwhelming sense of relief. The light at the end of the tunnel is expanding. Before long it will blaze forth gloriously. 'Then shall the righteous shine forth as the sun in the kingdom of their father. Who hath ears to hear, let him hear.' Matthew, thirteen, forty-three. Yes, indeed, the hour of decision draws near. The city will be saved. And like Jerusalem of old when Philip spoke, there will be great joy. Great joy!"

"You're cutting much too much meat. It dries out when it's sliced." Patently unswayed by his argument, Mercy shook her head. "You never cease to surprise me. I'd think you'd show at least a little concern about poor Ewing Bracy."

"Really, my dear, you make it sound as if I shot him."

"Who isn't important. He's lying near death while you're out collecting signatures. You should face up to it: you and your Vigilantes are responsible."

"We mostly certainly are not. One careless, thoughtless individual got carried away."

"Who shot him? You do know."

"I'm not at liberty to divulge his name."

"Somehow I didn't think you would be."

"It doesn't matter! It was an accident. Ewing knows that. Betsy did I mention that I saw a friend of yours early this evening when I was coming back from Fort Gunnybags? I was driving by police headquarters and I saw an army officer bringing him into the station. He definitely looked like he was bringing him in. It wasn't as if they were going in as equals, so to speak."

"Bringing in who?" Mercy asked.

"Loyal Devlin."

Betsy started. "Loyal's back?"

Mercy frowned. "Are you sure?"

"As sure as I'm sitting here."

"In jail," wailed Betsy. "Whatever for?" She threw down her napkin and scraped her chair getting up.

"Where do you think you're going?" her mother asked.

"Into town, of course. I have to see him, poor dear. How dare they lock him up like a common criminal? It's all a horrible mistake, it must be!"

"Now, now, I can't say positively that he's been locked up," said her father airily. "But that was definitely my impression."

"Betsy, sit down and finish your dinner."

"I can't, Loyal needs me."

She left. Tying on a scarf, she climbed into the buggy, snapped the whip over the bay, and sent it sprinting off.

Catherine sat in the cell with Devlin, reading his statement.

"It's exactly what I told you," he said, "you, the major, and your friend Westerfield. That's what happened, so help me. The question is, how do I prove it?"

"Maybe Robert can prove it for you."

"Why would he bother? I can't imagine he harbors any deep-seated affection for me. After what I did to him?"

"If anybody did anything, it was me. You don't know him, darling. He's not a child. He won't hold a grudge, he's honorable and decent. I spoke to him when he came back to the fort. He's leaving with them in the morning, maybe he can get the truth out of them."

"Why would either deliberately incriminate himself?"

"We'll see."

Loyal got up from the cot and began pacing the narrow confines of the cell. In the cell next door a drunk was loudly sleeping it off. Two other prisoners were playing checkers, occasionally arguing over the game. They were going at it like their lives depended on it. Devlin walked four steps toward the door, four back to the rear wall.

"What's really ridiculous is the way they keep tangling up their version," he said. "First they say Hennessy didn't shoot Tom, then they admit he did, only it was in self-defense. Then they claim I shot first when Hennessy and I confronted each other, another stinking lie. I'd love to see their sworn statements. I bet they're loaded with contradictions. And I bet they can't explain why they showed up back here without their weapons. They'll have to cook up some cock-and-bull fairy tale for that."

"You see, it'll all work out. Sit down, darling, relax."

"Darling? Darling?" Betsy Brannan stood staring at them.

"How dare you call him that, Catherine Bracy. Hussy!"

Devlin gaped in disbelief. "Betsy, what the hell are you doing here?"

"Eavesdropping, evidently," said Catherine, amused.

"Loyal, Loyal darling, why didn't you send word you'd come back? I've been counting the hours, wondering if you were all right, where you were, what you were up to."

"Betsy . . ."

"And after all my fretting, what do I find? You and this . . . this wicked, wicked thing. That's what you are, Catherine Bracy, wicked. Shame on you, trying to steal another gal's beau. We're engaged."

"We are not," exclaimed Devlin. "Nothing of the kind. There's nothing between us, Catherine, believe me."

"I believe you."

"Don't pay any attention to him, he doesn't know

what he's saying." Betsy eyed Catherine brazenly. "Did he tell you he had his way with me? Did you tell her, dear heart? And not just once, every night. He had his way, tell her. I let him because we're in love. It's not wrong if you're going to be married. Tell her, darling, tell her you took my body. You ravaged me."

"I . . ."

"Admit it, don't be afraid of her. There's nothing wrong with it, we *are* engaged."

"Get out of here," Loyal burst. "Guard, get this woman out of here."

The policeman who had locked him up came running in. "What's all the racket?"

"Get her out of here."

"She told me she come to visit you." The guard scowled at Betsy. "I told you he already had somebody in with him, that you was to wait."

"Get *her* out of here," shrilled Betsy.

They all began talking at once. The officer looked utterly confused. He finally acceded to Devlin's request and dragged Betsy out screaming and cursing. Catherine looked questioningly at Devlin.

"Did I sleep with her?" he said. "Yes. Only it's not what you think, it wasn't like that at all."

He told her what had happened. She listened without saying anything, but he could tell from her silence and her downcast eyes that she was hurt.

"There's no need to explain," she said quietly. "It's none of my business."

"I love you. It all happened before. I didn't want it to. It was the last thing I wanted."

"It does take two."

"Please listen. After I made such an idiot of myself at the house, I couldn't get you out of my mind. I tried, did I ever, but I couldn't. Then I got shanghaied at the Down Under and wound up at her house—only because her mother had taken care of me the night of the fire. I wanted desperately to see you again before I left to go looking for Tom. When we bumped into each other in front of the stables it was great, wonderful. Until Betsy came along. And you left. I have only myself to blame. I never wanted to hurt you, darling. Can you believe me?"

After a moment Catherine smiled. To Loyal, it was as if the stormcloud had passed, and the weight dragging his heart down vanished as suddenly as it had come.

"Am I invited to the wedding?"

"Not funny," he snapped.

He held her and kissed her. There was no reticence in her response, no holding back. She smoothed back his hair.

"I'll come by in the morning."

"I love you."

"I love you, Loyal Devlin."

"She'll be waiting outside for you. She carries on like a fishwife when she's crossed."

"I can handle her."

They kissed good night. She called the officer to let her out. As expected Betsy was waiting across the street. She came running over, fire in her eyes.

"Catherine Bracy!"

"Don't start, Betsy, just don't. You do, and I'll tell your preacher daddy just what a naughty girl you've been."

Betsy recoiled at the threat, her bravado rushing out of her like air out of a balloon.

Catherine walked away.

Mercy Brannan came to visit Devlin very early the next morning. She kissed him on the cheek in greeting and presented him with a fruit cake.

"Baked it myself. I hope you like it spicy. Now, what's this all about?"

When he finished telling her, to his surprise she laughed, but quickly sobered.

"I shouldn't, I'm sorry. It's a pity about your brother. But you sure do have a knack for getting into trouble." She lay a comforting hand on his. "It doesn't sound like the end of the world; you'll probably be out by the middle of the day. But, just in case they don't happen to unlock the door, perhaps you'd better think about a lawyer."

"I don't know any lawyer. I couldn't afford him if I did."

"I know an excellent one. Rupert Haddix, an old and very dear friend. Why don't I talk to him? Now, then, what on earth happened last night between you and my daughter? She came home crying her eyes out."

"I'm sorry about that, Mercy. She's gotten it into her head that she and I are going to be married, and nothing I can say is able to get it out. I swear I didn't lead her on."

"She doesn't need leading on. She's very good, exceptional at doing that herself, I'm afraid. I'm her mother, Loyal, and I love her dearly, but she can be a handful. When she comes to town the male population should duck and run for cover. I don't want to know what went on between you two. What I don't know won't hurt. But don't let her get to you. Matter of fact, I'm surprised she's still interested. Amazed, actually."

"What do you mean?"

"She seems to have become very interested in the Bowrigs' son of late. In fact, they've been practically inseparable."

"What happened to Gregory Miller?"

"Poor Gregory's in the throes of recovering from a broken heart. Another casualty in the battle for Betsy Brannan's affections. At the moment, Nathan Bowrig is the apple of her eye. Well, I should be going." She leaned close. "You be careful eating that cake, there's a hacksaw blade in it." She laughed and slapped his knee.

Captain Westerfield did not look forward to his assignment. Running down deserters called for a certain set of attitudes and convictions. For one, a strong belief that apprehending one—in this instance, two—provided a deterrent to others battling the same temptation. James Hennessy had had a flair for the job, probably because he enjoyed it so much. The corporal and the private obviously shared his enthusiasm. But it certainly wasn't his idea of fun.

The sun was not yet up as they rode out of the fort, heading toward the city to cross it to the Oakland ferry landing.

"You boys did an excellent job catching up with and collaring Sergeant Devlin. You're to be congratulated," he said.

"Thank you, sir," said the private. "We appreciate it, don't we, Billy?"

"Sure is good somebody appreciates us," said the corporal in a hurt tone. "Chrissakes, we go out and chew dust all day, with not so much as a decent cup o' coffee, and the thanks we get is a sneer from Downing. Boy, did taking over for the colonel ever go to his head!"

"Didn't it, though?" said Westerfield. "Nobody seems to realize how dangerous your job is. I mean, if the lieutenant didn't shoot first, the sergeant would have cut him down like a corn shuck. The same goes for when his brother caught up with you on the road. He came gunning, what's a man supposed to do, try to pacify him? Shoot first and ask questions later, that's my motto. You can be sure that's the way we're going to handle the Callahans."

"It's the only way, sir," said the corporal. "Them are desperate men out there, and Devlin was the worst. He would have popped us all if the lieutenant didn't get the drop on him. You should have seen the sergeant's face."

"You never seen a more surprised look in your life," the private went on. "Man looked like a mule kicked him from behind, right, Billy?"

"I'll bet," Westerfield said. "So what you're saying is in both cases it was shoot first or maybe don't shoot at all."

"Shoot first or don't shoot at all," repeated the corporal, laughing. "That's a right great way to put it. That's exactly it!"

"Keep it in mind when we catch up with the Callahans, boys."

They rode on in silence, crossing Sacramento Street in the direction of the ferry landing. Once arrived at the landing, they would have to wait at least half an hour for the next crossing, so Westerfield was in no grand rush to get them there.

"One thing about the scrape I don't understand," he said, assuming an innocent tone. "What happened to your weapons? You came back without them."

"Lost them," said the private.

"How?"

"Went over the side on the ferry coming home," said the corporal. "The captain asked us to take them off while we was crossing; sight of them made the ladies skittish. You know shemales. We set them on a chest at the back of the boat, laid a piece of canvas over them, but it was too close to the edge. When the ferry come in and bumped the landing, they slid off into the water. We already told Major Downing."

"So now they're at the bottom of the bay just beyond the landing."

The private nodded. "That's where they are."

"If anybody dived in and looked for them, that's where they'd find them, right?"

"Stickin' in the mud," said the corporal. "It's only ten or fifteen feet deep."

They crossed Kearny Street and Montgomery beyond it. Moments later they were approaching the dogleg that led to the ferry landing.

"Either of you boys know how to swim?" Westerfield asked.

"Are you serious?" The private scoffed. "I can swim like a damn fish. Billy here could swim clear 'cross to Oakland one arm tied behind him, isn't that so, Billy?"

"I expect if I had to," responded the corporal proudly.

"I can't swim worth a nickel," said Westerfield. "Look ahead there, you can see the turn leading to the landing. No sign of the ferry." He jerked the reins, picking up the pace. "Let's go."

"What's the rush, sir?" the corporal asked.

"You'll see, pick it up, move . . ."

That morning Colonel Bracy woke up feeling famished. A most positive sign, according to Dr. Wilcox. His patient hungrily downed beef broth fed to him by Catherine. He looked greatly, almost miraculously improved over the previous day. His color had come back, although in a paler version at the moment. He was regaining command of himself, and his eyes reclaimed their sparkle. All but his voice, a barely audible whisper, signaled a sharp turn for the better. Dr. Wilcox, nevertheless, counseled caution.

"Don't start kicking up your heels. You may feel chipper right now, but you've a way to go before you can even sit up."

"Don't be so optimistic, Byron," Bracy whispered. "My, but that tastes good." He signaled Catherine to hold up feeding him. "Dear, have you heard anything from your mother?"

"Not yet. It's too soon. Letters back and forth to Sacramento take at least a week."

"I'm dying to know how she's doing."

"Don't use that word," interrupted Wilcox.

"Just fine," said Catherine. "Don't start worrying about her."

"You mean you don't?"

"When you're back on your feet I'll run over for a visit, and bring you back a full report."

Wilcox cleared his throat, making it sound reprimanding.

"I wouldn't do that, Catherine. They probably wouldn't even let you in the door. Just seeing you could be harmful. By now they've already started her down a new road. Your showing up would only pull her back to all the uncomfortable realities she has to leave behind. You two are the ones she hurt—at least that's what she thinks. Give Slocum a chance to root it out. Give both of them time."

"He's right, dear," said the colonel. "We'll just have to wait for a letter. Byron, what's happening on the other side of the courtyard? How's Major Downing doing?"

"How would I know? I don't have anything to do with the army. I gather he likes your office. He hardly ever leaves it. I think he sleeps there."

"Go get him."

"Not a chance. Get him in here and you'll bend his ear talking shop."

Wilcox assumed a deeply disturbed expression—strictly for her father's benefit, Catherine was sure.

"You think nobody can run this place but you? What's so complex, so hard about it? The rawest recruit can sign his name forty times a day, bark orders, and walk down a line of men poking under their packs with the tip of his sword."

Bracy grinned. "He thinks he can get away with that

kind of talk just because we served together in Mexico. Pretty presumptuous, wouldn't you say?"

Wilcox sniffed. "Tell him to bear with me, Catherine. I don't often get a superior under my thumb. It's fun. Finish your broth, Colonel, sir."

"Can I take him home?" blurted Catherine.

Wilcox leered at the colonel. "When I say so, sir."

The corporal and the private stood in the colonel's office at rigid attention. Both were only partially dressed, looking a lot like drowned ship rats, despite returning from the ferry landing under a blazing sun. Captain Westerfield, perfectly dry, slumped in a chair glowering at them. Major Downing sat opposite them, and his expression was, if anything, even less sympathetic.

"Diving for something that isn't there makes about as much sense as blowing a safe you know is empty," growled the major. "It's clear you two have lied from start to finish. About the lieutenant's actions, your own, and about accidentally losing your weapons off the end of the ferry. Lied to make yourself look good, as if you'd conducted yourselves according to the book." He stood up. "Only, your conduct turns out to be as reprehensible as Hennessy's."

"Repre—" began the corporal mystified.

"Shut up! You're a disgrace to your uniforms. Your lying has put an innocent man behind bars. Captain . . ." Westerfield got to his feet. "Get up a note, Howard'll give you a piece of the colonel's official stationery. Request Devlin's immediate release. All charges dropped, army's wholly at fault, you know what to say. I'll sign it. Take it into town and bring him back here so I can apologize for these two clowns."

"Sir, if I may make a suggestion. Miss Bracy and Devlin are friends. I know she'd be delighted to be the one to tell him the good news. She and Chief Sanger know each other. She's over at the infirmary visiting her father."

"Okay, sure, fine. Give her the note. Howard! How—There you are. Give Captain Westerfield a couple sheets of the colonel's writing paper and an envelope, then buckle on your gun belt and escort these two over to the cells. They're to be locked up. Major Viselli has the keys."

"Yes, sir."

"Robert, don't go yet. We still have unfinished business. Get yourself a couple volunteers and go back out and see if you can find the Callahans."

Westerfield's reaction approximated that of a whipped hound. "Yes, sir."

Over a dozen boats moved along the Sacramento River, passing by the bustling capital of the not-yet two-year-old state of California. The City Hotel and the Eagle Theater dominated the block to the left. A three-story brick building with a blue shake roof stood on the corner, shaded by a towering oak. Between the brick building and the warehouse opposite it stretched a broad, unpaved thoroughfare. Beyond that small frame houses were scattered. Two thirds of the city's buildings occupied the area stretching to the right, standing in no definable pattern. Fronting the river were the Eldorado Exchange, Bailey's Groceries & Provisions Store, the Fremont House, General Jackson's Hotel, a drugstore, and J.B. Starr & Company, manufacturers of mining equipment. Dr. Donald Slocum's asylum was located behind the rooming house that stood next to J.B. Starr.

In a lovely, neat, if somewhat small room on the second floor, Doreen Bracy sat looking out the window. A rose garden sprawled below, and at the moment two large black-and-white magpies swept their long tails and chakked raucously. They stopped arguing abruptly and flew off, and were replaced by a robin that immediately raised its voice in song.

On the windowsill stood an empty glass. The bedroom smelled of lavender, the bed pillow suffused with the scent. Her clothes hung in the armoire, and peering out from under the bed were the pink puff and embroidered slippers Catherine had given her for Mother's Day three months earlier.

Doreen was beginning her sixth day under Dr. Slocum's care. The day before she had felt well enough to write letters to her husband and daughter. She lauded the hospital, the care extended her, and expressed the hope that she would be returning to them before the month was out. There were less than two weeks left in August and she had nothing concrete to base her optimism on, but the very fact that she could be optimistic impressed her as encouraging. But Dr. Slocum's cure—how effective it was for others, what it required of her—remained a mystery.

While she sat listening to her red-breasted visitor's pretty whistling, down the hall two men sat in a tiny office almost entirely walled in by bookcases. One man, in his fifties, was alarmingly overweight, his face as round and red as a ripe apple, his hands like bunches of breakfast sausages. Opposite him at the small rolltop desk, sat the founder and director of the facility, Dr. Donald Slocum. Physically, he resembled his older, cadaverous-looking brother in San Francisco not at all. Donald Slocum was tall, vigorous, athletic-looking. An athlete he was: weight lifter, distance runner, and superb swimmer. His condition and trim appearance contrasted sharply with those of his associate. Neither man, however, was giving any thought to how the other looked at the moment. Dr. Lionel Bystrom, former staff member at three New York City hospitals, held Mrs. Bracy's chart.

The office reeked of cigar smoke; a cloud of it nudged the ceiling. Dr. Slocum had just finished a Clandin's Imperator. He relit a second from the butt of the first and offered one to Dr. Bystrom. As they puffed away, they discussed the patient. Dr. Bystrom was sanguine about her chances for complete recovery. She was Slocum's patient, but he had talked with her at length on two occasions and was impressed with her attitude. His greatest concern was shared by Slocum.

"It's her heart that complicates things," said Bystrom. "And she knows it."

Outside, on the Sacramento river, a boat whistle shrilled; another, downstream, responded with an even higher note.

"Did she drink her whiskey this morning?" asked Bystrom.

Slocum nodded. "It's down to half and half."

"Did she say anything? Did she notice that you're watering it?"

"I'm sure she knows. She probably thinks it pointless to say so, since I'm doing the watering."

"I don't buy tapering off. She wasn't drinking every day before she was admitted. Now she is, and probably looking forward to her morning cup."

"It's not that much, Lionel."

"Any amount is too much."

They were silent, content for a time to puff and eye the smoke climbing to join the ceiling cloud. Slocum coughed, eyed his cigar accusingly, and resumed puffing on it.

"What you say about her heart is quite true," he said. "Of course. And in a way you're contradicting yourself. Her heart condition makes tapering off obligatory. Sudden deprivation could produce a dangerous exhaustion. You've seen it happen."

"How bad is her heart?"

Slocum indicated the chart in the folder in Bystrom's lap. "The results of her physical are in there."

"Not the usual nuts and bolts. I'm asking what you really think?"

"Not good. Erratic. Speeds up, pounds, slows, you can barely hear it. And without cause, apart from the pressure she generates inside. She was particularly nervous during her physical. Of course everybody is."

They discussed the heart's association with the stomach, the fact that it sympathizes strongly with the stomach. When alcohol reaches the stomach, it can throw the heart into a state of unnatural excitement. The long-range results of heavy drinking can cause enlargement of the heart, ossification of the valves, and other organic afflictions.

"What it comes down to," said Slocum. He shook his head.

Bystrom nodded. "We're walking on eggs."

"Not that bad, but we do have to be careful."

"What about adding tartar emetic to her daily ration?" Bystrom asked. "Now, before it gets too watered down?"

"I've never used it. I hesitate to start. I wouldn't even know how to prepare it."

"Eight grains dissolved in four ounces of boiling water. Half an ounce to half a pint of liquor. Taken daily in divided portions. Patients tell me it's absolutely foul, disgusting. I've had them drink it and swear off liquor right then and there."

"Miracle cure. It does cause vomiting."

"Back East we gave the patient laudanum for vomiting and diarrhea."

Slocum shook his head. "Vomiting scares me. It would put extra strain on her heart. Whatever we do, we have to consider the heart. We simply can't take risks. God forbid we cure her and kill her."

"Then you're dead against cutting her off as opposed to gradual reduction."

"Sudden deprivation can work more evil than dangerous exhaustion; her system could recoil from it, she could fall into a state of torpor. Melancholy, madness, delirium tremens. I've started her on alternating warm and cold baths. Not as extreme as usual, again her heart."

He set his half-smoked cigar on the ashtray, pulled open a drawer, and began poking through pamphlets and reports. Unable to find what he was looking for, he continued to search.

"I read something last night. Where the deuce . . . Never mind, I'll just tell you. Interesting. Some French veterinarian deliberately intoxicated a horse by injecting a pint of alcohol into its jugular vein, then immediately injected five grains of carbonate ammonia in one ounce of water in the same place. He claims the effects of the alcohol ceased immediately."

Bystrom laughed. "We're not veterinarians, Doctor. Mrs. Bracy's not a filly."

"I'm not trying to be funny, Lionel, just thinking ahead. Speculating. What if she turns out incurable? What if we have to throw in the towel and send her home? She'll start in again. But what if we can do something to prevent it?"

"The tartar emetic. Opium . . ."

"Not opium, that's much too risky. But something that'll turn her off of the stuff. Then restrict her to a milk-and-vegetable diet. I spoke with her daughter; she's very bright and conscientious. She'll cooperate in any way. Still, I sound like I'm giving up on her when we've barely started. That's not a very good approach."

"But there's her heart."

"Yes," said Slocum. "Dammit. Isn't this a good cigar, though? Great, just great."

They sat together on a stone bench surrounded by red and yellow roses in beautiful profusion. The robin still sang, joined in full throat by a determined black-capped warbler. Doctor and patient sat in the sun near an unusually tall red osier dogwood.

"I've been thinking, Doctor," said Doreen. "The way I see it there are three possibilities. One, I'm cured, I go home and that's that. Two, I'm cured, go home, and a month, six weeks later . . . Three, I'm simply incurable."

"I don't think we need worry about two and three,"

said Slocum, striving for confidence in his tone. "Let's go back to what we were talking about yesterday afternoon."

"The wedge."

"Yes. A good definition of it, I must say. Would it bother you if I smoked?" She shook her head, and he lit up a fresh Clandin's Imperator and got out a small notebook. Fishing out a pencil stub, he glanced over his notes, then spoke.

"You said you feel that as time goes on in your husband's career, the wedge drives you farther apart. The higher he moves up in rank, the more responsibility he accrues, the more time on the job, the farther apart you drift. Which, you say, he completely disagrees with."

She nodded. "Being a career officer's wife isn't easy. But it's not just the army. I suppose women married to businessmen share their husbands with his career. Lawyers, doctors," she said pointedly.

He chuckled. "I'm a bachelor."

She smiled. "Shame on you. You take sharing for granted. Just as I took his absence when he went off to the war. He left a captain and came back a major. Then he was promoted to lieutenant colonel and given command of Fort Point. We knew at the time it would be our last stop. Two more years and he'll retire. Knowing that helps, like knowing you have two more years to serve on your sentence."

"You blame the army."

"You think I'm being unfair."

"No, no. Only, you did marry him knowing he was a career man. You must have assumed he'd rise in rank, and like anything else, the bigger the job, the more responsibility, et cetera, et cetera. Your eyes were open, you thought you could handle it."

"I did. For years and years. But living with it has always been hard. It has for me."

"You made a conscious effort to accept it, but over the years it's worn you down."

"Exactly."

"So the fact that you only have two years to go doesn't help as much as it might."

The warbler ceased singing and rose, circling above their heads before winging off toward the river. The robin stopped singing, watched it briefly, and with the stage to itself resumed. Doreen cupped a large yellow rose with her hand. Slocum picked it for her; she twirled it and inhaled its fragrance.

"Lovely."

They went on. He agreed that her situation had drained her. She was getting older, which didn't help, plus her daughter was grown up and didn't need her constant attention. The cause of her problem was clear, but removing the problem looked to be impossible. She confessed that she saw no way of changing the things that made the coming two years seem more like ten.

"Would he resign now?" Slocum asked. "I mean this week? He knows the situation, its effect on you. What it's brought you to. He loves you."

"I won't ask him to quit."

"But if it means—"

"I don't care!"

"It's all right, we're just discussing it. Is it that you're afraid he'd never forgive you?"

"No, no, he would, he would. In a minute. But I can't put that on him, don't you see? I may be weak, but I'm no weakling. Dear me, that doesn't make any sense." She lay the flower down on the bench beside her. Across the way the fountain splashed, the water resplendent with sun diamonds. She turned and sought his eyes, peering earnestly into them. "I want to lick this as no drunkard ever wanted to. It's a dragon, I want to cut it down, kill it, rid myself of it forever."

"You'd never have agreed to be admitted if you didn't. But aren't you ignoring something very important? You hold the key, the solution. One word from you and he—"

"Tell me something, Doctor, if you were my husband, as proud, as patriotic, as committed to his career as he is, and you had a wife who adored you, but who—"

"Was suffering."

"Who turned into what I've turned into, a drunkard—what would you do if she asked you to quit? After twenty-eight years."

"I'd agree to it on the spot."

"So would he on the spot, and from then on I wouldn't be able to live with myself. I know, you think I'm being a martyr. Self-sacrifice carried to ridiculous extremes, unnecessary extremes."

"I think you're wrong. What you're doing is voluntarily erecting the one stumbling block that can prevent your recovering. What can I say to change your mind?"

"Nothing. You're wrong. I can kill the dragon. I will."

He offered no comment on this, instead rising from the bench, picking up the rose, and handing it to her. They walked. The robin, unwilling to lose its audience, followed them, swinging and circling about singing, singing. They walked in silence.

This, Slocum reflected glumly, was going to be a tough one. A wasted effort? Possibly, even probably. What about her husband? He got the impression, even without her alluding to it, that the colonel was as devoted to her as she was to him. Would he see the light? Would he quit without her asking him? Could their daughter persuade him to? He sighed.

"Anything wrong?" Doreen asked.

"No, no," he lied, and thought further that one of the most trying aspects of curing inebriety was that there were so many factors over which one had no more control than a drunkard has over his affliction. He flicked away his cigar stub.

"You enjoy your cigars, don't you?"

"Passionately, I smoke twenty a day."

"Are they good for you?"

He grinned. "They smell fouler than a ship's hold, I know. A true gentleman smokes a pipe, but I think cigars are healthier. I know nothing relaxes me like a good one. When I pause to light one up, those few seconds of concentrating on the match and getting it started break my train of thought, help clear my head. And once acquired, the taste is delicious. Smoking exercises the lungs, stimulates the heart, charges the arteries, warms the breast. A good cigar takes your attention away from the cares, the pressures, the world, if only for a little while. A good comfortable cigar helps a man get closer to himself. Want to know what's bad for you, harmful? Chewing gum. Bad for the jaw muscles, the teeth, the digestion. It's getting a bit sticky out. Shall we go in?"

Devlin helped Catherine into the buggy, then got on himself and took the reins. They drove west on Broadway Street toward Hyde. She hugged him and laughed happily.

"Didn't I tell you Robert Westerfield was honorable?"

"He's a prince!"

"Who brought you the fruit cake?"

"Mercy. Early this morning." He told her what Mercy had told him about Betsy's latest beau. "She's as interested in me as she is in the King of Mesopotamia. She just doesn't want you to have me. She's a little late for that."

"Betsy's quite a girl," she said. "It's hard to believe she's Mercy's."

"Some daughters take after their fathers. Did you know that she'll be seven on her next birthday?"

"She'll be twenty-one."

"Seven." He glanced at her archly. "Believe me, I know."

They turned right at Hyde. It was less than a month

since the fire, but not so much as a single charred timber could be seen as a reminder of the blaze. As they drove along the deeply rutted street, they noticed men carrying long sheaves of paper and stopping people to read them. They looked as if they were trying to get them to sign something.

"Did you hear?" Loyal asked, answering Catherine's curious glance. "The copper who brought me my breakfast said that Brannan's friends are campaigning to throw out the mayor and the chief of police. Brannan plans to take over as mayor, and I'm sure he'll pick the man who'll replace Sanger. Speaking of jobs, would you know anybody who might be looking for an examiner with a strong back and a weak mind?"

"Every merchant in town, every builder, everybody. Unemployment in San Francisco is confined to people who have no desire to work. Do you really want to stand behind a counter? Won't that be a little tame for you?"

"I've had my fill of wild. Besides, I'm not picky, anything'll do to start."

"You shouldn't have to work. You own a gold mine, remember?"

"I hereby bequeath same to the rightful owner: Mother Nature. Isn't it something? I own a gold mine and I've less than nine dollars in my pocket. I don't even have a room."

"You'll be our house guest."

"I wouldn't want to impose."

"I'd love you to."

"Invitation accepted."

As they drove on, the Vigilantes seemed to be blanketing the city.

"Do you think a petition'll work? Brannan'll be able to oust the mayor and the chief?" he asked.

"I doubt it. He'll need a majority. He certainly won't get any signatures in Sydney Town." She laughed. "And there are a lot of decent people who disagree with his methods, who plain don't like him."

They drove up to the house. A strange expression came to her face when they stepped inside. She stood on the oval rag rug in the foyer and looked about.

"It's so empty, Loyal, like a mausoleum. Mother in Sacramento, Daddy laid up at the fort. Last night I was so lonesome for the sound of another voice." She slid her arms around his neck. "Tonight will be better."

He was looking around also. "Last time I was here we had coffee and a fight."

"I have no desire for either."

She searched his eyes, hers gazing longingly. Without another word she took him by the hand and led him upstairs. In her bedroom, surrounded by pretty frilliness bright with sunshine, they stood facing each other, silently loving each other. She unfastened the top button of his shirt. He undid the top button of her blouse. Their hands moved swiftly; both began to breathe harder, faster; tiny pearls of sweat glistened on their faces. Outside, horses cantered by on the way down from the fort; somewhere far away toward the city a dog barked. A passing breeze lifted the curtain, then died.

They stood naked, eyes locked. She set her palms against his gently heaving chest. She slid them down to his lean stomach. There her hands separated, one to ascend and slip around his neck, the other to grasp his right arm and swing it around her. Their bodies clamped tightly together, causing her to begin trembling in delicious anticipation. She was panting now. He could feel her nipples harden against him just under his own. She rose on tiptoe, pushing her breasts up his chest, raising her lips to meet his. Their mouths worked slowly, deliberately, hungrily, drinking of the cup of desire. Neither said a word, but her gasping her soft moaning betrayed her rapidly mounting passion. Like a spirited mare it snapped its traces and ran. Faster, faster . . .

They were on the bed. His tongue danced slowly

down her quivering nakedness, exploring tantalizingly, singeing where it touched, taking some of the fire with it to ignite the next place. The fire spread throughout her, right to her rapidly dizzying brain. He licked, he nibbled, igniting her, lifting her through excitement into a realm that defied description, a state wherein frenzy mastered all other sensations. His manhood rose throbbing in her grasp; he was above her, poised on his limbs. She guided him, bringing it to her. When it touched her ever so lightly and fired an impulse to her brain, it exploded. Flashes of silver light flew in every direction.

He lowered, she bucked.

"Ahhhhh . . ."

Her feral cry shattered the stillness, then trailed off. All of him was inside her. He moved with the grace of a great stag. Incredibly gentle, his body marvelously tuned to hers, instinctively knowing every point to touch to arouse and linger upon. His feelings for her feelings were uncanny. He was fiercely passionate and yet tender and solicitous! So gloriously demanding! So glorious!

They lay separated looking at the ceiling, lost in the pink clouds that had materialized to envelope their rapture and conceal it from the eyes of the world. Now the cloud parted and the shreds softened into a mist. He kissed her. Their first words since entering the room came simultaneously.

"I love you."

---●◀ *28* ▶●---

At nightfall the signature collectors were summoned to Fort Gunnybags by the roof bell. Ten men were assigned to count the names. Sam Brannan and the other officers of the Committee of Vigilance waited with increasing impatience for the final total. Each of the ten arrived at his total; they put their heads together and came up with the grand total. All seemed cheered by the figure. Brannan waited atop his soap box, which raised him just high enough above his followers to enable him to command their attention. In his mind, it had long since ceased to be a common soapbox. It was instead the rostrum that Caesar mounted to address the Senate of ancient Rome, the palace balcony of beloved Queen Victoria from which she addressed her subjects, the rock on which Moses stood to expound the Ten Commandments . . .

"Sam," called Eustace Ward, breaking into his fantasy. "Here you go." He handed Brannan a folded slip of paper.

"I'll bet it's twenty thousand," crowed Brannan. "More. Gentlemen! Gentlemen, your attention. I have the result of the tabulation. The final total is . . ."

He paused melodramatically, the slip still folded in his hand, and held up. His listeners began shouting numbers.

"Quiet!" He opened the paper, read the number; a

frown shadowed his face. "Twelve thousand four hundred and seven. Gentlemen, gentlemen, brothers all, how disappointing. Can't we do better?"

"It's only been a couple days," Ward reminded him.

"Brother Ward is quite right. This is a start, an excellent start. But we must keep at it. By the end of this week I want twenty thousand signatures. Twenty thousand voices joined in one demanding we throw the rascals out."

The crowd cheered. He waved everyone silent.

"Well, what are we all standing around for? Let's get back out into the streets. We will not return until we have every signature. Twenty thousand!"

"Twenty thousand," roared his listeners, and began to disperse, heading for the exits.

"Wait! Wait!" Every man froze and turned to look. "One word, just one to speed you on your way."

"Just one," repeated someone. "Only one, Rev?"

Brannan smiled icily. "From the scriptures," he went on. "To fortify your zeal, to inspire every brother to exceed his quota. For, brothers, this is the hour of a new beginning for us all. Henceforth you are no longer merely men, you are modern-day apostles spreading faith in our purpose: to rescue our beloved city from the grip of the forces of evil. 'Came the angel out of the temple crying with a loud voice to him who sat on the cloud: Thrust in thy sickle, and reap; the time is come for thee to reap; for the harvest of the earth is ripe.' "

Cheering rose, muffling Revelations, 14, 15. The crowd dispersed, spurred by the bell on the roof. Eustace Ward and Sergio Scapelli came up to Brannan as he got down.

"They'll never get close to twenty thousand names," muttered Scapelli.

"They'll get more," Brannan said confidently. "More and more and more."

"I'd settle for fifteen," ventured Eustace Ward.

"I refuse to settle," burst Brannan acidly. "All we can get by Sunday midnight is my goal. Monday morning we move. You, Eustace, will take over as the new chief of police."

"Me?" Ward reacted more than mildly shocked. "What do I know about policework?"

"What does John Sanger know?" was the reply. "Besides, it's your civic duty, man."

"Sanger's a professional," Scapelli said.

"I don't care what he calls himself, what he's not is on our side. Eustace, you'll take over. I'll take over the mayor's job. It makes sense. I have seniority on the board of aldermen. In the event of Brenham's death, I'd automatically take over."

"Only until an election," Scapelli said.

"Automatically. Sergio, what's the matter with you? What are you all of a sudden, the devil's advocate?"

"What I am is fed up with our rushing off half-cocked, with you rushing us off."

Brannan eyed him as if he were a loathsome object. When he responded, his tone was even, unruffled, but discernibly cold.

"Me? Rush us off?"

"Let's not start bickering," interposed Eustace Ward.

"Eustace is right," said Brannan, mellowing. "This isn't the time. Our minds should be one, our eyes focused unwaveringly on the common goal. Ridding the city of every last Australian, driving them out and keeping them out. The only way we can do it is to take control. You, Eustace, as chief, I as mayor. Mayor Samuel Brannan—it has rather a nice ring to it, wouldn't you say, gentlemen?"

Four days later the Committee of Vigilance, working day and night, had succeeded in gathering more than eighteen thousand signatures. It was an impressive total. Even Brannan was pleased. It was shortly after midnight Sunday; Monday morning couldn't arrive fast enough.

Loyal Devlin, meanwhile, had taken a job with Olcott and Willensky construction and was working with a crew on an addition to the Parker House in Portsmouth Square. Nearly one hundred miles apart the Bracys were each improving. Doreen was driving herself mercilessly in an effort to snap the chain; the colonel was able to return home to his bed. Having turned the corner, he was recuperating so rapidly Dr. Wilcox professed amazement. Still, Catherine rarely left her father's bedside; only to bring Devlin his lunch at the worksite every noon and in addition to that only when it was absolutely necessary to go into town.

For some reason, known only to Betsy Brannan and Nathan Bowrig, Betsy and Bowrig broke up. They parted vowing never to speak to each other again. Mercy suspected that Betsy had demanded a ring as proof of his intentions and that Nathan had resisted the suggestion; it didn't take much to detonate Betsy; this was enough.

Somehow Betsy learned that Devlin was working in Portsmouth Square. She came around one afternoon, wearing a fetching red-and-white polka-dotted knickerbocker dress, short skirt with loose trousers gathered around the ankles. The outfit was the scandalous creation of a Mrs. Elizabeth Smith Miller, appropriated by the notorious Amelia Jenks Bloomer. Betsy drew whistles and catcalls, which she feigned to ignore. Twirling her parasol over her shoulder, she came up to Devlin. He was stripped naked to the waist, sweating profusely, wielding a ten-pound sledgehammer, smashing old foundation stone. He paused, leaned on his hammer, and swiped at his brow with the back of his hand.

"Betsy."

"My, my, aren't you the beautiful brute."

More whistles, more derisive comments. He lowered his voice. "Betsy, what do you want?"

"To see you, silly. What do you think? When are we going to get together. It's been ages; we have so much to talk about. I've been shopping for my trousseau, darling."

"Please, don't start with that nonsense. We're not getting married, we're not engaged, we never will be."

She positively grimaced, stomping her foot and pouting like a seven-year-old. "I like that!"

"So do I. Now will you kindly go away and let me work?"

"Only if you promise to meet me after." She indicated across the square. "In the Occidental Restaurant. I'll be waiting inside, out of the sun."

"Forget it, we have nothing to talk about. It's over; what am I saying. Go back to Nathan, to Gregory, or whoever. Stay away from me. I'm getting married."

"To that skinny stick Catherine Bracy."

"Beat it."

"I shan't. You can't make me. I'll stand here until I'm covered with filthy dust, and it'll be your fault. You don't have to talk to me, I'll just talk to you, and all your friends'll hear and you'll be embarrassed to tears."

"All right, all right, I'll meet you in the restaurant. It'll be at least an hour."

"I don't care. I'll have a cool lemonade and some raspberry sherbet."

"Five minutes. You can say what you have to say and then I leave."

"You're making a terrible mistake marrying her."

"Not now, Betsy. At the restaurant."

"You *are* a brute. You're cruel!" Up went her nose, sniffing disdainfully. She swung about and flounced off, sped on her way by cheers, jeers, and laughter. Devlin watched her cross the square.

"Seven years old, darling, seven."

*   *   *

To Devlin's surprise Betsy was nowhere to be seen when he walked into the Occidental Restaurant an hour later. To his chagrin her father was, sitting at the window table by himself. He recognized Devlin and waved, inviting Devlin to sit. A slender vase of dried daisies graced the table. Brannan was drinking a glass of milk.

"Loyal . . ."

"Reverend. Where's Betsy?"

"I sent her on home. We were discussing you, and she became very upset. She's extremely sensitive, poor child. She sets her cap for you and you knock it off her head. She's taking it very hard. This is becoming very awkward. Please sit."

Devlin sighed and sat.

"I have but one question," Brannan went on. "Did you or did you not ask my daughter to marry you?"

"I did not."

"She says you did. Are you accusing her of lying? Betsy is not without fault. Who among us is? But blatant prevarication is not one of her faults."

"I'm sorry, sir, but I'd remember if I asked her to marry me. I didn't for a very good reason. I don't love her. Now, if that's all you want to know, why don't I leave. If you'll excuse me."

"Wait. There's no hurry, you just sat down. I appreciate your candor. But, I love my muffin precious. She's all the world to me. To see her hurt, hurts me." He narrowed his eyes. "I hate it. Since you're the cause, I hate you. Were I ten years younger, I'd challenge you to a duel. Pistols at fifteen paces, sabers, foils—your choice—"

"Oh, for Chrissakes!"

"Here, here, no need to blaspheme." Brannan started up from his chair, his eyes blazing. "You're a scoundrel, sir, an Irish rogue."

A shadow fell over the table, stopping him. Both looked up. It was Mercy. "I thought it was you through the window," she said to her husband. "And it was your carrot top that caught my eye." She smiled fondly at Devlin and set her hand on his shoulder. "Who's an Irish rogue, Sam? Certainly not present company."

The waiter had come over, bringing a chair for Mercy. She ordered a peppermint squash. Devlin signaled two. Brannan sipped his milk, leaving its mark on his upper lip. Mercy wiped it away with his napkin.

"Arguing about Betsy, are you?" she asked, looking from one to the other and back.

"Not me," Devlin said. "I'm just here for the lecture."

"Sam, what are you doing to the poor man?"

"Now, my dear, this is man talk. It doesn't concern you."

"Stuff and nonsense!"

"My dear, do lower your voice. These people know me."

"This man's not interested in Betsy. They've about as much in common as a horse and a flounder, for pity's sakes. I'm surprised you can't see that. Don't you know your own daughter? She hops from beau to beau like a frog hopping lily pads. She hasn't the faintest idea of what true love is, and won't until she grows up, starts acting her age. She doesn't need a husband, she needs a hoop and stick. We've spoiled her rotten, and this is the result. Instead of badgering this poor man, we should both be home lecturing her on the obligations of young womanhood, the principles of fair play, social graces, and decent deportment."

The waiter arrived with two peppermint squashes. Mercy was on her feet. She waved them away. "Sorry, I've changed my mind. The reverend and I are going home. Loyal, do you like peppermint squash?"

"I . . ."

"Good. Enjoy them both. Sam, put some money down, enough for everything and a decent tip. We're going to our daughter."

"Sssssh, Mercy . . ."

"Fifteen years late, perhaps, but let's see what we can do."

29

The colonel had been moved home for the remainder of his recovery, and he was now able to sit up and receive visitors in the parlor. Feeling much better and looking it, he was able to eat solid food. He no longer had pain in his chest and was breathing normally. He ordered Catherine out of the house. "You're getting pasty-looking from lack of fresh air." On her way out, she met Majors Downing and Viselli at the front gate. They had been summoned by the colonel.

"The two men serving thirty days for deliberately messing up on MacGruder's firing squad have a little more than a week to go on their sentences," said Viselli, standing arms folded, leaning against the mantel.

"What about the Callahans?" the colonel asked.

"Nothing yet, sir. Captain Westerfield is still out hunting. You know about Sergeant Devlin."

"Catherine told me. Sorry business. Sorry . . ."

A shadow fell across the colonel's face; he slumped in thought. Downing and Viselli exchanged glances and waited.

Downing cleared his throat. "Sir?"

"Go on, go on."

"The muskets to replace those blown up in the quartermaster's warehouse in town by the fire are on the way from ordinance in Portland. We had to get them from the Department of the Columbia."

"Tom Devlin . . . What?"

Downing repeated his information.

"Okay. Remember, they're to be stored at the fort. In town is too risky. The Vigilantes might grab them. Besides, the QM's warehouse blew up in the last fire. Speaking of which, either of you know what Brannan's been up to lately? Up to no good, I'm sure."

"He's taken a new tack," said the provost marshal. He explained.

"Ye gods and little fishes," rasped Bracy, "what ails that man? What's the point? Why replace John Sanger? He's cleaning up Sydney Town, isn't that what they want? Has anybody bothered to explain to Brannan that two thirds of the Australians there don't trouble anybody except one another? And the police are weeding out the rest. Why in God's name can't Brannan keep his hands off? Let John do his job, goddammit!"

"Take it easy, sir," cautioned Viselli. "Don't get all worked up."

"You're right. I sure can't do anything about it sitting here. What else, Richard?"

Downing continued. Two men guarding the Sally Port door had been discovered playing cards by the Officer of the Day. As punishment they were forced to stand on barrels in the center of the courtyard with sticks over their shoulders from reveille to retreat for two full days. There'd been a fight in the mess hall. The two instigators were bucked and gagged and forced to sit on the north wall all day in the sun as punishment. Rats had gotten into the magazine and eaten into half a dozen powder sacks.

"We're out of arsenic," said Downing. "I sent a man into town to buy some. We could requisition it from Sacramento, but it'd take a week to get here. And I'm afraid mice have gotten into the flour in the stores again."

"Mice, rats, vigilantes, pirates." Bracy flung a hand. "We're under siege Oh, I almost forgot. The beach that runs along the approach road up to the seawall, I want it eliminated. Extend the rocks a minimum of four hundred yards. It doesn't have to be done tomorrow, and not by us; we can use local labor, if any's available. Long-term project, okay?"

"Yes, sir," said Downing.

With that, Viselli and Downing left.

The colonel had a brandy, checked the calendar, and decided—Wilcox willing—he would resume his duties one week hence. Half-days to start. He sat down at the secretary to write a letter to Doreen. He was just signing off when Loyal came home from work.

"You look worn to a nub," Bracy commented.

Loyal collapsed in a chair and clapped his stomach with the flat of his hand. "It's getting me into shape. Sir—"

"Please, don't call me sir. You're not in the army. Ewing is fine." He'd cocked his head; he eyed Loyal appraisingly, intuitively sensing that something important was coming up.

Loyal marshaled his thoughts and sucked in a deep breath. "Sir, Ewing, I'd like to, ah, I wish to, I want to, ah . . ."

"What?"

"Marry your daughter. I'd like your permission to."

"Granted."

Devlin gaped. "It's okay?"

"If it's okay with her. Have you asked her?"

"I will now. Thank you. Gee, that was a breeze."

"You didn't think I'd turn you down?" Bracy smiled. "You don't think she will? Relax, man, you're tight as a spring. Let's toast the happy couple. I congratulate my daughter, she's got good taste in husbands."

He got out a bottle of Madeira saved for special occasions. They followed the toast with another, honoring young love in general and young lovers the world over. It was his third drink in less than fifteen minutes.

"I'm starting to feel dangerously mellow."

Loyal put the bottle away for him, excused himself, and went upstairs to his room. He came back down with a letter in its envelope.

"It's to a friend over in Martinez. Where's the post office in town?"

"Not more than a couple blocks from where you're working in Portsmouth Square. On Washington next to the Garrett House."

Loyal told him about Ira Jack Fayles and all he'd done for him. He figured that his gratitude expressed in a letter would be more proper.

On the colonel's advice, Loyal left the house a half an hour earlier the next morning. The colonel cautioned him that the post-office lines were the longest in town. From a house on Telegraph Hill, San Francisco's highest point, a semaphore reported Pacific Mail steamer arrivals, sending people flocking to the post office.

The line was only fifty bodies long, and it moved steadily if not fast. Devlin was lucky in one respect: it was not a mail steamer arrival day, so the clerks would not be busy sorting out the mail, which could delay service anywhere from twelve to twenty hours.

Devlin finally stood at the window watching the clerk read his envelope.

"Martinez. That'll be twenty-five cents." Devlin pushed a quarter toward him. "Are you Loyal Devlin?"

"Yes." Devlin nodded.

"I've got a letter for you. Hang on."

The clerk located it and passed it to him. There was no return address. Devlin thanked him and walked away. Who in the world would be writing him? He tore open the envelope.

Dear Loyal,

I don't know if this will reach you. You didn't say where you'd be staying, so I sent it care of general delivery. Something important's come up that you should know about. You made it clear how you feel about the mine. But I can't get it out of my head that turning your back on a working gold mine is pretty foolish. I think of all the prospectors out here who work like slaves and don't find enough to keep body and soul together, and it's handed to you and you refuse it.

But if that's how you feel, I suppose it's none of my business. Only since we last saw each other, something's come up that sort of makes it my business. An old army buddy, Henry Wicklow (we fought side by side at New Orleans), came through with his two sons and two grandsons. Henry's done very well up in Oregon in lumber. He was passing through on his way to San Jose. We spent most of the day cutting up old touches. I ask you, what could be more boring to four young bucks than two old shakos swapping war stories?

But the war wasn't all we talked about. Henry was on his way south to invest in a fruit ranch. He's so rich it's sickening. I told him about the mine. I won't say he was interested, it was more like he caught fire. I walked him over to Bake Myers' assay office and Bake showed him the file copy of the assay report. That was the clincher. Oh, by the way, enclosed please find the certificate of ownership given me by Schaeffer, the local claim records clerk. Just sign it, have it notarized, and mail it back to me. I'll see that he gets it.

This is the deal, Loyal. Henry wants your mine. He'd love to buy it outright, but I told him I didn't think you'd go for that. I got the bright idea that he take it over and give you a percentage of the profits on a regular basis. You'd get a full production report every three or six months, and with it his check for your cut. I opened the hand with a bid of

25 percent. That was a little steep for him; we finally settled on 10 percent. It seems fair to me; you won't have to lift a finger, won't have to come out here, won't even have to meet him. He says if you agree, he can have his lawyer up in Medford draw up a standard contract. You'll both sign it, you'll be in business. If and when the vein peters out, the mine'll be abandoned, and the contract declared null and void.

It's up to you. If you like the idea, let me know. I can get in touch with Henry.

Sincerely yours,
I.J.F.

Devlin whooped, startling two women passing by and setting a poodle yapping. He spun around and ran back to the post office. He tried to crash the line, explaining to some very impatient-looking individuals that he had to get back a letter he'd just posted. He couldn't even buy his way back into line and finally gave up.

He'd write a second letter to Ira Jack—perhaps he'd go see him in person. He walked to Portsmouth Square and the construction site. He was more than twenty minutes late. The foreman started to bawl him out. He quit.

Within two days of the formal presentation of the Vigilantes petition to Judge Anson Galsworthy of the superior court of San Mateo County, Chief Sanger and Mayor C.J. Brenham were relieved of their duties. As soon as the news of the chief's dismissal broke, forty-one officers on the sixty-eight-man force handed in their badges. Sanger did his utmost to persuade them to stay on; he even praised his successor, Eustace Ward, as an able man, but nothing he could say stopped two-thirds of the men from quitting.

Brannan applauded the mass resignation on the front page of the *California Star*. As expected, he was appointed mayor.

Within twenty-four hours, Mayor Reverend Sam Brannan and the Committee of Vigilance declared war on the Sydney Ducks. The few policemen still in uniform reported to Chief Ward. Unfortunately, he didn't quite know what to do with them. He eventually decided to scatter them about the waterfront to watch for any crimes that might be committed while the Sydney Town war went on.

Not even Colonel Bracy could run interference for this confrontation. Even if he had been physically up to it, it would have been useless. The number of Vigilantes and their friends had quadrupled since the night he was shot. A hundred and seventy-five soldiers would be no match for four thousand armed civilians.

Though greatly outnumbered, the Sydney Ducks chose to make a fight of it. It went on for four days, the Vigilantes gradually wearing the Ducks down, chasing most of them out of town or down to the wharves and aboard ships. They killed nearly forty. Some of the Ducks hid elsewhere in the city or were hidden by friends. On the fourth night of the fighting Brannan ordered Sydney Town put to the torch. By midnight, nine contiguous blocks south of Telegraph Hill were engulfed in flames.

The sun rose on the ashes of Sydney Town. Most of the Ducks had fled town. Mayor Sam Brannan, sitting in the high-back posture chair in his new office in City Hall, presided over a victory celebration with fellow committee members. Spirits soared, champagne flowed, and Brannan puffed and strutted like an Atwater prairie chicken.

Unbeknownst to his honor, however, another meeting was taking place in Reverend Doctor Anderson's study in the Baptist church rectory on Filbert Street. Present at the meeting were ex-Mayor Brenham, Colonel Bracy, John Sanger and fourteen wealthy and influential business and professional men. All had one thing in common: none had signed Brannan's petition. They had just voted unanimously to remove Brannan from office, reinstall Mayor Brenham, and restore John Sanger to his old job.

A Committee of Safety was formed. Garrett Ryckman, the brewer, a former Vigilante who had become disenchanted with Brannan's leadership and quit, was appointed to head the committee. Ryckman was a florid, usually phlegmatic individual, but when his indignation level was high, as it was at the moment, he became as excitable as a small boy.

"Then it's decided, my friends. Reverend Doctor Anderson here and his people will draw up a list of Brannan's lawless acts. Olan Hatfield, Will Koski, and I will contact the governor. Judge Hemphill will contact the state's attorney general. I'm no lawyer, but I can't believe Judge Galsworthy's acceptance of the Vigilantes' petition has any force in law. What say you, Judge?"

Judge Rexford Pyle Hemphill was ninety years old and got about in a squeaky wheelchair. As feeble as he might appear physically, he was a sharp-minded, learned, man, and passionately honest. His honesty had earned him the affectionate sobriquet Upright Rex.

The judge leered demonically. "That petition isn't worth a match to burn it. I wish to hell I was thirty years younger. I'd love to get Anson Galsworthy into court on this one. He authorized a goddamn bloodbath, and I bet my ass against six barrels of vinegar he knew it'd turn out like it did when he put his blessing on it. What the hell, the sonovabitch is a Vigilante, isn't he?"

*   *   *

Events moved swiftly after that. Prodded by the Committee of Safety, Governor Peter H. Burnett issued a directive that ordered the Reverend Samuel Brannan to remove himself from the office of mayor of San Francisco or face immediate arrest and confinement. Police Chief Eustace Ward was given the same warning. Ward readily complied. Brannan balked. He demanded a meeting with the Committee of Safety, which was held at City Hall. He brought Judge Galsworthy and half a dozen Vigilantes with him. He also brought his bible.

Representing the governor was State Attorney General Hewlitt J.D. Thatcher, a sharp young lawyer originally from Los Angeles. Thatcher, who stood close to six and a half feet and was completely bald, was careful not to accuse Brannan out of hand. He had no need to. The meeting wasn't three minutes old before Brannan took the floor and began pontificating. In doing so, he unconsciously dug his own grave by pointing out his many lawless actions. Possibly, reflected the colonel listening, to justify them?

"My friends, desperate times call for desperate measures. And in the brief and tumultuous history of our fair city, alas, have times ever been more desperate?"

The small conference room was hot and crowded. Brannan's listeners, all in their shirtsleeves, fanned themselves impatiently, sweating furiously. Brannan, however, seemed unfazed.

"I ask you not to judge our methods, only our results. In every war there are casualties. Should our war with the Sydney Ducks be an exception? Men did perish—"

"They were murdered," snapped John Sanger.

"Casualties of war, John. A necessary sacrifice to success. We have broken the back of the monster that threatens our lives, our property, our pursuit of happiness. Gentlemen, we have purged our city.

"I stand before you accused of taking the law into my own hands. I agree—that is exactly what we did. And why? Because, gentlemen, the law refused to take the field against the enemy. Something had to be done. We did it, while you stood safely on the sidelines and watched. You, who stand to benefit fully as much from our triumph as we.

"And you dare accuse us of rashness? Of reckless behavior? You dare, you cowards. Shirkers."

The reverend was shaking his fist, reddening, his eyes bulging, jowls quivering. Quickly, he got control, just as John Sanger and two others started up from their chairs. Brannan continued, his tone milder, control intact.

"Do any of you think I assumed the office of mayor for glory and recognition? I took over because that man, the honorable C.J. Brenham, refused to lift a finger. Because Chief Sanger plodded like Aesop's tortoise dealing with the menace. I didn't reach for the crown, I accepted it as my civic duty—"

"Mr. Ward? Eustace Ward?" Thatcher interrupted.

"Sir?" Ward sat up in his chair, glancing sidelong at Brannan.

"I am speaking, sir," Brannan snapped. "You inter—"

"In a minute, Mr. Brannan."

"Reverend."

"I'm curious, Mr. Ward, did you also consider it your civic duty to take over as chief of police?"

"Of course he did," sang Brannan. "Tell him, Eustace, speak up, speak up."

"Somebody had to take the job," Ward said quietly. "It couldn't very well stand vacant."

"Thank you," Thatcher said. He paused and looked over the second page of the papers he was holding.

"May I proceed?" Brannan asked, his tone and expression as haughtily sarcastic as he could fashion them.

Thatcher didn't look up from his reading, only gestured for patience.

"Mr. Galsworthy," he went on, "when the petition was brought to you, you advised Mr. Brannan and his people that they were within their rights to replace the mayor and the chief."

"Definitely," said Galsworthy, according Brannan a benign smile. "Eighteen thousand plus signatures, better than three-quarters of the voting population."

"Close enough," said Thatcher. "So where are we? The petition was submitted, you gave it your blessing, Brannan and Ward replaced the mayor and the chief. After which the Vigilantes attacked Sydney Town. You, Reverend, led the attack. All told, more than forty people met their deaths, including four Vigilantes. Nearly a hundred were injured, many severely."

"We've already covered that," said Brannan, and fisted a yawn.

"He's right," Galsworthy said beside him.

"The police took no part in the fracas," Thatcher went on. "On orders, I presume, from you, Mr. Ward, you being in charge. Why did you keep them out of it?"

His eyes on the floor, Ward explained why he'd deployed his men to areas well removed from the battleground. The attorney general excused himself and interrupted.

"I didn't ask you what they did, it's what they didn't do. They didn't take part. You held them out of it. Why?"

"The police have been something less than the soul of cooperation throughout this sorry business," sang Brannan airily.

A small chorus of amens punctuated this assertion.

"I'm asking you, Mr. Ward."

"Tell him, Eustace. Speak up, man—"

"He was against it!" burst a voice from the side of

the room. "Against more bloodletting, innocent people getting hurt and killed!"

It wasn't Ward who had answered; it was Sergio Scapelli. He had shot to his feet. Brannan turned on him scowling, shouting, castigating him. He himself was quickly shouted down. Order was restored. Thatcher went on, keeping his tone mild. Throughout both Scapelli's and Brannan's outbursts his eyes had never left Eustace Ward's.

"Is what the gentleman says correct, Mr. Ward? Did you disapprove?"

"Yes." His voice was barely above a whisper.

"Eustace . . ." Brannan's voice was threatening, and his look even more so.

Ward ignored him. "It got too bloody," he said. "It was horrible. Every time we went in there was worse than the time before. The savagery, brutality—on both sides. People beating and maiming each other. Helpless women and children caught in the middle. It was a nightmare. A living hell. Last time I couldn't sleep, couldn't even eat for days. I'm a peaceful man, I loathe guns, bloodshed sickens me."

Brannan threw up his hands. "That's it. I've had enough of this mockery of justice." He glared at Thatcher. "You're not looking for the truth here. You just want to pillory me. You're all against me. 'And they spit upon him, and took the reed, and smote him on the head.'

"Listen to me, all of you, including you traitors. I'm going downstairs to my office. In my desk is a loaded gun. Yours, Brenham. Mine now to protect myself. Not against my enemies. Against all of you, my dear friends and followers! If any of you so much as sets a foot over my doorsill, so help me God I'll shoot to kill!"

Everyone sat stunned as he bolted from the room. One and all watched gaping, holding their breaths expectantly, listening.

Below, the office door slammed. Anson Galsworthy
was the first to speak. A muffled shot sounded, stopping him. Every man jumped up and rushed down the
stairs to Brannan's office. At the door, Thatcher set
his hand on the knob, turned it, and opened the door
slowly.

Brannan sat at his desk, the smoking revolver in his
right hand pointed at the floor. He turned scowling.

"It works and it's accurate. Remember what I said,
one foot over the sill . . ."

Up came the gun, still smoking, aimed straight at
Thatcher's heart. The men crowding behind him gasped.

Thatcher stepped back and closed the door.

30

Not many citizens questioned Brannan's decision to put Sydney Town to the torch. The majority of San Franciscans hailed the Vigilantes and their leader as bona fide heroes. Unlike Eustace Ward and Sergio Scapelli, most people were not in the least troubled by the spilling of blood, even that of innocents. Any blood would serve as long as it wasn't their own.

Two days after the meeting in the conference room at City Hall, the final results of the attack on Sydney Town were made public. The Ducks numbers had been reduced to about two hundred diehards, roughly 6 percent of the normal population of Sydney Town. And the cause of the depletion could be relied upon to discourage immigration from Australia for a long time to come.

Sam Brannan's loss of face in the meeting proved of short duration. Within hours his popularity was restored and with it his lofty self-esteem. His status assured, he celebrated with a long, boring speech to his loyal fellow Vigilantes. Only two members had defected: Eustace Ward and Sergio Scapelli, both immediately joining the Committee of Safety.

Sam Brannan remained as mayor. He nevertheless took to carrying Mayor Brenham's gun, although he had no occasion to shoot anybody for entering his office uninvited. Eustace Ward resigned as chief of police, and over Brannan's protests, John Sanger was reinstated.

Sanger did not want the job. He had to be talked into it by Ewing Bracy and others. But within two hours of his reappearance at headquarters, every policeman who had quit when he was fired returned to his job.

The Callahan brothers were not found. Captain Westerfield scoured the gold fields for nine days without turning up a single clue as to their whereabouts. The colonel hadn't expected him to find them and therefore was not disappointed. The effort had been made, the War Department would have to be satisfied. The firing squad rested.

Judge Rexford Pyle Hemphill officiated at the marriage of Loyal Devlin and Catherine Bracy in his chambers. Catherine's one regret was that her mother could not be present. Her father suggested that she and Devlin reaffirm their vows when Doreen returned home.

The colonel, meanwhile, now fully recovered, returned to his office, his desk and a small mountain of paperwork that a somewhat red-faced Downing freely admitted he simply could not keep abreast of.

"I can do a lot of things in this world, sir, and some pretty good, but paperwork isn't one."

Doreen sat in the garden alone reading late one morning. She was feeling good about herself for the first time in many weeks when she inhaled an ordinary breath that triggered an immediate severe squeezing pain in the center of her chest. It radiated through her left shoulder and down her arm. Suddenly she felt as if her upper body were being crushed and the black dread of imminent death exploded in her mind. The next breath did not come; she strained to take it in, her book tumbling to the ground. The garden dimmed and whirled about her as she struggled to breathe. Turning on the bench, she lay down. When her back found support, she found herself able to catch a breath, but just barely. She lay immobilized by wave after wave of pain, bundled in tension, dying in her mind, and gasping, gasping . . .

Dr. Slocum looked out an upstairs window, saw her in distress, and came running. Within thirty seconds he was by her side and shouting for help. He loosened her clothing and held her in a sitting position. She passed out. By now two orderlies, a nurse, and Dr. Bystrom had arrived. The orderlies ran for a stretcher and she was carried inside and upstairs to her room. She was put to bed in a sitting position. Her difficulty in breathing was by now somewhat alleviated. She regained consciousness, but the shock of the attack appeared to render her wholly unaware of anything other than her discomfort.

"Try to relax," whispered Slocum soothingly. "The more you relax, the quicker it'll ease off. You're breathing better and better now. In a few minutes it'll be back to normal. The pain's easing up now, isn't it?"

"Mmmmmm."

"It will more and more. Stay calm, relax, relax . . ."

"Want . . . to . . . lie . . . down," she murmured.

"No. That would be bad. This is the best position. It keeps your lungs expanded, your breathing easier."

In less than ten minutes the worst was over. The pain left her, her voice became stronger. She breathed normally, although hesitantly, patently afraid that a good deep breath would bring back the pain. Slocum stayed with her, comforting and reassuring her until early evening, when she fell asleep. He watched her sleep for fifteen minutes; her breathing appeared normal, her color had come back. He summoned a nurse to watch her and went to find Dr. Bystrom.

They sat in the little smoke-filled office at the end of the hallway.

"Out of the blue," commented Bystrom morosely.

"Still, that's heart trouble for you. You never know when or how hard it'll hit. You and your prophecy . . ."

Slocum blew cigar smoke, scratched a bit of tobacco from his lower lip, and restored the cigar to his mouth. "What?"

"What you said the other day. What was it, 'God forbid we cure her and kill her'?"

"We're in no position to do either. We can't take more than half a lick of credit for curing her; she's taking care of that. As for killing her heart, that's out of our hands. It'll do what it bloody well wants. Patient or doctor has no say. Still, you're right, it would be a terrible thing for her to lick her problem only to die of a bad ticker. And she's trying so hard." He puffed and mused in a silence, ending it with a shrug and a poor attempt at a grin.

"There's one bright spot. Her determination to quit the bottle won't spread itself thin trying to keep her heart going. I've never met anybody so firmly resolved to beat the devil. I'm willing to bet hard cash on her. What about you?"

Bystrom's expression brightened. "I think I'll wait till tomorrow morning before I reach for my wallet."

To no one's surprise the *California Star* was lavish in praise of its founder and editor-in-chief. Betsy Brannan basked in her father's reflected glory. Mercy, on the other hand, was embarrassed. She cornered Sam after dinner one night when the two of them happened to be home alone. She sat him down in the parlor and stood over him, fists fixed to her hips, looking down admonishingly.

"What's done is done," she said. "You've razed Sydney Town and there's nothing anybody can do about that. Plus you've made yourself mayor."

"Tut, my love, it wasn't my doing. I was the unani-

mous choice of the Vigilantes; I merely saw my duty
and accepted."

"Enjoy yourself, your honor. You want to be mayor,
fine; you want to be governor, go ahead. But one
thing you won't be because I refuse to allow it: a
gunfighter."

"What in the world are you—"

"You know perfectly well what I'm talking about.
You're carrying a gun, don't deny it."

"I certainly do."

Out shot her hand, whipping the left side of his
jacket to one side, revealing a shiny new shoulder
holster filled with Brenham's pistol.

"I saw it when you were admiring yourself in the
front-hall mirror before you went out this morning.
You carry it everywhere you go, isn't that so?"

She didn't wait for his answer; she tried to pull it
out. He grabbed hold of her wrist and pushed her
away. He buttoned his jacket. His eyes were suddenly
icy.

"Mind your own affairs, woman, and permit me to
mind mine. I'm not your child, I'm your husband. I
know what's good for me. The Ducks may have flown,
but there are still rascals abroad who'd like nothing
better than to see me dead."

"You plan to shoot it out with every Tom, Dick,
and Harry?"

"Hardly. I'm not stupid, just careful. I've no intention of provoking anyone. I mean only to defend myself. I've fired it just once to test it. That was four days
ago. I'll probably never fire it again, but I'm not going
out without it till things settle down." He lowered his
face into hers. "And don't reach for it again. It's
loaded, it could go off. This discussion is over. I'm
going into town."

"For what?"

"Business, my dear, what else? Being mayor is a
full-time job; it consumes the entire day. All I have

left is my evenings for committee business. And my nights for you—"

"Keep your nights, Sam Brannan," snapped Mercy, and walked out of the room.

Sam left the house, heading straight for Fort Gunnybags. The Committee of Vigilance had inherited a problem, small in comparison to the presence of the Sydney Ducks, but one that had to be dealt with. It was a natural consequence of the showdown with the Australians. A few had been seen drifting back into the city. Finding Sydney Town destroyed, they were forced to move elsewhere. They had collected around the bullfight ring west of St. Francis of Assisi Church, figuring that if they couldn't return to Sydney Town, they'd settle as close to it as possible. But Little Chile extended to the neighborhood surrounding the bullring, and the Chileans vehemently protested the invasion. Unwilling to order the police to deal with the problem, Brannan summoned his followers and mounted his soapbox.

"It's really a minor problem, brothers, nothing whatsoever like our recent encounter with and victory over the Australian scum. Our role will be more that of mediators, actually. Tomorrow morning at nine sharp we will leave here in force and march on Little Chile. Unarmed."

A loud sign of disappointment passed through his listeners.

"There'll be no confrontation, I'm sure, not after what we did to them."

"What'll we do, then?" boomed a voice from his audience.

"We'll discuss the situation with Señor Alvarez and the other Chilean leaders, determine precisely what is going on, and take the troublemakers in hand. Those we round up we'll put on a ship and send on home. Captain Avery Luckenbill, master of the *Dolphin*, which is moored right behind the Niantic Hotel, has agreed to take the Australians back where they came from for a fee. We will advance payment out of the treasury. If they refuse to cooperate, they'll be transported in irons. It'll be the last load of trash out of here. Those who escape our net and choose to remain will do so at their peril.

"And let me say this, brothers; for the first time in ages, peace is restored to my heart and my being. God willing all of you feel the same."

Huzzahs of agreement rose to the rafters.

"I carry no animus against our enemy. They are defeated and our city returned to us. Let us all kneel, hats off. Ahem, blessed Lord, we thank thee for thy gift and we shall prove worthy. The enemy is fled, the dregs of his presence will follow, and San Francisco will fulfill its destiny. Amen."

"Amen . . ."

The meeting broke up shortly before eleven P.M. Brannan left for home about ten minutes after. He was heading down Front Street toward Market when the buggy began behaving erratically. He stopped, got down, and inspected the rear wheels. He discovered that the left one had dropped its axle bolt. Thank heaven he had stopped. If he hadn't, the bolt might have fallen off, possibly injuring him. He was annoyed at the inconvenience and yet pleased it hadn't been worse. The Lord was on his side.

He lifted the seat, poking about in search of a bolt a bit smaller than the one lost, but usable. He found one. Its nut was twisted halfway up it.

He stood beside the imperiled wheel unscrewing the bolt, humming contentedly. His thoughts flew ahead to the meeting next morning with the Chileans. These were glory days. Events had set him atop the heap, and he was determined to stay there. He had a number of inspired ideas for improving the city, innovations that could only be implemented over the mayor's signature. Chief among them was Brannan Park; he smiled at the idea.

He had unscrewed the nut all the way to the end but for some reason there it stuck. He clenched his teeth and twisted with all his might, but that was as far it would turn. "Damn and double damn!"

"Somethin' wrong?"

He jumped in fright, his heart pounding in his chest. He'd been so absorbed by the work at hand, he hadn't heard the man's approach. He was unshaven and dirty. His breath was foul with the stink of stale liquor and he reeked of body odor. He was dressed like a tramp, and his toes protruded from one shoe. He looked drunk, but his words were not slurred and his rheumy eyes focused on Brannan clearly.

"Wha'cha doin'?"

Brannan stepped back, eyeing him fiercely. "Get away from me. Get out of here."

"Just ast ya—"

"Leave me alone, you filthy swine. Look at you, you're disgusting. How dare you creep up on a man and scare him half to death?"

"I jus'—"

"Never mind. Get out of here. Go on." Like steam in a boiler, Brannan's outrage was building fast. Impulsively, he stepped back and whipped out his gun.

The man gulped and started to raise his hands. "Hey, no, don' shoot, Chrissakes . . . Don', please . . ." He too backed off toward the corner street marker post some twenty feet away. "I didn' do nothin', honest . . ."

"Disgusting mongrel, filthy, stinking rabble!"

The man suddenly stopped cowering. He straightened, scowled, and leveled a dirty finger at Brannan. "You got no cause to talk like that to me. No right!"

Brannan was consumed with fury. How dare this mongrel reprimand him. Brannan yelled an obscenity and fired. The bullet struck the signpost inches from the man's head. He ducked and ran behind the post, trying futilely to hide himself.

"The next one I'll shoot to kill," roared Brannan.

In a flash, a gun appeared in the man's left hand. Up it came. It fired. The bullet drove straight into Brannan's heart. It was like being walloped in the chest with a shovel, knocking him over.

The man came out from behind the post. He looked about and fled into the night. Silence returned to the scene. The horse stood in the shafts, Brannan lay dead where he'd fallen, his gun inches from his right hand, the substitute nut and bolt still clutched in his left.

31

Reverend Samuel Brannan's death stunned San Francisco. The police rounded up the fewer than two hundred Australians still in town and questioned them, but to no avail. Whoever was responsible appeared to have gotten away with it.

Robbery was definitely not the motive: the victim's wallet was found with its contents intact. His watch and diamond ring were untouched. Had he and his killer argued? Had harsh words led to guns? Chief Sanger thought so; so did Colonel Bracy; so did Mercy Brannan.

The leaderless Vigilantes postponed their scheduled morning meeting with Luis Alvarez and the other Chileans. Unwilling to wait out the Vigilantes' period of mourning, the Chileans appealed to the police. Within two days the intruders were removed from their midst. Some of the Ducks scattered about the city; others left a second time, vowing never to return.

For pomp and ceremony, Sam Brannan's funeral rivaled that of any European royalty. Virtually the whole city turned out: friends drawn by loyalty and sympathy for Mercy, enemies drawn by curiosity and sympathy for Mercy. Colonel Bracy and six of his men paid their respects. John Sanger attended with eight high-ranking police officers. Eustace Ward and Sergio Scapelli were there. Judge Anson Galsworthy read the eulogy. San Francisco was a better city, more prosperous, more successful thanks to Brannan's tireless efforts, declared the judge. That it had also been the seat of turmoil for so long thanks to his machinations, Galsworthy chose to overlook.

Betsy Brannan stood with the thousands listening to the judge's praise. When the eulogy was finished, she screamed, threw herself across her father's casket, crushing the lovely sheaf of calla lilies, and sobbed loudly. She had to be gently pulled off by Reverend Doctor Anderson and Eustace Ward.

Mercy Brannan took her husband's death with the stoicism everyone expected of her. Anyone who knew husband and wife knew their relationship. Mercy was an unusually strong individual. This was not to say that Sam's death had not shaken her. It had, and visibly. Nevertheless, there was something in her demeanor that suggested it was not wholly unexpected.

Four days after the funeral, the Devlins visited Mercy to pay their respects. She looked worn out to Loyal, but she put up a brave front. She managed a characteristic quip or two. She was philosophical over her loss—and surprisingly candid. They sat in the parlor. Betsy was in town gadding about and shopping, and continuing to wear black.

"Betsy and I'll be leaving San Francisco," Mercy declared. "We're going back home to Maine. She was dead against it when I told her, but I think she's beginning to come around to the idea. Besides, it's not where we go so much as getting out of here. I stopped liking California a long time ago. I got discouraged at what San Francisco and Sam were doing to each other. This city changed him. He seemed to believe that it improved him. I'm not so sure. There was opportunity here and he seized it. I can hardly criticize him for that. I might not have agreed with his decisions, but he had the courage of his convictions. He never backed down. Challenge never daunted him; it energized him.

He was a most unusual human being. And I loved him."

Tears glistened in her eyes. Loyal lowered his to the contents of his cup.

"The way we went at each other sometimes, that might be hard to believe, but it's true." She paused, then resumed. "Anyway, now he's gone. And left me and Betsy amply provided for." She laughed lightly. "What am I saying? We're wealthy as Plutus. I'm arranging to sell the real-estate business and the *Star*, and the Brannan bank and the other businesses.

"He certainly did leave his mark. I wonder who'll lead the Vigilantes now he's gone? I suppose their work is pretty much done, though, now that the Sydney Ducks have cleared out. I must tell you two something: the night he was killed he left here with that stupid gun. I knew as sure as I'm sitting here there was going to be trouble. People don't make trouble, guns do. If folks disagree, they can only go so far with words, even with fists. With weapons, they kill."

"Live by the sword," murmured Catherine.

"Exactly." She shrugged.

"Is there anything we can do for you?" Loyal asked. "Just name it. Anything you need?"

She smiled and shook her head. "Everything's taken care of, thanks. You remember when I came to see you in the jail? I told you about Rupert Haddix, the lawyer. He was Sam's lawyer. He knows his business dealings. He's handled the contracts and suchlike. He's already started sorting things out. Thanks for reminding me, I promised to get Sam's papers together for him."

"We'd better be going," said Catherine.

After they left, Mercy went into Sam's study and sat at his desk. An odd sensation came over her as she sat looking at her picture on his desk. She could feel his presence. Wave upon wave of impressions of her husband swept through her mind. Sadness poured into her heart.

"Oh, Sam, Sam . . ."

She cried softly for a while then collected herself to weed through Sam's papers. Rupert Haddix wanted all papers relevant to his various business enterprises.

She got out his ledger. It was huge—it weighed at least ten pounds—and had a brass lock. She searched for the key and, unable to find it, broke the lock using the letter opener. She leafed through and found a large manila envelope glued inside the back cover. In the envelope were papers. She examined them. She was only partway through the first one when she gasped.

All the papers had to do with the area located just south of Telegraph Hill: Sydney Town.

"The battleground."

It was becoming clear to Mercy that Sam had been negotiating with various landlords for the past few months to buy their properties. All of Sydney Town. Located as it was in the center of the city, it was prime real estate. It would command an extraordinarily high price when resold.

"So this was to be his *pièce de résistance*."

By his order, Sydney Town had been all but completely reduced to rubble by the Vigilantes. The buildings removed leaving raw land. Mercy got out a map of the city and figured that her husband had already made arrangements to purchase roughly 60 percent of Sydney Town and was in the process of negotiating for the remaining 40 percent. She came across a sheet that listed potential profit figures for each separate block. He had estimated that the Vallejo, Broadway Street –Grant and Kearny Streets block was worth 2.1 million dollars alone. In the envelope as well was a long list of prospective buyers.

She got up from the desk, ripped the envelope from the inside back cover of the ledger, and restored the papers to it. She took them into the kitchen and burned them one by one at the stove. Emma the maid had been making the beds upstairs; she came into the kitchen, her eyes questioning.

"Just some worthless papers," Mercy explained. "Are you all finished upstairs?"

"Yes, ma'am."

"Do the parlor, would you? And beat the carpets. I have to go out. I have a meeting with Mr. Haddix at four-thirty. After you're done with the parlor, do Mr. Brannan's study. Top to bottom—it's needed a thorough cleaning for ages."

"He never let me, ma'am."

"I know, Emma; me neither. He had papers and things in the desk he didn't want anyone to see. Personal stuff. That's how it is with husbands and wives, dear. Each does have his secrets from the other. You'll see, when you and your Herbert get married."

"Oh ma'am, Herbert and me don't have no secrets from each other. Not a blessed one. We tell each other everything."

"*Every*thing?"

"Oh yes."

"My, my, I envy you, Emma."

"Oh, ma'am, how could *you* ever envy *me*?" She set one finger against a tooth, lowered her face, smiled shyly and swayed. "You're teasing . . ."

"Not really, dear, not really."

____ contains papers, Mr_ explained

___ the relief, would you? And bea_ the carpets

__ ___ He ___

___ use he didn't ____ enjoy _____

_____ himself ___ finish

●◄ *32* ►●

L oyal received a second letter from Ira Jack Fayles. In it was his copy of the contract with Henry Wicklow Associates, along with Wicklow's check for two thousand dollars. "Agreement money" was Fayles' term for it in his letter.

Loyal had never held anything close to that much money in his hand before. He handed the check to Catherine with the aplomb of Millard Fillmore presenting a presidential pardon. She read the check and fussed about how deeply impressed she was. But when she looked at him, it was with a puzzled expression. He looked troubled.

"You don't seem very impressed," she said.

"I just can't get used to the idea that I deserve it."

"You'd better try. I think you do. Tom and his partner gave their lives for that mine. Tom was your brother, you're his rightful heir. Apart from everything else, when they died, you were still a partner, remember? You told me you got back too late to tell them you were quitting."

"I suppose . . ."

"So, as the sole survivor, who deserves it more? Mr. Wicklow and Mr. Fayles don't seem to have any reservations." She handed back the check.

"I'm going to bank this," he said. "And when it clears, I'll take out ten percent and send it to Ira Jack.

He engineered the whole thing; if it wasn't for him, there wouldn't be any deal. He's my agent, he deserves to be compensated. Make that twenty-five percent."

"Ten percent, darling, that's what agents get."

They were sitting in the parlor. She looked about them.

"In case you haven't noticed, we're alone. Shall we go upstairs?"

They both smiled.

The sun streamed through the windows, drenching the bed with liquid gold. A flock of horned larks joined voices in a chorus of delicate music. Catherine and Loyal undressed and got into bed. Their lovemaking was still new to them with that special, marvelous glow of freshness. Their mutual exploration was as sweet as it was generous: captivating, blissful, beautiful subjugation to their senses. He played with her breasts, caressing her nipples, exciting her. His hand glided down to her velvety softness.

She stroked him, her breath coming faster now. Her hot moist tongue attacked, flicking down his body. He kissed her passionately. They made love, then made love again, climbing, rocketing to the heights, to climax. Again, again.

The sun was lowering when at last they surrendered to their exhaustion. They lay naked and panting.

She found his hand and squeezed it. "I love my husband."

"I adore my wife." He let out a long relaxing breath, tailing it with a quiet sigh.

"That blasted check," he murmured. "It makes me feel like a lazy slob. I shouldn't have quit my job; I guess Ira's letter just went to my head. I've got to get something to do. Anything but mining, as long as it's real work and I have to go to it every day. If I just sit around waiting for the checks to come, I'll wind up hanging out in places like the Blue Duck."

"Sure." She sat up, drawing the sheet up over her breasts. Bracing herself with one arm, she leaned over and stroked his hair, then lowered and pecked him lightly about the face and neck. "You'll think of something. Only not today. We're wasting precious time. We should be making love."

"You're insatiable."

"And you're desirable. Kiss me."

That evening at dinner, between the roast and vegetables and the apple pie, the colonel unwittingly suggested a solution to the problem that had now entrenched itself in Loyal's conscience.

"At the risk of ruffling your feathers, Loyal, there's something that's been preying on my mind. In a way, it has to do with your brother. I guess you blame the army for what happened, and I can't disagree with that, but if you can separate his death—"

"His murder," Loyal cut in.

Bracy nodded. "From your own situation. Let's say for the purposes of argument it never happened. If I asked you if you could consider enlisting, what would you say?"

"I've never thought about it."

"I'm talking about a career. At least twenty years. Application, physical, written exam, my recommendation for Artillery Officers Training School back East. Thirteen weeks' intensive study and training. And if you make the grade you'll be commissioned a shavetail—Second Lieutenant Loyal Devlin, a full-fledged wagon soldier—and be posted back here. Guardian of the Golden Gate. Artillery, best damned branch in the service by a long shot, no pun intended. What do you think, son?"

"I don't know."

"Do you out and out hate the idea? You find it attractive? Somewhere in between?"

"Daddy, you're rushing him," protested Catherine, coming in from the kitchen with the dessert. "And what about me? Don't I count? What makes you think I want to be an army wife?"

He waved away the question. "You're already an army brat, it's just one rung up the ladder."

"Or down."

"I like that! Loyal, you know it wouldn't be for the money. A hundred twelve eighty-three a month? And two dollars a month for forage for your horse? Of course, you realize nobody in his right mind joins the army for money. It's the other compensations, very special compensations. You might even say unique." He was suddenly eyeing him strangely. "The reasons Tom enlisted. Every man who fought in Mexico was a volunteer. No conscripts." He leaned over the table, setting his hand on Loyal's. "Think about it. There's no rush. Any questions you might have, I'll be glad to answer. Come to work with me tomorrow and I'll give you a tour of the fort. I'll—"

"Colonel Bracy," snapped Catherine.

The subject was dropped. Catherine's apple pie was delicious. The crust was so flaky, it fell apart at a touch.

Doreen made a remarkable recovery. She equated her heart seizure with the act of walking: she'd been walking along; she tripped, steadied herself, and went on. Dr. Slocum wished it were that simple, but hesitated to make issue of the comparison. She was up and about in a few days. She no longer had any desire for alcohol. It held no temptation for her. She recognized now that she had nothing to escape from. She loved her husband and wanted to go home. Life was too short for her to waste it on alcohol.

Doctor and patient strolled about town one afternoon. The Eagle Theater was preparing to welcome a touring company headed by the renowned character actor John Edmond Owens, born in Wales and arrived in America at the age of three. Owens' troupe would be presenting *The Live Indian*, in which the star would play three separate roles, including Miss Cordelia Crinoline, a mantua maker. On the same bill would be the popular *Peoples' Lawyer,* with Owens heading the cast as Solon Shingle. Doreen wanted to go.

"Not by yourself," said Slocum. "Doctor Bystrom might like to go with you. He loves the theater."

"What about you?"

"No, thanks. I'm not the artsy type. I'm much more fond of sports. The last two times I attended the theater I fell asleep. You wouldn't want me to embarrass you."

The box office was open. Doreen bought two loge tickets; she hoped Bystrom could make it. They walked up Main Street. It was undergoing repairs. Several large boulders had been removed and wagons were dumping dirt in the holes.

"When can I go home?" Doreen asked suddenly. "This weekend?"

Slocum stopped her. "That's only three days."

"When?"

"Next weekend. Hopefully."

"Next weekend. Definitely."

"On one condition: you go back by water. There's no earthly reason to exhaust yourself with a buggy ride. They've started a daily packet run that goes down the river to San Pablo Bay, down San Francisco Bay almost to your doorstep. I haven't taken it yet, but I hear it's a lovely trip."

Doreen could scarcely contain herself. "I can write Catherine and Ewing and tell them I'm coming home."

"Well . . ."

"Next weekend," she burst.

"Hopefully."

"Definitely."

Colonel Bracy stood on the top level with his son-in-law. Looking out over the Golden Gate, he thought

back to the pirates and the Vigilantes' armada, feeling
a dart of pain in his chest where the bullet had struck.
And feeling a twinge of conscience on the heels of his
and Loyal's conversation at dinner the evening before.
He had already written Doreen telling her of his intention to resign from the army; he hadn't heard back
from her yet, but he was confident she'd welcome his
decision. His conscience told him that he should have
told Loyal as well as Catherine, but he'd held back.
First he had to get Doreen home. Then he'd cross that
bridge and burn it after him. Actually, his resignation
had nothing to do with Loyal; he wasn't selling him on
an army career because that had been his choice.
Loyal had the makings of a fine officer, but it would
have to be his decision.

For Bracy, his decision was made. He was resigning.

"It's a beautiful view," said Loyal beside him.
"Sausalito looks about a hundred yards away.

"One and one-eighth miles."

"How deep is the water?"

"At its deepest point . . ." Bracy indicated. "Nearly
three hundred and fifty feet. What do you think?"

"I'm not sure yet. But you'll be the second to know."

"Loyal, you and I may not have the same likes and
dislikes, interests, preferences, whatever. Perhaps it's
not for you, but for me it's been a tremendous twenty-
eight years. To be perfectly candid, I can't think of
anything I'd rather have done with my life. I've been
happy, content, fulfilled. Not too many men can say
that."

The wind came up and the flag flapped briskly over
their heads. In the distance a freighter hooted greeting
as it passed, heading for the ocean. Captain Westerfield
appeared at the top of the stairs.

"Sir . . . Good morning, Devlin, I haven't had a
chance to congratulate you. Congratulations, the best
man won, eh?"

Loyal didn't know what to say in response.

Bracy rescued him. "You're both best, Robert. Who can figure a lady's heart?"

Westerfield looked quite grim. "Not me. Sorry to interrupt, sir, but Major Viselli and Major Downing are in your office. The meeting? We four have to go over the supply situation. The quartermaster has all his facts and figures."

The colonel glanced at Loyal apologetically.

"That's okay," Loyal said. "Catherine and I have to go to the docks to say good-bye to the Brannans. They're leaving for the East."

Twenty minutes later he held the reins as the buggy headed in the direction of the docks. When they got there, they saw that Mercy's things had already been taken on board the *Carthaginian*. She stood with her daughter. Betsy was attired in mourning, setting Catherine to wonder if she'd be wearing it until the *Carthaginian* reached port sometime next December.

About thirty well-wishers had come down to see mother and daughter off. Catherine pointed out Rupert Haddix among them. Two or three of the women were crying. Not Mercy—she appeared to be her old self: all smiles, bustling energy, and good cheer. She spotted the Devlins and made her way through the tight knot of people.

"I was beginning to think you wouldn't show up. Rupert . . . Rupert Haddix," she called back to the crowd.

A man a head taller than the late Sam Brannan but otherwise bearing a surprising resemblance to him, even to the identical beard without a mustache, came up beside Mercy, tipping his hat to Catherine.

"Rupert, this is the young man I was telling you about," Mercy said. "The one who shot the soldier. Which turned out to be self-defense. It did, didn't it, Loyal? I hope it did."

Catherine laughed. Betsy came running to join them. The others stood patiently watching the five of them.

"Loyal Devlin, meet Rupert Haddix. Rupert, you know Catherine Bracy. Catherine and Loyal just got married." She elbowed him. "Can't you tell?"

The change that came over Betsy's face at these words nearly sent Loyal into a gale of laughter. It was a look that transcended disgust and came ominously close to revulsion.

The ship's whistle blasted so loudly practically everyone jumped. Rupert Haddix's hat fell off and he had to catch it.

"Hello, Loyal," chimed Betsy. "Catherine. We have to get on board now, mother. Good-bye, Loyal, 'bye, Catherine, Mr. Haddix. Good-bye, everybody. We're going now."

She began dragging her mother toward the gangplank. By dint of superior strength Mercy was able to kiss the Devlins and Haddix and everyone else goodbye, deftly bussing her way from cheek to cheek before Betsy started her up the gangplank. They stood at the railing waving. A timely breeze bellied the sails; the wind arrived and took command and away sailed the *Carthaginian* with Mercy and Betsy. They waved good-bye to San Francisco, a city of sunshine, happiness, and tragedy, sailing off into the future thirteen thousand miles away.

"There goes my guardian angel," murmured Loyal. "I'll miss that lady."

Catherine nodded. "Won't everybody who knows her?"

Loyal and Catherine drove up to the top of Telegraph Hill, parking in front of the telegraph signal house on Greenbush Street. They could see the ship heading out of the bay toward the Golden Gate. Down the coast it would sail, down to Valparaiso, down around Cape Horn, up to Recife, up and up to Charleston, South Carolina, to New York, to Boston. An atom of envy surfaced in Loyal's thoughts as it grew smaller and smaller. It was nearly September, getting into fall in New England. The nights would be turning chillier, the mornings crisper, the trees would take on their autumn motley; Halloween, Thanksgiving, Christmas . . .

It dawned on Loyal that this would be his first Christmas ever without the anticipation of snow. Without all that was familiar, old friends, old haunts, old experiences revisited every holiday season. He'd miss his Yankee Christmas. He turned to Catherine, leaned over, and kissed her cheek. Yes, when Christmas came to this strange place he'd miss the world of the past. He took his love and his future in his arms and kissed her warmly, dispelling his nostalgia.

Yes, he missed the past. But not much.

Loyal and Catherine went to Sacramento to bring Doreen home. They were to return by water and were due to arrive back early afternoon on a Thursday. The colonel came home from the fort at two P.M. and sat on the stoop waiting, scarcely able to contain his excitement. He began to pace the yard, and when dust appeared down the road and out of the cloud came the buggy, he started for the gate.

Loyal helped Doreen down. She flew into the colonel's arms. Loyal and Catherine watched them joyfully. Doreen looked to be in superb health, glowing, animated. Husband and wife hugged and kissed, and over her shrill protests and laughter, he picked her up and carried her over the threshold. But once inside, his exuberance gave way to concern. She anticipated his question.

"I'm wonderful," she said. "I've never felt better. It's dead, darling, stone-dead. I killed it." She laughed. "Bare hands." She got a sealed envelope out of her bag. "This is for you from Donald Slocum."

He read the letter aloud for the benefit of Loyal and Catherine. Dr. Slocum pronounced Doreen cured, describing her as a "positively delightful patient," according her "the lion's share of the credit" for her triumph.

"You see?" she said proudly. "I did it."

Catherine hugged her. "I'm so happy for you and so proud. But we're not surprised."

"We knew you'd do it," Loyal said.

"You two deserve a little privacy," Catherine said. She took Loyal by the arm and started them for the stairs.

He eased her about and steered her toward the front door. "Let's go for a buggy ride."

Doreen walked about the house exulting in all the familiar sights, rearranging this and that, finding dust on a windowsill and clucking good-natured disapproval. They sat together in the parlor.

"How I missed you all and home. But would you believe that helped? It made me more determined than ever to get through it, get it over with so I could come home. What time is it?"

"Almost half-past three."

"I should start thinking about supper."

"It's too early," he said. "Relax, you must be tired."

"Not a bit. I feel like I'm full of fresh air, like I can walk without touching the ground."

He handed back Slocum's letter. "Keep that. It belongs with your school diploma, our marriage license. It's a precious document. Which reminds me, I have a letter for you to read."

He got it out of the top drawer of the secretary, unfolding and proffering it.

"I know what this is," said Doreen.

"It's what I told you in my last letter."

"I must not have gotten it—I mean, I can guess." She read sit, nodding knowingly. "You're resigning," she murmured.

"I should have ages ago. I should never have signed up for another hitch. I haven't told Catherine or Loyal yet. I wanted you to be the first to know. I know how much it means to you. That goes off first thing in the morning to departmental headquarters. I don't think

I'll have any problem. Not a lot of red tape. They'll be glad to get rid of this old war horse."

She finished reading, refolded the letter, and tore it up.

"Dorey, what . . . !"

"You're not resigning, Ewing; you don't want to, and I don't want you to."

"No, I've decided. And believe it or not, I do want to. Honestly."

She turned to set the pieces in the ashtray on the desk, then turned back to him. "You don't understand, darling, you don't have to. There's no need."

"It's got nothing to do with you."

"It's got everything. I'm the reason. Ewing, look at me. I'm cured. The dragon is dead, nothing can revive it. And"—she moved very close to him and emphasized each single word—"I don't need any help keeping it dead."

"Dorey . . ."

"I don't want any. I got this far almost all on my own. I have to go on the same way. You've twenty months to go. There's nothing in this world or in heaven you'd rather accomplish than to complete your thirty. It'll be the achievement of your lifetime, Colonel. Look me in the eye and tell me it's not. You're going to make your thirty years and I'm going to help you. And that, as they say, is that."

"Why don't we brew up a pot of tea," he said quietly. "Relax, and talk about it."

"No. Tea, yes. Talk about it . . . There's nothing to talk about." She put her arms around him and kissed him. "I love you for what you're trying to do. It's just like you, but you don't have to. If I were to backslide, whether you were out of the army or in wouldn't make a particle of difference. The army wasn't my problem; it was just a handy scapegoat. I had hours and hours in Sacramento to do nothing but think. I made up my mind that whether I succeed or fail is strictly and totally up to me.

"I fought it, I beat it. It's over. For you to resign is not only not necessary, it's wrong and could be harmful. Darling, I've enough on my conscience without adding that."

He stared at her for nearly thirty seconds. The light of understanding came slowly into his eyes. He smiled, he nodded. "Welcome home, Dorey."

◄ *Epilogue* ►

Lieutenant Colonel Ewing Bracy retired upon completion of his thirty years in the service. Prior to his retirement, Loyal Devlin had joined the army, was commissioned a second lieutenant, and posted to Fort Point. Ten years later, having been twice promoted, Captain Devlin was transferred to the XIII Corps under the command of Major General Joseph K.F. Mansfield at Antietam. Subsequently, Captain-become-Major Devlin fought with distinction at Fredericksburg, Chancellorsville, Gettysburg, and elsewhere.

Loyal and Catherine Devlin were the parents of five children, four boys and a girl.

Mercy Brannan and Betsy settled in Boston, Massachusetts. Betsy never married.

San Francisco survived its turbulent beginnings to become the chief seaport of California. Prior to the devastating fire and earthquake of 1906, the city's population had grown to more than 400,000. Its population today approaches three-quarters of a million.

Fort Point stands today as a classic example of a nineteenth-century coastal fortification—the greatest to be erected on the West Coast. The Civil War ended without the firing of a single shot by Fort Point. No Confederate privateer attempted to pass through the Golden Gate. Captain James I. Waddell, of the *Shenandoah*, planned to do so, but the war ended before he could execute his plan. Troops occupied Fort Point during both world wars.

During World War II, the troops were withdrawn in 1943 after U.S. forces had seized the initiative in the Pacific and the threat of Japanese attacks on West Coast cities evaporated.